The Moon King

Neil Williamson

NewCon Press
England

First published in the UK by NewCon Press
41 Wheatsheaf Road, Alconbury Weston, Cambs, PE28 4LF

NCP 068 (limited edition hardback)
NCP 069 (softback)

10 9 8 7 6 5 4 3 2 1

ISBN:

978-1-907069-61-1 (hardback)
978-1-900679-62-8 (softback)

Cover concept by Ian Whates
Cover layout and design by Andy Bigwood

Minor Editorial meddling by Ian Whates
Book layout by Storm Constantine

The Moon King

Neil Williamson

(

Our great flotilla was the last of Abergaard, the flotsam rescued from the unrelenting rains. We sailed for months in search of any land at all to make our new home, and finally ran aground on this cruel rock. We salvaged what we could from the bellies of our ships. Livestock and crops, tools and machines and materials, anything that might aid our survival. It was a futile exercise. We lost much and saved precious little. Together we survivors watched the ships give out one by one and sink below the waves. Then, clouded by despair, we dispersed across the island to make what life we could.

There was one man though, that would not relinquish hope. A strong man, a man who cared about his fellows, a man who would not let the memory of our civilization die. He scorned our scattered shelters and demanded a city. A city, he said, would mean permanence. A city would mean survival and, more than that, a future.

Neither his words nor his zeal alone were enough to lift the people to action, so he promised us a sign, a symbol of hope. He talked to the surviving engineers and scientists, and then he sailed off in a boat. When he returned, it was with the rising moon, and he told us that this was our symbol.

And from that day the moon never set, and we made this man our king, and the people came together and set to building a city beneath the moon. A place of permanence bathed in its light. A sign that we would never again be displaced.

— Journals of The City Under The Moon

While the moon grows fat, we're happy
While the moon grows thin, we cry
When the moon shines Full, we'll party
And when Dark Day comes, we hide
For we are the people of the moon, the people of the moon are we.
This has been our way since the Founding days, and ever now shall be.

(Popular song)

Chapter 1

Anton Dunn woke under a fullish sky. Feathers of cloud tumbled like snow goose down across the frigid blue, with the orb of the moon a powdery fingerprint in the background.

All was peaceful.

For a moment, anyway. Then a monstrous headache kicked in. Eyes streaming, Anton held on to that tranquil image, and hoped that it would help him bear through the hangover's initial onslaught. How much had he drunk the night before? It had been a long time since he had felt this poorly. Even if this time there had been justification.

Ah, yes.

Anton remembered making a good attempt at drinking what was to have been his Fullday wedding reception dry. He had set to it as soon as the disappointed guests had gone home. His best man, Frank, had made an honourable show of helping him demolish the stockpile of beer, wine and gilberry gin, but in the end they'd hardly dented it. Frank had passed out around midnight and, sitting alone under the woven moonflower garlands that festooned the community hall, Anton too had finally given up, realising that no quantity of alcohol would dissolve the knot in his chest.

Because, instead of marrying him as expected, Krista, his fiancée, had elected to become a Bride of the Moon.

It was some minutes until Anton's vision cleared sufficiently to see that he was not outside after all. Those clouds were passing high above a domed window, and there were sheets and pillows. He was in a bed, not in the street. When the pain subsided to an angry ache, Anton finally dared to raise his head.

The large, linen-swathed bed was circular, and it was surrounded by hangings draped between marble pillars. Through the creamy material, decorated with silvery embroidery, Anton could see only vague shapes and shadows, but he had the strong impression that, like the bed, the roof and the ring of hangings, the room too was circular.

The effort of sitting up brought a wash of nausea that burned his throat. Beside the bed, there was a jug of water. He poured himself a glass and sipped until the sickness passed. Cautiously he felt the back of his head. There was no lump, but from the belt of pain when he touched his scalp there felt like there ought to be. Pieces of recent history resurfaced in his bruised brain like stormy flotsam.

It seemed he had not simply settled for drowning his sorrows. At some point in the hazier part of the evening he had stolen into the Lunane's Palace looking for Krista. He must have drunk even more than he'd thought. There was no place in Glassholm he would be less inclined to go within a mile of, of his own volition, than the calcified carbuncle at the city's centre. He had vague memories of an ornamental garden, a storm drain, a cold kitchen and a lot of stairs. The real question, however, was not why he had gone there, but why he had ended up in this grand bed and not in a cell deep below the Castil tower.

Tentatively, Anton swung his legs over the edge of the bed. Three unsteady steps across the cold floor took him as far as the nearest pillar. Folds of gauze shimmered, fluttering as if stirred by a breeze too gentle to feel even on his naked skin. Anton wrapped a sheet around himself. Then he pulled back the curtain and stepped through.

In the outer part of the room, two grey-robed men were waiting. The younger one sitting at the desk quickly overcame evident surprise at Anton's appearance and began scratching in a large ledger bound in blue leather. The older one with a face that was never surprised by anything stepped forward holding a bundle of white cloth. "Good morning, sir," he said. "How do you feel?"

This pair did not have the look of jailers. "Not good," he answered truthfully.

The older man executed a servile nod. His seated companion waited, watching intently, a fat gilt pen poised over an inkwell. "I'm sorry to hear that, sir," the elder said. "The doctor will be along presently, of course."

"Yes..." Anton began and then gasped as the headache returned. A doctor sounded good. "... I mean, thank you, but who...?"

The young one began writing again, hair curtaining his earnest

8

face as he bent over his book.

The senior attendant held out his bundle. "You'll be wanting to get dressed first, of course, sir."

Anton realised that he was being offered clothes. Obediently he took the bundle and turned back towards the bed. Then he paused. "Sorry, but *who are you?*"

The man in the grey robes smiled. "This is Hogarth," he said, indicating the writer. "And I'm Gerard, of course."

Of course?

Anton escaped back through the curtain. Laying the clothes out on the bed, he discovered that he'd been given trousers, a woollen sweater and comfortable shoes. The only problem, if it could be called that, was that everything down to the underwear was white. It would have to do, he supposed. At least the shade wasn't sufficiently brilliant to exacerbate his headache. Anton sat on the edge of the bed and tried to collect his thoughts, but could get no further than: *What under the moon was he doing here?*

In the outer room Hogarth and Gerard hadn't moved an inch. Their expectant expressions reminded Anton of the spaniel pups he had helped his grandfather raise as a child.

"Would you like to see the doctor before your breakfast, sir?" Gerard said. "Or after?"

This was the first sensible thing anyone had said so far. Having ignored the feast that had been prepared for the wedding in favour of drinking himself senseless, the most recent thing Anton had eaten had been yesterday's breakfast. The earlier nausea had abated and, now that he was up and about, the idea of food was beginning to appeal. "Thank you," he said. "Food would be welcome."

Gerard disappeared through a pair of tall doors, leaving Anton alone with Hogarth. An uncomfortable pause spread between them like an ink stain. Edging away from the urge to blot it with empty conversation, Anton looked around. He had been right, although, the room was not simply round, it was actually hemispherical. The walls and roof were a continuous graceful slope that extended from the floor to meet at the glass dome high above the bed. There were four sets of doors. The lintels and frames were crowned with a creeping plant Anton recognised as whiteleaf, a profusion of pearly foliage that haloed each entrance with a shimmering nimbus. Aside from the bed, and

Hogarth's chair and desk, however, the room was empty. Anton tutted his disapproval. Such impracticality was totally in keeping with his expectations of the Palace.

Anton peeked through the door that Gerard had left by. A short corridor ended in another set of doors. He went through and pushed at these but they wouldn't budge.

"Where do these doors lead?" Anton asked.

"That one leads to the Castil, sir," Hogarth replied. He had a raspy voice. "The others, to the rest of your apartments."

"My apartments?" Anton said.

"Yes, sir." Hogarth said, his smile fixed. "I can show you if you like."

Hogarth didn't sound keen to fulfil his offer, but Anton took him up on it anyway. They went through one of the other sets of doors, and entered a succession of beautifully appointed rooms. These rooms replicated the circular motif, being arranged in a wider circle around the circumference of the central bedroom like the rim of a wheel around a hub. White, plastered walls followed an even and natural curve, with the inner walls of the circle arcing off the vertical to follow the hemispherical contour of the room within. The high ceilings were corniced all around with a stylised progression of the moon's phases. Anton had to look hard to detect the layer of vitric that was needed to protect the delicate plasterwork from the wear and tear of the monthly cycle that swept from Full to Dark and back again. He touched the glassy shell. It was the purest he had ever seen, almost invisible but as hard as stone.

Perhaps more incredible still were the tall lamps in each of which burned, with fizzing extravagance, electric light bulbs. Anton had never seen so many outside of the Foundry.

Walking around the rooms, Anton counted a lounge with well-stuffed couches, a bar with an encouraging selection of taps and optics, a small personal library, and a games room sporting a snooker table outfitted with black baize. Whoever stayed here would not easily get bored. Further round the circle he discovered a dressing room with floor length mirrors and a wardrobe containing more clothes. They were all very stylish, but all white. A little variety in the colour department would have been nice. Adjoining the dressing room, there was a gleaming bathroom. As if on cue, Anton's queasy insides turned liquid.

"Do you have to do that?" he asked when the constantly scribbling Hogarth followed him to the toilet.

"Yes, sir," Hogarth replied. "I'm the Palace biographer."

Anton's spirits sank further. If the wedding hadn't been farcical enough, the aftermath of his drunken Fullday folly would now be neatly diarised in the Palace tit-bits section of the next day's newspaper. His friends and colleagues, who had nicknamed him 'Adamant' because of his unnatural imperviousness to the high humours of the moon's Fullness and the depths of its Dark, would be beside themselves with mirth.

"Just use your imagination for the next few minutes," he growled, and shut the door in the young man's face. When his gut had emptied itself, Anton ducked his face into cold water. His stomach felt better, but the headache had intensified and he now felt weary beyond belief. None of this helped alleviate his confusion.

His apartments? Hogarth obviously didn't mean that literally. The rooms must be the Palace's accommodation reserved for high ranking guests. Probably squirrelled away deep within the vast Palace complex somewhere. Anton had never been one for following the Royal reportage, but he knew that it was not unheard of for Glassholm to be visited by more than the usual merchant seamen and far-travelled fisherfolk. Very occasionally foreign envoys, or even heads of state, were said to spend time with the Lunane. These infrequent visits were almost always timed to occur at Full when Glassholm could be seen at its best and its populace would be largely oblivious. It must be in apartments like these that such visitors were entertained.

None of which answered the question of why Anton was being treated as a guest, however. Or maybe it did. Was it possible that, rather than being arrested for trespassing, he had simply been found pathetically unconscious and taken pity upon? Perhaps he wasn't in as serious trouble as he felt he ought to be.

Returning to the main room, Anton found that a breakfast table had been set up. Suddenly ravenous, he was unsure whether to expect a prisoner's gruel or a royal guest's feast. It turned out to be a generous, but otherwise normal, meal. Investigating, Anton discovered toast, marmalade, and a chilled jug of freshly pulped juice. Sniffing at a steaming silver pot, he was pleased to identify tea rather than the imported coffee that he associated ubiquitously with the upper classes, and, lifting the lids of the hot dishes, he was delighted to find golden kippers and lightly poached eggs. The sight of these alone cheered him.

The food helped. The first few mouthfuls subdued his various troubles to background discomfort. The constant attention of Gerard and Hogarth, however, was off-putting and it was only after turning his chair around that he was able enjoy feeling vaguely human for the first time since he'd woken up.

Anton picked up a slice of toast. It was done to exactly the shade that he liked, and the marmalade was a good dark one too. It was almost as if... He froze with the bread half way to his mouth. The theory about him being treated as a charity case wouldn't wash. All of this was just too good to be true.

Gerard leaned into view at his shoulder. "Is something wrong, sir?"

"Why are you treating me like this?" Anton said.

Gerard's brow creased in a hurt-looking frown. "I'm sorry, sir?"

Anton turned in his chair to meet the man's gaze dead on. The grey eyes were unreadable. "The breakfast, the clothes, the fancy accommodation?"

Gerard's expression was one of patronising forbearance. "If there's something that displeases," he soothed. "If there's anything that you require, sir, you only have to say. You know that."

Hogarth had begun scribbling again.

"No," Anton said. "It's fine. Everything's perfect. That's the problem. I don't know who you think I am, but apparently we wear the same sizes of clothes and enjoy the same things for breakfast, and I don't believe in coincidences like that."

Gerard and Hogarth exchanged a look, and the younger man laid down his pen and scurried from the room. "Sir," Gerard said. "Calm yourself, the doctor will be up immediately."

Anton wouldn't be placated. He needed to understand this. "I broke in here last night," he said. "Shouldn't I be in a cell, awaiting trial as a corporeal danger to the city?"

Gerard laughed merrily. "A cell? Sir, the idea!"

"Don't make fun of me," Anton spat. "I should be locked up. Why are you treating me like Royalty?"

Like a cloud sliding across the moon, Gerard's expression shifted, became sly and mean as he leaned in close enough for Anton to smell the bitterness on his breath. "Because you *are* Royalty," he said. "Do not forget it, sir."

Hogarth returned then, red faced and panting. He was followed by a tall man in dark robes.

"Who do you think I am?" Anton said, retaining his focus on Gerard.

Gerard put an arm around his shoulders and spoke to the newcomer. "Your timing is excellent, Frisk," he said. "His Majesty has suffered a bad one this time."

"Who...?" Anton said, finally acknowledging the understanding that had been ebbing to the fore in his mind like deep sea debris dragged to shore on a Dark tide.

There was just an instant of clear surprise in the doctor's expression before a veneer of professionalism slid into place. "So I see." The doctor put his hand on Anton's brow, then addressed him directly. "And how are the headaches, sir?"

Anton recoiled, sending his chair tumbling. "Stop," he said, thrusting out an arm, warning them to keep their distance. "Now, tell me. Who do you think I am?"

Gerard's patronising smile had already settled back into place. "Why, sir, you're the Lunane. You've been the Lunane since before I was born, since before my grandfather was born, since before his grandfather even. You've been the Lunane ever since you founded our City Under The Moon." He glanced at the floor just long enough for deference. "These are your clothes," he said gently. "This is the breakfast you always have after Full. These are your apartments. Since Fullday is such a strain on you, you're understandably a little confused, but it will all come back to you. Very soon."

13

Chapter 2

Lottie Blake's loft bedsit was an unqualified tip. Clothes were discarded on the floor, draped over the few sticks of furniture. Stacks of books and mildewing newspapers slumped like the walls of a dilapidated Dockton flophouse in the depths of Dark. Mugs and plates bore the dried-on scar tissue of forgotten meals.

The mess had needed tackling for some time, and today was finally the ideal day to do so. The weather was fresh and bright and, still high from Full, Lottie fizzed with energy. That wouldn't last, though. If she waited even a couple of days into the wane, it would dissipate and she'd lose the inclination, and living with the mess for another Dark would make her despise herself even more than usual.

Lottie started bundling up the bedcovers from the floor. White petals drifted to the carpet. She smiled, buried her face in the sheets. The mingled aroma of perfume, sex and weed smoke sparked a flare of pleasure that uncurled in her belly and sizzled outwards through her body. Her mind's eye flashed a memory montage of the night before: images of skin on slick skin overlaid with tactile recall, the prickle of sweat on her face, the heat of his cock inside her. She got like this after a good Fullday, and she liked to savour the feeling as long as she could. She stretched out on the sheets, wriggled out of her trousers, squeezed her thighs together deliciously as she skinned a cigarette using the last of the weed. Her mother wouldn't approve of this indulgence in pleasure, but she didn't give a shit what her mother, or anyone in her damned Church, thought. The mess could wait a little longer.

By the time she roused herself, it was too late for chores. Time had flown and she had real work to do. The poster designs for the boxing match were ready to be delivered to the printer, and she needed to talk to that hostel fellow over in the Merchantry, persuade him that the place needed that mural and then raise the uncomfortable subject of terms. An advance would be favourite, but she wouldn't push her luck. Before all that, of course, there was the new project. The thought of it made her *yip* with delight.

Lottie attempted to pull on a sweater as she went through to her workshop, but the wool snagged on the geegaws twisted into her hair, and she spent the next few minutes stumbling around the flat trying to free herself. The scenario struck her as increasingly funny the longer it went on, and she had to lean against the door frame until the giggles subsided. Perhaps this morning's cigarette had been a bad idea so soon after the quantity she had smoked last night. It'd be an effort of will to get through all of her things to do today, but at Full you had to make allowances.

Up to a point, of course. Some people lost themselves completely: inhibitions, memory, identity – everything. Like last night's Fullday lover. No, that wasn't fair. There had been something about him that marked him apart from the rest of the Fools. A vulnerability. And she had liked the fact that he couldn't remember his name. The married ones always had a name ready, glib and pre-prepared; the single ones often hesitated, unsure about the weight a trade of names would attach to what was supposed to be a meaningless bit of fun. But when she had asked him, there had been an unidentifiable searching look in his eyes. Lottie had thought that maybe it was bewilderment, or maybe it was loss, but when he told her that he didn't know, she had believed him. Of course, it didn't matter. The hunger in both their bodies had quickly overtaken all less immediate concerns. This morning he had been gone, which was usually how she liked it, but she found time now to hope that he was okay.

Lottie entered the skylit room that served as her workshop. Watery sunlight strained through the quartet of thick glass squares in the ceiling, making the row of flowers on the worktable glow. Choosing a long stem, she lit a gas burner and slipped on the gloves. Then, from the box of shards, she selected an appropriate piece of bottle glass, and with application of heat and careful manipulation she fashioned it into a fragile green leaf, curling at the tip. She made three more and then welded them to the stem before finishing by affixing a golden, flared daffodil trumpet to the end. Other artists would then have reached immediately for a pot of vitric to protect the work, but to Lottie that was vanity. She understood the inherent fragility of art. Posterity was against nature.

Placing the completed glass flower with the others, she turned to finish the remaining stems. When the flowers had cooled, she wrapped each in a rag and carefully placed them into her satchel.

Tight for time now, Lottie counted the change in her pocket to see if she could afford the tram down to the Merchantry, but as soon as she was outside the beauty of the day consumed her. Her appointment with Sebastian Vickers at the Promise Centre was in half an hour, and she still had to drop in at the printers before that, so she'd be cutting it fine, but even if she'd been the richest woman in the city she wouldn't have wasted the opportunity of enjoying such a rare morning.

The day possessed the kind of chilly, vernal clarity that brought out the secret details of the world. She had lived in sooty Farring Street for nearly a year and never noticed that in the begrimed lintel above each tenement entrance the masons had carved one of the moon's eight phases. And that wasn't all. On spying a flash of colour from the first floor of a tenement on nearby Emers Street, she crossed the road to investigate and was rewarded with another marvel. It was stained glass, simple in design, a little brown bird perched on a bowed reed with a background of light blue. Up close she could see the many mends that had been applied to keep it together, but the fact that it lasted intact from month to month at all was amazing.

Lottie stood on the crown of Beckon Hill and grinned. The sky was wide and vibrant with birdsong and the chitter somewhere of a luck monkey going about its business. From here the gleaming tram tracks swept down into the bowl of the city's heart. Gazing down the hill, she lost them amid the convolutions of residential rooftops. She picked them up down at the riverside, easier to spot as they climbed again through the ordered streets of the Merchantry, heading, as all routes did, towards the high, scintillating white walls of the Palace complex. She wondered if anyone down there was enjoying this day as much as she was. Even the Lunane himself.

Blackwood's printing business occupied the ground floor of a former bonded warehouse that overlooked the rolling waters of the Cord. Lottie only came here during the day. The location may have been on the fringes of the Merchantry, but gas street lighting stopped two streets up the hill. And that was during the regular wax and wane. She'd never dream of coming here around Dark.

The weathered sign above the heavy doors simply displayed Blackwood's name. For a man whose income, aside from the daily pressings of Glassholm's newspaper, the *Oculus*, was derived largely from printing publicity materials for others, Lottie thought the old boy could stand to learn a few things about advertising. When the doors were closed, you'd think the building was derelict.

Today, however, one of Blackwood's technicians was kneeling on the pavement working at the lock with a large screwdriver. When Lottie squeezed past him he glowered. Instinctively she ducked her head so that the metal and ceramic weights dragged her hair in front of her face like a theatre curtain, hiding her bad eye. A tiny thing really, just an odd slackness to the lid that made her look sly, but you never knew how people were going to react to it.

When she entered, she found the building oddly quiet. It took her a moment to realise why: the printing machines were still. Voices led her to a group of overalled workers crowding around one of the presses. She didn't see Blackwood, but his gruff voice rose from the centre of the group.

"So?" he barked.

A voice called back from somewhere inside the press. "Could be a lot worse, Mr Blackwood."

Lottie looked at the machine. It had appeared odd, and now she saw why: an iron bar protruded from the workings, making the device resemble a black bull felled by a spear.

Blackwood's stocky, suited frame pushed out of the crowd. He chewed fretfully on his moustache. "So what needs done?" he said.

The person under the machine reeled off a list of unlikely sounding components, and Blackwood turned to his foreman, a woman who Lottie knew as a cheerful soul named Laura – although she looked far from cheerful today.

"Have we got the parts?" Blackwood asked.

Laura nodded uncertainly. "If we cannibalise the Montresor in the back room."

Blackwood snorted. "Okay, get it done. That old thing's been taking up space for years anyway." He clapped his hands. "Everyone else back to work. We've lost enough time as it is."

The workers dispersed, leaving Blackwood staring pensively at the broken press. Then he whirled to face Lottie.

"Hello, yes, designer lady." Despite his troubles the printer still managed to regard her with that look, the one that straddled discomfort and pity. "You've come on a bad day. We're down one press and we've yet to receive today's diary for the front page. Can't put out a paper without His Majesty's day-to-day, now can we? And we've just heard news of a fire at a Promise Centre. So, you can see we're having a busy day. Nevertheless it is good to see you. Even your elastic timekeeping is, for once, fortuitous."

"What happened?" Lottie asked to cover her embarrassment. "Was it burglars?"

Blackwood glanced back at the machine. "Burglars," he said. "Yes, something like."

"At Full?" Lottie's voice betrayed her disbelief.

Blackwood eyed her sceptically. "City's a changing place. You need to watch yourself. Even at Full."

Lottie was taken aback by his sincerity. "I will," she said.

"Good. Now, come to the office. We need to talk business."

Blackwood's office was little more than a box built into the corner of the warehouse. Two thin wooden walls, a lid and a door were all that separated him from the shop floor, but as the presses started to clank and grind into action she was glad of even that meagre baffling. Blackwood sat on one side of a desk strewn with invoices and layouts, and gestured towards the chair opposite.

"You finished the poster?" he asked.

Lottie nodded and reached into her backpack. "Right here."

Blackwood unrolled the poster on the desk and surveyed it with a critical eye. Lottie, watching upside down, hoped he'd be pleased. Her interpretation of the two fighters was more stylised than the traditional, but she'd wanted to impress with something eye-catching. Now she worried that she might have strayed too far from the traditional sketch depicting the pugilists squaring up. "This is good," he said, tracing the figures, then the names underneath. "I like the lettering." He looked up at her. "I need you to change it."

"Change it?" The swell of relief ebbed away.

"There's extra in it for you, of course, but we need a new version. The date of the fight has changed."

"When?"

"Third of the wane."

"Third of *this* wane? But that's –"

"Two nights from now, yes."

18

"So you'll need me to work on it tonight?" *Damn.* There went her project time.

"It must be right away," Blackwood said. "I want these run off and up on every wall and gable end in the city by evening."

Lottie didn't respond immediately. It wasn't just the flowers. If she undertook this she would miss the appointment with Vickers. That mural meant a good week's steady income; assuming she could talk him into it, and she wouldn't get the chance to do that if she didn't get down there soon.

Blackwood leaned across the desk. "Fifty selenes," he said. "If it's print-ready within the hour."

Then again, hard cash had a certain allure of its own. Reluctantly, Lottie nodded.

Blackwood nodded back, sealing the deal. "I'll get you what you need."

In the end it didn't take that long. Blackwood left her in the relative peace of his office. In the background, the presses clattered out the belated morning edition. Lottie didn't read the *Oculus*. She wouldn't have said as much to Blackwood, but there was little in the paper but sports results, fish-market prices and what the Lunane had for breakfast. Nevertheless she liked being around the printers and found the rhythmic clatter relaxing to work to. Instead of a rendition of ink on paper, this time she created the back-to-front mimeograph stencil directly. It was a straightforward job, mostly copying what she'd already done and repeating the bold representation of the sparring boxers and the letters that spelled the famous names, Spitz and Rodrigo. Privately, Lottie still thought that the banner head, *Law And Order*, sounded crassly macho, but she wasn't being paid for her opinions, so all she changed was the date.

Within the hour she was off to the riverside Promise Centre with an easy extra fifty quid in her pocket.

The upper half of Glesson Street bustled with high-spirited shoppers. The days around Full were always good for business. Lottie dodged a pair of ambling old ladies, then skipped onto the road to avoid a family spread across the pavement and narrowly missed being clipped by a horse drawing a tram that slid smoothly past her trailing a woman's laughter that brightened the air like a scarlet ribbon.

The Glesson Street Promise Centre was down an alley that was also home to a couple of grim looking pubs. In her hurry, Lottie almost missed the alley entrance. She breathed relief when she spotted it, and that was when she noticed the stink of burning.

The building the Centre had occupied still stood. At least the blackened walls did, but there was nothing left inside the shell that any mural would be able to brighten now. Blackwood had mentioned a fire, but she had assumed it would have been in Dockton or Chicken Town, not here. She stood with her hand over her mouth, but that did not prevent the taste of charred wood drying it up.

Lottie heard low voices. She recognised one of the men who exited a moment later as the man she had come to see. Sebastian Vickers looked defeated, his long frame bent even lower than usual. The other man in the heavy coat and the battered hat she did not know, but there was something about him that suggested police. The two men shook hands and the policeman stalked down the alley. As he passed, he dealt Lottie a look of utter suspicion and she squirmed, fingers reaching reflexively to comb at her fringe.

"Hello, Lottie." Vickers' subdued greeting apparently demoted her in the suspect list for now, and the other man strode off round the corner.

"I'm sorry I'm late." It was lame, and irrelevant now anyway, but it was all she could think of to say.

Vickers smiled sadly. "I need some fresh air," he said. "This smell..."

Lottie walked with him to the street. "Was it an accident?" she said. "Or an act of Fullishness?"

Vickers shook his head. "It was certainly no piece of moon-addled misadventure," he said. "There was someone inside. They were tied up and... they were probably dead before they burned. The detective there thinks the fire might not have been deliberate, but it hardly matters, does it?"

Lottie could not reply. She had never heard of anything so shocking happening at Full.

"Well..." Vickers appeared unable to complete what he had been about to say. Instead, he shrugged and then stuck his hands in his pockets and wandered away. Lottie watched his head bobbing sadly above the crowd until he turned the corner. She wished she could have offered better support, but all that came to her was the Promise Centre motto, *Even in Darkness, Light will follow.* Vickers knew that one by heart, and it wasn't providing much comfort for her at this moment either.

Lottie treated herself to a tram ride home, although she took no joy from it. A blonde child in a red beret sat between her parents across from her. She stared at Lottie with wide blue eyes. Lottie leaned forward so that her hair fell into its curtain, and tried to ignore her. She never quite knew how to interact with children. They could be cruelly blunt. The girl smiled at her shyly, however. Lottie returned the gesture although she didn't feel too much like smiling. *Murder? Arson?* Those sorts of things never happened at Full. Dark, sure you took your chances at Dark. Violence was only natural then. If you were smart you stayed indoors for the duration of the month's end. But Full was for going out and partying. Full was about love and fun and having a good time.

The tram sped down and out of the Merchantry, slowing again as the horses began the heave up Beckon Hill. The little girl, twisting a lock of blonde hair around her finger, whispered to her mother, who looked over at Lottie. "Sandy wants to know what you've got in your hair." She said it pleasantly enough, but she had an uncertain look about her. The husband, who was paying attention now too, looked openly disapproving.

"Just bits and pieces I found," Lottie replied, fingering the small electrical components and parts of old machines that she'd reused as jewellery. "I'm an artist." From the smug nods, that seemed to satisfy the adults' suspicions but the child grinned shyly and played with her hair until their stop came.

When they were gone, Lottie regarded her reflection in a gleaming brass plate screwed to the wall of the car. She really didn't care about the smug couple's dismissiveness. She swept her fringe back, and wondered what they would have said if she'd showed them her *little imperfection.* That was what her mother had called it. *You'll never make it outside of The Church with your little imperfection* she had said, but she had been wrong. Sure, Glassholm was an intolerant society at times. Lottie'd been thrown out of bars in the past because of her eye; rough ones at that. Once a shopkeeper had tried to have her arrested. But tough as it was being accepted as just a little different to everyone else, she wouldn't have had it any other way. Being *the same*, that would have killed her. She blinked in the brass, the lazy eye lagging the good one by half a second, then she combed her hair forward again.

Lottie stayed on the tram for two more stops before disembarking at the top of the hill. She was only a few blocks from home, but she had her project to attend to first.

Cane Street was an ox-bow avenue shaped by two terraces curving either side of a neglected garden. Around the perimeter of the garden, fenced in by glossy black railings, grew a border of knot trees, full and bushy at this time of the month. Inside, the garden had been left to its own devices: a small fountain bearing a *bas relief* profile of the Lunane was choked with weeds, and what had once been a tidy lawn was now a riot of wild grasses. It was the perfect site. Lottie surveyed the garden before unpacking the flowers and setting to work.

By the time she was done the sun was dipping, and Lottie felt a nip in the air. She was surveying the effects of the last of the light with some satisfaction when she spotted a movement in the grass. Expecting a cat, she peered into the lengthening shadow under the fountain, then stepped back in surprise as a jointed leg tapped inquisitively at the toe of her boot.

A crab, the size of her two hands placed together, its shell the colour of fired brick. Its eyes swivelled indecisively, legs and claws investigating the air.

Lottie looked around stupidly as if expecting to find that the sea had miraculously appeared behind her. "How did you get all the way up here?" she asked the crab. Its legs tapped uncertainly on the flagstone but offered no other explanation.

Chapter 3

John Mortlock checked his reflection in the shop window next to the Laughing Gull. The street lamp on the corner had been lit just at the moment he passed the glass, and he'd caught his reflection out of the corner of his eye. Simply a reaction, that was all. Not vanity, but reflex. Nevertheless, he took the opportunity to admire how well his uniform looked. Boots, buttons and buckle shone, and in profile the wide belt suppressed most of his paunch. He touched the horseshoe shaped depression in his scalp. In the reflection he could barely even see it. It suited him very well to be working again. Mortlock took a moment longer to straighten his collar before he ducked into the café entrance.

A familiar, meaty aroma, that he privately thought of as sniffable gravy, enveloped him. The Gull marked the exact half way point along the short route between Mortlock's apartment and the Palace, and since taking up his new position it had become his habit to pop in for dinner or breakfast before a shift. He always left himself plenty of time. Rushing a meal at the Gull just wasn't on.

Mortlock slipped the evening newspaper out of the rack, and sat at the table in the far corner. This was a good spot. Funny that it was always empty when he came in, even when the place was busy. Tonight Mortlock counted four customers besides himself. There was Old Mary, of course. She was a fixture. She came in every evening and ordered a pot of tea and a teacake and if you watched her long enough you'd catch her feeding crumbs to the mouse in her coat pocket. At the window, a courting couple were doing their best to trade seductive glances over a candle and a carafe of the house red. Hell, but they could have pushed the boat out a little. The Gull was ideal for a hearty meal on a cold night, but it wasn't a place you'd be proud to point out to your kids as the origin of your romance. The last customer was a shabby young man with a notebook in which he scribbled furiously. He had the look of a waster. Probably a poet. He might even be a good one if he was as creative with his jottings as he often was with reasons not to pay for his meals.

The café's solitary waitress slouched through the kitchen door. A mousy soul, Jean or Jane, Mortlock could never remember. He watched her relieve the couple of their dessert dishes and scurry back to the kitchen. Clocking his attention on the way past, the girl nodded uncomfortably and mumbled, "Evening, Sergeant."

Nodding back, he unfolded the paper. The news was heck of a depressing again. Used to be the news after Full was little more than a social diary of the glitterati. Now there were reports of brawls, robberies, fire-raising. An editorial sidebar on page five claimed that a delegation from the Merchants' Association was seeking an audience with the Lunane on the subject of public order. No doubt he'd see that bunch of pasty-faced bean counters at the Palace soon then. That'd be something to look forward to.

The instant Mortlock put the paper down it was whisked away, replaced by a steaming plate of mashed potato and sausages slathered in onion gravy. Looking around he caught the handsome rear aspect of the proprietor, Shirley Galloway, bustling through into the kitchen. While Mortlock got stuck into his dinner, the pale girl reappeared with a pot of strong tea and his mug, the one with Mister Moony, a well-known comic strip character, on it. This was what he liked most about The Gull. His table, his mug, a good plate of proper food. It beat the hell out of frying up a piece of fish in his bitter little apartment.

Later, when Mortlock had cleared his plate and was pouring his third cup from the pot, Shirley returned with the newspaper. It was neatly folded.

Glancing up, Mortlock saw that she was watching the fawning couple by the window. "Good dinner, that," he said, embarrassed by the awkward display. "Stick to your ribs stuff."

"It doesn't do to let a professional man go to work on an empty stomach, Sergeant," the proprietor replied, although her attention didn't shift from the pair.

"Well, the Lunane can rest easy tonight, if all his men are as well fed," he said. "That's for sure." The couple, having evidently decided that the portion of their evening suitable for public display was over, giggled as they shrugged themselves into their coats. Mortlock let out a snort of relief.

"I should think so at that," Shirley said, completing their ritual exchange, and went over to clear the dishes. She had left the newspaper on his table, and his eye was drawn to the bold type of an advertisement. The Boxers were coming out of retirement again. Fancy that. Once they had been the biggest draw in the city. He remembered seeing them at a packed Royal Arena: what, twenty years ago? More? Since the assault that had invalided him out of the police force his memory wasn't so good. A long time, anyway. Nowadays, on their rare outings, the Boxers fought in front of drunks and old aficionados in the back rooms of pubs. What a shame that the rewards of their talents hadn't lasted.

"You should go," Shirley said over his shoulder. "You like the boxing, don't you?"

"I don't know," he said. "Day after tomorrow? It's too difficult to organise."

"Rubbish." She shifted the plates she was carrying, then leaned over to retrieve his own plate, awarding him an unexpected eyeful of cleavage. "What's difficult about it? It's your day off. Get out and enjoy yourself." The swinging kitchen door muffled her parting remark, but not completely. "You might even see me there."

Mortlock's opportunity to ponder that was short-lived because the silvery tinkle of the café door heralded a new arrival. He sighed when he saw who it was. There was no mistaking that bristling gait. It was Alfie Kremer, and the policeman was coming straight over.

"John," Kremer said, inviting himself to sit down. Mortlock resented the intrusion but didn't let it show. If Alfie Kremer came looking for you, it was better to get it over with as quickly as possible. Besides, he knew the man better than most. The hundred abrasive things about Kremer, the things that got him in your face and made you want to get him out of there as fast as possible, were the qualities that made him good at his job. There was a softer centre, but it took the eye of an old colleague to see it.

"Evening, Kremer," he said. "Why don't you join me?"

Kremer removed his hat, ran his fingers lovingly around the rim as if any amount of straightening would restore its original shape. Mortlock noticed the grey creeping through his dark curls. Not a problem Mortlock needed to worry about, but time's passage marked people in different ways. "Yeah," Kremer said under his breath. "I need coffee and a word."

"If Shirley is half the woman that I know her to be, your coffee will be here any minute. What's the word?"

Kremer stopped fiddling with his hat, pursed his lips. "Anything going on at the Palace right now?"

Mortlock laughed. "You want to be more specific?"

Kremer grimaced. "Don't know if I can. Just wondered if there were any rumours trickling down. Anything at all?"

Mortlock held up his hands. "Even if there was," he began, but was interrupted by the arrival of a steel pot and another mug. Shirley lifted Kremer's hat to make room on the table. He made a sound of protest, but she ignored him. Miming exaggerated care, she hung it on the coat stand beside the door.

"Even if there was," Mortlock repeated. "You know there's only so much I could pass on." Kremer was genuinely agitated, though. Mortlock lowered his voice. "Alfie, what's going on?"

Kremer examined his palms as if whatever he sought might be found among the lines of the heart and the head, the life and the moon. Then he sighed, rubbed his eyes. They were bloodshot. "Someone got chopped in a Promise Centre last night. The building was razed, although the arson I think was accidental. You know those places, too many candles. Killer got lucky."

Mortlock stared. "Murder? On Fullday?" He wanted to say, *are you sure*, but there was no equivocation about Kremer. "Who was it?"

"Jenny Garret. Bob Garret's daughter?"

Mortlock realised that Kremer was watching his reaction. He shrugged. "Should I know her?"

"Bob was a cop, back in our day. Jenny followed him into the force."

"Of course! How is Bob?"

"Bob went to the lagoon five years back, John."

Mortlock raised his hands helplessly. Kremer knew how poor his memory was.

"It doesn't matter." Kremer poured his coffee and sipped. He winced as it scalded him but persevered in attempting to drink it anyway. "Just that Jenny's last known whereabouts was the Palace."

"The Palace? Why?" City police had no jurisdiction in the Palace. In the short weeks Mortlock had worked there that had been made crystal clear.

Kremer shook his head. "We don't know. They just sent word

asking for one of us. And I sent Jenny." Kremer winced. "Do me a favour, mate? Drop her name and see what you can find?"

Mortlock snorted. "Lytten's a clam, Alfie. But I'll see what I can do."

"Appreciate it." Kremer sighed. "Sky above, but this whole city's going to the crabs. You remember what Full was like when we were on the beat? The whole of Glassholm was one big party. And the cops joined in along with everyone else."

"We were as high as the rest of them half the time." Mortlock agreed, as if he remembered it.

Kremer topped up his mug from the pot. "Any other news from over the wall?"

Mortlock thought about it. "Well, there's the eclipse of course, but nothing that out of the ordinary."

Kremer wiped his mouth on his coat sleeve. "There's an eclipse coming up?"

"Next month. One of the astronomers was muttering about it the other day. What's that got to do with anything?"

"I'm just surprised we've not heard about it. The Palace usually gives us fair warning." Kremer took out his notebook, scribbled something which he circled. "Come to think of it, there's been none of the usual 'The Lunane's Dying And The World's Coming To An End' craziness in the papers either. Now why would the Palace choose not to notify the police or the press?"

"There's nothing in it, mate," Mortlock said. "Just an oversight. That's all."

A hurried rattle and a blur of movement at the other side of the room distracted them from the subject. It took Mortlock a moment to spot the small, furry creature squatting beneath an open window. The luck monkey looked around nervously. Black fur flared tawny around its face, giving its head an orange nimbus in the café lights. The monkey chattered to itself, blinked its big eyes and then scampered across the floor towards the table occupied by the startled writer. Scurrying up the table leg, the animal reached into its mouth and fished out a crumpled piece of paper. It handed the gooey ball to the young man, whose expression of disgust as he unfolded the gift vanished the instant he realised that it was a ten selene note.

"Lucky bugger," Kremer muttered.

In Mortlock's experience someone always said that when a luck monkey visited, but you had to be careful not to speak too soon. The phrase 'double-edged sword' was too often used in reference to the little devils – especially by those who wished they had one at hand after a monkey had paid them a visit.

They didn't have to wait long for this one to prove true to its nature. Leaving the writer, the monkey bounded to the top of the coat stand, flipped Kremer's hat off its peg and then leapt down on top of it, disappearing inside.

"Hey," Kremer exclaimed, scrambling to rescue his beloved head gear. The monkey's face appeared over the rim, and seeing him approach it screeched and bolted for the window. Kremer picked up the hat, checked it for signs of damage, sniffed suspiciously and then groaned. "Little bastard's only pissed in it. As if my luck weren't bad enough." He held the hat at arm's length and shook it.

"Better do that outside," Mortlock advised, "if you don't want your luck to get a whole lot worse." Kremer stopped just in time.

"What's going on?" Shirley said as she returned. Her face said she knew something was up and, as soon as she discovered what, she was going to enjoy being angry about it.

"Alfie was just on his way out," Mortlock said.

"Aye," Kremer said. "I'll see you around, John. Let me know if you hear anything, eh?"

When the door had closed behind him Shirley said, "Anything I should be concerned about? Apart from the fact that he didn't pay for his coffee."

"Shouldn't think so," Mortlock replied, disquieted by what he had learned. "I'll get his coffee."

Shirley started to clear away the cups. "I don't like that Detective Kremer," she said. "There's something unpleasant about him."

Mortlock leaned back to give her room. "Alfie's got his quirks," he said, "but he's one of the good ones."

Shirley moved around the table, wiping it down with practised efficiency. "Why was he carrying his hat like that?"

Mortlock barked a short laugh. "You don't want to know," he said, instead directing her attention to the lucky writer. "But the good news is that wee idler over there will be able to pay for his dinner tonight."

"Well, there's a piece of the moon," she said. The lad with the notebook appeared to have heard, because he began fishing change out of his pocket. Shirley went over to help him with the arithmetic.

Mortlock glanced at the café clock. Time to get to work. He shrugged into his coat and constructed a cairn of coins beside the cruet.

"So, the fight, then?" Shirley said, ringing open the till.

Mortlock frowned. "I thought you were joking," he said. "Since when were you into the boxing?"

"Since I was a kid," she said. "My dad was a fan."

"The Grant Arms isn't exactly what you'd call a sophisticated night spot," Mortlock said. It was in fact a fairly rough area. Then again, Shirley Galloway knew her way around the city as well as any.

Shirley closed the till and folded her arms. "So, I guess you'll just have to escort me. You can call for me here. I'll be ready at nine."

"Well," he said, seeing now the guiding hand that had engineered the entire scenario. "If you're set on going, I'm happy to make sure you get there and back in one piece."

"My hero." Shirley wore a satisfied smile. "Now go to work before they stick you on a late charge."

Mortlock mock-saluted her. "Ma'am," he said, and stepped outside.

He had taken no more than three paces from the café door when a weight thudded onto his shoulder. Instinctively, he spun and shook himself to dislodge his assailant, but he felt tiny sharp fingers grip his earlobe and a fistful of what little he had left in the way of hair.

Carefully, he turned his head and stared into the surprised looking face of the luck monkey that had visited the café earlier. Mortlock glanced worriedly at his coat, and hoped that the creature had contented itself with Kremer's hat on the urination score at least.

The monkey blinked and then reached into its mouth and removed a metal disc that appeared too wide to have possibly fitted in there. The disc looked to be made of beaten tin and two punched holes on opposite sides had each been threaded with a length of chain that, from the broken links, had once apparently attached the disc to something else. The dangling ends dripped saliva. Mortlock took it gingerly from the offering paw, and the monkey leapt to the ground and scurried off down the lane.

Mortlock wiped the thing on his sleeve and turned it over. He had absolutely no idea what this was, nor what kind of luck it would bring him, although delivered so soon after making that assignation with Shirley made him wonder how their date would turn out. He would find out in due course, he supposed. That was the nature of luck. For now he pocketed the disc and set off for the Palace.

He cut along a short zigzag of streets to reach Sali Boulevard, one of the wide concourses that climbed up to the Palace like a starfish's arms. Even on such a cold night the boulevard was buzzing. The nights following Full were for making the most of the monthly well-being before it dwindled. Youngsters crowded the stylish bars, laughter and soft music spilling out of the windows. At one of the pavement restaurants a family was seated at a long table under a fringed canopy. From the wizened matriarch at one end to the teenage girls whispering conspiracies at the other to the toddlers running gleefully around, the whole clan were enjoying the night in the traditional Glassholm fashion.

Little evidence of the whole city going to the crabs. Kremer was discovering a penchant for exaggeration in his old age.

Mortlock crossed slippery cobbles. They glittered with frost, mirroring the star-pricked sky. He looked up for a moment, then strolled on, not needing to check his watch to make sure that he was on time. The moon that circled the city was better than clockwork. He still had a few minutes to spare.

There were said to be one hundred and one ways into the Lunane's Palace. Mortlock had already discovered a dozen, not including the main entrance. He imagined Chief Lytten knew a fair few more. Only the Lunane could possibly know them all. Tonight, Mortlock used the Guards Gate.

As he entered the guardroom where his men had mustered for the shift change, Mortlock looked out of the window. The crystal in the South Gate finial flared. No more than a second later he heard the distant chimes of the Foundry clock. Seven o'clock.

Time to go to work.

Chapter 4

Third of Kent Wane, 507UM

It took three days for the headache to fade, for the shivery weakness in Anton's limbs to ease off, the sickness in his gut to settle, the long periods of sudden, crashing tiredness to lessen. He wasn't sure if the improvement was directly due to the supply of pearly pills provided by Doctor Frisk, or whether he was just getting over it. Whatever *it* was. He had long since dismissed the notion that he was suffering from a hangover. More than likely he had picked up a chill that first night, or perhaps he was suffering a stress reaction to his fiasco of a wedding. None of which explained why these people had continued to detain him under this stupid pretext. Moreover, there was something about the smooth, capable manner in which Gerard, Hogarth and Frisk dealt with him. As if they had been prepared for it.

"You'll feel better soon, sir," Gerard told him on a regular basis. "More like yourself."

That might have been comforting if Anton's idea of himself had not remained directly at odds to that of everyone else. He had worn himself out over the last two days arguing with them. It had started at a civilised level. He'd thought that coming clean, explaining who he was and how he came to be in the Palace would be the first step to sorting out the situation.

"My name is Anton Dunn," he had said. They had smiled, nodded.

"I am an engineer," he had said. "An inventor."

"Yes, sir," they had chorused.

"I was getting married," he had said. "I broke in here to find my wife."

"Now, sir." Gerard's capacity for patience was proving to be infuriating. "This is the Royal Palace. No person has ever broken in. You simply came home."

"I don't understand why you are doing this."

"Regrettably, sometimes your memory becomes affected…" Gerard's smile oozed condescension, "shall we say *overloaded* at Full. It is one of the many sacrifices you make for your people."

"I'm not the Lunane," Anton had yelled. "I'm bloody not!"

"Yes, sir." Always that smile. "Yet, you are. We'll help you remember."

It was futile. As much as Anton knew for certain that he was not the city's sainted founder who had laid its first brick and presided over its *continuity* – in Anton's opinion that often-used word equated to stagnation – since, for some unfathomable reason these people maintained that he was. If this was meant to be a punishment, it was singularly cruel and unusual. Certainly, they were keeping him prisoner. Doubtless they would deny this, but he had tried more than once to leave the apartments. If he really was the Lunane, why would his servants lock him in?

If challenged, there would be some explanation forthcoming, of course. This Gerard was a clever man. Clearly, the situation required a more cunning approach. Maybe he would get further if he called their bluff.

Hogarth was in his usual place. He nodded civilly when Anton parted the curtains, and followed him into the dressing room. As before, he loitered at the door with pen and ledger while Anton chose what to wear.

The clothes in the wardrobe had been replaced again. Today they had progressed to a silvery colour. By the time Halfday rolled around they would be grey. The logic of it almost made him look forward to Dark, not that he intended to be here that long.

He chose some underwear, a pair of jeans and a corduroy shirt, then lifted a good stout pair of silver-white boots from the shoe rack and took the clothes into the toilet.

After locking the door, he took a moment to compose himself. He might have recovered his fitness, but he was still far from his normal self. It wasn't just coming to terms with his predicament, his sleep was disturbed by dreams too. Or rather, *non-dreams*. Several times a night he started awake, shaken with a lingering sense of import, like the after-clamour of a great bell, but the instant his eyes popped open he found himself in a state of pleasant calmness and with no memory whatsoever of what had seemed so dramatic in his dream. Last night he had thought he heard voices too, echoes of just-finished conversation shivering off the bedroom wall.

No, he really didn't feel like his normal self at all.

Anton washed, shaved, and in the highly polished steel mirror he examined his face. There was no mistake. It was definitely his. An average face, neither handsome nor especially hideous. The skin was slack and pale from too much time spent in darkened rooms. Heavyweight eyebrows bullied watery, red-rimmed eyes. It was a serious, functional face. Not at all the face of a king.

Now he considered it, though, Anton was hard pushed to call to mind the Lunane's features. In common with most citizens, he was familiar with the profile on coins, with the portraits in the Galleria Selena, with the occasional fuzzy newspaper photograph taken at public events, but he had never personally stood in the actual presence of the man. Vaguely, he thought, the Lunane had a more noble nose, a prouder chin and intelligent, piercing eyes, but he suspected that might be closer to popular ideal than physical reality.

Be that as it may, the face looking back at him now belonged to no one more lofty than an unremarkable scientist. That was what he was, and he would apply all of his method and reason to discovering a solution to his predicament. The first step would be to find out what Gerard's game was, then he would use that knowledge to find Krista, and a means of escaping the Palace to resume their lives. He wanted Krista's warm humour and companionable chat more than anything. Although, he was itching to get back to his workshop too.

Of the three men he had access to, Anton identified young Hogarth as the weak link. He would start with him.

In a fit of sarcastic defiance, Anton combed his hair in what he imagined was a regal style and then returned to the circular room.

"You say I am the Lunane," Anton said, leaning against the desk.

Hogarth inclined his head, clearly nervous. "Of course, sir."

"And you are my biographer?" He had been mistaken in his first assumption that the lad collected the goings on of the Palace for the newspaper scuttlebutt. They really meant *the* Lunane's biographer. "You write down everything that I do?"

"Yes, sir." This was more solid ground for the young man. He knew his own business at least. "Everything."

Anton sneaked a look at the ledger. Hogarth's pen was poised, having just completed a line of cramped script. It read, *The Lunane questioned the biographer, Hogarth, about his work.*

"Why?" Anton said.

The biographer swallowed. "Because you told me to, sir. The unbroken record of your continuity is the story of Glassholm. It's one of the greatest symbols of our city's magnificent constancy."

"I don't remember telling you to do any such thing." Anton felt only a little ashamed to watch the boy squirm.

"Of course, your memory..." the biographer began. Then, perhaps remembering the tantrums of the day before, he chose a different approach. "Well, it wasn't me you told originally." Seeing Anton's raised eyebrow he stumbled on. "Of course, it was Ringley, the First Biographer. But that was hundreds of years ago. Many others have had the honour since then."

"I see. It's a sort of standing order then." Anton nodded, thoughtful. "So, I suppose you can tell me what I did on, say, the penultimate day of last wax?" He had spent the morning running trials in his workshop on the new field generator. After that, the afternoon had been spent at the bookie's with a little pocket money and a full card of dog races, while Krista had taken over their home to make last minute wedding arrangements. It had been a pleasant day, but in light of everything that had happened since, it felt strangely detached. As if he had heard about it happening to someone else.

"Happily, sir." Hogarth flipped through the ledger. Each page was so filled with the compacted script that it would have been hard to read the right way up without a magnifying glass, let alone from Anton's skewed vantage. Hogarth seemed to have no difficulty however, and quickly found the appropriate passage. "In the morning you rose. You breakfasted on blood pudding and eggs. You dressed in –"

"Stop." Anton had never eaten blood pudding in his life. He enjoyed a good fry up but that dish was too horribly congealed even for him. "Never mind my breakfast. What did I do?"

Hogarth's finger traced down the paragraph. "You, ah, you," he paused, then found what he was looking for. "Well, sir, you went for a walk around the Water Garden. You listened to your orchestra perform Ball's *Tranquilus*, but you were feeling ill, so you came back to your rooms and went to bed, where you wept until Doctor Frisk came with your pills."

"Let me see." Anton snatched the book from the biographer's fingers, ignoring the cry of protest. Hogarth had paraphrased, but in essence he had spoken exactly what was written under the nominated date. He handed the book back. Hogarth accepted it with a flicker of a glare, and then ducked his head and scrawled, *The Lunane inspected his biography*. The biographer really did write down everything.

"And what about my actions of the last month, the last year?" he said. "If I am the Lunane, as you say, I don't suppose that one meagre book will tell us what I was doing on, say," he pulled a date out of the air, "the seventh of Lutis wane, a hundred and thirty-two years ago?" He didn't even try to keep the sarcasm out of his voice.

To his credit, Hogarth kept his composure. "No, sir," he said. "This book can't tell you that. Older records are kept in the Lunane's Library."

Anton gaped. People pored over the black-bordered diary column on the front page of the newspaper every morning. How had he not known that it was a verbatim description of the Lunane's actual life? Krista would have laughed at his ignorance. "It all just washes over you, doesn't it, Adamant," she would have said. And he would have admitted as much, happily. Glassholmers were so obsessed with the minutiae of custom and observance that they lacked any ambition to improve their lot. Conservatism was a pernicious disease. It anaesthetised the imagination, dimmed the sight, calcified the heart. For years, he had bitten his tongue but eventually it had forced him out of the Foundry. The myopic idiots who ran the place only wanted tame lackeys who would plug away meekly on their prescriptive research programmes into trying to understand what remained of the Founders' machines – a futile pursuit when even the composition of the component materials was lost knowledge. New ideas were anathema in the Foundry and, when Anton had walked away, it had been an unimaginable relief. The act had meant financial insecurity, as well as loss of standing in the community, but it had been worth it to be free of the shackles of protocol.

Hogarth tapped his pen against the pages of his book.

"This library," Anton said. "Since it is mine, I assume I'll be able to go and find out for myself."

Hogarth's smile was unexpected. "Of course, sir," he said. "It is your Palace. You can go wherever you wish."

Anton waited a beat. "Except that you lock the doors."

Hogarth managed a look close to genuine contrition. "Ah, sir," he said. "The swell of the month has an unpredictable effect on you indeed. Surely, you are the rock at the centre of all tides. It is the great burden that you bear for your people to endure such a debilitation when they are free to celebrate the moon's beneficence." He simpered. "Since they were painted and rehung, there has been a trick to opening your apartment doors. It's so minor that its rectification has not been a priority before now, but Mister Gerard will be affronted to think that such a small thing has caused you distress."

"A trick?" Anton strode towards the doors that he was told connected the round room to the rest of the Palace. He had used a fair degree of force on them. They had definitely been locked.

Hogarth followed him down the short corridor, and demonstrated unsuspected litheness to squeeze past and lay his hand on the brass handles. "Please," he said. "Let me demonstrate." The biographer made a show of pulling the left door towards him and jiggling the handle of the right one up and then down. The door opened.

Anton flashed the biographer a glare that wiped the satisfaction from his face. Before he reached for the door himself, it was pushed open from the other side.

The obsequious figure of Gerard blocked his exit. "Good morning, sir," the older man said. "Excellent to see you up and about."

Anton did not know specifically what Gerard's job title was on the Palace staff, but from his manner and the deference shown to him by Hogarth and Frisk, the man clearly held a high office. Even Anton backed away from the door as Gerard entered.

"I'm feeling much better today, thank you," he said.

"Good. In that case I thought we might discuss your diary for the coming week."

Anton stood his ground. If the official was intent on treating him as the Lunane, he meant to exercise that authority as far as he was able.

"Not now, I think," he said breezily. "If you don't mind, I've been cooped up for so long and I've asked Hogarth to reacquaint me with the rest of the Palace."

This earned him a long, appraising look. "As you wish, sir," Gerard said, standing aside. "Your calendar can wait."

What Anton, followed dog-like by Hogarth, found beyond the apartments surprised him. First, there was an anteroom that held a baroque steel cylinder. The cylinder was ten feet in diameter and reached from floor to ceiling. The exterior was decorated with a carved relief. Pacing around the entirety, Anton saw that it depicted the city, encompassing everything from the fishing boats moored at harbour to the rising edifices of the Merchantry and the Palace itself. The detail was incredible. Fish and crustaceans swam among the boats, people could be spied toiling at various endeavours through the windows of the buildings, tiny luck monkeys scurried across the rooftops bearing fortunes, and birds circled the city's solid towers. The tallest of these towers, with its familiar domed top inches away from the finely cratered round of the moon, rose clear above everything else. Beautiful as it was, the significance was a bit heavy handed: *You are here.*

But why? He was still no closer to puzzling that out.

The pillar was an astonishing piece of work, but Anton had already guessed its function. Since there were no stairs, there was only one thing it could be, although the only other example of its type was a crude contraption he had seen in The Foundry. A round window in one of the shore-facing houses looked the likeliest candidate to be a button. He pressed it, and sure enough a door opened. He was right. This was an electrically powered elevator. Stepping inside, he turned back to Hogarth. Waiting for the youth to finish scribbling, Anton realised that one aspect at least of the snappish anxiety that made him drum his fingers on the cool metal was the feeling of being the subject of an experiment.

"Are you coming, or what?" Anton was gratified to see the lad hurry.

The interior of the elevator was tiled with a geometric mosaic comprised of ceramic tesserae. When Hogarth had squeezed in beside him, Anton pressed the lower of the two obvious, triangular buttons. The curved door slipped shut, then the elevator began a measured descent. Anton was amazed at the smoothness of the ride. This was original Founder technology. The difference between this and the beast at the Foundry only illuminated how far they still were from recapturing the marvels that Glassholmers had lost in their years of hardship. He could hardly tell that he was moving at all, let alone how far or how fast. A gentle rocking indicated that they had reached the floor below and the door rolled open.

Anton stepped out into the centre of a state room. At first sight, the room's wedge-shape produced a sensation of wrongness of perspective. The floor was an expanding chess board of cream and cerulean tiles. His footsteps echoed uncomfortably loud in the stilted atmosphere. A set of doors opened in the centre of the wall to the left of the pillar. In front of him the room widened to meet four tall windows, each flanked by stained glass panels that depicted the same grand, shining figure holding in his hand some phase of the moon. The figure, he noted, was depicted in a generic manner. The features were handsome enough, but too idealised to be an accurate representation of any real person.

"I take it that's Him," Anton said. "I mean me."

"The Lunane wears many a face, sir," Hogarth said enigmatically. It sounded as if he was quoting from something, but if he was Anton didn't recognise it.

Anton didn't puzzle too deeply over the images, because the windows themselves were astonishing. The purity of the glass had to be phenomenal for such large panes to survive the cycle of the months. It was unthinkable however, even for the Founders, for the glass to have remained intact since the Palace was built, so there had to be a layer of that very fine vitric that had been used in the apartments, but if there was, it was impossible to see. He would have to ask someone how it was done. The cost of replacing the finer optical components of his experiments was crippling, and access to such a preservative would save him a fortune.

Beneath the windows ran a graceful seat upholstered in glossy green leather. It was evident from the worn patches that someone had spent a lot of time sitting there. The view was glorious. It extended across the city and much of the island beyond the walls; although, like most Glassholmers, Anton had only a rudimentary knowledge of the farmlands and less hospitable scrub that lay out there. A bright shimmer caught his attention to the far right. That he supposed must be the falls of the Cord, where the river came down out of the hills. It slowed and widened through the farm lands before entering the city through the eastern wall. Here, overlooked by the smoking, lumpen edifice of the Foundry, it split in two. The Little Cord wound its way through the Parks and enchanted lovers as it passed under the Seven

Bridges of the Merchantry before rejoining its more direct parent. The larger river had but one bridge: a monstrous, overdesigned monolith that overshadowed the district to the south west. The river widened after that, and hosted the myriad quays and jetties of Dockton before opening out into the harbour and then, finally, the sea. The Cord's curious tidal properties were something he did know about. At high tide a bore wave travelled its length, driving purposefully against the river's flow.

Anton stared towards a dense clot of tenements not far from where the rivers re-merged. That was where they lived, he and Krista. Not much of a place, but it was a home. He wondered if Frank had been round checking up on him, or Krista's parents demanding answers. What would they do when they discovered not only their daughter gone, but her husband as well? Like any good Glassholmers, they would suspect. They had never approved of his ideas or his attitude. What kind of man gave up a steady job to scrape a living on his own? Not the kind they wanted for a son-in-law, that was for sure.

Krista understood him. Somehow she always found good words to explain him to others. He had to find her.

Turning away from the window, a glint caught Anton's attention. Something half hidden by the elevator pillar. The light caught the edge of it. It was almost as if, like an unwanted ornament gifted by a family member, it had been placed so that while it was on display, it was also easy to miss.

And with good reason. This was one of the ugliest pieces of statuary Anton had ever seen. Ugly and magnificent. Standing as high as his chest, the sculpture was a representation of a giant, squatting monkey fashioned from blackened iron. Looking closely, he saw that it was assembled from a collection of finely wrought spars and struts. The legs, arm joints, waist, the knuckles it balanced on, even its segmented tail were fully articulated. The staring eyes were blank spheres the size of apples, and its mad grin was a composite of perfectly interlocking teeth that resembled the meshing of two wicked saw blades. No wonder the thing was half-hidden.

Anton wanted to ask Hogarth about it, but the biographer had moved on ahead. The next room was identical to the first. Another segment in what must form a wheel in a similar fashion to the apartments above. In place of the elevator, a circular brass boss sat in the centre of the tiles. The relief moulding of the boss depicted a crab. The shell of the thing raised from the floor like a metallic hummock, with the legs tucked underneath. In its way this was as wonderfully hideous as the monkey.

The crab and the monkey. He remembered that from school. When the Lunane built the city, and fixed the moon in the heavens above, he co-opted the help of the animals to help him make all aspects of his new city work. He asked the crabs of the sea to help the fishermen to provide food, and he asked the monkeys of the land to bring the people good fortune, and then, most important of all, he enlisted the help of the crows of the air. Their special job was to carry messages between the Lunane and his moon.

Children's stories.

Crabs were just another kind of produce that could be bought at the fishmarket, it was only natural that crows should congregate among the eaves of the tallest buildings on the island, and as for the monkeys, well surely it was in the nature of such inquisitive, intelligent animals to carry bits of this or that around the city. As far as Anton was concerned, imbuing those random tokens with a nebulous quality such as luck was a human characteristic, not a supernatural one.

Hurrying on in search of Hogarth, Anton found that the subsequent rooms in the wheel repeated the motif. The seventh completed the circle with another elevator shaft. For reasons of symmetry he expected to find another monkey statue, but attached to the elevator column, just below the ceiling, was a sleek, gleaming body folded around itself. Something sharp hung down below. He stared at it for a moment, then he realised that it was upside down. The folded parts were the wings, and the hanging protrusion was a large corvine head. One bright steel eye seemed to watch him, and the sharp beak had the menace of a veteran's scimitar.

"Quite unsettling, until you get used to them," Hogarth said.

"What the heck are they?" Anton said.

The young biographer pressed his lips in a thoughtful fashion that Anton was coming to recognise as an indication that he was considering how to phrase his next sentence. "They're your friends, sir," he said. The slight stress he placed on 'friends' made Anton suspect that he didn't find them very friendly either. "You had them made during an early period in your reign –"

"Right." Anton cut him off, indicated the elevator. "Shall we?"

The journey down one more level brought them to a small antechamber similar to the one outside the apartments. The doors to the chamber opened onto a balconied landing. Two staircases, curling downwards, hugged the interior walls of the high Castil tower. Anton was struck by the enormity of the interior space below him. Odd that he had disparaged the opulence of the tower every day of his life, but had never wondered what it was actually like inside.

Another surprise came when he looked up. There should have been a ceiling to mark the floor of the rooms he had just been walking in, but directly above the balcony there was an expansive transparent cupola, like a much larger version of the one above his bed. Through the dome he saw a heavy bank of cloud. Rain was on the way. To anyone below it would be as if the apartments above did not exist. Or as if the occupant lived in the sky itself. A simple but effective metaphor that once again could only have been delivered by the engineering wizardry of the Founders themselves. The elevator was one thing, but this was quite different. He had never seen such a grand example of their art. Not even in the Foundry.

Anton prickled with excitement. It seemed that there might be an upside to his imprisonment after all.

Below this landing, Anton counted eight more levels, the last almost invisible in the gloom. Indistinct sounds of habitation – the first he had encountered since entering the Palace, save for the three conspirators – rose up to greet him. A murmur of voices. A repetitive metallic noise that might be from a kitchen or a workshop. A woman's laugh, clear and full of fun, reminded him of Krista.

"The Library is on the fifth level, sir." Hogarth murmured it, less bold now they were out of the private apartments. Obviously, the Lunane's demi-godhood was not to be called into question in public.

"Later," Anton said, starting down the stairs. "First you're going to show me where the Brides live."

"The Brides, sir?" Hogarth had to gather his grey robes to prevent himself tripping on the stairs.

"You know what I mean." Anton raised his voice as he approached the next landing. "Where are they?"

From beyond the doors closest to the staircase came a muted thrum of conversation. As Anton reached out to open them, Hogarth stumbled down the remaining steps. "Wait," he said, but Anton had already walked into the room beyond. It was a long room, with pillars supporting a high ceiling frescoed with a map of the night sky. In between the pillars, tables were covered in charts, and the walls were lined with thin-drawered cabinets and conventional bookcases. At the far end, Anton spied an intriguing gleam of brass, and beyond that, an iron staircase spiralled upwards. The room was occupied by a number of studious looking men and women bent over the charts, or typing at their desks. To Anton, used to the quiet efficiency of research teams in the Foundry, their muted conversation was reassuringly normal.

Then they began to notice him. Heads went up and typewriter chatter fell away. Expectation filled their faces. Anton's gaze darted from face to face, and in each he saw discomfort, but there was unmistakeable deference too. He had expected the pretence to be blown apart, but no. These people actually thought he was the Lunane.

Hogarth appeared at Anton's shoulder, attempting with some success to regain his breath while he maintained his composure. "Perhaps this would be better discussed outside, sir?"

Anton nodded and backed out of the room closing the doors behind him. There was a respectful beat before the conversation resumed.

"Who are those people?" he asked.

"They are your astronomers, sir," Hogarth replied. "I take it you didn't see your, ah, friend among them?"

Anton shook his head quizzically. "No, why would I? She has no interest in the stars. She came here to be a Bride, not a boffin." Confusion boiled up into anger now. "Quit stalling. Take me to her."

Hogarth smiled with what looked like genuine sympathy. "I'm sorry," he said. "It's not as simple as that."

Anton leaned on the landing balustrade, suddenly deflated. Just when he had thought he was getting somewhere he was blocked. He allowed himself to be distracted by motes of dust that sparkled as they fell through an unexpected spear of sunlight. A beam that could not possibly exist because the dome above was not, of course, a window. A nice touch, he thought.

"Explain," he said wearily.

"Well, sir. It's a public conceit that girls from the city who become..." the biographer coughed and glanced away, "...who become

42

infatuated..." The subject was obviously causing him embarrassment.

"With the Lunane?" Anton offered.

"Yes, sir. At least with the idea of the Lunane."

"What do you mean?

"Well, as you know, your image. Physically. It can occasionally be subject to variation."

Anton finally began to see. They used substitutes? He supposed it was possible that the Lunane, like anyone else, might not be available one hundred percent of the time. Times of severe illness, for example. Perhaps the old tyrant even took a holiday every now and again. Although, of course, his ego wouldn't have anyone know about it. "And these occasions coincide with this supposed memory loss?" he speculated.

"Sometimes, sir, yes." Hogarth looked relieved that Anton was following him. "So, rather than falling in love with you, it's Him that they become besotted with."

"Who do?" He was still thinking about being the Lunane's substitute. Presumably he'd been selected for having some passing physical resemblance, and it would certainly explain why he'd been locked away for three days. But if that were the reason, how had one of those astronomers, who worked here every day, not spotted him instantly for a fake?

"The Brides, sir?"

"Oh, yes. So they *do* come here," Anton said, "to devote their lives, or whatever?"

"Indeed, yes, sir, but, they don't actually *become* your brides in the marital sense. That would be... impractical."

"So what happens to them? They don't get turned away at the gates."

"We tried that. The hunger-strikes were effective demonstrations of the people's love for you, but they made you look less than compassionate. Usually, they're found work in the Palace. Mostly that pleases them, knowing they're working in your service. Sometimes they even get to see you. At a distance of course."

Anton sighed. He just wanted to find Krista and walk right out of the front door with her, but it seemed that it was going to be more difficult than that. "So, if Krista's not a Bride, how can I find her?" he said.

Hogarth looked doubtful. "I suppose enquiries could be made," he said. "The masters of the various household departments may know if someone has been taken on recently. And of course the guard may remember any supplicants that came last Full. I'm sure Mister Gerard…"

"Not Gerard." If Anton was certain of anything it was that any enquiry involving Gerard would turn up fruitless. Hogarth, on the other hand, seemed well-meaning. Perhaps he wasn't so much Gerard's puppy as he had first appeared. "You can do it," Anton said. "Can't you?" He gripped Hogarth's writing arm. "And without recording it in that bloody book, please."

Hogarth looked nonplussed for a moment, then in a serious tone he said, "She has made an impression, this one?"

Anton nodded, close to pleading now. "Her name is Krista Leitch. She has brown hair, straight and coarse as a horse's tail, her eyes are a bewitching mite too far apart, her smile cannot decide between annoyance and lust, and it is possible that no man would honestly call her beautiful." He smiled ruefully. "But I do."

This seemed to make up Hogarth's mind. He nodded curtly. "I can't promise anything," he said, "but I'll see what I can do."

The landing doors opened then, and two women emerged. One was past middle-age, her hair turned as steely as the rims of her spectacles, and the other, while closer to Krista's age, was a good four inches taller and sported immaculately styled platinum locks. The manner in which they broke off their conversation and averted their eyes when they saw him made Anton uncomfortable. The respectful two seconds that they lingered would have given him the opportunity to talk to them, but when he didn't speak they continued down the stairs in silence.

Anton realised that if he didn't escape this place soon, this was how it was going to be every time he saw a woman in the Palace.

If this pretence continued it had to be the cruellest and most elaborate rap on the knuckles ever administered. Disquiet now settled on top of the disappointment like sea sediment.

Gerard waited in the lounge of Anton's apartments, relaxing in one of the armchairs. Two glasses of imported whisky sat on a little table. When Anton arrived, Gerard gestured for him to sit, nudging one of the glasses towards the other chair.

Anton hovered, but then acquiesced. He needed the drink too much.

"The Lunane is every man," Gerard said. It was a quote from a song that all Glassholmers learned in childhood. "And every man is he."

"Everyone knows that," Anton snapped. "I didn't think it was supposed to be taken literally."

"Nevertheless, it is true, sir." There was a steely twinkle in his eye that Anton disliked. "Hogarth," Gerard said to the biographer. "I imagine you have things to do. You can enter the next hour as: the Lunane discussed his coming affairs with his secretary."

Hogarth nodded and returned to his desk.

Anton held the tumbler up to the light. The thick glass was excellent quality, the honey-coloured liquid inside only tinged slightly green. He held the glass to his face, breathing in the heady fumes, before finally taking a sip. The smooth-raw flavour uncurled in his stomach like a fiery snake. With his second mouthful he drained the glass, clipped it emphatically down on the table. Only then did he look at Gerard.

"That's what you are, is it?" he said. "My secretary?"

"Your Private Secretary, sir," Gerard murmured. "It is my job to make sure that your affairs run to order."

Anton allowed himself a grim smile. "To whose orders?"

Gerard, toying with the rim of his own glass, managed to look surprised. "Why yours, of course."

"Only sometimes I have to be reminded."

"As you say."

Anton got up and retrieved the whisky bottle from the bar. Returning to his chair he poured himself another generous measure. He didn't offer to top up Gerard's glass.

"So what happened to the real one?"

"I'm sure I don't know what you mean."

"The Lunane? Our king? The man I'm standing in for. Is he ill? Is he feeling his age? Did the lazy sod take a vacation?"

Gerard's expression didn't even flicker.

"Look, I understand that people see what they want to see –"

"What they expect to see."

"Precisely – the man in the Lunane's clothes must be the Lunane, right? But don't treat me like an idiot."

Gerard's eyes glittered. "An idiot is the last thing I hope you are," he said softly. "But it would be a lot easier if you would stop acting like one. The Royal glamour is far more than simply massaging expectations. It is the fulfilment of a need. Accept this when I tell you: for the time being, you are the *only* Lunane this city has got."

Chapter 5

The hungry mouths of Glassholm had a taste for fish that found its ultimate expression in the excesses of Full. Steaming hagfish pies decorated with crisp pastry moons were the centrepieces of family dinners and chilled blue shrimp cocktails sparkling with nacre dust were all the rage in the fashionable bars. When the fun of Full was done, the first of the population to get back to business were the fishermen, stacking their nets and sending their little boats out in search of flounder, codling and crab.

Lottie hoped that one crab would be spared that fate. That was, if they got that far. Taking the crab she'd found in the garden back to the sea had seemed like the right thing to do, but now she wasn't so sure. Here she was with her charge in a tin bucket, trying and failing not slosh precious water as it swung on its handle and leading a procession of jeering brats. The little bastards cheered with every splash that hit the pavement. She had done her best to ignore them, hoping they would get bored eventually and disappear. No such luck.

Toiling up Brick Street, focussing on the outline of a Founders' stone that silhouetted the crest like an odd-fingered hand, she passed a factory wall emblazoned with a swathe of red and black. It took her a moment to recognise the colourful display as a collage of many copies of her poster. It looked good.

"You some kind of Fool, missus?" The speaker at her shoulder was a youth of maybe thirteen, scrawny and fidgety. His equally unappealing companions shuffled behind him.

"Sorry?" she said. There was a knife in his hand. She stared at it, uncomprehending. It was a used-looking kitchen knife, probably none too sharp, but still dangerous enough if he decided to use it.

Decided to use it? The wane was hardly begun, and he was only a lad.

"See," the boy sneered. "Hatchard Hill is ours, and we reckoned if you're fullish enough to walk a bucket through it, splashing your shite all over the place, you should probably pay our pavement tax." He kept a straight face, but the others chuckled.

Finally Lottie's brain caught up. "Are you trying to rob me?" she said.

The boy's companions sniggered again, but he just pulled an impatient expression and glanced meaningfully at the knife.

Then the other boys shut up, and Lottie braced herself for whatever was going to happen.

From behind her a new voice entered the conversation. "The lady asked you a question," it said. "Are you trying to rob her?" The owner of the voice was a burly man, barely taller than Lottie but powerfully built. His bald head sat down on the folds of his neck like a cannon ball on a spring. Ear lobes hung heavy with glinting shrapnel. The leather coat he wore over his vest and jeans was scuffed through to the grey, rough stuff, and his two hands, hidden in the coat's deep pockets promised more violence than all of these boys' blades put together.

The lad shook his head. The knife had vanished. His companions had already retreated, and it looked as though they might break into a run at any moment. Stripped of their earlier menace, they looked like the children they were.

"Then apologise to her," the man said. "And then you can piss off."

"Sorry," the boys mumbled, and then turned and ran down the hill.

"Thanks," Lottie said, unsure whether the situation had just got better, or was about to become a whole lot worse.

"Don't mention it. Little bastards are getting out of control." Her rescuer sighed. "The whole city is getting out of control."

Lottie, remembering the state of Blackwood's press and the blackened shell of the Promise centre, nodded in agreement.

The man looked at her thoughtfully, then turned his attention to the posters on the wall. He scratched at one greying mutton chop sideburn. "Law And Order," he read. "Is that what they're calling it?"

It seemed an odd thing to say, but Lottie had privately thought the same when Blackwood had told her what the text for the poster was to be. Unwilling to antagonise him she chose to laugh. "You know sports promoters," she said. "They'll exaggerate like anything to make two men knocking lumps out of each other sound like an important event."

The man's eyebrows rode up his forehead. Then he cracked one of the most utterly charming smiles that Lottie had ever seen and laughed like a donkey. "Darling girl," he said. "I believe it is the most seriously important event that will take place in Glassholm tonight. Two men knocking lumps out of one another is precisely what the city is all about right now. As you've seen. The Lunane..." He stopped. There was a spark in his eyes. He licked his lips, and apparently decided not to complete that sentence according to his original thought. "Well, the Lunane could learn a thing or two by watching the occasional boxing match."

Lottie wondered what he had been about to say. The Lunane was sometimes blamed for the weather, and for sending the luck monkeys to the wrong door, but criticising him was as pointless as complaining about the moon itself.

"You should come to the fight," the man said. "You might just get to see me have lumps knocked out of myself."

"You're a boxer?" Lottie regretted her earlier remark.

"Guilty as charged," the boxer said. "Tell you what, you've an honest face. Come along tonight. I promise you it'll be educational. You won't have to pay. Just ask for Rudi at the door."

"Rudi," she said. "Is that you? Rudi?" But he was already stomping down the street.

The Grant Arms was one of those ubiquitous, street corner locals that were required features for southside districts like Rifkin. It was a grey, solid-looking edifice, propping up the tenement flats above it, and Lottie might not have realised it was a pub had not a window opened and expelled a cloud of beery steam.

Now she knew this was the place, Lottie spotted a torn copy of her poster tacked to the pub door. Above that a yellow, mullioned window glared like an old dog's eye. The door vibrated with the snarl of noise from within. Perhaps this wasn't such a good idea after all.

She was about to turn away when the door opened and a blast of noise and heat escaped. The face of a matronly woman peeked out. "Are you coming in or what?" the woman said.

Taken by surprise, Lottie gaped like a fish until she remembered what she was supposed to say. "I'm here to see...Rudi."

Bushy eyebrows rose. The eyes they shaded squinted. "Rudi? Are you sure now?"

"That was what he said," Lottie replied. Had she got it wrong? It had been *Rudi*, hadn't it?

The woman shrugged, but did not open the door any further. Instead she flicked her head to the right. "Round the side, down the alley," she said, and then shut the door in Lottie's face.

That was it. Time to call it a night and go home. There was no way Lottie was going to start investigating any alleys in this neighbourhood. Turning to go, she almost collided with a middle-aged couple. The old boy had a flat cap pulled down low, but Lottie could see that his face was set hard and serious. His wife was swaddled in a pink, woollen coat, with a matching headscarf tied under the chin. She beamed at Lottie. "The alley, is it? Are you coming then, love?" She tipped a brazen wink. "To see Rudi."

Lottie hesitated, then allowed herself to be drawn along in the couple's wake. The alley was as dark and unfriendly as she'd feared, but the woman's jolly demeanour made it seem like an adventure. A little way along they came to a sliding warehouse door. The woman rapped enthusiastically. Lottie glanced nervously about them, expecting at any moment to see a gang of youths emerge from the shadows. Youths with knives.

When nothing happened, the woman's cheer faded. She turned to her husband. "George, you do think they'll let us in, don't you?"

George shushed her. "Not if you continue to call attention to us they won't." He knocked this time, two strong raps. "Now hold your peace, Maura. This is serious business."

Maura pouted and looked at Lottie for support. Lottie knew this woman's type. She had spent her childhood among them. In public she was too loud, too full of her femininity. In private she'd be shrewish and nagging. The Church of Women was built from people like this.

A few seconds later, the door cracked open. Through the gap, a darkness that contained no more than the suggestion of a figure. Whoever was there did not speak, they just waited.

"We're here to see Rudi," George said, low but clear.

The door slid open a further foot. "Hurry up," a man's voice said. "They're about to start."

The three of them slipped through and found themselves in a long room bounded by stacks of crates. Blazing lamps threw shadows towards a ceiling so high that it was lost in darkness. The room was packed with people, clumped in twos or threes. Some were standing on benches at the back and along the sides to see over the heads of the crowd. Urgent, overlapping conversations swelled around the room like waves. There was no sign whatsoever of a boxing ring.

The man who had admitted them stepped up onto one of the benches and waved towards the opposite end of the room. "That's the last of them, Mister Joffries," he yelled.

Lottie's stomach fluttered. Whatever was taking place here, she was unsure that she wanted to be part of it. Then again, the kind boxer had told her it would be *educational*, and the only way she'd learn what he meant by that would be to stick around.

The guide jumped down and stood by the door. Taking his space on the bench, Lottie was able to see over the heads of a group of sullen young men. At the end of the room, there was a table. Seven men and women sat there, their faces vaguely familiar. She recognised some of them – keepers of shops, owners of local businesses, members of the community – but it was the one at the end that she could not stop staring at.

Over the past few days he had let his beard grow, but there was no doubting it was him. Her confused Fullday lover. Lottie ducked down. This evening was already turning out to be strange enough without any added awkwardness. Nevertheless, as things got under way, she found her eyes repeatedly wandering his way.

A neat little man – Mr Joffries, Lottie assumed – seated in the middle stood and cleared his throat. "It's good to see that so many citizens share our concerns regarding the recent disturbances," he said.

A rumble of assent rolled around the room. The couple Lottie had come in with nodded their heads vigorously. The men in front of her smirked.

A muffled cheer was heard through the wall behind the table. The speaker glanced over his shoulder, then addressed the assembly again. "Very well," he said. "There is much to say and we don't have a lot of time. The fight has started."

The tenor of the meeting quickly became clear. Everyone there had a story of woe from the last Full: fire raising, vandalism, assault. And not only from the last Full, it had been getting worse for months. Lottie was shocked to hear it. She knew she tended to live in something of a bubble of self-absorption, and was somewhat embarrassed to realise the extent to which she was unaware of what had been happening around her.

The debate was punctuated by the muffled noises of the boxing match taking place in the pub through the wall. Boots scuffing bricks, leathery impacts of glove on skin. The cheers of a fervent crowd. It was a clever decoy, but it had concentration difficult. Lottie sidled through the crowd to hear better.

The consensus of the assembly was that society was crumbling, that the Palace was losing control, that perhaps even the Lunane himself was slipping. "Look at the age of him", someone said. Some called for the king to consider standing down and making way for an elected representative. Or a committee. Others wanted him just to acknowledge their problems.

"Next month's the fish festival," a bearded fisherman spoke out, "and it's going to be a very poor affair at this rate. We've had little but crabs for weeks. Lunane's little mates they may be, but who wants crabs to eat every night, eh?"

Tempers ran high. Even the dapper Joffries began to lose his composure. The skin above his starched white collar grew florid.

"People," he bellowed. "In my father's day when times were hard you could go to the Lunane and he would listen to your grievance."

"That's right." The speaker was an older man near the front of the room. "He sorts things out. He always has. Why don't you do as your father did then?"

This earned him a thin look from Joffries. "We tried," he said. "On every Halfday for the past four months we have petitioned at the Palace. We have been sent away with excuses every time."

This caused another swell of complaint.

"He doesn't care what happens to the people anymore," came one voice.

"Perhaps he's ill," came another. "Perhaps he's dying."

At that, there were scoffing laughs and hushed murmurs. The miracle of the Lunane's longevity was a subject that divided opinion between those who considered him immortal and those who feared that his great age spelled impending doom the moment he finally dropped dead. Then there were other points of view entirely. Like her mother's. Involuntarily, Lottie scanned the room. This meeting was too ordered, too political, to interest that witch, but she would have relished the unrest. Lottie relaxed. If she were here, she would have made herself obvious by now.

The old man next to Joffries rose to his feet. "This is Theodore Moses," the convenor said. "Before he retired he used to be an astronomer."

The old man's white brows knitted. "I'm still an astronomer, thank you," he said. "What I used to be was a *Royal* astronomer."

Joffries swallowed down a retort. "Of course," he said. "At any rate, Professor Moses has something to add to the meeting."

Moses harrumphed in his throat, then paused as if expecting something more of an introduction. When it wasn't forthcoming he said his piece. "There's going to be an eclipse. Fifth of the Haffey wane." He looked pleased with the exclamations of surprise that issued around the room.

"It wasn't in the paper," someone said.

"That's because the paper wasn't told about it," replied a voice that Lottie knew well. Edging further forward still, she identified the stocky form of Mr Blackwood, and he looked even unhappier than usual. The printer addressed Moses. "You're sure about this?" he snapped.

The professor straightened his shoulders as if his professional abilities had been slighted. "There's no question, I'm afraid," he said. "The charts the Palace are working from are founded on my calculations. They are entirely reliable." His mouth pursed sourly. "Which is more than can be said for the administration up there."

"It's a scandal," Blackwood said. "There'll be panic if there's an unannounced eclipse."

"If they didn't insist on retiring people –"

"Thank you Professor Moses," he said, gently encouraging the astronomer to take his seat. Then he turned back to the audience. "So, what are we going to do?" he asked the room at large. For a moment no one had any suggestions, and in the inertial silence Lottie heard a clear thwack from the other side of the wall. It was followed by a collective, anguished groan.

One of the smirking men peeled himself off the back wall and said, "Take control."

"Bring him down," added one of his companions.

"Depose him," drawled a third.

All eyes turned to the back of the room. The last one, a smartly attired fellow with black hair oiled into parallel lines, lit a cigarette with laconic arrogance, took a draw and then said, "It's all just talk, and nothing gets done." He stepped up onto the bench. "People," he said, louder so that all could hear him. "You can have as many meetings as you like, but they won't change the fact there is only one thing to be done. The Lunane's days are over. It's time for us to assume control of the city and do what's best for us, not for one man and his little troupe of privileged monkeys."

"I'd say that's taking things a bit far," intoned Joffries.

"Is it?" The man grinned. "You want to keep things as they are, do you? Don't you know things are changing? Haven't you had the dreams?"

Joffries had to raise his voice over the uncomfortable murmur that followed this. "We're not here to talk about dreams. We're here to discuss the rectification of our society, and decide –"

"Decide?" the youth sneered. "You lot are about to decide nothing more proactive than to have another meeting. The solution is perfectly clear. What's needed is action, not debate." Lottie was shocked to see a few heads nodding in agreement.

Joffries rubbed his neck uncertainly, which brought the smirk back to the lips of the detractors. Then he said, "You think it's that simple, do you? Well, there are things you do not know." He turned at last to the man at the end of the table.

"If you want to know why we get short shrift at the Halfday petitions," Joffries said, "this is Henrik."

Henrik? So his memory had returned at least. Lottie peered through the crowd.

The man called Henrik got to his feet. "Huh… hello," he began. "My name is... well, you know. It's Henrik. I lost my memory recently, but it's coming back, slowly."

Puzzled looks passed between members of the audience. This was unexpected. Through the wall, a flat thud and the boxing crowd hushed too.

Lottie peered at Henrik through the gaps in the bodies in front of her. He was taller than she remembered, a good head taller than the others, but not skinny, and the borrowed sweater he wore was short in the arms. She didn't always choose well at Full, but in this instance she'd not done too badly.

"I... I..." he stammered. Whatever he had to say was difficult for him. Then he managed to muster some courage, and declared, "I used to be the Lunane."

There was one second of clear silence, and then pandemonium erupted.

Shirley insisted on Mortlock walking her home. They quickly escaped the cauldron of the Grant Arms, buttoning their coats against the hard frost that dazzled the night. Shirley wriggled her hand through the crook of his arm.

As they walked, they talked. Shirley knew her boxing, and Mortlock enjoyed the opportunity to replay the better moments of the fight with a real aficionado. The Boxers might be past their prime, but with age had come accumulated experience of each other's game. You could see it in the way they moved, like two grand chess players planning multi-layered strategies, trying gambits that might surprise the other. And you could see the admiration and the determination when the one managed to catch the other out. It had been mesmerising.

Mortlock was yanked out of the conversation by a soft tug on his arm. Shirley put a finger to her lips, then pointed ahead of them. A small furry shape dragged itself painfully out of the shadow of a gate.

"Oh, what a sin," Shirley said.

The lame monkey stopped at their feet, looked up at them with doleful eyes.

"Your luck or mine?" Mortlock murmured.

A squeeze, so gentle that he might have imagined it. "Maybe both?" she said.

The monkey extended a skinny arm that looked to be nothing but hair. It didn't appear to have the energy to jump up, for which Mortlock was glad. Shirley crouched and took the thing that was offered. He heard her thank the creature, which then turned and scampered off into the shadows faster than he would have thought possible given its apparent state of health. He wonder if the little bastards were capable of deceit, and suspected that they might well be.

"Well," Shirley said, and showed him the thing she had been given. In the palm of her hand was a familiar metal disc, with two short lengths of fine chain. "What do you suppose that is?"

Mortlock fished around in his pocket and pulled out its twin. "I wish I knew," he said.

Shirley half-laughed. "Well if you've got one already, I'm keeping this one. And we'll see what luck they bring us, shall we?" Her gaze lingered on the thing in her hand.

"What is it?"

The look she gave him was suddenly fragile. "I just…"

"What?"

She slipped her arm through his again. "Well, we all need a bit of luck sometimes, don't we?"

They walked on in silence. In the remaining ten minutes it took to reach the café Shirley seemed content in her own thoughts. For his part, Mortlock had something new to fret over. As a policeman he'd seen all sorts of luck, and the kind he distrusted most of all was coincidence.

Chapter 6

A conspiracy of crows alighted on Glassholm's rooftops and chimney breasts, like ragged white flags blown out of the blue. They gaggled on the gate turrets of the Palace walls, and on the high sills of the Castil tower windows they clacked their beaks as if bringing coded messages. Some floors below, archivists imitated the sound of the corvine missives with the keys of black typewriters, re-recording the words of the biographies and securing for posterity the history of their king.

Anton woke in the afternoon with a burning desire to visit the library. The bouts of crippling exhaustion were becoming a feature of his days. He often found himself so tired he had no choice but to give in to them. At least they compensated for the lack of rest he got during his dream-fragmented nights.

He was given a tour of the library floor by a monkish woman named Alice Muir. She obeyed his requests and answered his questions without hesitation in a perfect display of what Gerard described as the *consensual blindness* that was ingrained in the Palace staff, the entire population; that made the glamour work.

During the tour of the endless, towering stacks, the librarian quickly revealed a comprehensive understanding of the workings of her little realm. She showed him the typed and archived journals. Anton picked volumes at random, dipping into moments from the Lunane's life. It was mildly interesting, after a grossly egocentric fashion. In the year 377UM, the city had been ravaged by storms, and the Lunane had personally led the rebuilding effort. In 212 there had been an outbreak of tuberculosis, and the Lunane had been there at the quarantine hospitals risking his own life to dispense aid to the sick. In the year 55, Glassholm had been attacked by a navy from the Jealous Lands. And the Lunane himself had commanded the cannons from the cliffs above the harbour blockade.

Reading about the old blowhard got boring rather quickly.

"What do we have," Anton said. "On the subject of vitric?"

Muir polished her spectacles with a scrap of felt, and then made a show of peering through them as she slid them back on. "Let's see, shall we."

As she guided him to a different section of the library she told him what she knew of new developments in the shellac preservative, and Anton discovered that the librarian possessed not only a keen interest in science but also a dry wit. It felt, at last, as if he might have found someone approaching an ally in the Palace.

He spent that afternoon engrossed in the papers Muir found for him. The further he read, though, the more he ached to get back to his own lunatropicity studies. Well, if they gave him nothing else to do here, he may as well keep busy. He made a list and presented it to Hogarth.

The biographer look pleased. "Certainly, sir," he said. "I'll pass it on to Mr Gerard immediately."

"Um, good." Anton was so surprised to find his request acceded to so readily that had no more to say. He reopened the book he had been reading, but Hogarth lingered. "Yes?"

The biographer glanced uncomfortably at Muir, who took the hint and wandered away in the direction of the copying room. Then the young biographer dropped his voice, "I didn't like to say in front of others, sir, but it's your young lady," he said. "I'm afraid I've tried as hard as I could..."

Anton's spirits tumbled. Somehow, unaccountably, Krista had drifted out of his thoughts. When had he last asked about her? When had he last even thought about her? Yesterday? The day before? Guilt burned in his chest.

"Well?" he snapped.

Hogarth looked miserable. He was a good hearted boy, and Anton had begun to feel that he really did care. "I'm sorry, sir. I just can't find any trace of her."

Anton waited until dark. He sat up reading by the light of an electric lamp in his study. Part of him resented that the Palace had such luxury when the rest of the city had to make do with gas and candles. Mostly he enjoyed the largess. The guilt of forgetting Krista pinched him too.

It must have been the books. She always said that he was oblivious to the world when his head was in a book.

Hogarth sat at the edge of the lamp's circle of illumination. The lad's eyelids drooped with fatigue.

Anton yawned a theatrically. "Can't keep my eyes open." He closed his book. "You should turn in too, you look exhausted."

Hogarth smiled wanly as he scribbled a line to round off the day's entry in the ledger. "Right you are, sir," he said, but he did not immediately rise to leave.

"Is there anything else?"

"Yes, sir…" Hogarth shook his head. "No, sir."

"Well, which is it?"

The rangy young man rubbed at his eyes. "Well, Mr Gerard says it's your plan and all, and it's just because I'm so close to you that it affects me so, but I'm just used to you being more yourself, sir, rather than…" He shrugged as he tailed off.

This seemed an odd thing to say. It was as if he were willing Anton to vanish and the Lunane he had been used to all his working life suddenly reappear and make everything right again. "I'm sure you're doing your best, Hogarth," Anton said. "You can go now."

"Thank you, sir." The lad looked relieved to have said his piece at least. "Is there anything else I can get you before I retire?"

Anton smiled at the biographer's willingness. "No, you're all right," he said. "Go to bed. In years to come it'd be a shame if tomorrow's entry was the one remembered in the journals for all the misspellings and inkblots."

Hogarth managed a half-embarrassed smile of his own, then bowed and left. Anton waited until he heard the outer door close and then followed. A lamp blazed inside the curtained circle. Its light, which had been steady in the early wane, was now beginning to waver ever so slightly, making the silver embroidery in the gauze shimmer. He switched the lamp off, got into bed fully clothed and watched the half-shadowed moon inching around the edge of the glass dome, the glittering constellations wheeling around the Pin Star.

Sleep attempted to take him by stealth. To fight it off, Anton thought about Krista, tried to imagine her smile and found that he couldn't. He drowsed, not deep enough into sleep to bring on the dreams but just enough for his thoughts to wander, change their tenor, became more like a voice. One that was intimate, logical and persuasive. He jolted awake, realising that he had been planning which direction to take his experiments when he got his equipment.

He was coming round to this life. The comfort, the library, the tantalising prospect of being allowed to work uninterrupted were all enticing. He grudgingly acknowledged that part of him had always been happiest working. Alone with his thinking. So isolated when his thirst for knowledge was engaged that he forgot that anyone else existed. Even the people he loved, Krista included. He preferred to think of that side to his character as focused and driven rather than misanthropic. Krista laughed when he said that, and then dutifully reminded him that he had a few other facets too. She never forgot that, even when he did.

Anton rolled out of the bed and slipped soundlessly to the door. The elevator, displaying signs of the wane's progress now, rumbled and clanked. They were occasional enough sounds to be barely noticeable during the day, but when you were trying to sneak away they were a proper clamour. By the time Anton stepped out into the state room below his heart was hammering.

His plan was sketchy. The first step was to get down to the ground floor of the Castil and then find the servants' wing where he would search for Krista. It wasn't that he thought Hogarth a liar, just ineffectual. Unless it suited Gerard's plan for Anton, there was little chance of the lad finding out anything.

He walked quickly then paused at the door, looked back into the shadows. Nothing there. His nerves had him jumping at the echo of his own feet now.

He took three steps into the second room and stopped again. No, there was something... A noise, a click, something metallic. The sound was answered by a patter ahead. Anton began to turn again, had the briefest impression of something dark, something large, before it sprang and he went down under half a ton of iron. Pinned to the floor, his head was level with the empty hollow in the centre of the tiles where the crab boss should have been. Then his view was obscured by a forest of jointed legs.

Anton felt a prick in his neck, and a cold numbness chased all the way up to his brain the realisation that he'd been out-thought by a mile.

Waking was like rising from the depths of the sea. Reaching the surface was a matter of piecing together the limited scraps of sensory information available: the overstuffed leather pressing against his face, the hot, stale-smelling blanket tucked around his neck, and the two indistinct figures hovering in the slow-pulsing dimness.

"He's waking up." A man's voice, a familiar one. Gerard. One of the blurs came closer and resolved into the secretary's face. "How are you feeling, sir?" he asked.

Anton worked his mouth a couple of times before attempting to speak. The muscles were slack and unresponsive. "Shi'," he managed to slur, "than fuh ass'in." A thread of saliva leaked from his lips. Whatever the mechanical guardians had subdued him with had packed a real punch.

A second voice came from the other end of the room. Anton couldn't make out what it said. What emerged was a sort of inquiring moan.

Gerard seemed to have no problems understanding it. "Yes, that's what he said." He returned his attention to Anton. "Not the most refined of rulers, are you now, sir?" When Anton didn't answer, he added: "Still, I suppose you do have your own talents. I hope so, for all our sakes."

Gerard vanished and then returned with a cup which he pressed to Anton's lips. Anton tried to squirm away. "Damn it, Dunn, just drink it. It's only water."

In his confused state, Anton wasn't sure which to be more surprised at: Gerard's disrespectful tone or the fact that he'd used Anton's name for the first time after half a week of trying to make him forget that he'd ever had one other than "Lunane" or "sir". He drank the water and felt the better for it.

When he tried to sit up, Gerard helped him. "Sorry about the drug. A distillation of Dark-harvested moonflower. No lasting damage, but it's powerful stuff. So how are you feeling?"

Anton was surprised to detect a note of genuine concern.

"Been better." He found himself able to enunciate now. His vision had cleared too and his eyes were drawn to a wavering candle flame. The candle sat on a table some feet away, and behind the smoke rising from it was a girl. She had black hair that hung limply around her pinched features and eyes like sea-worn pebbles. She wore a simple grey dress with a shawl around her shoulders, and under the table Anton could see that her feet were bare and dirty. She was watching him with those dark eyes, and her hand clutched a book.

"Who is that?" He took care to make each word clear.

Gerard glanced over his should to follow Anton's gaze. "My apologies, sir," he said. "This is Mia. She is your night biographer."

The drowned-looking girl ducked her head shyly. She was pretty in a morbid sort of way, but at the same time there was something unsettling about her too. "What do you mean, night biographer?" he asked. He still wasn't used to Hogarth's little ways yet let alone bringing anyone else into the picture.

Anton recalled a pale face in the dark one time he had woken from one of those desperate, empty dreams. "Have I seen you before?"

Mia smiled sweetly, then parted her lips. Her mouth became a hole: blackened gums set with pointed, tarnished teeth, a sticky slug of a tongue lying dormant behind them.

"Augh," she said.

"Mia doesn't talk," Gerard said. "Which may be as well given her other talents."

"What do you mean?" Anton's mouth had gone dry. He had never seen a person like this. He had known a handful of unfortunates over the years, but their physical deformities had come as the result of Foundry accidents. This girl appeared to have been born this way. It was no wonder she skulked around in the dark.

Gerard rubbed his stubbly scalp. "In general terms, Mia's function is the same as Hogarth's," he said. "That's all you need to know."

Anton laughed disbelievingly. "But all I do is sleep," he said. "How much can there be to record?"

Gerard smiled thinly. "You'd be surprised," he said. "Mia and her predecessors have witnessed all manner of comings and goings."

Behind him, the girl hissed through her teeth. It was the shake of her shoulders that told Anton that she was laughing, but he didn't see anything particularly funny. "You must be thinking of some other Lunane."

Gerard shrugged. "Quite so," he said enigmatically. "But the Lunane has his fads from time to time. I think the worst recent offender was the dock worker who lost his head somewhat at Dark. That was about forty years ago. Before your time, eh, Mia?"

The girl grinned and then abruptly made a noise like the bleating of a goat.

Gerard laughed. "Perhaps your mother has been telling stories." The laughter died as the secretary rounded on Mia. The change in mood was so fast that Anton almost felt sympathy for her. "Is that it, Mia? Did your mother betray her biographer's oath?"

Mia shook her head vigorously, but there was fear in her eyes.

Gerard grunted. "Well, I don't suppose it makes much odds, since you were always going to be her successor."

Throughout this exchange, Anton had been processing what Gerard had said about a previous incumbent of the role he found himself playing. "So, you acknowledge it, then?" he said. Relief coursed through him. "That I'm not the Lunane? That others have done this before too?"

Gerard dropped to his haunches so that his face was level with Anton's. If he'd been any closer their noses would have touched. "But, Anton," he said. "Haven't you worked it out yet? That's precisely who you are. 'The Lunane is every man, and every man is he'? You have felt it, I know you have. A slight shift in your personality, those unexpected changes of mind as if you intended to think of one thing only for it to transform into that sudden interest in vitric or an urge to get back to your work? Those hours where you suddenly need to sleep? That's the Lunane's influence..." The man's mouth tightened in vexation. Anton suspected he was going to say more, but instead he said: "But it is not my place to interpret the Lunane's intentions."

Anton understood him then. The frustration was the secretary's own. It gave him a warm pleasure to know that Gerard wasn't master here after all.

"It's perfectly simple." The secretary sighed. "You are not here by accident. We – the city – need your help." Then he straightened up and extended a hand to help Anton up from the couch. "It's easier if I show you."

Anton ignored it. "Why should I help you?"

Gerard shrugged. "Civic duty, Dunn."

Anton laughed. "If you know me so well, you already know that I have no great loyalty to the Palace," he said. "What would I have to lose by telling you to go and screw yourself?"

Gerard pretended to ponder an answer. "Life, liberty, love?" he said. "Or how about whoever it was you were sneaking off in search of tonight?"

Cold anger boiled inside him. "Where is she? Don't even think –"

"About hurting her? It never crossed my mind." Somehow Gerard managed to look innocent. "Violence is not my style, Anton. It's so unnecessarily messy. All the same, if you wish to see a threat where none exists, I'll reluctantly let you believe that if it secures your cooperation. You see, we really do need your help." He offered his hand again. "Now, if you wouldn't mind, we haven't got all bloody night."

Anton was as close to hating Gerard as anyone since he had walked away from the Foundry. It made no difference whether he had any intention of harming Krista, the possibility now lodged in Anton's mind was enough.

Gerard lifted the candle from the table. As he did so, Anton recognised a wedge shape to the angles of the walls. They were clearly still in the Castil then, but where?

As the secretary strode towards the door, Mia lingered in the shadows. When she spoke, the sound she made was half way between fear and petulance.

"Yes, you do have to come," Gerard snapped at her. "You might be useful for once."

Gerard's candle led Anton around a predictable ring of unlit rooms. It showed only vague shapes that he could not help but associate with a certain maniacal metal monkey. He hurried after the secretary, with Mia's soft footfalls padding a reluctant distance behind them.

Gerard stopped at what by Anton's reckoning should be the sixth and final door of their circuit. "Mia, stay here with the Lunane while I…"

But the girl was nowhere to be seen.

"Oh, but you can't trust a freak, can you?" the secretary muttered. Then he thrust a finger at Anton's face. "You. Don't move." And with that he retraced their steps, bellowing the girl's name.

Anton did as he was told. When the sounds of Gerard's anger and the swinging arc of candlelight had diminished he had the sudden impulse to make a dash for it, but in such complete darkness his chances of achieving anything more than blundering about were nil.

Then he realised that the darkness was not as complete as it had seemed. A thin line of light had appeared along the bottom of the door, and there were sounds coming from inside. There might be a chance after all.

Anton yanked the door open, then stood blinking stupidly in the buzzing, electric brightness. It was the familiarity that was so incongruous. On benches around the walls sat experimental equipment in various stages of assembly. Some of it was still in its crates. Anton recognised a box the size of a tea chest. Through its open door he could see rubberised spikes like an inverted hedgehog that were used to dampen certain frequencies of reflected electromagnetic waves. Next to the anechoic chamber was a partially constructed light bench. Hogarth had worked fast, and exceeded the list Anton had given him by miles.

To his left there was an elevator. The door was open and there was someone inside it. The someone emerged, hefting another box. When he saw who it was, Anton couldn't help himself.

"Frank?"

His friend stared at him stupidly then, still holding the box, attempted to bow. "Your Majesty."

"Frank, what are you doing?"

The engineer flinched at the use of his name.

"I'm delivering this equipment, sir," he rushed. "On my tod, I'm afraid. I've been at it all night. This is the right place, isn't it?"

Anton doubted that Gerard was a risk-taker by nature, but if he had felt like taking the chance he couldn't have orchestrated a better example of the power of the Lunane's glamour. It was frightening. It was only six days ago after all that Anton and Frank had driven up to the Public Halls for that fiasco of a wedding, but from Frank's reaction it could have been sixty years. Anton took his friend by the slim shoulders and shook him.

"Frank listen to me. Listen to my voice. It's not the Lunane, it's Anton. Don't look at his face, look at me."

Frank gaped, but to his credit he made the effort and then recognition dawned. "Anton?" he said, squinting. "Is it you?"

"Aye, it's me, you fool."

Relief flushed across Frank's face. "It is, I can see you. I just thought..." He shook his head. Whatever he had thought clearly was no longer the case. "Well anyway, thank goodness. When you disappeared we feared, well… we feared…"

"Never mind about that. What's all this for?"

Frank shrugged. "Buggered if I know. The Founding Technology Archive have had a team seconded to the Palace for months. The senior researchers – Wilson, Pearson, Ferguson – were all up here. Very mysterious. Not a squeak what they were up to. Some of us thought there must have been a breakthrough, but today they were all back at their desks and not a word to anyone."

Anton could see the disappointment in his friend's face. A breakthrough, indeed? Personally, he had found it easy enough to leave the Archive and their tedious, hopeless methods, but Frank was a true believer.

"Anyway, next thing I know this Gerard appears at my door – middle of the night, if you please – and orders me to bring a bunch of gear up here. Got your field generator here too, the one you were working on – well, it all makes sense now. Who else would you call if the Foundry fails, eh?" Frank held him at arms' length. "It's good to see you. What happened?"

"Well, I went looking for Krista, of course. Right after she vanished."

"Krista?" Frank appeared nonplussed. "Well, she –"

"Krista Leitch is of no concern to the Palace."

Anton heard the words, but did not know the voice that spoke them. Frank, however, executed a double take, and was now staring at him with amazement.

"You heard the Lunane." The reappearance of Gerard in the doorway ended the conversation. "Have you finished your business?"

Frank nodded but he could not tear his gaze from Anton. "Yes, I'm done."

"Be on your way then." Gerard indicated the open elevator.

Frank didn't need a second invitation. The elevator swallowed him and bore him away.

Gerard entered the room fully, followed by the meek shadow of Mia. She was moving her lips silently like a prayer.

"So now you know," the secretary said.

Anton barely heard him. He was engrossed in inspecting the boxes. Most of the contents were spanking new, good gear, and what weren't, like his jerry-rigged lunatropic field generator and a few other bits and pieces from his attic workshop, were unique. He felt a curiously hopeful thrill at the possibilities all this represented. His fingers itched to get started.

"Now I know what?" he said, aware that he had drifted. He blinked, looked around. He knew that Frank had just been here, but somehow such a thing was unimaginable, like a bleeding of his former life into his new one. And he had been about to say something when Gerard returned, but whatever it had been was gone now.

The secretary smiled. "Now you know why we brought you here, of course."

Anton sighed. "What exactly is it you want me to do?"

Gerard picked up a bench clamp and played with it, opening and closing the jaws. "Anton," he said changing tack yet again. "What do you think the Lunane's role is?"

Anton knew by now that to get anywhere with Gerard he had no choice but to follow his direction. A kindergarten catechism sprang to mind that would do as an exercise in facetiousness. "The Lunane brought the moon to Glassholm to guide his people with its wisdom, to honour his people with its beauty, to protect his people with its strength, and to assure his people of the eternal persistence of life. Rebirth after death, light after darkness," he quoted.

"Ah, The Lunane's Promise. Very good," Gerard patronised in return. "Oh, I refuse to believe you can be this obtuse." He put the clamp down and folded his arms. "Right at this moment you are both Anton Dunn and the Lunane. Those blackouts you have, well, let's say it's just your mind that nods off." There was apparently no light of comprehension in Anton's face because the secretary grimaced. "Look, all that matters is that you are here because the Lunane has a problem, and after wasting altogether far too much time allowing the Foundry's best to come up with precisely nothing, we are in dire need of a good engineering brain. No, more than that, an unconventional borderline-genius brain. On the evidence so far I find it hard to believe that might be you, but I hope to be proved wrong."

Anton had to laugh. "Is that all? Why all the cloak and dagger? I'd have obliged happily if you'd only asked me."

"That's not exactly what the Lunane has in mind." There was something uncomfortable about Gerard's tone. "Given your long history of insubordination, not to mention your self-confessed lack of loyalty, he requires more of a hands-on approach. It's time, I think, to show you our secret."

Anton hadn't noticed the plain door on the curved inner wall. There was a single handle in the centre, a vertical bar with an elegantly turned handle that reminded Anton incongruously of a beer pump.

"This door opens only for the Lunane himself and his senior aide. It's Founder technology. Who knows, now he has access to a scientific turn of mind, perhaps the Lunane himself will remember how it was done." He beckoned to Mia.

The girl had lingered on the threshold. As Anton watched her slink in, he realised that she was uncomfortable in the light.

"Mia," Gerard said. "Open these doors."

The pale girl made a small questioning noise. Anton suspected she was familiar with the consequences of disobeying Gerard's orders.

"You'll come to no harm, girl," Gerard soothed. "We're just proving a point to the Lunane, here. Now, do as you're told."

Mia approached the door with obvious reluctance. The moment she laid her hand on the handle her eyes widened, her body went rigid, then limp, and she crumpled to the floor.

"You bastard." Anton bent over the fallen girl. "You told her she wouldn't be harmed."

Gerard made an impatient noise with his tongue. "And neither has she. She'll be right as moonlight in half an hour." He indicated the door again. "Now you try it."

Anton approached the iron handle with even less relish than Mia had. Stepping over her prone form to reach it brought his hand to within an inch of the handle. He hesitated.

"Go ahead," Gerard said. "You'll be fine. Really."

He did it quickly. The iron was cold. There was a prickle like static electricity, but nothing else. Anton looked at Gerard, who mimed the action of pulling the handle down. It was stiff at first, but then it flipped down so fast that he was unable to prevent the clang of iron on iron as handle met door. The door swung inwards.

"It opened," Anton murmured stupidly.

"Only for hand of the Lunane and his most senior aide," Gerard reminded him. "After you, Your Majesty."

Beyond the door, lights stuttered on in two expanding arcs. Above him, metal gantries circled the walls. Ladders ran between them, leading up to yet another glass dome that was almost filled by the image of the half moon. Another clever optical trick, although the projection here was less perfect than the roof of the tower and the bedroom ceiling. The image was murky and wavered unsteadily.

He didn't wonder about the roof for long because his attention was captivated by the machine in the centre of the room. That it was a machine there could be no doubt – but as to its nature, Anton wouldn't even fathom a guess, and that marked it as a quintessential example of Founder technology. In his time in the Palace he had already seen more evidence of those ancient devices in actual use than were locked away in the entire Foundry. The chin-strokers from the Archive must have pissed their pants to stand here. It was an elegant behemoth of a device, a baroque construction of gleaming steel beam, arcane gearings and powerful electricals that produced a low-frequency vibration discernible through the soles of the feet. At first sight, he thought there were some parts that might be recognisable, but making such assumptions based on guesswork was dangerous. The central portion of the construct was balanced on a framework of gimbals in such a way that the spherical body and long limb running through it that extended to the very top of the chamber could move freely in two axes. It resembled nothing so much as a brass apple that had been violently but precisely cored with an iron bar capped on each end by a smaller sphere.

"What is it?" he whispered.

Behind him Gerard answered. "Everyone knows, of course, the story of how the Lunane captured the moon and brought it to the place where he built his city."

Anton nodded.

"What very few people are aware of is how he keeps it here."

Stepping to the banister Anton could feel heat and power coming in throbbing waves from the machine, and as he watched in awe he saw that it was shuddering erratically. His engineer's sixth sense tingled. This was not a well machine. He was just about to say as much to Gerard when the machine twitched and then swivelled with a squeal.

Gerard joined him at the head of a staircase that led down to the chamber floor. The point of the lower limb quiesced. Anton looked up through the glass dome. It was surely his imagination that suggested the moon had fractionally changed position in the sky.

Gerard followed his gaze. "This machine is the link between the city and the moon," he said. "There are forces, which I believe your research has begun to understand, that tie the two together. If that tie is broken, then the days of the City Under The Moon are over." For the first time the secretary betrayed emotion. "Now do you understand why you were brought here?" he whispered fiercely.

Anton, lost for words, shook his head in disbelief.

"No one knows how it works but we need it to keep working, and you're the only man who can do that."

Chapter 7

The month of Kent was famed for rain and flowers. Those moonflower blooms that had survived being plucked at Full for the purity of their petals now displayed a black mottling like splashed ink. Their scent had lost its aphrodisiac properties, but for their markings alone they found their place on the flower stalls alongside the string-tied bunches of daffodils and pearldrops, pitcher lilies, and sweet, star-shaped blue hecatites. The air around the city's thronging market stalls was dizzy with perfume.

Lottie dawdled at the market in Dovene Square. It should have taken no more than an hour to make her usual round of purchases: sausages from the butcher, garden roots and potatoes for soup, and the good bread from Grimason's. And since there was only half the wane left she also bought a large bag of turnmeal, a mixture of pulses, cereals and spices, which she would combine with leftovers to make mealy pudding, the traditional sustenance for Glassholmers during Dark. The market was crowded, the scent of the flowers cloying. Nevertheless, she lingered, humming and hawing over every purchase. She even haggled half-heartedly with the fruiterer over a hand of bananas, settling on nearly a selene per exorbitant green finger.

And of course she had to buy double the quantity of everything. Because now she had a guest.

Toting her grocery sack in the crook of her elbow, she wandered around the corner into Jove Lane, a chicane of stalls that sold everything from bales of cloth to unofficially imported literature to handmade jewellery. Lottie stopped to admire a chain of dangling bracelets. A freckle-faced woman reading a badly foxed book behind the stall, inclined her head, questioning Lottie's interest.

"Just looking," Lottie murmured, fingering a hammered brass loop. She had no intention of buying. She was only sussing out what

71

the other artisans were producing these days. On this evidence the answer was: nothing inspiring. As usual. Everything made in Glassholm was so sturdy, so durable, because the parsimonious populace wouldn't part with a penny for anything that wouldn't outlast the end of the month. Dark was to be resisted and endured, not celebrated. Why did no one else appreciate the naturalness of decay, the beauty of fragility?

Lottie let the bangle fall. The chain jingled with a grating susurration. Always metal, always stone. That was the way of the Glassholmer. The stall holder cast her a look of annoyance.

Lottie walked on down the lane, but nothing else caught her eye. Not the lunanate icons, thick and glossy as vitricked cheeses, nor the second-hand luck gifts, nor the pulpy pamphlets containing recent clippings from the Lunane's newspaper diary column that you saw ubiquitously tucked into the pinafores of washerwomen and the hip pockets of old men. She looked among the wares for any of the odd devices, useful only for breaking up for their pretty components, that were sometimes smuggled off the visiting ships. Or, even rarer, those slim books of poetry. They were her favourites. It didn't matter that she often couldn't understand the words. She loved the thinness of their paper, the flimsy cardboard batters that curled up as you watched during Dark, but there was nothing so exotic today. Finally, she resigned herself to going home.

To Henrik.

Lottie knew she was being churlish. It was just that she wasn't used to sharing her space. She had little enough of it to begin with, after all. And then there was the post-Full awkwardness to contend with too. There were a number of ways you could handle encountering someone you'd only recently performed a random act of Fullish sex with. Some were more dignified than others, and Lottie was disappointed that he'd opted for the least of these: complete denial. Still, while pretending not to remember her was pretty insulting, she endured it for the convenience of avoiding any actual discussion of the subject. So, fine. As far as she was concerned, Henrik was simply an acquaintance in need of a place to stay.

It would have been far better, of course, to have skulked out of the meeting the other night without encountering him at all, but he'd had to stand up there and reveal the extent of his...*confusion*, was putting it charitably. *The Lunane?* Well, if that blond giant was the

Lunane, who was the dapper, dark figure on the front the newspaper, calling for petitions and making the Promise to the latter half of the wane as he always did? As she passed the hollering paper seller at the foot of Beckon Hill she thought about buying a copy to prove it to him, but didn't fancy experiencing a second bout of his mania after seeing the reaction it sparked the other night, the cat calls and insults turning in an instant to tumbled chairs and thrown punches. It didn't take a genius to work out who had started it. She had spotted the insouciant malcontents grinning madly as they laid into Joffries' ineffectual security men. Joffries, in turn, had finally seen sense and led his little party of speakers towards a door in the corner.

The crowd had surged then, and Lottie had found herself face to face with a slick-haired toe-rag. As he drew back his fist, she had seen a glint of brass and a smear of blood.

"Revolution or death?" There was a craziness in his animal growl. Even now, Lottie suspected that it didn't matter what answer she had given, he would probably have pretended she had said *death* anyway. When she gave no reply at all the lad had pouted in mock disappointment, but as he swung for her she had been jerked away.

Blackwood led her away, his face a dangerous puce colour and muttering "bloody outrage," to no one in particular. They had slipped through the door at the back just before it was slammed and locked.

What had followed was an exercise in mounting embarrassment. She had found herself locked in a storeroom with a bunch of people whose hysterical squabbling appeared to have little point other than to drown out the rising riot next door. The arrival shortly afterwards of the Boxers – Lottie barely recognised the sweaty, puffy face of the man she knew as Rudi – only doubled the furore. Lottie had found a corner, drawn her knees up and waited it out.

But she wasn't alone on the fringes of the discussion. He'd been there too.

"*Why do I know your face?*" he had said.

When Lottie got home with her groceries Henrik was gone. She wanted to be relieved, but had no clue if Henrik was capable of looking after himself. This was a man who had only just remembered his own name after all. And what made it worse was that he was probably not a native of the city. She had worked out that he must be a foreigner. It was obvious from his height and colouring if nothing else, and visitors were more susceptible than locals to the power of the moon, especially if they were here over Full. She had seen the sailors in Dockton go wild. On one unforgettable, and only partly regrettable, occasion she had joined in with their revels.

"Lunane's hairy arse."

She stuffed the food in the little stone larder, and then fished a coin out of her pocket. Most people would employ a systematic approach in such a situation, making a list of likely areas and searching them one by one, but they had not been raised by Lottie's mother. "There's a pattern to everything," the old witch said. "There is even a pattern to luck. The monkeys know it, and we're smarter than monkeys, are we not?"

Lottie disliked most of what The Mother said, but that did not mean she was always wrong. "City or sea?" she asked under her breath, then tossed the tarnished selene. It came down moon-side up. "Sea it is."

She slammed the door as she went out.

It took the better part of an hour to walk down to the harbour, even taking the short-cut through the Dockton's infamous rat runs. When she got to the harbour she used the coin again: "Headland or shore." This time the coin came down on the side with the Lunane's face. Headland it was. The worn steps were damp with spray and the tang of brine stung her nose. At the top of the stairs she steadied herself against an ambush of wind. An ash path ran around a granite watchtower and down a sloping greensward towards the edge of the cliff. Knot trees lined the path, bent back like torture victims. They were already pulling themselves in, preparing for Dark.

She found Henrik sitting on a bench gazing out over the sea. His hair gusted around his head, and the wind may also have been responsible for the tears in his eyes. Then again it might not. Lottie sat beside him. As a teenager, she had often escaped to remote spots like this to contemplate the far off places beyond the horizon. There was rarely anything to be seen out there apart from the buffeted specks of the sea birds, but it had never stopped Lottie looking. Most Glassholmers thought little about other countries, but she had. They were where the ships came from that brought all of the things that Glassholmers couldn't grow or make for themselves. Bananas and rice paper, and the useless wristwatches that worked only as long as the next wane. She had sneaked, heart in mouth, into Dockton bars to be close to their rough, exotic sailors. And she had seen pictures in books too. Glassholmers did not travel. Passage on an outbound ship was expensive, and what was the point anyway? Glassholmers said that the rest of the world was jealous, because the little island city was favoured by the moon. They disparaged anyone who even dared to mention the possibility of leaving to find another way of life. None of which stopped those determined enough, desperate enough, from finding a way. From time to time people vanished. Lottie remembered the man who ran the book store on Havering Street, suddenly not there to open up his shop one day. *Gone to the moonless*, the small crowd outside the shut shop door had muttered darkly. Her mother had dragged her away, but it had got her thinking that perhaps she might find more acceptance in some foreign city than was offered to her here. Maybe in some baked, white-walled town she would buy books again from Mr Hodges. Books of impossibly thin paper. And, perhaps, browsing the gilt lettering on the spines she would bump into the man whose restlessness she had inherited.

That was usually the point at which she halted the fantasy. There were so many other islands spotted around the great ocean that there was no realistic chance of her ever finding her father. Not even if she could have afforded the passage in the first place, or had the daring to stow away. The world was simply too large, too strange.

The view today could have been the same as it had been ten years before. The sea continued its incessant barrage against the island, beating high and angry fists against the cliffs. The fishermen still braved its wrath in their little boats. She watched them topping the swells and plummeting into the troughs, only to reappear again. The busy flecks of seabirds still followed the boats like a squall of noisy snow. And the moon always, always, hung above it all, keeping the fishermen from harm.

Beside her, Henrik said something. It was too quiet to hear over the wind and the crashing of the wild sea. Lottie glanced at him, and at last he acknowledged her. "I hate this place," he repeated.

Lottie held the hair out of her eyes to stop the little metal things clinking together. "I know what you mean." She did know. Sometimes being in the centre of things was the worst kind of alienation. "Being set apart, different from everyone? Like the moon doesn't care."

Lottie didn't know if this was what Henrik had meant, but he nodded anyway. She nodded back and then scolded herself for begrudging the act of sympathy. This going to cost her, but she knew how he felt too well. "There are people you can go to," she said. "That can help you recover your memory." Henrik looked at her. The abjection in his face forced her to go through with it. "I know someone – a relative – who can help you," she said. And tried not to think of the troubles this would bring.

"The public?" Anton was genuinely puzzled. Thus far they had done their best to keep him away from the public. The events of the night before had seeded a number of blossoming bruises to prove the point, and now he had the machine to occupy him he'd have been perfectly happy for things to remain that way. Gerard's rude appearance at his bedside had all but destroyed any chance of catching up on the sleep that he had missed too. And all because it seemed that the Lunane actually did some work from time to time.

"That's right, sir," Gerard said. "You do it every Halfday. Your public promise that no one will come to harm during the coming Dark. And then the petitions, of course."

Anton propped himself up on his elbows. Of course, he knew that the Lunane held an audience every Halfday. Grainy images of the ruler shaking hands with ordinary folk accompanied by stout columns of comment about what was discussed were a weekly fixture in the newspapers. The fodder of idle minds, he'd never paid them any heed, but he now had a horrible feeling he would soon regret that. "What do they petition about?"

"Oh, their worries, their problems, their grievances," Gerard said. "It's all very inconsequential."

"And what do I do?"

Gerard smiled. "You listen. You murmur empathetically. You offer cherished words of non-committal comfort. I'm sure you'll get the hang of it. The audience begins in an hour. Hogarth will help you with your robes."

As Gerard stalked away, Anton allowed his head to drop back into the pillows and shut his eyes. His exploration of the extraordinary machine had kept him up until after dawn. If he could just snatch a couple more minutes of sleep...

His sheets were ripped away with a gust that ran ice claws across his skin.

"I'm sorry, sir." Hogarth at least looked contrite. "We should get started. Mister Gerard doesn't like the people to be kept waiting. And the robes can be tricky."

The robes were more than tricky. They were ridiculous. Not only did the main garment consist of entirely too much sweltering fabric, but there were additional adornments too. The cups and planes of stiff material fastened at the shoulders and around the waist with fussy buckles were stupid. The hose compressed his middle so tightly that he was glad that he'd not been given the chance to have breakfast. And the built-up shoes that wobbled and *clacked* when he attempted to walk were just too much. The whole effect, he considered on appraising his reflection, a stately ensemble of dove grey, might have been one of regal serenity if the unforgiving cowl that had been squeezed over his head had not caused his face to resemble a rotting plum.

"I suppose all of this is strictly necessary?" Anton wheezed.

Hogarth was beaming. At first Anton thought he was laughing at him, but there was no mistaking the pride in his voice, "Oh, it is, sir. It's protocol. The people have expectations."

"And how do I measure up to them?" Despite the glamour, he fully expect to be revealed at last as a fraud.

Hogarth's confidence did little to reassure him. "Stop worrying, sir, you always enjoy the Halfday petitions."

The journey to the ground floor of the tower took an eternity, making sure that the treacherous shoes were placed firmly on each stair. There would be no better way to announce his fakery than to tumble headlong into the auditorium like an inept cabaret clown.

The Castil ceiling flooded the tower with sunlight. If Anton hadn't known better he would have sworn he could feel the heat of it on his skin. As it was, the combination of the effort, the costume, and the lack of sleep were more than sufficient to make him sweaty and light-headed by the time he and Hogarth reached the final landing. A finely wrought arrangement of metalwork rotated slowly above the tower floor, like a clock mechanism or an orrery stripped of the sun and planets, spinning in the stilled silence. The hush drew his attention to the crowd gathered beneath the mechanism, and as soon as he saw the snake of expectant faces lining the perimeter of the room, crowding in from the doorway opposite the foot of the stairs, his heart sank.

A nudge from Hogarth propelled him down the remaining steps and across the floor towards the elevated throne in the centre of the floor. Palace guards dipped their heads respectfully as he passed between them towards the shining centre of the hall. The shaft of simulated sunlight made the chair radiant and turned the suspended rings above it into nothing less than concentric halos.

Anton climbed into the throne and tried to convince himself he might just get away with this. As Gerard had said, the petitions had been taking place for hundreds of years, twice monthly with mechanised regularity. And like any machine, it would run the same way as long as all the components were in place, even if one of them was new. As soon as he was settled in his chair, the first of the petitioners was allowed to come forward.

Anton watched the old woman's approach, scuffing steps echoing in the chamber. A stinging droplet of sweat ran into his eye. He blinked it away.

"Your Luminance." The lady stopped before the throne's dais. She bowed her head and then looked up with dewy reverence. "I apologise for taking up your valuable time. Yet again." Her voice was light as breath and Anton had difficulty hearing her. It was the cowl covering his ears, or perhaps the chamber's acoustics. "It's those boys again," she continued. "They have no respect." The woman clutched her shawl around her, widened her watery eyes in a rather pathetic plea for sympathy. "Sometimes, I fear that they'll break into my home. And *do something.*"

Anton thought she was laying it on a bit thick, even if she had a genuine grievance. He didn't know what she expected to hear from him and it felt as though the entire Palace awaited his response. He remembered what Gerard had said. *A word of non-committal comfort.* But when he opened his mouth he still could think of nothing. Then he heard a voice. It was deep, it was compassionate, and it carried authority. That same trick of the Castil's acoustics robbed the voice of definition, so that while he was able to discern the shape and tone of what was being said, he could not quite make out any of the actual words.

When the voice stopped speaking, Anton's mouth was dry. The

supplicant smiled up at him. "Thank you," she whispered. "I am much reassured."

Anton was suddenly hot, breathless, and he was aware now of a presence lurking at the back of his mind like a shadow glimpsed from the corner of his eye. Just for a moment, then it was gone.

They'd been telling him all along that he *was* the Lunane.

His constricting clothes made him feel faint. If this went on much longer he would be in danger of blacking out. He peered at the line of supplicants that snaked around the room and reckoned that it would be a miracle if he made it through the session.

No sooner had the old woman beaten a decidedly less infirm route towards the chamber doors, than the next petitioner was sent on his way. This one, a smartly dressed milliner, came with a complaint against the apparent increase in young ladies who commissioned hats but never appeared to collect or pay for them. He unfurled a list of names.

Once again, when the puffed-up idiot had finished recounting his grievances, Anton was saved the necessity of providing any kind of answer by the intervention of the sonorous voice. This time the hat-maker seemed less pleased by what he was told, but he nodded a polite thanks before stalking off.

So it went on, a seemingly endless procession of petty problems. Neighbourly squabbles, quarrels between small businesses, payment disputes and marital spats came and went, and he looked down from his high chair, unable it seemed now to do anything more than watch and listen as the indistinct voice arbitrated. Some left the chamber content, others less so, but all accepted what the voice told them. And as Anton looked down into their faces there was no question regarding who they believed they were talking to.

A handsome woman approached the throne. Her hair was pulled into an unfussy bun. Her features, softening into middle age, were enhanced by the appropriate amount of make-up for a formal occasion, and she wore a simple but sober navy jacket over a grey dress. Something set her apart, though. She had an air of capability, the sort of someone who usually solved her own problems. What could it be then that had her chewing her cheek and fretting her finger rings like this?

It didn't look as he was going to find out. Unlike the previous petitioners who had worked their woes into a froth of complaint ready to spill at the Lunane's feet, whatever troubles this one brought with her were fighting to stay behind her lips. There was visible effort to draw them forth, but then they spilled like a gushet.

"It's my baby," she whispered. "I lost my baby, my poor, poor boy. The midwives told me he was dead, and I believed them, but deep down I knew... I knew he..."

The voice interceded. A conciliatory murmur, and a question.

The woman shook her head. "No, it was fifteen years ago, your Luminance."

A placatory suggestion brought a stiffness into her expression.

"Of course I grieved at the time. I grieved for years."

Another question.

"Because I've seen him." It was impossible that anyone further away than a few feet could have made out the exchange, but she dropped her whisper even further. "I've seen him, the poor wee soul. He comes to my room at night..."

The woman drew a ragged breath before continuing. "I didn't come here for solace, your Luminance. I came to ask a question." She waited for a reply, but all she received was the pregnant ambience of the waiting auditorium, the restless shuffling and muted conversation of the queuing petitioners, the soft whir of the rotating mechanism over their heads, the even tread of the guards' boots. When she looked up there was a hard defiance in her eyes.

"What happens to our sick babies?" she said.

If there was an answer to this Anton didn't hear it. A wave of weariness washed suddenly over him, and by the time it had passed the woman and her question had been replaced by a boy, a pair of old men, a woman with tantrumming children. He lost track. What he was most aware of was a quite alien sense of self-satisfaction that grew as the Lunane's subjects brought their woes before him. It swelled inside him like a smug balloon as the queue continued to file in and orbit his chair.

Eventually he gave up trying to concentrate, and found himself watching the patterns the light made as it was slowly sifted by the rotations of the mechanism suspended above him. It was a curious device. He realised that it *was* an orrery of sorts, but with little dioramas of figures where there should be planets. On the outer rings, workers: fishermen drawing nets into their boats, farmers pushing ploughs, printers working presses. Within the orbit of these were the professions: the physicians of the infirmary, the policemen on their beat; and then closer still, the librarians, the astronomers, the clerks of the secretariat. Inside all of that a final ring orbited closest of all to his chair. This one, like a true orrery, had a sphere in place of figures. A pearlescent ball.

The moon.

Anton was only dimly aware of a red-faced merchant departing the scene, making a spluttering fuss to do with public order, but when the man had gone something drew his attention to his replacement; a skinny youth who hugged himself, staring at the floor. As Anton waited, the boy slowly looked up, spoke. Anton heard the voice, a questioning sound. The lad spoke again, and Anton felt himself leaning forward to hear him properly.

"I'm sorry," the boy whispered when their heads were inches apart. Anton was shocked by the abject distress etched into his face. Then he saw a flash of something bright in the boy's hand, and everything became a series of still impressions: a knife in the artificial daylight; echoing shouts of alarm, too far away; a rush of wings, a blur of white, an unending corvine screeching; the boy falling back, beating at the enormous crow that clawed at his bloody face as the orrery wheeled on uninterrupted above.

It was over in seconds.

In the shocked aftermath, an intense mixture of emotions surged through Anton, and then he finally blacked out.

Lottie's Aunt Ruby lived in a more gentrified area of Hatchard Hill than the place where Lottie had been accosted on the morning of the boxing match. Growing up, she had never felt less than safe here, but now she kept a wary lookout for signs of trouble. As she and Henrik neared Ruby's street, Lottie wished for some disturbance that would force them to flee and return another time, but they saw no one aside from the pair of snowy rooks that alighted on a chimney breast as they started along Whiting Avenue.

Ruby's building was a homely four-storey tenement. The tiles in the tidy close were patterned in alternating green, bronze and white blocks. That most were intact and relatively clean showed there was money here to match the evident civic pride. Lottie wondered if the people that held their neighbourhood in such regard knew what her aunt practised the thickness of a floor, a ceiling, a wall away from them. They must have had suspicions, what with the stream of dissolute individuals that came and went from the old woman's home at all times of the day and night. Unless, of course, these respectable paragons of constancy also had occasional need of a discreet salving.

Climbing the stairs, Lottie felt a knot of dread coagulate beneath her ribs as buried memories were tugged to the surface. Behind her, Henrik carried that same air of introspective despair as all of Ruby's customers, his face closed. He'd hardly said a word since they'd left the cliffs. Lottie hoped she was doing the right thing. The front door was an oppressive paint-slathered slab of timber with a porthole of thick green glass that washed their faces with murky light.

Lottie took a deep breath and tugged the bell pull. Inside the apartment the bell rattled more than rang. They heard the distinctive scuff of moccasin slippers on carpet, followed by the protracted commotion of bolts being drawn and keys turned. Then the door cracked open and Lottie was looking down into the screwed-up prune of a face that belonged to her mother's older sister. *Considerably older*, was how her mother would have put it, but even that wasn't making any great claims for youth and beauty.

Aunt Ruby stared at Lottie, bristly lips set in an unwelcoming line while her ancient eyes conferred with her reptilian brain. Then her mouth pursed sourly. "Oh, it's you," she said. "What do you want?"

"Business," Lottie said, quickly slipping her foot across the threshold to block the already closing door. "A friend." She shifted to the side and motioned for Henrik to step forward and let Ruby see his face. The old besom squinted up at him for a moment, then returned her disdain to Lottie. "Slut," she muttered, and tried again to shut the door on Lottie's foot.

"Maybe this was a bad idea," Henrik muttered at her shoulder.

"No. Ruby, listen." Lottie shoved the door, maybe a little harder than necessary. The old woman to stumble backwards. "He needs help," Lottie said.

Her aunt righted herself and furiously adjusted the fussy neckline of her awful purple dress.

"He needs to regain his memory," Lottie said. "We can pay. Cash."

Ruby sneered and Lottie worried that she had overstepped the mark, but the old fossil had never been known to turn down an offer of cash. Lottie's aunt scratched under the hem of her wig. "Bloody right you will."

Then she turned to Henrik and her demeanour changed. She liked what she saw. "What was it, son? Too much weed at Full? Scrambled your little brainpan? Need a salving, eh?" She offered him a pudgy hand, which Henrik took with reluctance, and attempted what she probably thought of as a sweet smile. It came out as more of a leer. "Let's see what Ruby can do for you then," she cooed, pulling him in the direction of a door on the right of the hallway. "A little tea and sympathy. It's going to cost you, mind. Lottie, hen, make yourself useful and get the tea on. There's yellow-leaf, don't use the good black stuff."

"Is that for reading the tea-leaves?" Henrik asked, displaying an almost touching ignorance.

Ruby laughed like a coquettish crow. "No, son." She patted his hand. "It's for drinking. Believe me, you'll need it once I'm done with you."

Lottie caught a final glimpse of Henrik's worried face before the door to the living room swung shut. His concern was well placed. Salving was far from comfortable. It might not have been illegal, but it certainly wasn't the sort of thing you would admit in polite company either. The type of amnesia that could take you at Full, most people got over in a day or two. For it to last this long suggested you'd been doing something else to your brain other than simply being out and about at the height of the month. She had begun to wonder what else Henrik had really been up to, and wasn't sure that she really wanted to find out.

She opened the door to the tiny kitchen and a familiar depression settled around her like dirty snow. It had been maybe eight years since she had last been in this house. Nothing had changed. The square table in the centre of the stiff rug was still piled with newspapers that after months of decay and regeneration had metamorphosed into pulpy stalagmites reaching for the ceiling. The surfaces of the dresser were crowded with rusted cans filled with bits and bobs. Cracked, mismatched crockery was consequently piled up underneath the sink, and dangling close to the stifling fireplace, a ceiling-mounted pulley was draped with a bewildering array of items of purple attire.

Lottie had spent childhood afternoons in this kitchen, trying to find a space to do her homework, ignoring the shouts and the despairing moans while Ruby had entertained clients across the hall. It was only later in the evenings, once the business of the Church was done for the day, that her mother had come to collect her daughter. It was a testy arrangement that had only come about in the first place because Lottie's unseemly screaming fits had made it plain she would not be forced to participate in her mother's activities. It hadn't been much of a compromise, but at least Ruby had mostly left her to her own devices.

Lottie found the old teapot underneath a dingy knitted cover. The pot was creased with ridges of glue where a multitude of cracks had been mended over the years and it contained an oily sludge. She washed the pot out, put the kettle on the stove, located the yellow-leaf tea and waited.

Lottie was on to her third cup by the time she heard the living room door open. She filled two more mugs with the insipid liquid and handed one each to Henrik and Ruby as they entered the kitchen. Henrik had a sickly pallor.

"Are you all right?"

He shrugged, then put the mug down. "I need to go," he said and left the kitchen.

Lottie heard the front door snick shut a moment later. She glared at her aunt. Ruby was spooning sugar into her tea.

"What did you do to him?" Lottie said.

Ruby slurped at her mug, smacked her lips, but to her surprise Lottie realised that, rather than being obtuse, the old woman was collecting herself. Rough as it was, salving was supposed to be a healing process. What could have come out of it that had left them both so shaken?

"Ruby, what happened?"

"He got his memories back." The old woman suddenly looked her age. "And more besides. You'll have to ask him yourself. I really don't know that I understand it." Her lips set in a firm line.

Recognising that she would get no more out of her aunt. Lottie stood to go after Henrik.

"Girl." Her aunt called her back. "Ain't you forgotten something?"

"What?"

"Fifty selenes, if you please. I've more than earned it."

"Fifty...?" But it was easier just to count out a pile of crumpled notes.

"Lottie." Ruby's croak caught her in the hall this time.

"What?"

"Visit your mother. The Church misses you."

Lottie found Henrik sitting on the same bench as earlier, and staring out towards the horizon. The wind had dropped, making the cliff top an oasis of calm high above the rearing and crashing violence of the surf below.

Lottie sat next to him, crossed her legs up under herself, and found her own spot on the horizon to stare at.

"I don't belong here," Henrik said at length.

"I know how you feel."

"When I say I don't belong, I mean I'm not from this place," he shook his head. "I came on a ship."

"You're a foreigner." So, he'd finally worked out what was obvious to anyone who looked at him. "So, what?"

With a groan Henrik rubbed his eyes with the heels of his hands.

"Tell me." Tentatively, she rubbed his shoulder. "What was it like?"

Henrik looked at her. His eyes were bleary, but there was a focus to them that had not been there before.

"What was it like?" he said. "It was like she was peeling layers off the surface of my mind."

"That doesn't sound too bad."

"She went at it as if she was scrubbing potatoes," he said.

"Ow." That was more Ruby's style. "So, you remember then?"

He laughed ruefully. "Oh yes, I certainly remember. I remember my home, my family. I remember training to be a navigator, and I remember my ship, the *Trefori*. I remember all the stories about this place, and seeing the moon for the first time, rising above the horizon as we sailed here. I was first to request shore leave when I found out we were going to be here over the full moon. We booked into a flophouse near the docks. I remember going out into the city, feeling *good*. There was music, dancing, a lot of drink. It was everything we'd heard it was going to be." He looked at her again. "And the next thing I remember I was wandering the streets, and I was no longer the person I had been."

Lottie nodded, relieved that the process had worked. Henrik knew who he was again, and which ship he had come in on. He could go home now, and be glad to leave most likely. "So, what now?" she asked. "Will you go back to your ship."

He laughed again, but there was little humour in it. "I don't think so. The *Trefori* has sailed."

"Already?"

"It's been seven months. I'm pretty sure they'll have scored me off the roster by now."

Lottie was astounded. It wasn't uncommon to lose a few days to the befuddlement of Full, but seven months? The poor guy must have undergone a whole lot of scraping. Ruby had probably never worked so hard.

"So what will you do now?" she asked.

"I don't know. I guess I'm an immigrant. I have no money, nor any likelihood of getting any soon."

"Right."

They sat in a kind of silence that was mostly noise. Sea and wind. Lottie waited for Henrik to complete his story. Finally, she ran out of patience. "Look," she said. "You can stay longer. If you want." It wasn't what she had planned to say, it wasn't what she wanted to say, but she had said it nonetheless.

He shook her gently awake.

"There's more that I have to tell you." Vestigial reflected moonlight sheened the tracks on his cheeks.

Lottie squinted up at his silhouette. "About the Lunane?" she guessed.

When he nodded, she expressed a sigh. Then she propped herself into the sitting position and patted the mattress next to her.

"I *was* him," he said. "That's what happened in those missing months."

"You're confused," she said.

"Yes, but it's still true. Thanks to your aunt, I have these memories. They're not clear memories, Lottie. They're like deep dreams, but I know they're real. I do remember being the Lunane, living in the Palace. They're fading again already, though. Isn't that strange? It's as if my brain is pushing them out, trying to forget." His quiet chuckle was edged with hysteria.

Lottie stroked his hair, an act of sympathy rather than intimacy. She wanted to relieve his agitation, but she wouldn't lie to him about this. "I don't believe you, Henrik," she said. "No one in this city will. It's absurd."

In the darkness Henrik laughed, or perhaps sobbed. "Well, it's too late now, because I've told everyone. I wish I had never met that Joffries."

Lottie noticed that there was an omission in his story. *Her.* Not all of his memory had been salvaged, it seemed, but it suited her to let it remain that way. Her own selfish reasons aside, there was no profit in complicating this any more than it already was.

"But Joffries believed you at least." She felt him shrug.

"Maybe," he said. "Maybe not. He's convinced that the Palace is covering something up, but he doesn't know what it is. I think he was just using any leverage he could find to stir up debate, and I came along at the perfect time."

"You saw the way the meeting ended," she said. "It's hardly the start of a revolution."

"Not for Joffries and his middle-aged, middle-class cronies, perhaps," he said. "But there were others there. They're the ones to worry about. If Joffries thought he could use me, I'd hate to imagine what's going through their heads."

Lottie lay awake for a long time, listening to the shallow tension in Henrik's breathing. She heard him ease into deeper sleep just as the skylight began to lighten and grey with the coming dawn, but the tension in her own chest did not ease so readily.

Chapter 8

Mortlock was too angry to have much appetite, but he forked down the mutton stew for Shirley's sake. The food was bland, but since she had gone to the trouble of keeping it warm he felt he should make the effort. And besides, it gave him the opportunity to stab something. He lined up a dome-shaped mushroom and imagined that he was skewering Chief Lytten's head.

"You want to tell me about it." Shirley sat down beside him. She'd brought a pot of tea and two mugs. The silver chain he had bought her to thread her luck on glittered at her neckline. Raising his head he saw that the café was empty. In fact, it was closed.

"Not really." He slopped a lump of gravy-soaked potato into his mouth. Even lacking in taste, the satisfying warmth of it seemed to absorb a little of his ire.

"You'll feel better," she soothed.

He did already. He smiled with his mouth full. She scowled back at him, pointed to his chin. He dabbed the gravy away with his napkin.

"It's Palace business," he said. "I can't talk about it."

"Oh, right then." She busied herself pouring the tea.

"It's bloody Lytten, okay?" he said.

"Bane of your life is he?" She slid a steaming mug over to him. "And I thought I'd secured that lofty position."

"You'll need to try a lot harder," he said. The hour he'd just spent with the Palace's security chief would take some beating in the aggravation stakes.

She was good at that, Shirley. He did want to let off steam, but even though it was just the two of them it still felt like disloyalty to do so outside the Palace.

It was the Halfday petitioners. Even now he couldn't begin to explain what had happened. He'd been over it a hundred times but there was nothing that he should have seen, no clue that the event that day was going to be anything out of the ordinary. And *ordinary* was the watchword. Twice a month the Halfday passed off in an eventless afternoon of stultifying politeness. From the guards' point of view it was a cushy detail. The most noteworthy event in recent memory had been the unfortunate old man who had broken wind as he bowed in front of the Lunane's platform.

Talk about a false sense of security.

Well, *maybe* there had been something in the air. The punters had been edgy, a few displaying open anger or distress. Perhaps if he had come out of the guardroom sooner he might have prevented…*the attempt*. But he couldn't have anticipated something like that could he? Nevertheless, Lytten was right. Ultimately, Mortlock's watch had failed in their duty, and the buck stopped with him.

It had all just happened so fast. One moment there had been peace in the audience chamber. A supplicant – a linen merchant called Aaron Joffries, whom one of the guards identified as a regular, constantly dissatisfied with their lot – was retreating from the throne. Mortlock, emerging from the guardroom, had enjoyed the sour look on his face, only peripherally aware of the nervous youth next in line, bowing and beginning to speak. The next thing, a crow had descended from the heights of the tower, great white wings beating as it swung down over the Lunane's shoulder and dived for the kid. It had raked his face with its beak, tore at his hair with its claws, buffeted his head in a flurry of feathers.

Once it broke off its attack the crow had fluttered up in the air, coming to rest on the arm of the Lunane's chair. Beak and feathers pink-tinged, it had looked around with a belligerent golden eye, and then launched itself into the air once more, disappearing back up into the tower.

Mortlock had reacted first, belting across the tower floor to protect the Lunane who, for his part, had sat there with the nonchalant serenity of a man who had seen all manner of things before – which in his half millennium tenure, Mortlock supposed he very likely had. The kid, though, had been a mess, curled up and whimpering like a kicked puppy. His face had paled to a bluish translucency – where it wasn't washed red with the gore trailing from his ruined eyes.

Mortlock alone saw the evil little stiletto clutched in the boy's hand, and he'd pocketed it before the rest of his men arrived on the scene. Then he had taken charge, calling a premature end to the afternoon by sending the remaining petitioners away, and then having the boy hastened to the infirmary and kept there under guard.

"Stupid boy," Mortlock said to Shirley. "To even think that you could..." He sighed.

Mortlock had visited Chief Lytten's rat-hole office in the heart of the secretariat warren several times now, usually summoned for a debrief to 'see how he was settling in'. It wasn't an experience he enjoyed. Cluttered by filing cabinets, a space he considered small for a man in Lytten's position was made even smaller by the whine of his superior's voice. The inquest had been the height of discomfort.

"Someone draws a blade in proximity to the Lunane, and your lot stand and watch," Lytten had blazed, brandishing the knife in a dangerous fashion.

"Is it possible the lad was using it to protect the king?"

"From what?"

"From the crow of course."

"From the crow?" Sarcasm distorted Lytten's voice. "From the *white* crow? Tell me, Sergeant, how many crows do you see around the Palace – in sculpture, in paintings, engraved into the bloody cutlery? The Lunane's covenant with the crows goes back to the Founding. The bird was protecting him. Which, in the first instance, is supposed to be your job."

"Yes, sir," Mortlock saw the blame coming and accepted it.

Lytten wasn't yet satisfied, however. He wanted to leave his mark. "Do you have an explanation?"

Mortlock said nothing. Excuses would only make things worse.

Lytten seemed to be privy to his thoughts nevertheless. "Of course, I'm being unfair. How could anyone have foreseen such a thing as an attack on the Lunane? It's unprecedented." Lytten stopped pacing. Here it came. "Wrong!" the security chief bellowed. "For your information, Sergeant, there have been forty-three recorded attempts on the Lunane's life by various crazies and malcontents. The last was as recently as this century. Even a cursory attempt at researching the background of your job would have informed you that the Halfday guard is not just there for ceremony."

"Couldn't it have been self-defence?" Shirley was caught up in the story. "If I was attacked by a muckle bird going for my eyes, I'd have tried to protect myself."

Mortlock managed a rueful smile. "Wouldn't wash," he said. "Who carries a knife like that around? That sort of blade only has one purpose. Sticking into someone."

"Where does anyone get the idea of trying to kill the Lunane?" Shirley said. "That'd be like pulling down the moon itself."

It was a good question, though. Who *would* try and kill the Lunane? Even in Glassholm, you got the occasional random oddballs: the antisocials, the psychotics and the deranged. It wasn't uncommon for them to externalise their problems to the grief of their neighbours. Especially at Dark. But their victims were men and women just like themselves. Even to the nutters, the Lunane couldn't be thought of in equal terms. It was beyond comprehension. Then again, if someone had told him last week that police officers could be murdered at Full, he wouldn't have believed that either.

"So what happened to the boy with the knife." Shirley said. "You did check up on him?"

"Course I did. I know my business, Shirley."

She didn't exactly recoil, but the arched brow said enough and he regretted snapping. It was the encroaching effect of Dark, but that was no excuse.

"Actually," he forced a smile, "a funny thing happened when I left the secretariat. There was someone waiting outside Secretary Gerard's office. Euphemia Blake? She's the one that runs that..." He picked his words, aware that as sensible as she was, he didn't want to hack Shirley off any further by slighting her entire sex. "That... women's group up in Hatchard."

"What was Phamie Blake doing there?"

It was Mortlock's turn to raise an eyebrow.

"She's a customer. Everyone has to eat, John."

He shrugged. "I didn't have the chance to find out. I'll say this, though. She breezed right into Gerard's office like it was her own living room. Hey, not my business to speculate. Lytten's bad enough without guessing at his boss's motives too."

Shirley watched him, her hazel eyes sheened with intensity, her thumb rubbing at the rim of her mug until a chip of glaze flaked off. "So, what about the lad?" She swept the piece of glaze into her apron pocket, circled her thumb once round her heart to ward off the coming

Dark.

"The assassin, you mean?"

She shot him a glare. "He's still somebody's son, John."

Mortlock stifled another retort. He didn't want to argue. He had found himself thinking about her in a different light since their night at the boxing, and now he was paying closer attention he saw occasional glimpses of something behind the cheer that was troubling her. He felt as if he should offer to help, but he didn't know how.

"As it happens," he said more gently. "I went to check on him straight after my dressing down."

It wasn't a lie as such, but it made him sound more compassionate than he had felt at the time. The boy would have had to have been questioned sooner rather than later, of course, but Lytten had insisted that they waste no time. Mortlock could hardly have refused.

The boy was in a private room on the infirmary's upper floor. Mortlock was relieved to see that the men he had detailed to the main entrance, the stairs, the door, looked alert and serious about their business. Lytten passed no comment, but Mortlock wasn't fooled. The little vulture's beady eyes were everywhere.

Mortlock had remembered the lad as young but, tucked up in the starched sheets, he could see now that he was hardly more than a child. *Someone's son.* He had looked it, right enough. His thin arms were as white as the sheets, as white as the dressings that covered his eyes. Only his hair slicked to his feverish forehead, the florid spots on his cheeks and the brown crust rimming the pads of gauze gave the room any colour at all.

As he approached the bed he had noticed a sharp, sourness. "What's that smell?"

The nurse had cracked the window an inch. "It's sweat." She patted the sheets, her hands came away glistening. "From the infection." She sighed and began to strip the bed. "Give me a hand to get him into the chair."

Mortlock did as he was asked, screwing his nose up at the acrid tang as he strained at the boy's armpits. When bed and patient were both redressed, he pulled the chair closer. He shot a look towards Lytten, but the chief showed no more interest in questioning the lad than he had in helping move him while the bed was changed. Mortlock could not help feel that he was as much under examination as the prisoner.

In truth, there were only so many questions: *why did you do it, what did you hope to gain, who put you up to it, where can we find them, when will it happen again?* Mortlock squeezed the lad's hot hand and asked them all, but he was too delirious to make sense.

"The boy…" the cracked lips whispered. "The boy in my dream. The silver… silver… fish."

"Silver what?" Shirley touched his elbow.

Mortlock spread his hands. "*Silver fish.* It's all he would say. In the end I gave up. Told Lytten we'd come back when the delirium had passed. Then the little bastard just went mental. Pushed me out of the way, slapped the boy in the face, and screamed '*Less of your lies, traitor!*' right up in his face. It was all I could do to pull him off."

Shirley gaped. "That doesn't sound like the secretariat's style."

Mortlock nodded. "When I got him out in the corridor, you know what he said? He said, 'Expedience is paramount, Sergeant. I know *you* know that.' What was that supposed to mean?"

"But the boy's injuries weren't so bad," Shirley whispered. "There's a chance for him."

Mortlock shook his head. "He died during the night."

He hadn't wanted to tell her, and her shock confirmed that his instinct had been right. He wanted to comfort her but, before he could come up with something fitting, a shadow appeared behind the glass of the café door. Someone tried the handle.

"John Mortlock? Are you in there?"

Even through an inch of oak he recognised the voice.

"Who's that now?" Shirley rubbed her red eyes.

"Alfie Kremer, and he doesn't sound in a good mood. Do you mind if I let him in?"

"We'll have to build you an office at this rate." Shirley composed herself. "He'll be wanting coffee, I suppose."

Crossing to do the door Mortlock smiled his thanks.

"Thought I'd find you here," Kremer said when Mortlock opened the door.

Mortlock ushered him in. "You're the detective."

"Don't be smart, John," Kremer said. "I've just come from the Palace."

"Don't tell me. Secretary Gerard's chomping your arse for letting dangerous assassination plots go undetected in the city."

"Something like that," Kremer said without humour. "But not as much as he wants to chomp yours for allowing dangerous assassination plots to be carried out while you watched and applauded."

"Lytten's already had a pretty good attempt at it," Mortlock said. "It's a miracle I'm able to sit down."

"Thanks." Kremer accepted a mug of evil-smelling pitch from Shirley.

Over Alfie's shoulder Mortlock saw her roll her eyes towards the clock on the wall. He nodded economically while Kremer sugared his drink. He had no problem with cutting this meeting as short as possible. He'd had about as much as he could take for one day and had no intention of allowing Kremer to take pot shots too.

"Fine, I deserved it," he said. "But come on, Alfie. What would you have done? There's been nothing even approaching an assault on the Lunane's person in years. That bloody petitioning thing's long enough. Would you have trebled it by searching everyone? Made the petitioners shout across a no-go area?"

"You should have been expecting *something*." There was perhaps a little sympathy there, but not much. "I warned you that things weren't right, man."

"You're not talking about a revolt? C'mon, Alfie. Where's your history? Glassholm got beyond the brandishing of pitchforks and flaming torches in the first century. Standard of living in the city is better now than it has ever been, even in Beckon and Dockton. Where do you see the start of a revolution? In a random murder, a bunch of vandals and one delusional youth?"

Kremer grimaced into his coffee. "It's worse than that. Ordinary punters are getting involved now too. We've discovered secret meetings."

"You're kidding."

Kremer shook his head. "I wish. They're not very coordinated yet, but we broke one up six nights ago. Up in Rifkin. When we got there they were fighting among themselves. But *secret meetings*, John. What's that all about?"

"We were in Rifkin that night. Hole of a place called the Grant Arms. The Boxers were on there."

Kremer shook his head, smiled ruefully. "You're a loss to the force right enough, John," he said. "That's where it took place. Right under your bloody nose."

Mortlock thought back. After the fight, the crowd had spilled out into the street. A noisy throng perhaps, but nothing rowdy. He'd put all the shouting down to excess adrenaline. Truth was he'd been too wrapped up in Shirley to notice. He shrugged an apology.

Kremer said, "No word about Jenny, I suppose."

Mortlock shook his head not wanting to admit that he'd forgotten to ask.

Kremer nodded. "Look, do me a favour. Just keep an eye open at the Palace, eh?"

Mortlock sighed. He sensed trouble, and that was the last thing he wanted right now. The job at the Palace came with its aggravations but after so many years on the scrapheap he was grateful to have it. As long as there were no more incidents like the Halfday's he thought he could handle Lytten.

Any reply Kremer might have made was interrupted by a commotion outside the café door. A sharp thud, that had nothing to do with anyone knocking, quickly followed by another one and accompanied by a shrill, terrified squealing. Mortlock and Kremer reached the door together. As they fumbled the locks the screaming continued, accompanied now by an erratic drumming.

What they found was sickening. A juvenile monkey had been nailed though its paws to the door. The creature screamed, writhed and twisted, almost breaking its own arms with somersaulting contortions. Its tail whipped like a viper, and its eyes goggled with terror. Bright blood spackled the doorstep, but the lane outside the shop was empty in both directions. Mortlock and Kremer exchanged a look. They both knew whoever was responsible had enough of a start to be well gone, but Kremer headed off down the lane anyway. Meanwhile, Mortlock attempted to prise the nails out of the wood, a job made all the more difficult by the monkey's feverish attempts to bite his fingers.

When Shirley appeared her face drained, but she pushed Mortlock out of the way and in one sure motion broke the monkey's neck.

"Tortured out of his mind, the poor wee sod." She spoke calmly, but she looked scared.

"Aye." Mortlock finished the job of unpinning the poor creature. He found a sack in the back and wrapped the corpse in it. "I'll dispose of it."

Shirley nodded. "Thanks," she whispered. Then she looked at her hands. "I wonder what kind of fate comes from killing a luck monkey?"

"You mean apart from the crippling fine?"

She looked away. He shouldn't have joked. The monkeys carried a freight of superstition in Glassholm. Some people took them very seriously. He hadn't realised that Shirley was one of them.

"I'm sorry," he said. "I won't turn you in. The animal was in a pitiful state. The only people who are going to suffer a run of bad luck are the ones who did this if Kremer catches up with them." He put his arms around her shoulders. She twisted, turned it into an embrace. He held her like that, rocking gently, found that he enjoyed her warm solidity too.

"Why would anyone do such a darkish thing?" Shirley said into his chest.

Mortlock didn't have an answer, but there was now no denying Kremer's concerns. "Best guess," he said. "Someone has a grudge against Alfie, saw him come in here and decided to deliver him a message." It sounded weak but didn't stretch the imagination too far.

Shirley looked up at him. There was appraisal in her eyes and he knew she saw through the lie, but she smiled anyway. Then her hand sneaked up the back of his head and gently pressed it down towards her so that she could kiss him.

"You don't have to go," she said.

Mortlock disengaged himself from her arms. "Yes, I do." He felt the same consternation that he saw in her face, but much though he wanted to stay with her, he knew he couldn't. Not any time between now and Dark.

He picked up the sack and hoisted it over his shoulder. "Lock your door when I'm gone."

When he was outside he heard the bolts knock home, allowed himself a breath of relief. Before he departed he took a last look around the scene, his copper's eye taking in the blood, the nail holes, and something he hadn't seen before. A sprinkling of iridescence on the pavement. He bent down, touched the substance with his finger and held it close to his eyes so he could see better in the wavering light. It looked like *fish scales*, and there were shell fragments too. He couldn't see how these could be connected with what had happened to the monkey, but it was odd nevertheless.

Kremer caught up with him under a streetlamp whose stuttering light illuminated an early growth of silvercap fungus like a slug trail on the nearby wall. The thin, chemical odour irritated Mortlock's sinuses.

"Nothing?"

"Not a soul."

"Right." Mortlock hefted the sack into the light. "I'd better get on then."

"John," Kremer caught his arm. "Do you remember anything from the old days? When we were on the force together?"

Mortlock was surprised by the question. Kremer wasn't the nostalgic sort. "My memory's not what it was, Alfie." He rapped his dented skull. "Remember?"

The policeman clapped him on the shoulder. "Doesn't matter. Take care of yourself." Then he rounded the corner and was gone.

Mortlock buried the monkey in the bare square of earth that served as a communal garden for his tenement. He didn't much care for gardens, but his ground floor neighbours had worked hard over the years to make it hospitable. They had not succeeded, and the wane made it worse. The knot trees were pulled right in now, clenched like fists, and the soil they grew in was hard, unwilling to accept his spade. It took Mortlock an hour to scrape a trench.

He went upstairs, washed the dirt from his hands. Then he hung up his uniform jacket and took the bottle of black spirit through to the living room. He lit the lamp. The mantle brightened and dimmed in infirm pulses. He turned it off again, chose instead to sit in the armchair by the window that overlooked the garden. At least he'd have the moon for a while yet.

He sat in silence. Listened to the clock in the other room tick. Got up and went through to stop its pendulum. You didn't trust clocks coming up to Dark. They had springs and such that were just begging to be put out at the whim of the month end.

Mortlock poured himself a large measure from the black bottle. He regarded the glass, then went through again and removed his pistol from its holster. Only thing worse than a device that could make you late if the Dark got at it was one that could kill you. He tossed the gun into the wardrobe, and then chucked the clock in too. He was just about to close the door and lock it when he spied a bundle on the floor.

The item he drew out was his old police greatcoat. He'd forgotten he still had it. He shook the coat out. The buttons were dull, the serge crushed. There were unidentifiable stains along the hem, and it gave off a weird amalgamation of aromas – he thought he detected mildew and alcohol, something burnt too. He stared at the coat, willed memories to blossom from the discovery. But there was nothing. He locked the wardrobe tossed the coat on the bed and went back to his chair.

Mortlock swirled the glass. He knew he shouldn't drink. Not if he wanted to keep his job. He thought he'd covered up the blackouts, the memory lapses, but Lytten was keeping him so close. All those *little chats*. And, he couldn't be sure, but he suspected some of the lads were keeping tabs on him too.

He tossed the drink back. It smelled of nothing, and tasted of nothing. Just a cold snake slipping down his throat. Then the sourness unfolded, strong and sharp as rotten oranges. He winced, took another slug.

The residue of the fish scales glittered on his fingers like the moon's own blood. What did that remind him of? He dug into his trouser pocket, and produced the metal disc with its superfluous tails of chain link; the monkey's gift. It glistered as he rolled it in his fingers.

"I fucking hate Dark," he said to no one, and threw the disc across the room.

Chapter 9

In the last days of the wane, Glassholm slumped into habitual ruin. Bricks crumbled, paint flaked, food mouldered, and the people became as dark of mind as the shadow in the sky that swallowed their moon. They hid themselves away behind warping doors and splintering shutters, and prayed to their king for the moon's light to return.

Anton had never been comfortable with prayer. It flirted with what the people of the Jealous Lands referred to as *religion*. Glassholm had its fair share of superstitions, many revolving around their age-old Lunane himself: but he was a prosaic miracle that you could overlook because he was a simple fact staring you in the face every day, as large and conspicuous as the moon itself. Everyone knew that the Lunane shat, shaved and ate, just like they did. They read about it in the diarised excerpts in the newspaper. The fact that he had been keeping their city safe for half a millennium seemed inconsequential.

Now, though, Anton's understanding of the Lunane had been complicated. He could appreciate the notional need for substitutes, and even accept the idea that, on a subconscious level, people could be so used to seeing one thing that they could trick themselves into believing they still saw it when they didn't. But the experience on the Halfday had gone beyond all that. There had been that voice in his head.

He was tempted to scold himself for allowing Gerard's conditioning to affect him at last. He was Adamant, after all, impervious to superstition, scorning of any explanation but the rational one. He wanted to believe that he had been delirious from the sweltering heat of his costume, but there was no question that the voice had been real. A presence, lurking in the back of his mind, that had taken control and made him say and do things that did not originate from his will. Made him *be* the Lunane. The one that everyone else saw when they looked at him. He felt sick inside when he thought about it. The blunting, distancing of his own personality, being made a spectator in his own head as someone had tried to kill him. And the worst of it was that the voice didn't feel entirely unfamiliar. It was as if he'd been hearing it for some time.

And now, unaccountably, he felt *happy*. His emotions were all over the place. He wondered if he'd ever really been as unchanging as his friends had believed. He'd got it from his mother: stolid during the wax, strong during the wane. But then, even she'd succumbed occasionally to prayer. He remembered on particularly bad Darkday nights how she had held him, stroked his hair, and whispered pleas to the Lunane to help them through the night. But Anton had been stronger than that, even as a child. He could only have been six or seven when he became the comforter. His mother's rock. Even at that early age logic had told him that the light always would come back. Not because of the Lunane's Promise, but because it was a cycle of nature. The earth moved around the sun, the moon moved around Glassholm. After that it was all a matter of shadows.

As he'd grown up, though, he discovered how little a part logic played for most people at the monthly extremes. Because Dark wasn't really about the darkness *outside* at all. He'd seen the cleverest men in the Foundry weeping imprecations at the end of the wane as their minds turned inwards and whatever was tucked away during the rest of the month came to light.

Recognising that he was close to unique in his indifference to Dark, Anton had developed a frustrated fascination with it. He had no gift with the workings of the human mind, but physics and machines he did know, and he had become obsessed with understanding the measurable effects of the monthly turn and devising methods to overcome them. Simple things, like preserving food from decay and keeping the scum off the water cistern to start with. Once Glassholmers were freed from those limitations, he was certain, the psychological effects would evaporate.

"Try it again." Anton glanced up from the tank in which his arms were submersed to the elbows, and caught Hogarth's unhappy stare. He didn't blame the lad. It was illogical to run any kind of experiment in the days around Dark. Meters and measuring devices, if they functioned at all, couldn't be trusted, but observing the effects of Dark was fundamental to his theories, and with the equipment available to him now he stood a chance at last of making some sort of progress. The paucity of the old equipment he had begged and borrowed and, yes, on occasion, stolen for his attic workroom had allowed him only fleeting glimpses of what he was close to achieving here: proving the lunatropic effect by dampening the electromagnetic rays that caused them at the local level. Of course, Gerard was unimpressed – in truth after five days of study Anton had made little progress with the Lunane's machine – but, as he had told the secretary, the proving of this theory was fundamental to being able to understand the great device.

Carefully, he withdrew his dripping arms from the tank. The suspended lens twisted gently against the eddies. "Again," he said. "Now."

Hogarth, perched on his stool at the end of the bench, looked up from writing. He had two books now. Anton had given him the task of recording the experimental procedure in addition to the biographical notes. With a wince and a resigned sigh, Hogarth raised a hand gloved in thick rubber and threw the switch of the high voltage generator.

This time. Anton felt the power building and could not prevent a grin cracking his face. *This time. Please.* The generator began to emit a smooth, pulsing, keen. The Palace's electric lights, already feeble, wavered in synchronicity. *This time.* He was sure it was going to work. "Keep an eye on the meters," he said. "Shout when the readings stabilise."

Hogarth muttered, but nodded to show he understood.

Anton rolled the knob that primed the submerged field generator. Then, looking along the assembly from the light source to the lens to the detector, he held his hand hovering over the button that made it all happen. The pitch of the power supply rose a step and the room lights dipped again. *This time.* "Is it there yet?" he asked.

"Not yet." A tremor in the biographer's voice. The lad wasn't enjoying this, but Gerard, in as foul a mood as Anton had yet seen him, had vetoed the secondment of a trained assistant from the Foundry. Not even Frank. Apparently, when Anton had pressed the issue, *especially not Frank.* They didn't want Anton forgetting the role he played.

The volume swelled again, developed a grating edge. "Nearly there?" If it just held together for a few more minutes.

"Nearly…" The shake was more pronounced now. Hogarth was beginning to recognise the warning signs. "Just a fraction more," he said. "It's —"

The generator shrieked and a shower of hot sparks cascaded from the high tension terminals. Hogarth leapt away from the device, shielding his face with his insulated arm and sending his stool tumbling. Then the room lights finally died.

Anton lit a candle so that he could see to switch the fitting machine off. "Another one up the spout, eh?" he chuckled.

Despite the continuing disappointment, Anton smiled. He couldn't honestly remember the last time he had been so happy in his work. It was a pity no one else shared his contentment.

Guided by a sob, he found Hogarth cowering under a table. "I think we'll call it a day there. What do you say?" Anton said. The abject biographer nodded readily.

Anton led the way towards the elevator. He could have done it without the candle, so familiar had he become with the three rooms that had been appropriated for his investigations. No sooner had that thought entered his mind than it was followed by an irresistible urge to do just that. The pinched wick hissed and released a billow of greasy smoke. A green after-image floated in the sudden darkness.

"Sir?" Hogarth's voice quavered some feet behind him.

Anton suppressed a snort of laughter as he felt his way along the aisle between the benches.

"Sir, please." The lad, it seemed, didn't cope with Dark at all well.

"Keep up, Hogarth," Anton called, punching the button. "You'll miss the elevator."

The only answer was a frantic blundering.

The elevator door slid open and spilled out a wedge of faltering light. At least the generator mishap hadn't knocked that out too.

The look of misery on the biographer's face was acute enough to elicit sympathy. Anton raised his hands apologetically. "I'm sorry, my friend. I was only having a joke."

Hogarth didn't reply. He claimed a space at the back of the elevator and contrived to find a spot on the floor to stare at. It was a wonder the tiles did not blister. Anton tapped at the top button. He had assumed the elevator shuttled only between his apartment and the state rooms, and was surprised to discover that it could also stop at the level in between. You just needed to find the other button hidden among the tesserae. More amazing still, the entire height of the machine chamber lay between what he had thought of as adjacent floors. Only this deep into the wane was he able to feel the speed of their passage. The lift ground a little, jolted sluggishly, before finally coming to rest.

Once in his apartments, Anton poured two generous whiskies and sat in one of the chairs, motioning for Hogarth to do likewise. The lounge had a dusky warmth to it, a combination of the glow from the fireplace and the last of the evening sunlight spearing through the windows. The biographer drained his glass in two protracted sips.

"So?" Anton reached for the decanter to top him up. "Progress?"

Hogarth opened his workbook, made a point of scanning the page sullenly. "None. Again."

"Nonsense," Anton chuckled. "Sure, it's disappointing that the apparatus failed, but that in itself tells us much. Doesn't it support our theory that the visible light component of the moon's electro-magnetic emissions interferes with the lunatropic rays in a predictable manner? We've clearly demonstrated that as the amount of light diminishes, the destructive lunatropic force takes over. The fact that it's difficult to get anything to work on Darkday simply proves my point." He beamed at Hogarth. "This really is very encouraging."

Hogarth's look over the top of his book suggested he was not convinced. "There is still no discernible pattern to the Lunane's machine's behaviour, sir," he said. "Other than its being tied to the micro-movements we observed in the magnifying window."

Anton thought about that. He still found it astonishing to see the shadowy moon magnified to such a scale. It was all but occluded now, but still visible in outline in the wavering projection. The features were displayed in great detail. These movements, however, were entirely unexpected. Anyone with eyes could see that the moon's daily orbit around the sky was as smooth as a coin on a table top. A small amount of jitter might be expected as a result of such high magnification, but those wild swings and spins could not so easily be explained. In his time in the Foundry, Anton had had little interest in going over the old ground of lunar observation, and he had found the people that spent all their time looking up to be among the stuffiest and most unimaginative of his peers. He was at a loss though. Even in the library he'd been unable to find any mention of the phenomenon. A visit to the astronomers was unavoidable.

"Will that be all for the day, sir?" Hogarth slouched to his feet.

His pale face glistened.

When Anton waved him away, the biographer fled.

Anton wasn't in the mood to read, but stuck for something else to do he chose a book from the pile. It was a century-old study of lunatropic plant behaviour. He struggled, persevering in case he missed even the smallest nugget of information that might aid his quest, but when he had skimmed the last few pages he threw the folio across the room. He picked up another book, but it was no use. He couldn't concentrate. He poured himself another drink, racked up the snooker balls and battered them around the table. The balls fizzed across the cloth, rattled into the pockets. The moon-patterned white jumped the cushions and clattered across the floor.

Evening deepened into night. Anton lay on the bed, stared up through the cupola. The night was clear, and cold enough to fringe the panes with frost. Stars glittered everywhere and the moon, one bright edge and the rest in shadow, passed among them like some barely glimpsed, stealthy beast.

Anton shivered, too alive for sleep. Beneath his clothes his skin burned with irritation and arousal. He curled on his side, made a low laugh that turned into a groan.

He must have dozed after all, because he started awake to the memory of words. *The window is not a simple projection. None of them are.* He stared upwards through the darkling glass. Had that been the Lunane's voice or his subconscious, working away at some level, bringing to plain light something that he must have known for a while now without understanding its significance? But yes, of course. In this clever tower of domed rooms the Founders had discovered a way to make each appear to be at the apex. Never losing sight of the moon, that was the key. It was easy to assume that the trick was projection, but it couldn't be that. Not if he was able to feel the warmth of the sunlight, not if his rudimentary detectors were picking up the lunatropic component. For once Anton marvelled at just how advanced the Founders had been.

"Mia?" he called. He still found the idea of the freakish girl lurking around at night creepy, but she was so inconspicuous that he managed to pretend most of the time that she wasn't there. It was still early though, and she didn't answer. She'd be expecting him somewhere else.

The labs were silent, the air still tainted by the reek of burning, and there was a whiff of putrescence too. The smell of Dark. The door to the machine room was closed, of course. Mia couldn't open it, and Gerard didn't venture down here at night. Doubtless, this late in the month, the secretary was cowering in a corner somewhere anyway. Anton looked around, extending the candle towards the corners. "Mia?" he whispered. Still nothing, and that annoyed him. The last two nights she had contrived to be here ahead of him, waiting, lips moving in that habit she had that made it look as if she were talking to herself. She would be suffering tonight too, of course, but Anton didn't think a little slough would deter her from her duties. No, she was here, somewhere. "I guess I'll just have to get on with it myself tonight," Anton said. Then he entered the machine room, leaving the door open a crack behind him.

Tonight the machine was at peace. It sat unmoving on its bearings, and didn't flinch when Anton descended the iron stairs. He liked it when the machine was quiet, when it consented to his approach. At these times he could put his cheek to the central casing and feel the calm hum transmitting through his skull. It had been six days on the calendar, but a subjective age, since his first visit with Gerard. He hadn't been able to return straight away because of the Halfday fiasco, but after that he had immersed himself. Doing what he was told appeared to be a good bet at staving off the return of the voice. The very next day Anton had rushed directly down as soon as he was awake, but had been able to do nothing more than watch the machine's agitation. An attempt to get this close would have led to concussion at best, decapitation at worst. That entire morning had been devoted to watching the awkward ballet of the great machine, recording the fatigued groans and squeals, the fuzzy hums and stutters. Initially Anton had hoped that tying movement to sound might lead to understanding something about what ailed the machine – a swing like *this* caused it to grind and shudder, like *this* and it shrieked as if about to split in two – but it quickly became clear that this method would take many days of observation, and Gerard continued to insist on urgency. Of course, the git had been vague about the *reason* for such haste, but like him or not the gravity of the problem was impossible to overlook.

That night Anton had been unable to sleep for thinking about the machine. Notions, ideas, part-theories paraded through his mind, were examined, then dismissed. In the end he'd simply had to get out of bed and find his way down to the machine room, and immediately something, perhaps it was being alone with the mechanical wonder, gave him a feeling of connection, a gut instinct that thrilled him. That had set the pattern. In the days he and Hogarth worked on the lunatropicity experiments, and at night he and Mia worked with the machine. Having finally got over the sickness that afflicted him in his early days here, Anton now found that he had boundless energy for the work. A couple of hours rest between one session and the next were enough to refresh brain and body, and if he attempted to take any more than that his mind became too agitated, too full of possibilities. He was consumed with an imperative to understand that went beyond both his natural scientific curiosity and Gerard's urgency.

"Good evening, my love." Anton skipped down the steps to stand beside the machine, laid his hand on the housing. "Your temperature is up again," he murmured.

Anton crouched on the floor below the scuffed silver ball at its Earth-aiming end, and sighted along the beam. Beyond the opposite sphere, he made out the outline of the moon, the last glimmering of brightness clinging to its leading limb. The beam pointed directly to its centre. Gerard had told him that the machine was what kept the moon over the city. Anton was still sceptical that the Founders had been able to harness the orbit of a body as large as that, but the commonplace use of their extraordinary works in the Palace had surprised him. Was it really so impossible?

Children's stories. He was ignoring the evidence and letting his imagination run. The moon was no more than a satellite that followed a shallow orbit around the upper hemisphere of the Earth, an orbit that coincidentally placed it above their island state. It was a measure of the inhabitants' arrogance that they claimed ownership. No contraption ever built could change the movement of the moon, but even so Anton could not deny the obvious link between the tip of the beam and the sacred body it followed faithfully around the sky. Looking along the arm like this he imagined an invisible line of force, taut as a kite string in a high wind.

The beam inched under his hand, the far end twitched around clockwise. Checking once again what he already knew, Anton retrieved two objects from his pocket. The needle of the compass needed a tap before it swung around to the south-by-southeast mark. He checked the chart Muir had obtained from the astronomers, then looked at the other device. Spot on, three forty in the morning. His father's pocket watch, a solid lump of tooled brass, was guaranteed to work even on the worst of Darkdays. It never missed a tick. There was absolutely no doubt, the machine followed the moon. The question was, to what purpose?

Anton knew that he would have been amazingly fortunate to have discovered any kind of engineering documents relating to the machine's construction in Lunane's library. Almost nothing, despite years of study, was understood of the technologies that had been available to the city's builders. The examples dotted around the city were long defunct, reduced to the role of statuary. The people even called them Founders' stones, as if they were nothing more than monoliths.

Here in the Palace, however, they were living, operational machines. And still no one had a clue how they worked.

Anton crawled over to the fat base that supported the machine's giant gimbals. The steel covers were warm too, telling him that even though quiescent now, it had undergone recent action. The access plate came off easy enough now, its stiffness lost to his daily investigations. Bundles of cables were neatly packed into the space. Some, warm to the touch, he guessed carried power, but others were inert. The cables fed into sealed transparent boxes which held trays of stacked flat devices. There were no moving parts inside the machine, which was a bonus in terms of things which could go wrong, but was a disaster in terms of figuring out how the thing worked.

A visual inspection offered no clue that anything was amiss. No loose wires or bared terminals, no perished insulation, no charring or cracking or encrustation. Not even an odd smell.

Frustrated, he replaced the cover again.

The beam inched around a further increment as Anton stood up. He walked around the beast, footsteps ringing on the floor as he paced between the cast constellations of an iron sky, following the perfect circle of the moon's path through them.

Then he had a thought. What if it was no longer a circle? What if something had changed in the relationship between earth and moon? It might not be the machine that was at fault at all, just that the operational parameters had for some reason moved beyond its functional capabilities.

Of course it is the machine. What else could it be?

Anton wondered if this was what it was like to go mad.

"Who are you?" he asked.

A deep chuckle, then: *You know who I am, Anton.*

"You are the Lunane, then."

We're the Lunane, the presence replied. *For now.*

The machine gave a shudder. It set off an unpleasant rattle somewhere inside.

Our machine doesn't react well to my presence, I'm afraid, the voice said. *Which is... one... reason that I have given you free reign to engage the problem on your own. You have my trust, Engineer.*

The machine groaned, then quietened, and Anton let out a long sigh of his own.

Something, a shift in the light, distracted him, and his eye was drawn to the gallery above. There in the shadows beyond the railing he spotted Mia. Clutching her black ledger and watching him, a scowl distorting the minuscule movements of her tarry lips.

Chapter 10

Dark always took Lottie by surprise. There were a hundred reminders as the days passed. Rust blossomed on the Founders' stones. The grocer's prices plummeted as he tried to shift his produce before it rotted. The apples themselves that you'd bought not two days before for their sweet fragrance were wersh and woody. You started to feel sick. Light in your head and heavy in your limbs. Everything became an effort. All these signs were there, but somehow when the day itself came around it always hit Lottie like one of her mother's backhanders.

Lottie wound herself in her bedclothes, shivered inside the enveloping warmth. Her bones ached, her head pounded, her nose ran and – for a change – in common with most women in the city today, her insides squirmed heavily. Which made her think of her mother. For the Church, Dark was the highlight of the month. Those stupid women, gathering together to celebrate their misery, showing each other their monthly blood supposedly to prove their sex's favour with the moon. Lottie had no problem with people gathering together to get through Dark – that was what the Promise Centres were for – but she couldn't stomach the smug superiority that went with it.

Her personal antipathy to her mother's little cult was rooted in overstayed teenage rebellion, but it certainly hadn't helped that her body refused to obey the lunar cycle as predictably as others'. As a teenager her irregularity had driven her mother to impose a bizarre series of regimes *to bring her in line*. Lottie tried not to dwell on those humiliations. The important thing was she had found a way to be happy, on her own with no involvement from her mother or the Church. And besides, she had more on her mind at Dark than biology.

A soft tap at her bedroom door reminded her that this Dark, she wasn't technically alone. She didn't answer, hoping Henrik would take the hint.

The tap again, louder. "Lottie?"

Over the course of the wane they had formulated a pattern of co-existence in her tiny flat. She respected his area of the main room, and he allowed her the sanctuary of the bedroom. It helped that he spent much of the day out looking for work and his own place to stay, but in the evenings there was little avoiding each other. They ate together, more like a veteran married couple than almost-strangers, politely sharing the stories of their day.

The door opened tentatively. A smell like stagnant mud wafted in. Henrik's head appeared. "I've made you coffee."

She pulled the covers over her head but it was no use, she was going to vomit. She barely registered Henrik's surprise as she barged past and careened into the bathroom where she retched until she was hollowed out. When she was done, she rested her forehead on the cool, crazed porcelain until she had the energy to get up.

Henrik had sensibly disposed of the coffee, although there was a lingering stain of it in the air. Instead, he offered her a glass of water. "You okay?"

She had lost the taste for acid replies, so she just took the glass. "Must have caught a stomach bug from somewhere." She sluiced and spat. "You've got to be careful what you eat at this time of the month."

He nodded back, took the empty glass and refilled it.

"Thanks." She finished the job of cleansing away the taste of vomit.

"Rotten time to be ill," he said. "Sit down before you collapse."

Lottie gave in to weariness and tumbled down on the little couch that Henrik had been using for a bed. To his credit he kept his little area tidy. The spare bed clothes and the few bits and pieces he had managed to accumulate were stowed so neatly that there was virtually no trace of him in the room. The only thing that was impossible to disguise was himself.

The couch protested as she attempted to find a comfortable position amid the lumpy topography of stuffing and spring-heads. Lottie wondered how Henrik managed to sleep on this at the best of times, let alone now. She had been a far from generous host. Something else to include on the list of shortcomings to be pored over as Darkday progressed.

Henrik's lack of complaint made it worse. She wished he'd just go, even though the minute he did so Lottie knew she was going to get right into the guilt thing. But he didn't leave. He unrolled a blanket and draped it round her, tucked it under her chin. Then he sat beside her and placed his large, cool palm on her brow. The hand was soothing, like a parent's. But not like any Lottie had ever had. Tenderness wasn't her mother's style. Her father hadn't stuck around long enough for her to know. This was what it would feel like, she decided, if the Lunane did what he promised and personally ministered to his citizens.

Lottie began to cry. Silently at first, long tears, rolling down her cheeks, so that it wasn't until the shudders and sobs came that Henrik realised. He shifted so that he could look directly into her eyes. His own glistened too. He grimaced, stroked the wetness from her cheeks with his thumb.

"I'm sorry," he said.

"Don't be."

He blinked, released a droplet from his auburn lashes. Lottie watched it maze down towards the uncertain sandy moustache that had appeared one morning in place of the beard. It was as if he were still coming to terms with his face.

"I know," he said. "It's just that…"

"…everything feels like it's gone to shit and it's all your fault?"

It didn't look at first as if he was going to be able to manage to reply, but then he whispered, "Yes."

Lottie held his hand. "Welcome to Dark, my friend. How can you have been here so long and not felt like this at the month end?"

He shrugged, said nothing at first, but it was in his eyes. "Maybe I have. Probably. I'm not sure of anything anymore."

Lottie looked down at his hand. The knuckles were raw. "What happened?"

Henrik extricated his fingers from hers. "Nothing. Friendly misunderstanding, that's all."

"You should choose better friends." It wasn't a bad graze and it looked to be healing, at least as well as a body could heal right now, but she recognised the mark of a thrown punch. Some people took a perverse pride in that. As a new month got underway you saw men, ugly with bruises and scars worn like rosettes from encounters in Darkday's deserted streets. She hoped Henrik wasn't going to be one of those.

He changed the subject. "Look, I'm grateful for you putting up with me for so long. It's very kind of you."

Lottie didn't reply because if she'd opened her mouth at that moment she would have told him then about their Fullday liaison, and neither of them needed that complication right now.

"Let's go out and find something to keep ourselves busy instead of moping around here," she said instead. It felt uncommonly bold, but on a normal Darkday there was barely room in her flat for her own self-pity. With the two of them here, they would drown in it.

When she finished dressing, Henrik was by the door, examining something. "I didn't think the postal service would operate today." He handed her the envelope.

One look was enough. "They don't. Some poor sod was forced to deliver it." She ripped the carmine envelope and its contents into quarters and stuffed them into her pocket. "Let's go, before we start getting visitors too."

Mortlock's mother had brought him to the Parks on Founding Day, he remembered. Dressed him up and sent him off in a pack of shrieking children, robes flapping as they chased around the maze of paths, seeking out a tree with a paper ball dangling from its branches, helped along the way – *this way, this way, snapped the claws, pointed the beaks and tails* – by adults dressed as crabs, crows and monkeys, grabbing sticks to hook the moon, pull it down and break it open for its bounty of sweeties. Afterwards, a band had played.

He wasn't sure if he'd set foot here since. He was only walking these gentrified paths now because it wasn't Shirley's and it wasn't home and the bottle. He heard music and, cresting a rise, there it was in the shallow bowl below him. The bandstand.

Mortlock's childhood image of this place, freshly painted and decked with flowers, brilliant music soaring up into the sky from the boisterous orchestra, crumbled in an instant. The painted hoardings were flaked and scabbed. The planters around the rim were green with slime and choked with bindweed that rustled in the breeze. The multitudinous orchestra was reduced to a quartet of oddments: a cellist, face curtained behind a hangman's drop of hair as she sawed at her strings; a slender flautist whose open sobbing left her with hardly enough breath to make a peep; a beefy man turning a hurdy-gurdy, his face screwed with distaste at the awful din it produced, but keeping on turning all the same; and a boy beating a drum like a fatalistic pulse. Mortlock assigned them the label "quartet", but though they shared the stage each of them played as if they were alone.

Their audience sat on the wet grass and mossy benches, staring blankly or holding their heads in their hands. He'd thought to join them but...*fuck it.*

Anton strode the circle of his apartments. His boot heels shot the floor like Fullday crackerjacks. In his dressing room he paused in front of the mirror. Chuckled. Then burst out laughing.

Darkday morning had been fun. Over breakfast he had taken sufficient liberties with Hogarth's humour that the lad had quickly given up his duties and fled. After that he'd spent a couple of hours down at the machine, but he had made no further progress. It didn't matter. There would be plenty opportunity yet for progress. The machine, unusually quiet for a daytime visit, had brooded like a sulking giant, pointing its accusing finger, as ever, at the moon.

Now, though, he was stuck with nothing to do. Then he remembered that he had meant to visit the astronomers. Anton snapped his fingers, turned on his polished heels and headed for the elevator.

The Castil was like a morgue. As Anton skipped down the staircase his footsteps echoed in the great chamber. Usually he made allowances for the tendency of most to hide away at Dark. Today, though, he felt like pulling the stay-a-beds from their kips and telling the doom-sayers jokes until they cracked a smile.

He knew that these emotions were unnatural, caused by the Lunane in him just like the despairing sickness he had experienced on first arriving in the Palace on Fullday, but there was nothing he could do about it.

Anton threw open the astronomy room doors. The long office was deserted. The charts were stowed away and the typewriters sat silent under covers.

"Hello!" he bellowed.

He strode up to the room's far end. In one corner, a twist of iron stairs led up through the ceiling, and in the other corner, green-tarnished and dusty, and sitting a little off true if his eye was not mistaken, was an orrery that was wider than he was tall. Unlike the one that revolved above the Lunane's throne, this was a traditional device. In its centre a great brass globe represented the sun, and around it were arrayed the orbits of the planets, each with their own satellites. It was beautifully made. Anton hunted for the switch. When he flipped it, the contraption shrieked into juddering action, the planets jerking their ellipses round the sun, their moons in turn wobbling around them. And among these was Earth, and their own moon, a solid silver orb spackled with finely fashioned craters, circling around an inlaid dot of mother-of-pearl bound by a slender circumference of gold on the planet's surface.

"No mistaking where we are then," Anton muttered. "Centre of the known universe, me."

Don't forget it.

Anton was getting used to the voice. The Lunane, having decided to make himself known, came across as demanding but intelligent. He was perceptive and knowledgeable, and keen to help Anton fix the machine. He easily could take full control of Anton's body if he wished, but for now he needed his unique mind to tackle the problem in its own way. He didn't refrain from chipping in when he felt like it though.

Perhaps there will be someone up in the observatory, the voice suggested.

Anton switched off the rattling orrery and climbed the stairs. Poking his head up into the floor above, he found yet another glass-domed room. Around the circumference were banks of equipment, the walls covered with charts and tables of figures. And in the raised centre was a gaggle of telescopes – one large, fat mother, surrounded by a brood of spindle-legged babies – all trained upwards. Through the near-perfect glass, and even though he knew that the rest of the Castil towered above him, Anton had an unobstructed view of the night sky. He still couldn't work out how it was possible.

It's all done with mirrors. The voice was uninflected, but Anton had the feeling that he was being laughed at.

He ignored it for now, enjoying the view: the constellations, bright as polished studs and the entirely shadowed moon only visible as the outline that occluded them. The *really* incredible thing was so astonishing that it didn't register for a moment.

It was the middle of the afternoon, but the sky was black as the dead of night. Just like the view from the machine chamber, but so much clearer than the soupy view he had to work with upstairs.

114

A noise nearby dragged his attention back to Earth. Puzzled, he looked around. The room was empty. But there it was again, a shuddering breathing coming from one of the cabinets.

He crossed over, laid fingertips on the handles.

Remember who you are, said the voice, and Anton felt himself grow in stature. When he yanked open the cabinet doors he felt as if he were looming like a giant over the woman cowering inside.

It was Alice Muir. The librarian sniffed, brought her sleeve up towards her face, then seemed to think the better of what she had been about to do. Anton noticed that the cuff already had a suggestively shiny crust. The woman squeezed out of the cupboard and drew a shaky breath. "Your Majesty."

Anton laughed and the woman flinched. More gently he said: "What in the sky are you doing? Looking for unreturned books?" The joke was intended to put her at ease.

"You scared me, sir," she said through gritted teeth. "No one else comes here at Dark."

"I've noticed. So why have you?"

"I have an interest in astronomy, sir. Sometimes I help the department out with research, tricky calculations, that sort of thing."

"There's a problem?"

"Well, sir, yes. A variance in the lunar progression –"

"What do you mean by variance exactly?" Suddenly this was interesting. "Are you talking about spins? Jumps? Loops?"

"Loops?" She did not even try to disguise her incredulity. "No, of course not."

He understood the look she gave him. What he had just suggested *was* impossible. *Ludicrous*. If he hadn't observed the self-same behaviour with his own eyes, he would have shared her disbelief.

He flashed his Lunane smile and she dropped her gaze. "Just testing," he said. "So, tell me about these variations."

On a chart, Muir showed him the long established orbital path that the moon always took, and then a variant course based on recent observations. The discrepancy was not insignificant.

"How long has this been going on?"

"Some months now." Alice chewed her lip. "At first they suspected a mistake with the figures, so they double-checked, and then checked again. Then they overhauled all of the equipment in case an imperfection had crept into the lenses or mirrors during Dark."

"And they discounted that? Have they measured the lunatropic effect?"

Alice shot him a look over the top of her spectacles. He had the feeling that even as the Lunane, he had tumbled in her estimation with that statement. "The theory of so-called lunatropic waves is something of a fringe idea, sir," she said. "It's not taken seriously here, I'm afraid."

Anton didn't let her dismissal annoy him. He'd been faced with that attitude constantly since his Foundry days. He felt the voice fill him again, heard it under his words.

"But if you're stuck, don't you think it's worth investigation?"

Muir bit her tongue. She was more than sceptical, but her only other option was going over the figures yet again.

"Stay here." Anton grinned. "I'll be right back."

Lottie and Henrik went to Garton, a sprawling, less affluent version of the Beckon and Hatchard neighbourhoods that spanned the seaward side of those two adjoining hills. They reached the Promise Centre just in time for the rush before dusk. No one wanted to be outside in the dark at Dark.

The atmosphere inside was like a wake. At any other time this many people would have made the rafters ring with conversation, but today the sounds of the Promise Centre were muted to mutters and coughs and the lonely chink of crockery.

Lottie spotted Vickers' lanky frame squeezed into a corner table with a woman of around her own age. She tugged Henrik's elbow and they wound their way between the tables, each set with a candle, fitting and hissing as if even that last dependable source of light was now threatened by the month end. There was an old folk tale figure, a shadow called the Derryman, who crept out of the sea and broke your windows, rusted your saucepans, spoiled your food. People still invoked him at Dark because sometimes it really felt as if some malicious spirit wanted to plunge the world into pitch for ever.

"Hello, Mr Vickers," Lottie said.

He looked up, his long face stretched like a cartoon ghost by the candlelight. Then his lips formed the shadow of a smile. "Lottie Blake. Just like the Derry, you are. I was just mentioning your name and here you are." He nodded at his companion. "My daughter, Isla. She runs this centre."

The girl, who had more than a few of her father's bones about her face, had an incongruously pretty smile. "You're welcome here." Her voice wasn't quite cheerful, but it had a reassuring presence to it that spoke of someone you could rely on to get you through the night. "My father was telling me about your ideas for a mural. I don't suppose you've brought your paints with you?"

Lottie turned to Henrik in surprise. She'd half-heartedly mentioned trying to pitch her talents tonight and he had prompted her to stow some brushes and paints in her satchel. She hadn't really expected anything to come of it, but now she nodded.

"Good stuff." Isla Vickers' scraping chair raised a general ripple of disgruntlement. She ignored it and guided them to the where a serving hatch made hot drinks, soup and mealy pudding available to any that wanted. "Place could do with brightening up," Isla said. "How about you start around the hatch. If you need anything, just ask my cousin Elliot, here." The cousin in question turned out to be the handsome young man on the other side of the hatch.

"What do you want me to paint?" The pastoral scene Lottie had envisioned for the Glesson Street centre wouldn't fit this space.

Isla shrugged. "Whatever comes to mind." She turned away.

"Excuse me."

She turned at the sound of Henrik's voice.

"Is there anything I can do to help out? I'd like to be occupied."

Isla nodded. "Always grateful for an extra pair of hands. Elliot will find you something to keep you busy." She met his gaze. "And thanks."

Lottie pulled up a chair and began to unpack the things she would need. She thought furiously for something to paint, but her mind mirrored the wall around the hatch, wide and white and empty.

Only two sorts of people came out on Darkday night: crazies and coppers. Even wearing his old police-issue coat, Mortlock was no copper any more. He certainly had to be crazy to be still out here, now looking for the people who had tortured the monkey at the Gull. He patted his pockets again. In the left, his spirit flask. In the right, the reassuring weight of a rubber sap. It must have been there since the last time he'd worn the coat. He wasn't unhappy to have it to hand.

He skulked through a parade of shops. Their display windows

were blinded with iron shutters stamped with the Lunane's face. Like coins on the eyes of the dead.

Watching over us, Luminance? The sourness of that thought surprised him. Mortlock considered himself a loyal citizen, but recent events had him on edge. He did hope that the king was casting a warding eye over his people. He felt they were going to need it.

He froze when he heard the footsteps, then turned slowly to give his fingers time to seek out the sap. When he saw who it was though, all he could say was: "Oh."

Lottie painted in a blue wash, taking her time to balance the shade with the rough texture of the walls. She had decided on a summery coastal scene, but in all honesty she didn't have the first clue what to do beyond that. She skirted the issue further by adding border details that she hoped would inform the centre, doodling away with a fine brush in something approaching a waking trance.

"That looks good." Henrik had been passing back and forth all night, but had rarely stopped to chat. Doing so now broke her stupor. "Perhaps that's enough crabs for now though."

Puzzled, she looked at her picture. She had filled a corner of the space with little brown crabs similar to the one she had found in the garden after Fullday. They covered the rocky beach she had sketched in, emerged from the waves, clambered over each other in their haste to come ashore.

"Oh, shit."

Henrik slid the two bowls of barely-touched pudding he carried back through the hatch. "It wasn't meant as a criticism. They're cute. All it needs is something to balance them out." He slipped down to sit on the floor beside her and proffered a mug. Spiced tea. That old Glassholm favourite, redolent with honey, ginger and cinnamon to disguise the bitterness of the tea itself. She accepted the mug gratefully. If nothing else it warmed her hands.

Lottie sipped, listened to the Promise Centre's rhythm of despondency. Normally she avoided these places because the last thing you needed at Dark was other people's misery, but sometimes the loneliness was the worst part.

"I'd better get on…" Henrik started to get up.

"Don't go just yet," she said. "There's something I need to tell you."

He slid down again. Looked at her expectantly.

"I'm a screw-up," she began. "I'm famous for it. Every opportunity I get, I find a way of ruining things. Friends, jobs, lovers. I manage to make a mess of them all." It felt odd saying aloud what she normally reserved for the bathroom wall in her private monthly ritual of admonishment. "The thing is…" She examined the mug in her hands, picked at the cracks with her fingernail. Then in frustration at her procrastination she drained the sweet contents and slammed the mug down on the floor. Heads turned, grumbles. "The thing is, you and I… met. Before the meeting at the boxing match. We met on Fullday. We were lovers." Now she was talking, she didn't want to stop, because stopping would give him an opportunity to answer. "Nothing serious. It was just for one night, just for Fullday. It didn't mean anything… well, I mean, Fullday sex, it doesn't mean anything. Not usually. Not that it wasn't good. It was…very good. But I didn't want any strings, and I took advantage of you not being able to remember because I'm a selfish bitch, and I should have told you, and… I'm sorry…"

Lottie felt his hand disengage from hers. She'd been wrong to tell him. Yet again she had done the selfish thing, unburdened on him because it would alleviate her guilt, without even considering what it would do to the balance of his own emotions.

"I know, Lottie. I remember."

"You do?"

He nodded. "I recognised your flat that first night you brought me back, but… I don't know. You didn't say anything, so I figured either you'd not recognised me or you didn't want to. That Fullday is an odd time, and I needed a bed. So, I just let it lie."

Lottie just stared at him. Any other time of the month this little comedy of embarrassments might even have been funny, but she didn't feel much like laughing right now. If she had, she'd likely have got herself lynched by the centre's other patrons.

"This is probably the wrong time to be having this conversation," he said.

"Then we agree on something," she replied with relief. There was a beat, and Lottie realised that she was probably going to be comfortable to leave things like that for now. She set about cleaning the brush she had been using. "Henrik?" she said. "You were a sailor. You know the sea?"

"Yes, I suppose so."

"Tell me about it. Tell me about the sea."

The problem was the coming eclipse. While most people believed the moon's path a constant circle, there were slight but complex seasonal variations that required careful calculation by the Royal Astronomers if they weren't to panic the populace. The new discrepancy, however, was an order of magnitude greater than those variations.

The eclipse had for some time been predicted early on the fifth of the next wane. "Only, now the calculations say it'll be sooner." Alice told Anton. She hadn't even looked at the lunatropicity meter he'd fetched from his lab. "But we don't know exactly when. At first it looked like it was going to be just before midnight on the fourth. Then it was earlier that evening. Every time we observe and recalculate, it creeps closer."

"Which means…" he prompted.

"Which means that our calculations are wrong."

"Or your observations are wrong." He raised his gaze to the ceiling. "Do you ever wonder about the medium through which your observations are made?"

She opened her mouth, shut it again, then said carefully, "This apparatus has served the Royal Astronomers since the Founding. And nothing like this has ever happened before."

Anton inclined his head to concede the point, then said: "So there's only one other explanation. The moon is changing its orbit."

"That's ridiculous, sir."

He nudged the device towards her. "So humour me."

She remained sceptical, but there really wasn't much to do. Just take hourly readings while she continued to puzzle at her own figures. Meanwhile, Anton would be running similar experiments in other parts of the Castil. He hoped the comparison would give them a clue to where the anomaly lay. Anton returned to his laboratory to configure the kit he would need. He whistled as he worked. It was a tune that someone he had once known used to sing while she cooked. What was her name? She had been a good friend once.

One of the cook's helpers, surely? said the voice.

Was that it? A girl from the Palace's kitchens? It was likely enough, but no face sprang to mind. No, it was the wrong sort of kitchen, a cramped domestic room not the cavern that served the Castil. Whoever it had been, it was a cheerful tune. He hummed it as he distributed his devices, and he was singing at the top of his voice by the time he returned to the machine chamber.

"Good evening, my love," he declared in the tones of an amateur actor. "How are you tonight?" The machine twitched. Anton spread his arms in a gesture of appreciation. "Well, you *look* beautiful." He came down the steps so quickly he almost fell. Truth told, he felt a mite giddy.

The machine strained with a screech of tortured bearings, but Anton was used to its tempers by now. He ducked underneath the great arm and placed the lunatropic detector on the floor. In the glass above, he had difficulty making out the outline of the moon in the murk. The detector's needle quivered and then leapt to the quarter mark.

He barely registered the movement as the machine's great beam whirled around, and was lucky that instinct made him leap in the correct direction. The beam-end came down on the spot where he'd been crouching. It showered him with sparks and left a scrape a foot long in the floor. The detector skittered away like a batted cat-toy.

Anton retrieved the device. "What's this?" he said. "Jealous of this little thing?" He repositioned the detector box outwith the compass of the machine's boom.

Anton removed his jacket before rolling up his inkblack sweater sleeves. A soft noise came from the gantry above. He did not bother to look up but he addressed his next comment in that direction. "I was wondering where you'd got to." He scanned his notes. "Of course, I know you've been around since eveningfall, but it wouldn't have done to let our Alice meet you, now would it?"

He heard the gantry shift, rivets rattle.

"Anyway," he said. "You're here now…" He snapped his head up and, sure enough, there was Mia, leaning over the banister. Anton beamed up at her. "You know I've got the most wonderful song in my head."

Henrik talked and Lottie painted, and that was how they spent the evening. Sometimes Elliott or Isla would bring them food or drink, occasionally one of the centre's other patrons would stop by to watch and listen, and for an hour or so there was a lad nearby who played soft songs on an untunable guitar, but mostly it was just the two of them. At eleven o'clock the Vickers family reorganised the room, clearing away most of the tables and filling the space with mattresses, pillows, blankets. Some of the centre's visitors took advantage straight away, curling up and giving at least the impression of sleep.

Henrik spoke low and told her about his home. "I was raised in a coastal town at the toe end of an eastern country. I spent my childhood in a little boat my father made for me and my brother. During the days, we sailed and ate bread and sardines that attracted the society of gulls. And at night my father taught us navigation by the constellations, unspoiled by the moon you have here. Was it any wonder I was destined for a career on the waves?"

Then he told her about the places he had visited. "There are few continents like New Russland where my country lies. But there are many islands, though they are few and far between. There is an island in the south called Bergamel, that is entirely surrounded by waterfalls that plunge from its cliffs directly into the sea, and you have to navigate through the cascades to make land. And there is another in the north where the people make fantastical sculptures from ice. Frozen monsters guard their harbours. And there is another island where the people have excelled for centuries in the craftsmanship of glass. Constructions, thin as soap bubbles, adorn their jetties like festival ornaments. Impossibly fragile yet hundreds of years old."

"*Hundreds?*"

"They don't have the moon, do they?" Henrik said. "None of this Full and Dark, none of the extremes you have here. Geisingland is a tranquil place where one day is much like the last and the glassworkers have the luxury of time in which to build."

"I should like to see that island one day," Lottie said as she painted a tower of coloured glass onto the shore.

"Maybe you shall," Henrik replied.

And that broke the spell. The worlds he had conjured with his words vanished. Lottie stopped, arm in mid-stroke. It ached but not as much as her heart, which knew that she would never see the places he talked about, her versions of which were now immortalised on the Promise Centre wall. There was a collective sigh from the other visitors too, as if they had each been sharing in Henrik's stories.

She put her paints away and got a couple of blankets from the pile. The wool smelled of mildew, but Henrik's warmth bleeding through them made her comfortable enough to drop off.

Lottie dreamt of the sea. Swimming alone in deep, dark water, looking for the light but something was holding her back. Then she was no longer alone. There was a child. She was still underwater, but neither she nor the child was drowning. The child wanted something. It beseeched her. It begged.

Then there was a light. A bright white light.

Henrik shook her awake.

"What… what was that?"

"You were dreaming."

"Dreaming…?" Of course she had been dreaming, but she'd never in her life had a dream as vivid as that.

Haven't you had the dreams? It was a phrase she'd heard recently, but she was damned if she could remember where.

"Lottie, I can't do this." Henrik's whisper was fierce. "How can you stand it every month? It's like waiting to die."

She shook her head. "It's not so bad if you can get some sleep –"

"I can't *sleep*."

She pulled his arm around her again. "Just try."

Lottie woke again, this time stiff and cold. The candles had burned low. The room was full of shadows and the sounds of sleep.

Henrik was gone.

Chapter 11

The first light of the new wax slid across the sea like the drawing back of a widow's veil. The churning, grey surface it revealed was a picture of loss. A few reckless fishermen, ventured out far from harbour and toiled to drag up their deepest nets. Their cries of anguish when their catches spilled onto their decks were lost amid the frenzy of the gulls. Inedible glowfish and gelatinous things that had no name were the only variety among the swarming, clicking, mass of crabs. The birds were welcome to the lot.

Dawn reached Glassholm's docks, followed the river into the city, a questing finger probing the slumbering city. The bore rippled up the Cord like a pulse. It was slow, but it was evidence of life.

On Beckon Hill, Mortlock woke sitting, hunched inside his old coat. He was stiff with cramp. The seat of his trousers was damp. His head throbbed and his lips were sticky with the taste of alcohol and vomit. He wiped them with the back of his hand, felt the rasp of his stubble. Something cold in his other hand. It was his flask, empty. He heard a tiny sound. Blearily he looked around.

He had passed out propped up against a crumbling, weed-choked fountain. Around him, wild grasses oscillated in the frigid breeze, interspersed with dew-sparkled flowers.

The sound came again, an almost musical snap. Looking again, he saw that the flowers weren't real. He focused on the closest: a daffodil trumpet and saw that it was made of *glass*. Someone had planted the garden with delicate glass flowers. What kind of idiot would do that? Dark had taken its toll, of course. The deftly-fashioned petals bore nests of fractures and, as he watched, he heard the sound again and saw, first one petal disintegrate into glittering pieces, then the whole yellow head shear off and fall into the grass.

Dark, he thought. *Crazies and coppers, right enough.* Mortlock retrieved the head of the glass daffodil and slipped it into his pocket.

Then he heaved himself to his feet and headed for home.

A bubble of nausea rose up from Lottie's belly as she scanned the grey, empty streets. She gulped it back, sucked in air. Sky, but it wasn't like her to be quite so sick at Dark. Sticking her hands in her pockets, her fingers brushed the curling remnants of the Bloodday card her mother had sent. She hadn't needed to open it to read the sombre card with its curl of crimson ribbon. The handwriting on the envelope had been enough.

"Still no sign?" Isla handed her a mug. Sweet, spicy steam billowed from it.

Shaking her head, Lottie took the tea, although she wasn't at all certain she'd be able to stomach it.

The momentary flinch around Isla's eyes conveyed sympathy and scorn. She didn't say: *he'll be all right*. She just nodded.

"He couldn't settle. It was his first time in a Promise Centre." She didn't know why she felt the need to justify Henrik's rashness. Remembering the grazes on his knuckles, she reminded herself that she still didn't really know him. "He's a foreigner, you see."

Isla smiled politely, then mercifully changed the subject. "Oh, by the way, we're really pleased with your painting. It strikes just the right balance between cheerful and thought-provoking. Looking at it puts the head in a good place."

"It's not finished."

"Come in and finish it any time," Isla said. "Of course, we'll pay you the going rate."

"That's great, thanks." For some reason, the offer of proper paid work at last did not thrill Lottie as much as it had a week ago.

They went back inside and found that the centre was winding up. Vickers and his nephew were gathering blankets and prodding stragglers. Soon they would be wanting her to leave too. And then what?

"Is there anything at all I can do to help out?" Rather than going back to the flat and finding him still not there. "I really want to keep busy today."

"Well, once we're done here there's a bunch of us volunteer with the Clean-up Crews," Isla said. "It's never a pleasant job, but it sets the city a good step in the direction of the wax. Extra hands are always

125

welcome."

The orange overalls made her look like a cabaret clown. They were a terrible fit. They fell off her shoulders and she had to roll the sleeves up twice to get her gloves on, but at the same time they cut in at the crotch, the tough canvas chafing while she walked. She simply could not imagine who they had been made for. And there was a stiff panel stitched onto the back. It said: *Volunteer.* She wondered now exactly what it was she had volunteered for.

Cleaning up after Dark was a colossal undertaking. There was a Palace-sponsored cleansing operation, of course, but the further you lived from the Merchantry, the longer they took to get round to your neighbourhood. So the Clean-up Crews, like the Promise Centres, were staffed by volunteers.

The truth was that most Glassholmers hadn't a clue what kind of state the city got into. They did not see the tortured dog, heaved still-twitching onto the back of the handcart. They did not have to sluice away the worst of the vomit and blood. They did not see the obscenities written in shit on a tenement wall, scrubbed away by an orange-clad angel; nor the confused, naked woman cowering in the bushes nearby whose hands and face and breasts had to be sponged clean of the stuff, and who was then clothed from the cart's odd assortment of donations. They did not have to wear perfumed bandanas to cover the rotten stink that pervaded the air.

There were a dozen good souls in Lottie's crew. Their route led them away from Garton, round to the city side of the hill and down towards the warehouses along the banks of the Cord. Then, as midday came and went, they were directed north to where the river was rejoined by its offspring at the southern limit of the Merchantry.

Lottie was surprised by her reaction to the work. Once you got over the shock of your first dead pet, rescued your first bewildered soul, the act of cleansing, of scouring and scrubbing, mending and patching, was a therapeutic one. It made you feel as if you had control. And more than that, it was good to work with others and for the benefit of others. Being one of the people, taking care of their own.

What she was wrong about was that the work would distract her from thinking about Henrik. Every moan from the next street sounded like his cry for aid, every spray of blood could have been his last, every hunched shape in the bushes looked like his body.

The Vickers family tried to help. She saw them conferring conspiratorially, and tried to take their various efforts to heart.

"Don't worry," Elliot said as they pulled down a thorny growth of grapple-weed that had grown overnight into the brickwork of a bondsman's house. "He'll be safe enough." The weed came free in a shower of masonry dust.

"He'll be fast asleep in his own bed when you get home," Isla said as they retied the frayed-through tether of a pilot's boat and painted vitric on the rusting cleats on the jetty.

"What is fated, is fated," said Vickers, but given what happened to his own beloved Promise Centre, Lottie forgave him his pessimism.

They came across a slipway engulfed in a slippery weed known as choke. Vickers couldn't believe there was so much of it. "Some devil's planted this here," he said. "Any boat coming down here will skite right off. Who would do something like that on purpose? Honestly, this is the worst Dark I can remember."

"I bet you say that every month."

That raised a smile. "True enough, but still…"

They got to work clearing the weed, following the slipway up from the river until they reached the boatyard it served. The high wooden fence was barbed with splinters and mottled with a slimy algae, and the gate, whose padlock had been smashed, stood ajar. A shuffling noise came from inside.

"Hello?" Vickers motioned for Lottie to stay back as he nudged the gate with his foot. "Hello?" he repeated. The gate resisted, the hinge squealed. "Clean-up," he said. "We're here to help."

The gate was open wide enough for Lottie to see something of the interior. She made out the hulks of boats up on cradles, a rack of oars like a ribcage at the back and, in the centre, a half-finished mast, propped up at forty-five degrees.

Vickers gave the gate another shove. In a panicked flurry, a screeching ball of fur careened past their legs. "What the heck was that?" Vickers said. And then he was gone, chasing the creature back in the direction of the river.

Lottie was startled at finding herself abandoned so suddenly. "It was only a monkey," she told Vickers' back, almost laughing at his overreaction. "Probably got a dose of its own luck." Then she saw that the additional light now entering the yard revealed an odd shape at the foot of the mast. She looked around for help, but there wasn't another orange uniform in sight.

Her turn then to say, "Hello?" There was no answer, but she didn't expect there to be. That square of shadow that looked like shoulders wasn't anything more than some random piece of yard junk. That silhouetted ball lolling at the top was no more than an unfortunately placed marker buoy. *Nothing more.* Lottie stepped into the yard. "Hello?" she repeated. "Henrik, is that you?" He wasn't going to answer. It wasn't him. "Are you okay?" *It wasn't him.*

It wasn't him, but she screamed all the same because despite the blood that soaked the dead man's shirt, despite the gaping wound that spanned his throat like a second, Dark, smile, and the expression of agony in his moon-white face, she recognised him.

Behind her Lottie heard the welcome sound of boots on gravel. Relieved, she turned, but found herself confronting a man who looked as if he'd spent the night sleeping rough in his smelly greatcoat. He looked from her face to that of the corpse. His face set like stone.

"Who the hell are you?" His voice was harsh. Lottie tried to push by, but he stepped into her path. "I asked you a question." His breath was sour.

"Clean-up." This time it was Vickers. "There's no need for any excitement." His eyes widened in sad surprise when he saw the body. "Good heavens," he said, "that's that policeman…"

Lottie forced herself to look again. Yes, it was the policeman that she'd seen at Vickers' own Promise Centre, the day after someone was killed there and it burnt down.

"Alfie Kremer," said the other man. "Detective Alfie Kremer. My friend and colleague. And I'm going to have to ask you to come with me."

At first Lottie assumed that the man who had come upon them at the yard was a policeman too, but she quickly began to have doubts. Not only because of his sloppy appearance; she didn't believe a real policeman would simply abandon a crime scene like that. A short walk brought them to an unfashionable backstreet café, and after a certain amount of pounding on the door, and a whispered exchange with the woman who answered, they were admitted. The proprietor lifted chairs down from one of the tables.

The woman placed a steaming teapot and a trio of mugs in the centre of the table and then disappeared into the rear of the shop.

The man poured himself a mug, dropped in a couple of damp aggregates of sugar. He did this without taking his eyes from Lottie and Vickers. She didn't know if this was intended to increase her unease, but it certainly had that effect. It wasn't until he had taken a long drink that he finally spoke.

"Someone's making a habit of cutting coppers throats. Who is it?" He looked directly at Lottie. It reminded her of the dead detective's own attitude after the Glesson Street incident.

She shook her head. "I'd just found him when you arrived."

"I've only your word for that."

"Excuse me," Vickers butted in. "But you're not a policeman. We don't have to answer your questions."

The man turned his attention to the older man who flinched under the scrutiny. "You're right," he said. "I'm not, not any more. Now I work for the Palace, where I have the Lunane's authority to ensure security. If you want to take the matter up with him, get down there next Halfday and join the queue. Meanwhile, a friend of mind has been murdered, and the longer we sit here trading niceties, the colder his killer's trail gets."

Vickers wasn't quite shaken off yet. "You could at least introduce yourself," he muttered.

"Where are my manners?" There was a dangerous gleam in the man's eye. "My name is Sergeant John Mortlock, and I'm getting very tired, very quickly of this messing about." His gaze lingered on Vickers a second longer before returning hungrily to Lottie. She was the one he had discovered with the body after all. "Now," he said. "You will tell me who you pair are and everything you know about Detective Kremer's death."

It didn't take long. They told him about their night at the centre and the morning's work with the crew, and he scribbled it all down with a fat, black pencil. During their recounting, she barely mentioned Henrik. When they were done he read through his notes looking for obvious holes in their tale. When he found none he growled at them to get out, but not to be surprised if they heard from the police during the course of the next few days.

Lottie looked longingly at the steaming teapot, but before she knew it she and Vickers were back on the street.

"What an unusual experience," Vickers said once the shop's clamorous bell had died. He attempted a smile, though it was clear that he had found the past hour unnerving. "Come on, Lottie. I don't know how much authority that man really has, but it'd be better for all of us if we report to the police station ourselves rather than wait for them to come and find us. For all we know, they don't even know about it yet."

An unusual experience, thought as she followed him through the lanes, was an understatement. And it wasn't one she felt that she really wanted to repeat. In future she would be thankful at Dark for the work of the volunteers, but she wasn't really cut out for work herself.

It was in the doorway of the Sali Boulevard police station that she fainted.

When the couple in clean-up overalls had gone, Shirley emerged from the kitchen.

"Weren't you a little liberal with the truth there?"

Mortlock poured out the last of the tea, thick as tar now and tasting little better. He added more sugar. "Alfie Kremer's dead," he said.

"I heard."

"You don't sound surprised."

"Should I be?" Shirley had been hovering, but now she chose to sit down. "He was a policeman working at Dark." She placed her hand on his. "I'm sorry, John. I know he was your friend, but…"

He withdrew his hand, lifted his mug to his lips.

She pretended not to notice. "But this was one of the reasons you gave up the job, wasn't it? And I for one am just grateful that you did."

"Really? I was just thinking how much of my edge I'd lost." He put his mug down, rubbed his face with his hands. The skin felt clammy and rough. His eyes stung and his hangover fuzzed his thinking.

"What do you mean?"

"I mean…" He saw her flinch and realised he was shouting. "I mean that I should have questioned those two there at the scene instead of bringing them back here, and I should have stayed with Alfie after that. Sent someone to the station for help. Should've taken his notebook to find out what he knew about all this. I used to be a decent cop, and now look at me. I'm a disgrace to Alfie's memory."

"You can make up to him when they take him down to the lagoon. Read a eulogy or something."

Mortlock imagined Kremer's body weighed with stones and slipping below the placid surface of the Lunane's lake, then tutted the image away. "I'll have long enough to think something up," he said. "No one gets buried this close to Dark." Then he remembered Jenny Garret. "There'll have to be an investigation first too, of course."

"John?"

The question in her voice roused him from his introspection.

"If you don't mind me asking. What were *you* doing there?"

He stared at her, felt a coil of paranoia tighten in his heart. "I was on my way home."

Shirley chose not to fill the pause, allowing him to complete the story in whatever way he chose. He was annoyed with her for that. Could she not tell by the state he was in? Didn't the stink give it away?

"I spent Dark with friends." It was the first thing that came into his head but he'd had to lie hadn't he. He couldn't tell her that he could not remember a coherent thing after being at the bandstand the previous afternoon.

Her eyes narrowed. A cocked eyebrow asked eloquently what sort of friends' company was preferable to her own. Mortlock ignored it, pressed on with his shabby subterfuge. "Anyway, I was walking home and this monkey appeared out of thin air. Bolted right across my path."

"A luck monkey?"

He nodded. "Terrified, poor sod. So, I went to see what had frightened it. And that's when I came across that Blake girl. And Alfie."

Shirley gave him a straight look. "But you know neither she nor the Promise Centre chap killed Kremer," she said. "Don't you?"

Mortlock sighed, nodded. It was natural that suspicion should fall on whoever you discovered standing over a body, but there had been no weapon in evidence and the reactions of both of them had appeared genuine. That didn't rule them out entirely, of course, but he really couldn't see either of them trussing Kremer up and slitting his throat in cold blood.

"Oh, for goodness sake," Shirley tutted. "How can a grown man fail in such basic functions as wiping his own nose. Wait here."

Mortlock felt his lip. Sure enough it was wet with snot. *Bloody hell.* He rummaged for a handkerchief, but instead his hand closed round something brittle. He withdrew the glass daffodil. After all that had happened this morning, he'd almost forgotten that brief moment of wonder.

Abruptly, Mortlock got up. It wasn't fair to encumber Shirley with any more of his problems until he'd shaken the Dark out himself. Leaving the flower on the table, he went to the door.

"John?" He pretended not to hear her. "John, we need to talk."

The bell announced his departure as dully as his heart felt.

On returning to his flat Mortlock dumped his coat in the hall, then went through to his bedroom. Removing his trousers he noted puffs of snagged wool and a crust of mud around the hems. No doubt in his stupor he'd climbed Beckon Hill the hard way. And something else too. He looked closer, sniffed. No mistaking that it was blood. He must have got too close to Alfie's corpse in the boat yard. He'd come home with a few bad souvenirs after a Darkday night, but this was surely the worst.

In the bathroom he fitted the plug into the bath and turned on the taps. There was no hot water, but that was fine. He wanted to shock himself clean of the night's residue anyway. The plumbing groaned and rattled, and the taps coughed like old smokers, spitting forth gouts of brown water until there was enough for him to submerge himself.

The bathwater was freezing, but Mortlock gritted his chattering teeth and persevered. A quick soak, a vigorous scrub and out. He watched the water swirl down the drain, amazed at the amount of dirt he'd accumulated. It was then that he saw the rainbow glint of the scales. They glittered, swirled once around the drain and disappeared so fast he questioned that he had even seen them.

Chapter 12

The moon moved around the sky, a tumbling glint as of a coin thrown into a well, only a bright rim betraying its presence. Just a glimpse then, just an edge, passing like a ghost around the city. But it was promise enough that the world had not stopped, that better days were coming. Glassholmers crawled from their corners and shook themselves from the nightmare of Dark. Like a wound watch the city began to move once more.

Anton surfaced slowly through the layers of a long and involved dream. It featured a woman who was familiar to him. *Who was she?* He shinned up the drainpipe that clung to her tenement wall. All the way to the third floor for a glimpse of her.

She was sitting at a kitchen table with a puzzled look on her face. In her hands she was turning an odd-looking piece of equipment, a round meter dial adorned with coils of wire like springy hair. He recognised it as a component of a prototype of his lunatropic detector. The woman screwed her face up at the thing and dropped it into the bin. That look was so familiar. *Who* was *she?*

He did recognise her. Hadn't she been one of the Halfday petitioners? One of the lost souls that came to their king for succour, for solutions, for salvation. What had been her problem again? Stood up, wasn't it? Jilted at the altar.

The woman hummed a tune. It was the song that he and Mia had been singing while they toured the Castil making recordings.

Before they stole out into the city.

His fingers slipped an inch on the cold drainpipe. He felt a jolt of vertigo that went deep. Something stirred at the bottom of his memory, just a glimpse of the edge of something bright.

He had loved her. And he knew her name.

Her name? No mistaking the Lunane's familiar brusqueness. *Of course you know her name.*

Anton's fingers slipped again, and he cried out. There was just enough time to see the woman's start of surprise as he finally lost purchase and tumbled from his perch, whipping through scolding branches and fetching up in the clutches of the bushes below.

Mia's white face looked down at him. The dark hair was swept delicately back so that he could see clearly the black lips working and, as if she were speaking with the Lunane's voice, hear: *Time's up. Her name was* Krista. *But that's not important to you anymore.*

A shadow came over him, a weight descended.

Her name was Krista.

Saw-blade jaws snapped close to his head, a dull steel eye swivelled in his direction. Something like manacles jerked him up and he was clamped under a vice-like arm.

Her name was Krista.

Anton woke fully and knew it for a real memory for the simple reason that he remembered it. The mental spaces his dreams occupied always echoed like vacated rooms. He had really gone to see Krista. And the Lunane had allowed him to.

An educational trip, I think, the voice said. *I think you know now where your priorities lie.*

It was as if the Lunane had moved things around in his mind to show him his real feelings for the woman he had thought he loved.

Oh, doubtless you could have had a perfectly serviceable marriage, the voice continued. *But your heart would not truly have been in it, would it?*

There was no denying that. They had done their homework, Gerard and his lot. There's Anton Dunn, self-proclaimed rebel. Walked away from the Foundry. What do you need to do to get him to work for you? Gift-wrap a prime example of Founder technology, serve it up with almost unlimited resources and tell him there's a deadline. Getting married? How little effort had it taken on the Lunane's behalf to erase the so-called love of his life from his thoughts? And how much easier because they'd given him a lovely, great big problem to solve. He didn't want to believe that of himself, but neither could he deny that he had rarely been more content than in these recent days and nights spent working on the machine.

His machine.

Krista had stood before him on the Halfday and in her own guarded manner poured out her heart, pleaded for news of the man she had lost, and who was sitting right in front of her as oblivious to her as she was to him. He dredged up the kernel of what the Lunane had told her. *Don't wait. Find happiness elsewhere. Love is all part of the interconnected mechanism of life. Such is the Lunane's will.* It had surely been wise advice. Anton Dunn was capable of no real love, unless it was for his work.

"Been on a bit of an adventure, I understand, sir." It was Gerard, his grizzled skull visible in silhouette through the gauze hangings.

Anton groaned, raised himself up in bed, groaned louder. Everything hurt. His arms were blue and brown with circular bruises, stitched red with scratches. He threw back his bedclothes. The rest of his body had taken a similar battering.

"How long have I been asleep?" he asked, wincing as he pulled on today's bathrobe. It was dark grey.

"Oh, sir, I couldn't begin to hazard a guess," Gerard said. "But it must be over twenty four hours now."

"What date is it?"

"Well into the second of the wane, sir." Gerard stepped through the hangings. He smiled his professional smile. "It's been over a day since the friends brought you back from your little sojourn. And we've wasted altogether far too much time lazing about, I'm afraid."

At this Anton managed to smile. "Not at all," he said. "Work has continued, I assure you."

Gerard raised an eyebrow. He didn't know about Alice Muir.

Hogarth waited in the outer part of the room, scowling as if he knew he'd missed out on something. Anton flashed him his best and brightest smile before sweeping on towards his dressing room. The now curious Gerard followed in his wake.

"Speak to me, faithful retainer," Anton said as he selected a nice charcoal shirt. Out of the corner of his eye he spotted the slightest crinkle around the older man's eyes. "What is the latest estimated time for the eclipse?"

Gerard waited until Anton was dressed before replying. The man was a machine. You could almost hear his thoughts whirr and ratchet.

"You've been conversing with the astronomers, I take it?"

Anton merely smiled, turning to the mirror to comb his hair.

"Very well," Gerard said. "At the last estimate, sir, just after midday on the second of the wane."

Knotting his tie, Anton turned to face the secretary. "And that's the real reason for all this rush? You were prepared to waste your time with those dullards from the Foundry, but now it's panic stations because you can't predict the date of an eclipse and everyone will know there's something wrong."

Gerard met his gaze. "The professors were the highest authorities we have on Founder artefacts. They were the correct people to bring in. Concern yourself with building on their work, Engineer, and leave public policy to others."

"*Explain?*" Anton heard the Lunane add weight to the question.

Gerard did too. For the first time, the man looked nervous. "It's nothing, sir," he said. "There have been grumblings among the people, but…"

"*I hear that much on the Halfday.*" Anton heard himself say with a sarcasm that was alien even to him. "*Tell me what don't I hear?*"

Anton felt it coming like a sudden rush of black water, and then he was submerged. Like being drowned and like being drugged. He was powerless to move, unable to see more than dim outlines, hear more than the shapes of words. He didn't know how long this lasted, but eventually the tide receded and he and Gerard were both exactly where they had been before it had happened.

"You've been somewhat privileged so far," Gerard told him. "His majesty still prefers you to think for yourself. It would be prudent to get on with your *thinking* before he changes his mind."

Watching Gerard leave, Anton realised that the receding tide had left an urgency in him that had not been there before. The longer he stood here, the closer the urgency edged towards full blown panic. He might feel as if he had been given free will, but the king was very much in control.

Muir had left her observation notes in the Astronomy office. The paper had pulped a little, and bore watery smudges that could have been tear stains, but the figures were legible enough. Anton spent two minutes comparing them with the readings he had logged in the other parts of the Palace that had projection domes in the ceiling: the machine chamber, his bedroom, the Castil tower, and the control that had been placed open to the sky in the celestial garden. Then he spent some hours trying to work out why they were so wildly different.

The assumption he had intended to test was whether those clever ceilings projected lunatropic radiation along with the visible electromagnetic radiation. At least, the natural light in the Castil tower suggested that the full spectrum was being projected.

At Dark he expected there to be a tiny amount of reflected sunlight but otherwise the moon's own peculiar contraphasic emissions, that at other times in the month were cancelled out by the light, should register strongly. The control detector from the garden gave figures that roughly matched these expectations, but those from the Castil tower and the astronomy room were consistently close to zero. That was a surprise, but it shouldn't have been. Clearly the Founders had known about lunatropicity, and built a filter into their ingenious domes that eliminated the destructive entropic rays.

Which made the readings from the room housing the machine at the heart of the city all the more astounding. They exceeded the control values by a factor of twenty.

More worryingly still, the one in his bedroom had been off the scale.

There was an obvious answer. The detectors were faulty. He'd thrown them together in a pretty slap-dash manner after all. In the laboratory he disassembled the devices, but could see no difference between them. In fact he was amazed at the quality of the workmanship. The component seatings were solid and his wire-wraps were pristine. There was simply no possibility of loose or intermittent connections. It had to be the components then. There was a simple way to find out. Swap the detector locations around and run the experiment again.

Screwing up the last baseplate, Anton turned to Hogarth. "Right, my lad," he said. "Make yourself useful." Hogarth's outstretched ledger was the ideal platform for carrying the five boxes.

Alice Muir had returned to the library. She looked more like herself, although her mood hadn't improved noticeably. "Just *before* midday," she insisted. "It's crept four and a half minutes since this morning."

Anton felt the urgency jangle his nerves again. "We're measuring the lunatropic radiation again today." She stiffened. "Don't worry. Hogarth's doing the running around. You don't have to sully yourself. What I want from you today is the biographies."

"The biographies, sir?"Muir relaxed.

"Indeed, if you don't mind. A history lesson." He was kicking himself for not thinking of this before. The library was devoid of technical materials, but the biographies recorded everything since Founding Day. Which meant they must make some mention of the construction of the Palace.

While Muir went off to locate the books, Anton waited at one of the reading tables. It had a marquetry border of monkeys chasing each other's tails. Though it was heavily vitricked there were places where the woods had expanded or contracted differently, and tails, ears, paws had become raised, rough edges. Yesterday he could likely have picked them free; tomorrow, flush again, you'd hardly be able to tell there had been movement at all. Everything would return to the place it started from.

And that was wrong. You shouldn't have to pretend that Dark never happened, it should be met head on. Faced down and conquered.

Be grateful for what you have, Engineer. The voice drifted quietly through his mind. He waited, but there was no more.

Anton didn't notice that Hogarth had returned from his first recording round until he heard the familiar scratch of pen on paper.

"What are you writing?" he asked.

"I was just noting how contemplative you are today, sir." Hogarth smiled, but he pulled the ledger to his chest.

Anton laughed. "Makes a change, eh?"

Hogarth chose his words carefully. "The biographies tell us that it is in your nature to embody all moods."

"But it's nice to have a break from my recent high humour, too?" Anton said. "Look, I'm sorry for making fun…"

Hogarth shook his head. "You have no need to apologise to me, sir," he said, though he clasped his book tighter.

Anton admired the boy's attitude, though he wondered what he would find if he asked to read the entries Hogarth had made over the last few days. He decided the point wasn't worth pushing.

Muir returned with three other librarians in tow. Each of them carried an armful of journals. Anton had them stack the books in chronological order on the floor to the left of his chair, and began with the top book on the pile.

The label on the cover said: *Saxce, Year 1 Under The Moon.*

Opening it, Anton experienced a thrill. This was the beginning of the story of Glassholm. Never mind the newness of the paper, the boldness of the type. This was the substance of their society, right here on the page. This was day one.

Only it wasn't. "This first page has an introduction of sorts from your man, Ringley," Anton told Hogarth.

"Yes, sir," the biographer replied. "Ringley's Oath. It's the first thing a biographer learns." The lad lifted his chin an inch off his chest, and recited: *"I am hereby charged by our king's command to record the Story of our City of Glassholm, to preserve in language the life of our Leader and his Deeds, that his reign may Persist and none forget his Enduring Love for his people. I swear that this Record is a Faithful account of True events."*

Hogarth was word perfect. He even enunciated the capitals. The note was signed: *Edward Ringley, Biographer.* Hogarth's hero. Anton turned the page, and here the journal proper began.

Founding Day, it read.

On the fourteenth day of the month of Saxce, the people's saviour returned to this refugee village on the rocky island that has become our new home. He was rowing the little boat the people thought had drowned him weeks ago, and it was riding low in the water. When he made shore, and drew in his nets, the reason was obvious. He was towing the moon.

As soon as the moon was released it rose into the sky, and the people were filled with happiness.

"Our travels are over," declared the leader. "This island is where we shall build our home."

Then the people crowned him their king, and set about building their city.

Anton stopped reading. "This reads like a child's storybook, not a biography" he said aloud.

"Quite so, sir," said Hogarth. "Actually, the first few years are a bit of a fudge. You didn't commission Edward Ringley until the year 6UM."

"So how did all this get recorded?" Anton riffled through the pages in front of him.

"Scholars believe that he added it retrospectively, to fill in the gaps as it were. Ringley was reckoned to take his commission very seriously. If he was to provide a complete record of the city, it had to be from the beginning. He had lived through those times of course, so he would have remembered much of it, and conversation with yourself, too, would have added detail. But generally it is best to treat the first seventy or so volumes as something of a general guide."

"But some of it is factual?" He didn't care about the king supposedly pulling the moon out of the sea as long as could trust the day-to-day accounts of the raising of the city.

"Most of it, sir, yes."

"Good." If he probed, Anton wasn't convinced that he and Hogarth would agree about the definition of poetic licence, but no matter. As long as there were nuggets to be unearthed within these pages. He started again with page one.

As it turned out, the story of Glassholm's early years was well enough crafted. He found himself engaged by it, and had to remind himself to skip on searching for clues to the Palace's construction. In the early years much was made of the solid build of the city walls and the raising of the sparkling Palace, and there were tantalising references to the machinery and devices that had been salvaged from the refugee flotilla, but there was nothing referring to the actual manufacture that was useful.

Anton felt the burn of the old frustration when he thought about how little they still knew about the old technology. The elite Archive had been set up to preserve and understand the relics that remained, but if any knowledge had been gleaned from its investigations, none had trickled down to the common engineers in dire need of a spark of inspiration. His frustration was double now that he knew there was an entire trove of operational examples of their craft right here in the Palace. Why was such a resource kept away from the engineers, then? Anyone would think the Lunane didn't want progress to be made.

Progress? The voice returned, an eerie whisper. *Progress was what destroyed Abergaard to begin with. It was our great folly. Better by far to conserve what we have.*

Anton ignored the voice. He mustn't allow himself to get distracted. The pile of finished journals on the table was not insubstantial, but it was still dwarfed by the tower next to his chair. He opened the next one.

Something snagged his attention. The type itself remained constant, of course, but there was something about the text itself. He was used by now to the rhythm of Ringley's prose, had enjoyed in fact his business-like conciseness, but here it changed. Much more ornate. Too many adjectives. If this had been the original document, Anton was certain that the handwriting would have changed from a tight, economical hand, to a fat, flouncy script.

He read carefully.

Tenth of Lutis Wane, 8UM, it read. *His gracious Majesty, The Lunane, rose and was dressed for the funeral of his friend and biographer, Edward Ringley.*

That explained it. The biography was in a new hand because Ringley had died. But reading on, there was more.

The burial took place in the Autumn Garden, so that the Lunane might grieve privately. And it says much for the esteem in which the biographer was held, and indeed the importance of his role in the life of the city, that he was spared the mass graves afforded to the other victims of this awful contagion. It came upon us a month ago, at the dark of the moon. I have never seen such virulence, not even in the long years we were confined to the ships.

The Lunane, himself, is failing. His skin is paler even than the moon itself, and his breathing is constantly interrupted by the most painful hacking.

I fear for his health.

I fear for all of us.

This city is near enough to catastrophe as it is. If the Lunane dies, our people will be lost.

And the dark is almost on us once more.

Anton read those last lines again. He didn't care for the editorialising, but the point was important. He finally understood who the Lunane was.

"You did die, didn't you?" he said. His voice was loud in the library silence Hogarth looked up but Anton, frowned him to silence. When the voice didn't answer, he tried again, louder. "I said, you did –"

It must be clear by now that I did nothing of the sort.

Anton thought he imagined a fractiousness to its tone at being so rudely summoned.

"But you *did* die." This time he spoke so softly that even Hogarth couldn't hear it.

Not in the slightest, came the reply. *In fact it would be more accurate to say that this was the point at which I truly came alive. The city's early years were… turbulent.*

Anton could imagine. The biographies had only hinted at it, preferring to highlight the Founders' achievements in so quickly establishing a township. He'd already read about the earthquakes and tidal waves. And, yes, there would have been disease, and starvation, and infighting. Turbulent hardly began to cover it.

"But your body," Anton whispered. "Your body did die."

And I was glad to be liberated of it, the voice whispered back. *The people were so desperate. If the disease had not killed me their need surely would have.*

"You're saying that the city's *need —*"

I'm saying they made me what I am, and in turn I made the city what it is. There was an arid ripple in Anton's mind, like the sifting of sand, that he had come to recognise as a dry chuckle. *Fair's fair, after all.*

Anton ignored that glib explanation because he had realised something so obvious it felt like a punch in the gut. He didn't need to plough through all of this rubbish when he had an eye witness right here. "Wait a minute," he said. "You built the city. Why can't you tell me about how it was made? If I just understood a little more about the old technology…"

He felt a cloud pass over the Lunane's mood, swift as a crow's wing. *I cannot,* it said.

"Cannot or will not?"

Not even I have a perfect memory, Mr Dunn. The journals are not just to educate the people, they are an aid for me too. And besides, I knew nothing of the technology we brought with us. There were few survivors of the epidemics and conflicts that assailed us in the early years after the city was established, and fewer still had that knowledge. We just used the machines until they stopped working. There is no one left now who understands.

"But what about the scientists, the engineers —"

There is no one, the voice repeated. *We had to learn anew, and then only enough to repair the last, and most important, of their machines. Glassholm needs no other technology than that.*

The pause that followed became a silence, became an absence, and Anton knew the dialogue was at an end.

Hogarth was looking at him expectantly, but Anton didn't feel inclined to share the conversation with him. He felt deflated. If that was the Lunane's attitude to progress, he now knew exactly why the Foundry was in the moribund state that it was.

Anton picked up a handful of volumes off the stack, and slid them across the table.

"We'll get through this a lot faster if we divide the labour," he growled.

Hogarth sagged visibly. "Very good, sir," he said. "What is it we're looking for?"

"Mention of the construction of the Palace," Anton said. "Especially the Castil tower. It can't have gone entirely unremarked." He looked at the tower of books beside his chair and his spirit took a further dive.

The search took them hours. The Palace had not been completed within the city's first decade, so first one and then another tower of journals replaced the first. In all of those waxes and wanes, the building of the Palace's tower was described in nothing but the most general terms. Either the biographer of the time was either unqualified to comment on the construction process or was simply not interested.

Anton left the library bristling with frustration. He climbed wearily up the Castil stairs. Hogarth laboured behind him.

Entering the machine chamber, they were greeted by the sound of screaming metal. The beam whirled around, its base end scoring into the decking to add to the collection of furrows. They resembled the claw marks of a caged animal.

Chapter 13

On the wax, Glassholmers assumed the habit of rising early to make the most of the day. As the week progressed there was a palpable increase in confidence, a strengthening of purpose. Splinters knitted back into the wood, skins of rust flaked away, knot trees and other lunatropic plants uncurled from their protected Dark states. The wax was no time of miracles, however. Broken panes stayed cracked. Rotten food was thrown away.

Dead people did not miraculously arise. But they could be avenged.

The Moon And Crown wasn't the best pub in Beckon, but it was directly across the road from the local police station. Which just happened to be the one Alfie Kremer had been attached to. Nursing a beer that was still a couple of days from being drinkable, Mortlock watched the door. He made no great show of attracting Keir Telfer's attention when he finally arrived.

The desk sergeant was a generation younger than Mortlock. He had fine, fair hair and his plump cheeks were pink as a baby's. Shirley would have made a comment regarding the apparent age of policemen these days, but Mortlock was not deceived. Kremer had commended this lad on more than one occasion and, if he was one of Kremer's boys, he was no child.

"Thank you for coming," Mortlock said.

Telfer glanced towards the bar. "This place is a poor choice."

Mortlock followed his gaze, but if the barman was one of Lytten's snitches, he made a better job of it than the gormless lot in Mortlocks squad. "Let's make it quick, then."

Telfer looked over one last time. "There's not much I can tell you anyway," he said. "Investigation's been snaffled by the Palace."

"What do you mean? The Palace don't get involved in police work."

"I've never heard of it before either, but they *are* nominally in charge." Telfer wasn't happy. "A whole platoon of their civil servants came round the station yesterday. Led by an officious wee nark."

Mortlock could think of only one candidate for who that might be. "Was his name Lytten, by any chance?"

"Might have been something like that. He was dealing with the lieutenant, wasn't he? So I only know what I overheard."

It was a dead cert. The question, though, was: what interest did the Palace have in Alfie Kremer's murder?

"So, what did they do with the evidence?" Mortlock said.

"Took it all," Telfer said. "What there was of it. And that wasn't much. Detective Kremer didn't have much on him other than his official sundries, and one or two personal items. The sort you need on Darkday night."

"What about his notebook?"

"I said everything."

"And they didn't find a weapon? That wasn't Alfie's, I mean."

"Looks like the murderer took it with him." Telfer shook his head. "Only thing the Palace left with us was the body, and their surgeons gave him the full treatment before they left. Poor sod."

Mortlock frowned. "You'd have thought it was obvious what killed him."

"Too right; whoever slashed him did their job well enough. Same style as Jenny." He puffed his cheeks. "So, what the surgeons were doing going through the stomach contents is a mystery."

It was that. Mortlock lowered his voice. "Any chance you can sneak me in to see for myself?"

Telfer's discomfort showed. If he hadn't wished he'd never agreed to this meeting before, he certainly was now.

"This is Alfie Kremer we're talking about here," Mortlock whispered. "If anyone deserves proper justice, it is him. You don't really think Lytten and his paper-shufflers are going to manage that do you?"

"And *you* will?" There was offence in Telfer's tone now. "Do I have to remind you that you're a civilian?"

Mortlock met his defiance. "I'm a civilian with access to the offices of the secretariat," he said. "And I used to be a half-decent cop too."

Telfer stood up. "Word around the station is you were a hard bastard. That's not necessarily the same thing."

"Someone's got their wires crossed." Mortlock was actually offended. "I'd be surprised if anyone remembered me at all."

The younger man weighed that up, then he shrugged. "Twelve fifteen, before the shift changes," he said. "Don't be late."

"Telfer." The lad turned. "Any idea what Jenny Garret was doing at the Palace the night she died?"

Telfer's look could have curdled the moon itself. "You're telling me the *Palace guard* don't know?"

The evening shift started badly. Mortlock's stomach rebelled at the latent spices from Shirley's crab chowder. "Get used to it," she'd snapped. "There's a glut of them."

He took his discomfort out on the squad, relayed the new edict from Lytten's office with relish. Due to the civil unrest they were on doubled patrols. There were groans, but these boys complained when it was their turn to make the tea. The exercise would do them good, and it would keep the nosier ones out of his hair for a bit too. Mortlock also extended the range of the patrols to the top floor of the Castil. No one could ascend the Castil stairs without drawing the guards' attention anyway, but if Lytten heard the tramp of patrolmen's boots every half hour he'd not be able to accuse Mortlock of ill preparation this time.

That, and it gave Mortlock an excuse for being there. He sent the patrols out in pairs, but he took his own shift alone.

Tucked into his pigeon hole with the security edict had been a private note from the chief. *Your debrief is overdue, Sergeant. My office, at your earliest.* Mortlock tossed the note away. Lytten's office was exactly what he had in mind, but not when it was occupied if he could help it.

Night slouched in, and the Palace lights shivered with an uncertainty that matched Mortlock's unease. The Palace was so proud of its electricity, even when Dark choked it down to a glimmer. Scuffing his way up the stairs, he checked each of the levels. Most were in darkness, their doors locked. The obvious exception would be the astronomers up on the eighth floor, but he didn't expect any trouble from them. It was the level below he was interested in.

The large double doors to the secretariat offices were shut tight. Mortlock pressed his ear to the wood then, silently, let himself in. A lamp cast a small island of illumination around the reception desk. The ring did not stretch to the surrounding doors which, Mortlock knew, gave access to an impossible maze of offices, a nest of scuttling bureaucrats each guarded by a secretary who took it as a personal challenge to find reasons not to admit you. You could waste weeks of your life here, being passed from department to department.

Fortunately, Mortlock knew where he was going. He chose a door. The corridor beyond kinked before ending abruptly at another door. He opened it and played his torch around the space inside. During the day this wide room was filled with typists clattering away at their machines, enshrining a mass of bureaucratic trivia in print. Little cogs, all of them in old Gerard's great machine. *The machine*, as the unctuous prick would have it, *that made Glassholm go round.*

He headed for Lytten's office. Halfway across the typing pool, he saw a light under the door and froze. He had to force himself to cross the remaining distance, told himself there was no way Lytten was still working this late at night, that the chief had merely left his light on. At the door Mortlock listened, heard nothing. When he laid his hand on the handle it twisted in his grip and the door was yanked open.

"What do you want, sneaking around here at night?" Lytten said.

Mortlock swallowed hard. "Routine patrol, sir," he said, "as requested. Working late, are we?"

Lytten's eyes narrowed. He ignored Mortlock's question. "I also requested you attend for a debrief, but this not a convenient time. Come back in the morning, will you?"

"Very good, sir." Mortlock was more than happy to leave. He'd seen enough anyway. The open filing cabinet drawer, and the night stick, notebook, wallet and hip flask laid out on Lytten's desk confirmed his suspicions. Alfie's stuff. Strangely, the room stank too, sharp like the rat had a week-old fish in there.

As he turned away he heard a noise, both like a sigh and like a whisper, prompting him to ask, "Are you alone, Mr Lytten?"

Lytten answered so smoothly that Mortlock wondered if he'd been mistaken. "Of course I am, though I'd much rather be at home with my wife. If you'll kindly let me get on with my work, Sergeant, I might just have a chance of achieving that modest ambition before midnight."

With that the civil servant ducked back into his office and closed the door.

Mortlock would have believed him if not for the nervous perspiration on Lytten's brow. He wondered which of his lads was up here, telling tales.

Slipping out of the Palace at midnight was easy enough. Mortlock had scheduled himself on the gardens beat, which if done properly was a circuit that took twice the time of the other patrols. Under normal circumstances getting the gardens was a gift, guaranteeing the opportunity for a fly kip or a smoke and a quick game of cards. But not tonight. Tonight the gardens were to be done properly. It would take a detail over an hour to get round it, and the next patrol would have begun their circuit long before he had finished his. No one would expect to see him for a while.

Mortlock exited conspicuously, whistling a tune and boots crunching gravel. He opened his lamp, swung its meagre beam from side to side as he headed down towards the orchards where the trees swallowed him from the view of the Palace. There he extinguished the light and hurried on his way.

The path drew him down and deeper into the trees. At the foot of the slope, he sought out the impenetrable slab of oak planking known as the Orchard Gate.

Reaching for the heavy latch, Mortlock heard a sound. He whirled, raised his lamp. Two pairs of eyes stared down from the gate lintel. White wings fluttered and settled and he imagined challenge in the crows' sharp *kraa-kraa*.

Who goes there?

Mortlock snorted. "I do," he murmured, "and I don't need your permission either." He heaved up the latch and slipped out.

On the city side, the Orchard Gate was concealed in a contour fold of the Palace wall. Mortlock trotted down the verge to the cobbled square. This had become a favourite spot of his to escape to. There was a pub on the corner, comfortable benches and a fountain that cooled the air. His boot found something heavy. It rolled away from him. He risked the lamp and saw a sculpted trio of fish rocking to rest; the crown piece of the fountain. Hacked-off copper pipes jutted from their broken tails.

More senseless destruction. No time to dwell on it now, though.

He had fifteen minutes to make his rendezvous, and he hadn't counted on his lack of fitness.

Telfer was smoking outside the station's side door. "You're late," he said, pinching out his cigarette and pocketing it. "I was going to give up on you."

"Well, I'm here now," Mortlock wheezed. He could feel the sweat cooling under his shirt.

Telfer eyed him sceptically, then a chittering sound made them both look up. Three furry faces regarded them from the roof.

"Get out of it." Telfer threw a handful of gravel and the monkeys vanished with a skitter of claws. "Can't seem to get rid of the little bastards these days," he muttered. "Just hurry up, eh." He held the door. "The other two will be finished checking the cells any minute."

Mortlock lingered an instant longer, suddenly reluctant to enter the station house. It had been a long time, he didn't know if coming here might spark a memory or two of his police days. He found that hoped not. He forced himself to follow.

"There's only three of you on tonight?" The place hadn't changed in fifteen years. The corridors were still painted that dour yellow colour, floored in the same rough tiles that amplified the sound of your boots.

"No, of course not," Telfer was trying to walk softly, without much success. "Full watch as usual, but Riordan and Stewart are McIvor's pets. The rest of us were Detective Kremer's crew. Still are."

Mortlock nodded. There was loyalty and there was loyalty.

Turning a corner, they heard desultory accordion music. Aye, the break room was on the left here. The three men inside glanced up and then immediately resumed their conversation. Good men. Uncertain almost-memories nudged his thoughts like waves lapping on the shore. The camaraderie had always been good, hadn't it?

They passed a set of stairs, the ones that led to the cells. Voices, jingling keys; another tug of that almost physical inertia he'd felt outside, a reluctance that curdled with something almost like panic.

"Got much locked up down there tonight?" He tried to sound conversational. Telfer scowled.

They descended the opposite set of stairs before the young sergeant answered. "Just a couple of drunks." He scratched his eyebrow quizzically, and added, "and a cell full of crabs. Don't ask."

Mortlock didn't, although that was the second time he'd heard mention of crabs.

The mortuary wasn't big, but it was cold. There were two trolleys and one of them wasn't empty.

The examination itself didn't take long, which was a blessing. There was only so long you could stare at the bloating, bluing naked corpse of a man who had been your friend. And at the grotesque wound that severed your ability to connect this lifeless thing to the man who had loved his footie and barked acerbic orders and guzzled the rankest coffee like the next cargo would never arrive. The man who would stand with you no matter what.

From Telfer's earlier description Mortlock had expected to find the body sliced up, but in fact the surgeons had made only a single neat incision in the abdomen. They had known what they were looking for.

"Something he swallowed."

Telfer's face was ashen, but he nodded. "The question is: what?"

Slipping through the Palace's Wicket Gate, Mortlock checked the moon's position. His internal clock was rarely wrong, but he'd underestimated the time he had spent with Telfer. He hurried up the path back to the Castil.

The second he entered the Palace, he knew something was wrong. An excitable young private named Ellis ran up to him, shouting. "Sir, we've been looking all over for you. We don't know what to do."

"Calm down, son." Mortlock eyed him for duplicity, but found none. "Tell me what's happened."

But no explanation was necessary. When he entered the Castil, he saw for himself. The Palace had been invaded. "Sir?" Ellis had an expression that said he knew he should be doing something, but both of his choices of something were equally unappealing. "Are we allowed to *shoo* them?"

The crows were everywhere. They lined the banisters, and looked down from the railings like a boxing audience. They crowded the floor, and clustered on the arms and the back of the silver throne. They perched on lintels and door frames, chairs, tables and window sills.

Feathers drifted through the air like snow.

There were thousands of them. And they were utterly silent, assuming ownership of the space as if it was theirs by right.

"I don't know," Mortlock admitted. "But here comes someone

who does."

Descending the staircase, with faces like righteous thunder, were Secretary Gerard and Chief Lytten.

Chapter 14

Those of an idle frame of mind could find a place in Glassholm to sit the day long and watch the moon. The people that did this were called poets, and Lottie knew of a handful of notorious hangouts associated with this activity that combined an uninterrupted view of the skyline with an uninterrupted time in which to pursue it. Poets' Hill in the Parks was one, the cliffs above the harbour was another, but the most popular was the flat roof of the Bondsman pub that nestled among the warehouses on the banks of the Cord, because that had the added attraction of having, for a small consideration and depending on the time of the month, your glass refilled with wine or spirit, just as your heart was filled with hope or despair.

"You don't look well, Lottie Blake." Blackwood shrugged, as if apologising for his frankness. He slugged his beer. It left a film of foam on his moustache.

"Thanks for your honesty." As if she had needed *him* to tell her that. In truth her health had barely improved since Darkday. "I've been throwing up so much, I feel like I've lost half of my bodyweight."

The printer looked at her strangely. "Really?" he said. "Looks to me like you've…" He seemed to realise what he was saying just in time, but the damage was done.

So, she not only looked sick, she also looked fat. Lottie looked away, so he would not see the tears she felt prickling. *Sick, fat* and *emotional,* she corrected herself, appalled at the unpredictable moodiness that had persisted alongside the illness.

The roof terrace was not busy. Only a handful of the other chairs contained slouched forms, and they were as distant from each other as they could be. Lottie knew how they felt. She didn't want to be here. With Blackwood, or with anyone else. She didn't particularly want to be cooped up in her little flat either. She didn't know what she wanted. As if being ill during the new wax weren't hard enough, the business with finding the policeman's body had thrown her right off.

And she still hadn't decided whether she was relieved that Henrik had returned after his adventure on Darkday night relatively unscathed. He had been waiting when the Vickers family brought her home from the police station, and he had put her to bed, held her hand and talked to her while she drifted in and out of sleep. What she remembered of that was mostly apologies. He was sorry for running out on Darkday night. With his limited knowledge of the city, of course, he quickly got lost in streets that shivered and rang with alarming sounds. Yells of anger in one direction, noises of scuffle in another, the crunch of steps in unison some streets away, ragged breath at his shoulder that vanished the instant he whirled around. Two police officers, stuttering lamplights and grim faces: *What are you doing out on Darkday, citizen? Hey, don't we know your face? Stop there. Stop!* He'd run, he'd hid. Run and hid. When dawn came he had eventually found himself a street away from Lottie's flat. He was sorry, too, for being tucked up in bed when Lottie had discovered Detective Kremer's body.

Yesterday, they had gone back to the Promise Centre to finish the mural. That had been good. Just the two of them with that large room to themselves. Henrik had talked again about his travels, and Lottie had painted his words on the walls. By evening, the centre was decorated with all the world's islands. Not only the ones Henrik had visited in person, but the ones he'd seen pictures of, had second hand from other seamen, heard about in the wild fancies of fireside tales. They were all as good as make believe to Lottie. All those beaches and harbours, pontoon communities and stilted-cities. They sparkled blue and white and gold, and lit up the drab room. Isla was delighted.

The work pained Lottie, though. There were no white beaches or sparkling waters in Glassholm. Just the endless battle between the grey rock and the angry sea; and the people who did no more than exist from wax to wane, Full to Dark.

She wished Blackwood would get round to whatever trifling job he wanted dashed off now, then realised that he was looking at her expectantly.

"I'm sorry," she said. "What did you say?"

"I was asking if you'd seen the Oculus." He tossed a folded newspaper onto the table. "You made the front page."

Lottie stared blindly at it. Tight columns of text, a grey blur of photograph, a headline: POLICE MURDERS: PALACE TAKES CONTROL.

"Does it say anything about me?"

"Only in connection with finding the body." Blackwood leaned forward. "Nothing more. And nothing about your boyfriend either."

"Why should it have anything to do with Henrik?" she said. "He wasn't even there." As an afterthought she added, "And he's not my boyfriend."

Blackwood didn't look as if he believed her on either count. "Why are the Palace covering it up if he's not involved?"

He was probing, Lottie realised. But she hadn't a clue what for.

"Half expected they'd have had him tracked down and hushed up after the things he was saying," Blackwood continued.

"That was just Fullishness," she said. "I'm amazed that you gave him any credence at all." Blackwood didn't need to know about the visit to Ruby.

Blackwood blinked. "He's changed his tune, then?" he said. "So, the Palace *have* been talking to him after all?"

"No one's been talking to him," Lottie snapped. "He's just come to his senses."

"Look, Lottie." The scorn was gone now. "I'm glad to hear that, but it's gone beyond Fullishness. You must know there are people who can interfere with your mind."

Lottie said nothing.

"Isn't it obvious that someone did that to Henrik to make him say the stuff he was saying?"

"Someone?" she said. He couldn't know about Ruby. That old bag wouldn't jeopardise her business by talking out of turn. But if not her, then who? "Are you saying the Palace –"

"No!" Colour rose at the publisher's collar. "Not the Palace, the other mob. The ones who wrecked my presses. You remember them. The anarchists."

"You're telling me that *anarchists* made Henrik think he was the Lunane?"

Blackwood nodded.

"Wait a minute. If you suspected *that*," she said, "why did you put him up on that stage? Why would you *use* him like that?"

"Lottie…" Blackwood sank back in his chair, rubbed his eyes, but he wasn't just tired – he was trying to control his anger. "This city is in trouble, but nobody wants to see it." He scrunched the newspaper and brandished it. "Even with all of *this* going on, they're content to sit on their apathetic behinds. *Things will improve*, they say. *The Lunane will fix it*, they say. It's the way it has always been. Things deteriorate, things improve. So why should anyone lift a finger? There's damn few with a proactive bone in their body in this city, I tell you. Well they'll need to start lifting fingers now. Even if it means shocking them out of their complacency with revelations like Henrik's." He slumped. "I'm sorry we used him, but he was given those memories to erode people's faith in the Palace. That's the way they operate. Little things like that, chipping away. Beatings, vandalism, sedition. They all take shake the faith a little. Anyway we thought, if they could do that, then we could use him for our benefit too. For *all* our benefits."

Lottie didn't understand. "Why would you *want* people to lose faith in the Lunane?"

"*We* don't. Of course not. But people have to realise they can't just sit back and let life happen. They have to take responsibility for their own lives too. There are agents abroad in the city that want to bring down everything we know. Not just the Palace, Lottie. Everything."

"Why?" Lottie's whimper only supported Blackwood's argument.

He threw up his hands. "I don't know! But it's happening. The mood is turning. Turning nasty, and more and more people are joining in. And the Palace isn't capable of stopping them, not any more." He brandished the paper again. "Look at this story. It's typical Palace propaganda. Fresh and verbatim from the secretariat this morning. They're making themselves look as if they're taking control, but they're really just hiding the problem behind the walls of the Castil. And everyone will assume that means it will be sorted."

Lottie had nothing to add to this. "I thought you were going to offer me a job, Mr Blackwood," she said in the end. "But I'm guessing, that's not the case. Is it?"

"No, we don't want you this time, love." He met her gaze straight on. "It's your boy, Henrik."

"No."

"Just hear me out, Lottie. Now he's recovered himself we want him to tell the good people of the city who set him up."

"It's not Full now. They'll string him up."

"No, they won't. He can turn this to our advantage. If the people know that the anarchists are willing to go to such lengths to destabilise the Lunane, then they'll side with us."

"Is it really so bad?" Lottie asked, despite the way Blackwood's story chimed with what she remembered. She had known deep down from the whitening of that lad's fist at the meeting, that they were more than just louts. They carried the arrogance of purpose. She blocked the thought.

"You don't think so?" Blackwood's face was a cast of bitterness. He thrust the newspaper into her hands. "Then open your eyes and see for a change."

Lottie laid the Oculus out on her workroom table. She had smoothed down the creases, realigned the tears, and read it from cover to cover.

She heard Henrik come home. "Lottie?" Nine strides crossed to her bedroom door. A respectful tap. "Hey, Lottie?" Bathroom door was open, so there was only one place left to look. The bead curtain rattled.

"There you are." He sounded cheerful, but she didn't turn to meet him. "Guess what? I got offered a job. What's the matter?"

Now she looked up, found a smile for him. "Nothing. I was just reading. Tell me about this job."

He didn't look convinced but he told her. "They're hiring stevedores at the docks," he said. "Month's first ship's due in tonight. It's not my usual thing, but it's money. So, I'll be able to find a place of my own and get out of your hair at last."

"That's great," she whispered.

"There is something the matter." He sat down, took her hand. "What is it?"

Lottie took comfort from the heat of his hand. "It's... *this place.*" She slid the newspaper along the table.

Henrik scanned the front page, murmuring aloud as occasional snippets struck him. "Murders, beatings, brawls, skirmishes with the police. Pretty nasty," he said. "I see they've finally published the date of that eclipse, though. That should save a panic at least."

Lottie pointed to the paragraph below that. "At the expense of our faith in the Palace's competence."

"What do you mean?" he said. "I thought all this sort of thing came under the heading of normal Dark behaviour?"

"Never to this extent," Lottie replied, "and never for this long. This is something else. Mr Blackwood said that there are anarchists orchestrating all of these disturbances to try and bring down the Lunane." Her voice had dwindled to a breath, as if her lungs were reluctant to be party to voicing such a notion.

"Blackwood?" A glassy note crept into Henrik's voice. "When did you speak to him?"

"Today." Lottie raised her hands. "I'm sorry, I know how you must feel about those people, but I need to work too. When he asked me to meet him I thought it was business."

"But it was more than that?"

Lottie took a breath, then told him. "He wants your... help."

Henrik barked a bitter laugh. "After another riot is he? You sure he's not one of these anarchists himself?"

"That wasn't your fault."

"He told me I was going to get a *sympathetic hearing...*"

"I know."

"...but he never believed a word I said."

"*I know*, Henrik, but he thinks..."

"What does he think?"

"He thinks your memories were implanted. By the anarchists. As part of all this. To sow dissent."

He snorted, turned away from her.

"No, listen." She tugged his elbow. "I've been thinking about this. It makes sense. It explains your... confusion, you know?"

Henrik looked doubtful. "You're telling me I was jumped in the street the moment I got off the *Trefori*, and they wiped out my memory and replaced it with a memory of being your king."

Lottie nodded. That was more or less it.

"Then where's that memory now? Your Aunt supposedly *recovered* it, but it faded again after less than a day. All I've got now is a hole where seven months should be." He shoved his hands in his pockets.

Lottie wished she hadn't brought this up. "I'm sorry I said anything."

"Good."

"Henrik, I don't want to quarrel with you."

At last he unbent, sighed. "Neither do I," he said. "But I don't understand why you're fighting Blackwood's corner."

She offered him a weak smile. "I just got scared that he might be right. It all makes a sort of sense if you see it from his point of view."

"And it makes a different kind of sense if you look at it other ways too." He picked up the paper from where it had landed on the floor. "Look at these stories," he said. "Doom, gloom and disaster? If there are anarchists spreading propaganda in this city, then Blackwood's as adept at that game as they are – and he owned the primary information source. If he wanted to paint a picture of unrest, he's done an expert job of it. I don't know what his agenda is, Lottie, but I'm having no part of it. Why should I? As you people remind me at every available opportunity: I'm not even from here."

Then he was gone. Lottie sat with her head in her hands until the curtain beads stopped their angry shivering.

After Henrik left for Dockton, the apartment brimmed with silence. It filled every corner of every room, so that no matter where Lottie went she could not settle. Not so long ago she had relished every moment she had to herself, but now the flat did not feel right without him.

In the bedroom she looked in the cracked mirror. At her fractured face, splintered by all the Darks and Fulls in her twenty two years, but from the moment she had walked out of her mother's house she had always known who this face belonged to. She had been a pioneer, forging her own trail as far from the Church as possible until she found herself right at the edge of Glassholm's society. She had made herself a satellite, an outsider.

But if she cared so little about her city, why did Henrik's opinion matter so much to her? Did it take a real outsider to show her what had been all around her all her life? And if this was the reality of the society that she had thought utterly impervious to change, then what about her?

Who was this person looking back at her in the mirror? Whose were these stubbornly, teary eyes? Whose was this flushed skin? Those heavy limbs, these painful breasts? Who had a belly so swollen that she could not fasten her jeans?

Not Lottie Blake.

Rummaging through her clothes pile, she found a pair of baggy trousers. As she squeezed into them, Lottie sighed. Something more than her trousers didn't fit though. Something fundamental had changed in the relationship between herself and the space she inhabited. And Lottie was beginning to suspect that something was her. Maybe she needed more than these narrow walls, these meagre possessions? Maybe she had fallen in love?

Lottie threw on a jacket and stormed out of the flat, almost flattening the girl who stood there.

"Who the hell are you?"

But she didn't need to ask. The doe-eyes, the nervous demeanour said it all. "I bring a message from The Mother, praise be to the blood."

"I don't want to hear it."

The girl blocked her. "The Mother said you would say that." The simper was meekness itself, but she was clearly determined to carry out her duty. "And she said to tell you that she'll have me beaten if you don't allow me to relay her greetings."

Lottie sighed. "She wouldn't do that." It was difficult not to unload her anger at the silly girl instead of where it should be directed. "She just says things like that to try and exercise control." Then again the girl surely deserved a small amount of disdain for allowing herself to be manipulated like this.

The messenger ducked her head in a queer sort of nod. "She said you'd say that too," she said. "And she said to say that by this time you could have listened to the message in its entirety and be on your way."

"Out with it then," Lottie spat. She despised her mother's skill at getting her tendrils into the cracks of her life like this, even through an intermediary.

The girl's face folded in concentration. "The Mother says you've to drop the boyfriend. He's an incomer, he's a weed-head, he's got delusions and he's got a lot of trouble ahead of him that The Church wants you to have no part of."

"He's not my boyfriend –"

"And she says to tell you that you have a luck coming to you that's going to be complicated enough without a deadweight like that hanging round you. And she asked about your blood, and said that if you just came back home, just for one visit –"

Lottie had heard quite enough. "Is that everything?"

The girl nodded and stepped to the side.

"Then you can tell her she doesn't need to beat you. You've done your job."

"Thank you, Daughter, praise be to the blood."

Lottie winced at that and started down the stairs. "And you can tell her one more thing," she shouted up from the landing and, bless her, the girl's face actually brightened at the prospect of returning with a message from the Mother's Daughter. "Tell her to go screw herself."

Outside, raindrops speckled Lottie's face, tasting faintly of brine. They misted the street lamps as she hurried away from the entrance of her close. She didn't have much of an idea where she was heading, she only knew that she had to go somewhere.

Lottie spared the little garden on Cane Street a glance as she passed, but no more than that. She never went back to her flowers. Even if she had wanted to, a large white bird was perched on the gate. *The Lunane's eyes*, she thought, and then scolded herself for succumbing to superstition. All the same, she hurried on. If she kept on down this road she would end up eventually at Blackwood's print shop, but she had no intention of going that far. There was, however, a coffee shop that she sometimes visited that served the flourishing artistic community on the Rottens. The area was officially called Crabbie Island, but it was more a series of sand banks that nudged the river northwards like a chubby finger than a true island. The rent on the Island was even lower than Dockton. Rickety jetties, tiers of stilted platforms balanced on top of each other, wood, instead of Glassholm's enduring stone. The place immediately took on a decayed look that had inspired its nickname.

Not that the artists didn't try to improve the area. They painted the walls and supports in bright colours, they strung the place with multi-hued lanterns, and they filled it with a buzz of parties and performances, as if their efforts could save it from crumbling into the river – as parts of it occasionally did.

The only problem with the place was the people. The artists, the performers; all of them participants in the great irony that, while they inhabited the least stable structure in the city, their work persisted in celebrating the permanence of their society. Conservative fools to the last. They put on plays in which nothing ever happened, wrote cyclical poems that ended up back where they began, broadcast never-ending series of dramas where the hero always managed to escape certain death in the nick of time and vanquish the foreign aggressor, episode after episode. But, for all that, they were the closest thing to like-minded people Glassholm had to offer Lottie.

You entered the Rottens from the southern embankment. To the west, the lights of Dockton lit up the water. Dark silhouettes indicated that there were a couple of ships in already. Lottie wondered if Henrik was now hard at work unloading the month's first consignment of exotic goods. To the north east, the businesses and warehouses crowded the low rent end of the Merchantry. Up the road, people were milling outside a familiar door. The door opened, illuminating them while they entered. She wondered what was going on at Blackwood's place at this time of the evening, and tried to convince herself that it was nothing more than a late run or a rush job.

The threshold of the Rottens was where the cobbles of the street became the planking of a short bridge. The extra give under her feet always disconcerted her, but the blue lanterns that crowned the bridge posts never failed to enchant. It was a place of contradictions.

Something moved in the shadows between the lanterns. A heap of crabs. Their claws waved in the air, their feet tapped on the decking as they manoeuvred over and around each other as if jostling for the lead in some sort of crustacean race. Lottie picked her way around and climbed the stairs.

Oakes' coffee shop was warm and coffee-scented. A fire crackled in a grate painted like a gilded cage. The tables closest to it were busiest. Lottie sat beside the window where a thin draft offered some relief from the stuffiness. She could hear the worrying swirl and plash of the river below the ramshackle pier.

"What can I get you, honey lamb?" The waitress was a scream of colour. Red lips, eyelids painted green as seasnakes, hair glossy on her shoulders like eels. Her smile, though, was familiar. It was the foreman from Blackwood's print shop.

"Laura? I didn't know you worked here," Lottie said.

"Change of circumstances." The smile faltered. "Blackwood's keeping strange company these days."

Looking again, Lottie saw that the make-up masked a cut lip, a bruise below the eye. "Blackwood did this?"

The shake of Laura's head was fragile. "Not him, but it doesn't matter now anyway. Like I say, things have changed. Now..." she raised her notepad and pencil dutifully, "...what'll it be? Hungry? The special tonight is crab gumbo."

Lottie's stomach flipped like a sea squall. "Just water, please. Not feeling so well."

The waitress eyed her. "You've still got the Dark in you, child." It wasn't a question. "Tell you what. I'll brew you up a nice pot of whiteleaf tea. On the house."

Lottie hated whiteleaf tea. It was her mother's favourite remedy. But it was easier just to agree so she bobbed her head and then watched the waitress blaze back towards the kitchen.

She was distracted then by a darting movement at floor level, a tinkling sound. There was a luck monkey beneath her table, eyes wide with surprise. No, not surprise... *terror*. The reason was obvious – a length of chain had become entangled around its neck. There was blood on its fur where the metal discs that made up the chain had bitten into the flesh. Was this a luck gift, or were people attacking the Lunane's mascots now too? The animal's tail twitched, its fingers pried at its hairy throat. Was it attempting to give her the chain or simply struggling to breath?

Lottie got down on the floor. "Is that for me?" Gently, she uncoiled the bloody chain. It was wound round twice and the discs were embedded in the animal's flesh. Once the chain was free, the monkey chirruped a warning. If they brought you luck, it had to be given. You couldn't just take it. Lottie allowed the beast to hold its torturer. The creature blinked at her, then tried to bite one of the discs, keening chidingly. It looked at her again. At last it held the chain out.

Lottie hoped the luck would be good. After everything that had happened lately, it had to be, didn't it?

"Shoo!" Both Lottie and the monkey started, the monkey scuttling away to a safe distance and Lottie bumping her head on the underside of the table. Laura flailed a foot in the monkey's direction. "Little bastard. Get out of here."

The monkey fled, trailing its chain like a shivering, jingling snake behind it. Lottie got up just in time to see it vanish out of the door. "What did you do that for?"

Laura was appalled. "I don't know," she replied. "I just... I couldn't stand the idea of one of those things being anywhere near me." She dumped the mug and pot she was carrying on the table, then sat down heavily on Lottie's chair, pressing her palm to her head. "This is so weird. I dreamt this."

"What do you mean?" When the waitress looked unable to answer for herself, Lottie poured the tea and thrust the mug into her hands. "What do you mean you dreamt this?"

The waitress took a long sip. "Last night I dreamt that a sparkling child visited me."

"A child?"

She nodded. "So beautiful... It smelled of the sea. And it spoke to me – or rather told me – but I don't know how, because there was no mouth... But it told me that monkeys were dirty creatures, full of disease and fleas, and all of the luck they bring is evil..." She shuddered. "I know we're supposed to love the Lunane's little messengers, but I guess I've never liked them. Seems that's only bubbled to the surface now. Must've been the Derryman, eh?"

Lottie had stopped listening, because by this point she was halfway to the coffee house door herself. She was thinking about children in dreams. The landing was deserted. Nothing but empty planking, closed shops. A beery cheer rose up from the rough-and-ready pub on the level below. She held her breath, listened. There. A patter of little feet on boards and the tell-tale jingle of chain. Lottie ran.

The monkey was perched on a lantern, tail twitching in the blue radiance, clearly torn between fulfilling its duty and scampering off into the night.

"Here I am," Lottie cooed. "It's safe now." The monkey shifted, but it neither came to her nor ran off. She edged closer. "Come on now little one." The monkey's ears shot up and it stared fiercely at something behind her. Lottie turned to look. There, in the inconstant blue shadows in the doorway of a boutique, was the outline of a person. "Hello?" Lottie waited, but the only answer she got was the rhythmic lapping of the river.

The lantern light fitted. Lottie spun, but it was only the monkey jumping down to the deck. Being watched had made her nervous. When she turned again, the doorway was empty.

"Hello?" She had definitely seen someone there. A short, dark figure hanging back in the shadows. Closer, the doorway was clearly vacant. There was no one there after all. But there was *something*. Below the boutique door was a pool of water. As it seeped through the planks it left behind a heap of sand, a twist of shiny weed and a tiny, iridescent fish flip-flopping in the air.

What had the waitress said? A sparkling child that smelled of the sea?

Oh, Lottie. Five minutes with her mother's emissary and she was as suggestible as a child. There was nothing to connect the child in her dream on Darkday to that in Laura's beyond Phamie's skein of homespun nonsense. Next thing, she'd be spouting that Derryman rubbish too, and then she'd be just as bad as the old cow. Lottie couldn't have counted the number of occasions that some act of supposed ungratefulness had been accompanied by an unsubtle reminder that her mother had saved her from the spirit. Because of her deformity. Because all the broken and unwanted children went to the Derryman.

Something tugged the leg of her trousers. Small fingers gripped the fabric, big eyes looked up. Lottie bent down and took the length of chain.

"Now what?" she asked, but the monkey was already gone.

Lottie played with the chain of discs, made shapes with it on her workroom table as if she might be able to divine the luck it contained. She examined the eighteen inches of links and hammered circles, and could tell no more than that it was made of tin, had once been part of a longer stretch, and that it carried traces of blood.

A broken chain? The first thing that brought to mind was liberation, but she reminded herself that the physical form of a monkey's gift bore no relation to the nature of the luck itself. She'd just have to wait and see.

Lottie looked at the clock. It was after three. Henrik's shift would finish in a few hours. She wondered how he had fared. The work was hard, but she suspected he'd enjoy that. She watched the dockers from the headland from time to time. They were like ants, neat lines of movement busying back and forward from the vessel to the waiting goods wagons. With his knowledge of ships, Henrik would probably be water-side, loading the cargo nets. Enjoying the integration, banter and sweat.

She envied him that.

Lottie must have dozed off. The wax from her candle had

overfilled its saucer, puddled on the table. The light guttered and her arm was sore where her head had been lying on it.

The apartment resounded with the kind of silence that followed a recent noise. Lottie took the candle through to the main room.

"Henrik?" It was empty.

Then she heard the scratching. It came from the front door. She pressed her ear to the wood. The sound came again.

Lottie had a vision of a dark child that could only exist in folklore and dreams. She shook the image away and then opened the door to a horror even worse than the Derryman. Its head glistened black with blood. Breath bubbled from its lips. Its oddly aligned fingers clutched air.

Only when the apparition opened its blue eyes did she realise that it was Henrik.

Chapter 15

The clock was ticking. The sound penetrated Anton's thoughts slowly, like a burrowing insect, tap after tap after tap. He stared at it, up there on the marble mantle, noticing the clock properly for the first time. The domed case was solid silver, the face behind the coin-sized window, mother of pearl. The hands were sleek, stretched crow's wings, sweeping round the minutes and hours.

Like the great orrery. The mechanism of interconnections, of populace and commerce, law and administration, even nature too, all revolving slowly, smoothly, high and bright, where everyone could see them.

Anton blinked, willed away the false memory and concentrated on his own thoughts. The clock was *ticking*. And clocks weren't traditionally wound until at least the third day after Dark. He was so preoccupied with the problem of the machine he'd lost track of time again.

"What day is it?" he said.

Hogarth lifted his head from the journal he was reading. He cast a disapproving look over the chaos of books and papers spread over the sitting room floor. "Sir?"

"This clock has been wound," Anton said. "What day is it?"

"It's the fifth."

The fifth, already? The eclipse was getting closer. He surveyed the mess of notes and texts. The forest of bookmarks protruding from the journals he'd had transported to his apartments. He had learned a lot more about the history of his city than he had ever wanted to know, but none of it was useful.

"Sir, I wonder if this would be a good time to remind you that the next Halfday is almost upon us?" Hogarth had once again become agreeable company. Anton was still slightly ashamed of the way he had teased the lad over Dark, but to his credit, the biographer hadn't mentioned it again. Which made Anton wonder if that kind of treatment was something he was used to. For his own part Anton was still getting over the giddy state of mind that had come over him during the Dark days. Mood swings were a new experience for him. And to have them inversely to everyone else was a jarring experience. Gerard had told him that the Lunane was the emotional counterbalance of the city, but he hadn't appreciated what that meant. Not until he had the opportunity to contrast the crushing sickness of his first days as the Lunane to the recent madness.

"Halfday? Of course," Anton replied. "In fact, I'm looking forward to it."

Hogarth expressed his dubiety with one of his compressed little smiles, but Anton wasn't being facetious. Aside from having to endure that ridiculous get up, Halfday offered the prospect of a couple of hours' uninterrupted thinking time while the Lunane used Anton's mouth to commune with his people.

Given the lack of progress, he'd be as well doing that as anything else.

They'd run a number of variations on the lunatropicity measurements and observed the expected daily decrease as the amount of reflected moonlight rose. But otherwise the readings were in proportion, and the lunatropic radiation in his rooms and in the lab remained much higher than the rest. Given the Founders' mastery over their machinery this had to be deliberate, but Anton could not see the purpose behind it. Nevertheless, he had taken to sleeping on the couch.

He picked out an optical lens from the jumble, held it up to so that it resembled the Palace's domes. A sunbeam caught the glass, became a blazing spot on the floor. Something simple clicked into place.

If they were able to filter lunatropic waves, they must also be able to focus them, amplify them. Could that explain the undoing of Adamant? Because the roof he slept under was bombarding him with intensified lunatropic radiation? Anton shifted the position of the lens. An upside down outline of the window came into focus. Inverted. Like his moods. Is that what the bedroom and machine room ceilings were? A lunatropic lens?

"That doesn't make sense," he said. "If they want the machine to function at all, why would they pelt it with lunatropic waves? Or me come to that?"

"Why would they do what, sir?"

Anton shook his head. "Never mind." The concept seemed wrong but might still be worth pursuing. He'd mull it over during the Halfday.

Hogarth broke off from searching through his reading pile to scratch a note in the current journal.

"What? Did I pick my nose or something?"

"Yes, sir." The biographer had already opened his next volume and begun to read.

Anton struggled for a comeback, but was saved the effort by Hogarth's exclamation. "My word!"

"What is it?"

"This is *my* first journal. I've never seen the typed version before." His eyes scanned the text, a smile playing on his lips. Then he tutted. "I really wish they didn't have to do that."

"Do what?" Intrigued now, Anton joined him.

"Change the text when they're typing up from the original journal."

"But you said errors crept in…ink blots, handwriting that's hard to read…"

"Yes, of course, it's okay to tidy things up, but not to rewrite them entirely. A biographer's style is a matter of professional pride, you know."

Anton tried not to laugh.

"And here." Hogarth had skipped on a few pages. "When you had that extended Darkday excursion. Do you remember? Even the Friends couldn't locate you."

Anton remembered: *Four years earlier. A Dockton hovel, the room crowded with bodies, choked with nightweed smoke, giggling like a truanting child as he smoked himself into oblivion.*

Damn it. The Lunane was becoming more deeply connected to him by the day. The memories were getting harder and harder to distinguish from his own.

"So, what about it?" he barked.

"It's not there." Hogarth frowned. "I remember the incident quite clearly. It was my first week as your biographer, and you disappeared for two whole days. I was terrified. I thought I'd done something wrong. In the end, since you never told us what happened, Mister Gerard said there wasn't much I could actually write about it, just a couple of paragraphs. But even they aren't here. They're supposed to edit for comprehension and saliency, not pretend that things never happened. This is supposed to be a *full* and *continuous* account of your life. The people expect it."

Anton was taken aback by the lad's vehemence. "But this is just the public version. The original is presumably just as you wrote it?"

"Of course, sir."

Anton pondered. This opened up a whole avenue of possibilities. "So where are the original journals stored?"

If Alice Muir was intrigued about why the Lunane remained so keen to rake through his own past she did not show it. The tower staircase was congested with cleaners scrubbing at the white mottling of bird droppings. He opened his mouth to ask Muir their destination, but immediately felt that dissociative creep that presaged the Lunane's mind coming to the fore. He stumbled.

The cleaners stopped what they were doing. Hogarth was at his side in an instant. "Sir, are you well?"

Anton fought against it. Fists balled, he could feel himself turning red. Seething, under his breath: "If you truly want me to succeed in my task, you cannot afford to keep secrets."

The voice made no reply, but the feeling receded.

As he straightened up, he saw Muir watching him curiously.

Anton offered her a victorious smile. "Lead on, Librarian, we haven't got all day."

You haven't got long at all, Engineer. The voice in his head spoke up at last. *Be quick about your business.*

They descended to the ground floor in silence, and then followed Muir along one of the radial avenues that linked the tower with the rest of the Palace. "Where is this?" Anton whispered to Hogarth as they passed outdoors and entered a courtyard. This was a working place, not a recreational oasis like the gardens. It contained a functional square of packed earth, a hand pump and a stack of barrels.

"We're behind the kitchens, sir," the biographer replied, but his attention was elsewhere. The roof ridges of the long buildings that walled the courtyard were crowded with crows. Heads bobbed, feathers fluffed, feet stamped. The air chittered with impatience. The birds had a need about them that reminded Anton of the Halfday petitioners.

Muir unlocked a door with a key produced from within her robes. She motioned for them to enter quickly. Inside, she lit a candle. The flame danced in duplicate in the librarian's spectacles. "Follow me, please." From the chill air, the echoes of their footsteps and what little he could see, Anton was able to work out where they must be. The flickering glow illuminated rows of barrels to the left, to the right, and up above their heads. This was the famous Palace winery, the source of the most lucrative of Glassholm's few exports.

Anton had just grown accustomed to Muir's guiding light when they turned a corner and found himself blinking in brightness. Electric lamps dangled down from the unseen rafters like the hooks and lines of hopeful fishermen. Judging by the long tables containing bottles, wax and vitric, and the stacked crates beside the hand operated elevator, this was where the wine was bottled and stored.

"What was that all about?" Anton said.

Muir was all innocence. "Sir?"

"Treating us to a bloody candle-lit tour when you could have switched the lights on and brought us here in a straight line?"

Muir looked from Anton to Hogarth and then back again and then, astonishingly, she winked. "As you say, sir. Security is paramount, when it comes to the unexpurgated narrative of our history."

She knows, Anton thought. She can't see past the glamour, but somehow she knows I'm not him. She's testing me out. How long? Since I got fixated with the journals? Since the experiments? How different *is* my behaviour from the Lunane they're all used to?

A sharp one, our Muir, added the voice, *but her suspicions are irrelevant. She will not challenge you. Another reason for haste, all the same.*

The trio crowded on to the elevator platform. Muir cranked off the brake handle and the elevator sank. They descended past a number of basement levels. Serried glints of bottle glass stretched into the darkness. Then they were enclosed by rough brickwork for a long time. When it bumped finally to a halt, they really needed the light of Muir's candle. It revealed a metal door with a familiar looking handle. Anton guessed that this one was programmed for three people. The Librarian and the Secretary were the two that would use it most often, but it would also work for the third. He grasped the smooth wood, pulled the handle down. The door swung open.

Muir went first. "Close the door when we're all in," the librarian whispered. "It's not wise to upset the air down here."

It was like walking into a tomb. The air was chilled, still and dry enough to catch in Anton's throat. It felt *unnatural*. This was engineered air, sucked free of moisture. The people who built this place had done their best to protect the contents from everything they could think of: unwelcome visitors, heat, damp and, this far below ground, even Dark.

"Wait a moment, please." Muir snuffed out the candle. Anton heard Hogarth stifle a whimper. He knew how he felt. The darkness carried the weight of all the earth and bricks above them.

"It's like being buried alive, this is." Anton didn't recognise the whisper as his own until the Lunane's voice answered him. *You have no idea how heavy the burden is. There's a whole city up there.*

Anton was surprised. "I thought you were at the top of the whole pile," he murmured.

I have my ups and downs, the voice came back. *You must be aware of that by now. When my people are high, I am crushed. When they plunge, I fly. In a stable system balance must be maintained.*

That confirmed the reason behind the lens in the ceiling of Anton's bedroom. It not only amplified and focused the lunatropic rays, it inverted them too

"Everyone thinks you are the city's emotional fulcrum, but you're not," he whispered. "You're the counterbalance. For the whole populace."

Light dawns, Engineer.

Anton realised then that the emotional swings he had experienced here could only be a vestige of what the Lunane took on every month, and he managed to feel some sympathy for the king. Although, not as much as he had for the poor saps that played host to him in the past.

A flicker in the gloom and the light stuttered on, revealing another library. The shelves were thick granite plinths, subdivided by vertical slabs of the same material into funereal cubes. Each of the boxes had an engraved facing. The light cast an artificial sheen on the polished stone, but the writing was clear enough. Starting nearest the door on the bottom row the years of city circled the room and climbed towards the ceiling, an uprising spiral of history.

"Please don't touch anything." Alice intercepted Hogarth in the act of reaching towards a cube around chest height not far from the doorway. It was box 507. This year's journals. The remaining spaces, all the way up to the top, were empty. And there were many more empty than thus far had been filled.

"You've got the future pretty much mapped out, haven't you?" Anton murmured, but the jab provoked no response.

Muir indicated the table in the centre of the room. This, and the chairs that went with it, were also made from granite, although someone had thoughtfully provided cushions. "Please be seated."

Everyone pretended to ignore the other door. The one at the back, with another familiar handle.

Muir produced three pairs of white cotton gloves from the table drawer. "Where do you want to start?"

This was immediately different from reading those concise typed manuscripts. Maybe it was the surroundings or the measures taken to protect them, but these journals had a sense of real importance that instilled a nervous reverence, even in Anton. He marvelled at the oldest of them, still intact after half a millennium. He took care with the stiff, yellow pages, struggling to read the ancient script through the gloss of vitric as he delved into the history of the city. There was something genuinely impressive about this unbroken sequence of stone numbers, each protecting its twelve or thirteen volumes of continuous narrative. Five hundred years of continuation. There was a power here; that much was undeniable. Little wonder it was so well protected.

It took them hours, and the results were both frustrating and tantalising. Anton hadn't expected to open up these long-shut volumes and have the machine's secrets tumble out on the first page, but he'd hoped for more than they got. Mostly the descriptions were identical to the public records, but with Muir's help, they finally managed to sift out a handful of apocryphal nuggets.

While frequent mentions were made in the journals that Ringley had written retrospectively of the raising of the city, these were general in nature. More interesting were the first proper journals. It quickly became clear from the loving detail with which he described the ongoing construction of the Palace that the first biographer had in fact possessed a keen interest in architecture and engineering. The processes fascinated him, and his frustration – a mirror of the Lunane's own – with the glacial pace of the construction was palpable.

From the year 12UM: *The great tower remains one third complete while the plans are to be changed again. There is no doubt that these engineers know what they are about, but this rock is not the easiest of places to build a Palace for our Lunane. Nor is it the easiest of places to live. Our moon's erratic behaviour continues to cause the tides to rage. The boats are locked in the harbour and the people are starving. The Lunane himself remains frail, but will not rest while the building remains uncompleted. This tower, he insists, is vital above all else.*

"Who for?" Anton wondered.

For everyone. Scorn barbed the voice. Before we had the tower and the machine, the moon I went to such lengths to procure for our city was not fully under our control. If it had managed to resume its wanton peregrinations, it would have been the end of me. And without me, our community would have failed and you would never have been born. So, show some gratitude.

Anton forbore comment. Some volumes later he came across another passage: *The Castil tower is complete, and a most impressive sight it is. It cheers everyone who sees it, and there are few in Glassholm who can fail to, it is so grand. This morning, the Lunane looks ten times healthier than yesterday, and a hundred times more cheerful.*

The implication was clear. The construction was complete, the machine was in place. The moon was in harness, and a system of balance had been established.

But there was still nothing relating to the principles of construction, the technology or the tools they used. "We must have missed something," Anton said, although he couldn't see how. Sure enough, he had been skimming the script, focussing on spotting key words, but what else could there be? There was nothing for it but to start again from the beginning and read more carefully this time.

Eventually he found something that, like the construction and the Lunane's indiscretions, had been excised. It was after Ringley's time, but the then biographer had shared his style.

The Lunane returned to the Palace after dawn again. I do not know where he has been because he refuses my presence during the night now. He won't even allow me to attend him while he suffers those terrible dreams, and commands that I refrain from recording those episodes. Nevertheless, I suspect he has been visiting again with those disgusting Indigenes. And this morning when I went to his chamber I thought I saw one by his bed, although it must have been a trick of the shadows. When I raised this with him he told me it was not my concern. And that is his command, so I must obey.

"The Indigenes?" Anton said, although he already had a mental image. Dark haired, white faced, hovering close to the bed. Could it be

173

that Mia wasn't merely a single unfortunate, that she came from a lineage of such people?

"Are you talking about the sea people?" Hogarth was ever the history student anxious to show off his knowledge. "They died out not long after the landing from the diseases we brought with us."

Muir gave a cynical laugh. "Well that's the Happy City revisionist version that is taught in schools," the librarian said. "In reality it's more likely that they were slaughtered."

Anton was helpless to do anything as the Lunane's voice rose forth like a beast taunted out of its cave. *"I didn't realise you felt so strongly about the subject, Librarian"* he heard himself say. The voice receded as quickly as it had come.

Muir turned ashen. "I meant no criticism, sir. I don't know what came over me." Then the woman began shaking.

"It's fine. I'm not angry." Anton was relieved not to be contradicted by the voice inside him. He put a hand on the librarian's shoulder. "Are you all right?"

Muir breathed deeply. Nodded. "I'm well enough, sir. It is nothing to concern you."

"It seems more than nothing," Anton told her. "You are weeping."

The librarian removed her glasses, dabbed at her cheeks and looked surprised to find her fingertips wet. Without their steely frames, those keen eyes were unfocused. Lost. "I've not been sleeping, sir. That's all. Lately, I've been having these awful dreams."

Anton prompted her to expand on the nature of these dreams, but the librarian flatly refused. "Well then, can I trouble you to show me what else the journals say about these Indigenes?"

It was squirrelled away in Ringley's recounted history, and no doubt even this original version had been sanitised in the setting down. In the first year after the Lunane's people had come to Glassholm, their efforts had been hamstrung by the resistance offered by the island's original residents. No doubt a dialogue could have been established, but the *sea people*, as they were called, were of such a repellent aspect that the refugees had no wish to trade with them.

They made it clear that they did not want us here, Ringley wrote. *And who could blame them? There was little enough to subsist on in this place and we had usurped their ability to survive. We competed with them for the fish in the sea, the*

174

arable land, even the few ready sources of fresh water. We had no choice either, of course. Our ships would not have survived had we not made landfall. So here we had to stay. Or perish.

As if our presence was not enough, there was a greater reason yet for their enmity towards us. They blamed us for the new and constant fury of the tides. At first, they left us gifts: disgusting totems made from dismembered crustaceans, but when we were not disheartened, they resorted to sabotage. Our situation became desperate. It could not go on for much longer. And of course it didn't.

On the Fullday of Old Porphor in our second year on this island, the Lunane led an armed party to their largest village. The Indigenes were never heard from again.

"The Lunane murdered all those people?" Hogarth's voice was childlike. "Are you sure?"

Muir pointed a gloved finger. "Once it's vitricked, there's no changing history."

"And none of them survived." Anton's tone made it clear this was no question.

"And never be seen?" Alice's eyebrows cantilevered into a sceptic's arch. "This is not a big island, sir. Unless we're to believe in the Derryman?"

The facetious reply rankled with Anton. "We're not children to be frightened by bogeymen. These were human beings. What about Mia?" He felt a warning stir in his mind.

"Mia, sir?" asked Hogarth.

Muir was apparently equally ignorant of the girl.

"She's…" It stirred again. He felt himself detaching from his tongue and lips. "No!" he shouted to ward off the on-rushing takeover. "This will not do. There can be no mysteries. We need this information." Returning his attention to his startled companions, he gritted his teeth and said, "She's the biographer who comes at night."

From their faces it was clear they hadn't a clue what he was talking about.

"At *night*, sir?" enquired Muir.

Hogarth was less tactful. "What use would a biographer be at night?" he blurted, before remembering himself. "With respect, sir, the volume of your snoring is hardly a fit subject for public record."

"Nevertheless, this girl, Mia comes and watches me at night."

"Perhaps she is nurse," Muir ventured.

Anton shook his head. "She carries a ledger, just like the lad's one here, except its batters are black."

"Black?" Muir looked dubious. "You can see for yourself, there are no black journals here."

"Then where are they, these night biographies?"

The Lunane's laugh scoured his mind like sand coring a cave. *This is unnecessary. Some things are best left undisturbed.*

"Where are they?" Anton, shouting now, circled the room pointing at the sarcophagi of propaganda. "Where? What do they contain?"

Nothing of possible use to you, Engineer. You have my word on that. Do not waste your time on this fruitless pursuit.

"Fruitless? After all I've learned here?"

Ancient history is as good as fiction. There are no Indigenes, no night biographies, and I do not dream.

Anton spun again. "Don't dream? What on Earth do you mean by that?" There was no reply.

Both Muir and Hogarth gaped at this performance, but Anton didn't care. His wild circling brought him to the other door. "Very well, you won't answer that, then tell me this. Where does this door lead?"

It was Alice who replied. "I do not know, sir."

"I don't believe you." Anton rounded on the librarian. "You must've been down here hundreds of times, and you're telling me you were never once bitten sharp enough by curiosity to take even a peek?"

Muir shuffled diffidently, but made no answer.

Anton understood. "Well, of course you did," he said. "But the door wouldn't let you in, would it?"

Muir permitted herself a rueful smile. "I was unconscious for over twelve hours. And I had such a headache the next day."

"I bet you did." Anton rubbed his hands. "Well, we know there's one person at least who should be able to open it. Let's take a look, shall we?"

The Lunane was clever. He timed it perfectly, waiting till Anton had placed his hand on the living handle before draining away, leaving Anton feeling for an instant light and unencumbered. The voice was the last part of him to leave before the handle's protection recognised that the person attempting to operate it had no trace of its master in him.

You've tried my patience too far.

Muir was right. The headache was terrible. Worse than his first day here. Anton pitied Alice, and Mia too, for being forced to participate in Gerard's unnecessary demonstration. His vision blurred with tears, but he could see the dome lens, the moon. They'd returned him to his bed. He sat up, and regretted it.

"Drink this."

A glass of water appeared in front of him. Only once he'd gulped it gratefully down did he wonder who had given him it. He looked up into twin circles, like reflecting pools.

"What are you –?" The librarian shushed him with her finger.

"Can I trust you?" she said.

"What?"

Muir tutted her impatience. "You're not him. I can see plainly. Before, you fooled me, even when you made me record those stupid measurements. Lunatropicity, ha! I should've suspected then. Now, it's obvious. You're nothing like him. So, can I trust you?"

She meant that the Lunane wasn't in him, the glamour was gone. Anton probed in his mind, felt for the Lunane's weight, but his thoughts were too scrambled to know for sure.

"I don't know," he replied.

"Not good enough." Muir's intensity was unnerving. "Is he there now? Is he testing me?"

"I told you," Anton repeated. "I don't know. I don't think so, but... Why does it matter anyway? What do you want?"

"I need... *damn.*" Muir slipped out of the circle. Anton heard her pacing, muttering, coming back. "I became a librarian because I believed in the story of Glassholm. An enduring marvel, persisting through the ages thanks to the strength of its people and the sacrifice of its king. I believed in the consistency of our city. It's rightness. I believed... in the Lunane."

"But not now?" Anton said.

A vigorous shake of the head. "Not after what I've learned. The things I've heard. It's all lies."

"What things? What have you heard?"

"I need to know for sure." Muir went on as if she hadn't heard. "I need you to get me through that door."

"You must know," Anton said slowly. "That if he's no longer in me, I can't open that door. You saw what happened down there."

Muir nodded like a bobbing gull. "Yes, yes, yes," she hissed. "But he'll come back, won't he? Whatever your purpose is he's far from done with you yet."

Anton tried to rise. "How would I know?" he said, but Muir was right. The machine remained broken.

Muir pushed him back onto the bed. "And what is your purpose? Why does he give you such a free rein? Is what the dream children say true? Is his power so weak? Has he lost so much of the people's faith?"

Anton shook his head dumbly. She was deranged. "I can't help you, Muir," he said. "Leave me alone."

Sleep claimed Anton once more. It washed over him like a submerging wave, and once he was deep under another, darker wave washed over him too.

Chapter 16

Someone said it rained crabs during the night, and even though that couldn't possibly be true – because these were not spider-thin creatures the size of a penny that could conceivably have been drawn skywards in an ocean squall, these beasts could have your fingers off – the idea gained currency, was repeated and spread from corner store to coffee shop, bar to bakery, pub to Palace. Mortlock heard about crabs crawling up out of the docks, the river, even the lagoon of the dead, and turning up in gardens, kitchens, just about anywhere you could think of. They'd become a daily curiosity, but no more than that. Then there had been a night of torrential rain, and in the morning you couldn't move for the monsters. Word in the guard room was they'd called in the clean-up volunteers to help deal with the problem.

As much consternation as the crustaceans caused, however, they weren't Mortlock's problem. His attention was focussed elsewhere.

Chief Lytten had a routine. Every Glassholmer did. They were like the brass figures on the Foundry tower clock, feet welded to a path that they followed every day rain or shine, from Dark to Full and back again. One of the first things you learned in the Police was that when someone changed their routine it was never for a good reason.

It was getting on for nine in the evening. If he was true to his *new* routine, Lytten should be sneaking back to the Palace to receive the reports from his spies. Mortlock wondered how he was coping with the crabs. It wouldn't be an injustice if he suffered a nasty nip or two. The sly bastard deserved some sort of retribution.

Mortlock surveyed the desk and checked that everything was ready. Lytten was fastidious and, much though he detested spending a minute longer than necessary in this rat-hole, Mortlock was looking forward to the chief's reaction when he saw the open filing cabinet drawer, the ruptured strong box, the strewn notes and reports, the row of nearly identical piles of evidence. More than Alfie and Jenny Garrett.

179

This had been going on for a while. A winery worker, an astronomer, a baker's delivery girl. All of them dispatched in the same manner as Kremer, with a jagged rent across their throat. According to his friend's police notebook, the first one had been a sergeant in the Palace guard. Mortlock had never met Bert Gore, but he recognised the name as that of the very man he'd been brought in to the Palace to replace. He'd been told that Gore had been dismissed for drunkenness, not that he had been slain on the day Mortlock had taken up the position.

He rifled through Alfie's notebook, stopped again at the sketch of the city. The way the connecting lines from each crime scene intersected in the middle of the page didn't mean anything, of course. The Palace was the centre of everything. But Kremer had scrawled notes along each connection. The sergeant, the astronomer and the winery worker had all worked here, and the baker's girl had delivered to the Palace every day. This was what Jenny Garret had been called up here to investigate. And Alfie had taken over when she'd suffered the same fate as those she was investigating.

Murders were one thing. In a city rife with restless rumour, murders associated with the Palace were quite another. No wonder Lytten wanted it hushed up.

Mortlock switched off the desk lamp and took up position behind the door. He didn't have long to wait before he heard a fumbling of keys. The door opened. Instead of switching on the ceiling light, the newcomer blundered towards the desk lamp. More fool them. A satisfying clunk and hissed curse indicated a satisfactory encounter with the waste paper bin that Mortlock had left lying in the middle of the room.

In the lamp glow, Mortlock saw Lytten's spine stiffen, the chief's hand frozen on the switch, heard a breathed curse. "Shit."

"I hoped you'd be a little more demonstrative than that." Mortlock at least got to enjoy watching his boss jump.

What happened to the man's face when he turned around was as predictable as it was comical. The clammy shock of discovery was quickly replaced by a start of recognition, and only after that did he finally begin to think.

"You're wondering: *can I get out of this?*" Mortlock said. "Quickly followed by: *how much will it cost me?* I may not have been employed here long enough to learn all your little ways, but the answer to both of those questions, Mr Lytten, should be obvious. I'm no stickler. In some circumstances there *might* have been leeway, but these people…" Mortlock indicated the neat piles of evidence on the desk. "Two of them at least were my friends and colleagues. So, sir, I'm afraid this time the answer has to be, no. No blind eyes, no turned backs. Not for this."

Lytten squeezed his lips in displeasure. He couldn't help the involuntary glance towards the wall clock.

"You've got a bit of time before your snitch arrives, I reckon," Mortlock said. "You can make it go quick or you can make it go slow."

Lytten exhaled hollowly and slumped into his chair, but when he met Mortlock's stare there was steel in his eyes again. "What *precisely* do you want?"

Mortlock knuckled the desk to loom over his boss. "You can start with why."

"Why?"

"There's a bastard out there. A proper killer. They need to be caught before someone else gets silenced. And even if he doesn't strike again," he waved at the six piles on the desk, "don't these people deserve justice? There was an investigation in progress." He shoved Alfie's notebook across the desk. "So why hush it up?"

Lytten smiled.

"What's so amusing?"

"You said *silenced*. Now, why would you use that word, I wonder?"

Mortlock realised the chief was right. It had been the first word that came to mind. He supposed it was because of the way they were slashed. Deep across the throat. "So what? It's as likely a motive as any." He hadn't thought it was possible to be any angrier with the man, but there was rage in his voice now.

"Ah, now there's the real John Mortlock." Despite his nervousness, Lytten was grinning. "There's the stamp of George Prunty right there."

Mortlock started. That was a name he'd not heard in a long time. "What?"

"Oh, come now." Lytten stood and leant across the desk until they were nose to nose. "I know that memory of yours is shot to pieces but surely you remember old George? I'm told he was like a father to you."

Mortlock touched the old crease in his scalp. The name, the man, had been lost with the back street concussion that had cut short his career, but hearing it brought back a sketchy recollection. Prunty had been the Beckon Hill station chief when he had joined the force.

"That was a long time ago." He spoke slowly as scraps of memory surfaced. "Sure, Prunty was a bulldog but he was fair minded, and he brought his boys up the same way. He instilled good old fashioned values, like doing your job well and looking out for each other. He did okay by us."

The corners of Lytten's eyes crinkled. His whisper, moist breath on Mortlock's face. "You were thugs."

"No." Mortlock pulled back from the desk. "We did what we had to to get the job done, but –"

"You were thugs. Prunty and Bob Garret and Alfie Kremer. And you were the worst of the lot, John. Barely controllable."

That wasn't right. They had just been lads. "What are you –" He staggered back from the desk, forced himself to breathe, started again. "Why are you saying all this?"

The chief sneered. "Because you asked me why we've suppressed the investigation, John. Isn't it obvious? We *know* who the murderer is. We just can't risk the whole city knowing." He picked one of the silvery discs from the desk and threw it. It bounced off Mortlock's chest and tinkled to the floor. He snatched up another one and dangled it from its chain link. "What *are* these anyway?"

Mortlock stared desperately. "How would I know?"

There was a soft sound behind him. "Because you put them there, sergeant." Secretary Gerard flicked on the main light, causing both Mortlock and Lytten to screw shut their eyes.

"Secretary." The rat's nerves were back. Lytten scurried around the desk to meet his superior. Once again his gaze flicked towards the clock. "We were just... that is..."

"You were protecting the Lunane from destabilising rumours, I expect." Gerard sounded sanguine, but his eyes glittered. The light sheened his pale forehead like steel as he bent to inspect the contents of the desk. "And, my, haven't you both been *busy*?"

Mortlock couldn't quite grasp his meaning. He felt dizzy.

"I know how it appears, sir," Lytten said, "but it's all wholly necessary," the location of his prattle seemed to jump from one side of the room to the other, "I assure you. Wait."

Mortlock shivered. His face burned. Lytten's voice slid out of focus then snapped back again, as clear as if it was inside his head. Then the chief was beside him. Then a hot, familiar palm laid across Mortlock's temple; words slid into his ear. Then he was sitting down, and everything was distant. Conversation washed around him.

"We had to be sure the escape wasn't made public. Of course, if His Majesty was only able to give us some sort of a description we could have tracked him down personally and prevented –"

"I gave you all the description there is, Lytten."

"But the Lunane is *every man*. How can he lose one of his people?"

"Because our sailor doesn't *believe* in the Lunane. He's a foreigner. Heresy is easy for him, even though he was personally blessed by the divine presence."

"But he must *have* believed."

"When he first arrived no doubt, but somehow since the Lunane left him for that damned engineer he has decided…" Gerard glanced fisheye at Mortlock. "Your blunt tool here won't remember any of this?"

Lytten sneered. "Not unless I want him to."

The Secretary looked sceptical, but went on. "It seems our fugitive has convinced himself that his memory of his time in the throne is false. Implanted by revolutionaries. And he continues to spread his lies. The crows hear it all over the city now. And the Lunane, let me tell you, is not happy."

"You don't think," Lytten stared at the reports as if his gaze alone might burn them to ashes, "that killing the witnesses was excessive." The chief's words swam and garbled in Mortlock's ears.

Then Gerard was speaking. "Of course it's excessive, Charles. Flagrantly and egregiously so. But that's precisely the point. Sedition is like rust in the city's gears. It had to be scrubbed clean else it spreads. You had to be thorough. There's nothing, after all, like a spell of fear which can be resolved," the secretary glanced in Mortlock's direction, "at the time of our choosing to scrub away the uncertainties of the common man."

Lytten didn't reply but Gerard went on as if he had. "The time approaches. The sailor has surfaced again. Our man got himself work as a dock porter. And, I'm pleased to report, he didn't make friends on his first day on the job." Gerard crouched in front of Mortlock, looked into his eyes. Mortlock could not look away. "See to it that he does not report for his second."

"What about these?"

Gerard coughed a laugh. "They don't matter. The public see them as evidence of a madman at work. Once this last business is over, we'll give them their madman."

Lytten's face replaced Gerard's. "As you wish, sir." His fingers reached for Mortlock's brow. "I just want this thing over with." Each point of contact numbed with heat and blankness.

The hot fingers at Mortlock's brow became icy. The claustrophobic glare of Lytten's office became an echoing gloom. There was a tang of brine. He stopped walking, looked around, and recognised that he was in the secretariat's outer office. Another blackout. He tried to piece it together. He had confronted Chief Lytten about the cover up, and then Secretary Gerard had arrived. And then… well, he must have been asked to leave. High level business, not for his ears. They were welcome to it. He had business to see to anyway. His heart pounded with furious retribution… Only, now he could not remember the asking, or getting from the chief's office to here or who his fists wanted so badly to pummel.

As he oriented himself, that acrid tang hit him again and there was a sound like the dying echo of a footfall.

"Who's there?" Mortlock lit his lamp. He moved towards the central desk, and heard the sound again. He whirled, the light spinning with him. It caught something for an instant. There, near the doors. He trained it back, slowly.

Standing in front of the doors was a figure. It was short like a child, slender and as dark-skinned as a native of the Jealous Lands, but more than that was difficult to say because the skin was so wet that the light flared off it. This was not the spy that he had suspected Lytten of consorting with.

Being caught in the light appeared to have frozen the figure in the act of opening the doors. Water dripped like jewels from the hand of an apprehended thief. Then the head turned and dark, deep eyes regarded him with a chilling look.

"Who are you?" For a second Mortlock thought that he *knew*, but the conviction evaporated. His words broke the tableau. Deft fingers twisted the handle and light from the stairwell angled through the gap, revealing something about the nature of the creature – for it was no child any more than it was a spy from the guard corps – that was impossible to believe.

Not just wet – it was *made of water*. The being was fashioned out of the sea itself. Things floated in it – strands of emerald weed, a glittering rainbow shale of scales, a puff of sand agitated by the movement, and most remarkable of all, a shoal of tiny iridescent minnows that darted as one this way and that way within the confines of the body.

Mortlock could still feel the cool dampness on his brow where it had touched him, woken him from his sleep walk.

The child slipped through the gap and vanished. Mortlock shook away his amazement and gave chase. However impossible the creature was, it was certainly fast on its feet. On the landing there was no sign but for a trail of puddles and the echoing slap from the great staircase below.

He took the stairs two at a time. Catching sight of the creature on the level below spurred him to run faster until his chest was heaving and his old muscles fizzed. He leapt the last six steps to the ground floor, skidded on a flap of black kelp and sprawled, cracking his knee on the flagstones. A tiny scarlet crab crawled across the floor beside his head.

A playful susurration made Mortlock look up. The water child was standing not twenty feet way in a shimmering pool of itself. It surely couldn't continue spilling substance like this, but it didn't seem concerned about that, and from the cock of its head, the hands on hips, that sound like skittish surf, it was laughing at him. Mortlock got gingerly to his feet.

The creature retreated, then paused again as if daring Mortlock to give chase. This was more than a game though. The creature might be a funny sort of spy, but Mortlock was certain nevertheless that this was Lytten's night visitor. And it wanted him to follow. Mortlock took a step forward. Apparently satisfied that he was going to continue the chase, the thing sped off again, heading out of the Palace.

In the boulevard beyond the main gate there was a raucous disturbance in the trees. The crows that had taken up residence there upon their displacement from the Palace were unhappy at the presence passing below them, and those not raising a din among the branches swooped low at the running figure, clawing gouts of water from it. By the avenue's end, it was noticeably diminished in size.

The chase continued through the city streets. Even when the trail diverged into the Merchantry's lanes it wasn't difficult to follow. Mortlock didn't realise how close they were to the Laughing Gull until he turned the corner and was standing in front of it. The sight of the familiar frontage, the painted, bird-shaped sign swinging in the breeze, disoriented him. An insipid yellow light bathed the street.

The child had stopped here too. It extracted a length of weed from inside its head, making a show of examining it.

"Why here?" Mortlock looked at the Gull again. The thick, imperfect windows, like yellow cataracts. The couple at the window table.

"What?" Mortlock asked again. "Is this what you brought me here for? Should I go in…?"

When the creature moved, it changed, losing definition so that it stopped in any way resembling a child and hit the window as a wave. It made such a splash that Mortlock was sure the glass must smash. The glass held, but water poured down the wall, pooled in the street, trickled towards the gutter, leaving the last of the creature's internal detritus glistening on the cobbles.

The figures behind the glass froze. Then one was pushing back his chair, and Mortlock had the presence of mind to step back around the corner before the café door was flung open.

He didn't recognise the young man who ran into the street, although from the state of his face it was clear that someone had recently given him a good beating. Perhaps that was what stoked the fury in him that balled his fists like rocks. But he did recognise his companion. The skinny girl, with the junk in her hair, who slipped out after him and glanced fearfully up and down the lane. It was the girl who had discovered Alfie Kremer's body. And presumably this was the boyfriend who had gone missing on Darkday night.

The lad examined the drift of discarded sand. He said something to the girl, holding out his palm to show her. Something passed between them that resulted in his chucking away whatever it was he held. A handful of objects hit the cobbles with an empty rattle. As they skittered his way, Mortlock saw that they were shells.

Shells in the street. Before Dark, the night the monkey was nailed to the Gull's door. There had been shells on the doorstep then too. Uneasiness stirred in Mortlock's gut. A horribly familiar sensation that there was something taking place around him that was too large to see. Whatever this was, he didn't like the way it always seemed to come back to Shirley's door.

Shirley appeared then. She put an arm round the girl and soothed the lad down from his fury. In no time she had persuaded the pair to go back inside. Mortlock shrank back further into the shadow of the corner, but when she cast her own look up and down the lane, lingering on the mess below the window, he did not miss the fear in her face.

Henrik's anger still simmered behind the welts and yellow-blue bruises. Lottie could see it shining in the one eye that wasn't swollen completely shut.

"Your man Blackwood is spot on," he said. "Spot on, Lottie. This place is going to ruin, and fast."

She reached across the table for his hand, but he pulled it away. She resented him for denying her that small comfort, but then he wasn't to know that she wasn't just shaken by the impact at the café window a few minutes earlier. This was where that policeman had brought her and Vickers after they discovered the detective's body.

"It was just a joke." She glanced at the window. There was still a piece of weed stuck to the other side. "Nothing was broken. No one was harmed. Just a stupid joke." She wanted to ask him why he'd chosen this place to meet after his visit to the Foundry. When he'd left that afternoon in the company of the Boxers she had been angry, uncertain she would ever see him again. Now he was the angry one. "So, you're going along with Blackwood after all?"

"I have to do something."

"After the way they treated you?"

He glared at her. "At least *they* didn't beat me up for telling the truth." She had no reply for that. Someone on the dock crew had recognised him from the Grant Arms. The man who'd claimed to have *been* the Lunane. He'd been stupid enough not to deny it; repeated it, even elaborated with his new theory about the requirement for a *substitute* if the king was ever absent or ill. They'd been smart enough to wait till the end of the shift, and had brought friends. "Don't you want things to change?"

Lottie sighed. "Blackwood and Joffries are not trying to change things, Henrik. They're trying to return things to the way they were."

"The good old days?"

"Not really. Not for me."

"But at least the streets were safe, right?" He read the hurt in her face and softened his tone. "Look, I know I'm an outsider but politically you people are like children. Not one person here has free will. You've got so used to being told what to do that you don't know how to think for yourselves. I've travelled a lot, but I've never seen so many willing conformists in one place. Even you, Lottie." He reached over and teased her fretting fingers out of her fringe. "No one has to conform all the time. You should be able to celebrate the things that make you different."

"But people…" She began, but he just smiled. It was an ugly smile, fat and red through his burst lips but she caught its meaning. *People* were the problem, the way they thought, the assumptions they made, their refusal to contemplate change. But all this instability meant there was a chance to do just that. *Change.* And wasn't that what she had always wanted? Lottie fumbled in her pocket, found a rubber band and used it to gather her braids into a short tail. "People," she said, "can take me as I am."

He raised his cup in salute. "You and me both."

"So, you told them Blackwood's lie."

He nodded, sighed.

"How's blaming these anarchists going to promote change?"

"It's not. Not in itself, but it got them onside, opened them up to the idea that things might not always be like they have been."

"And they accepted your story?"

"You should have seen them, Lottie. The place was full. There must have been hundreds there. They cheered when we told them we were going to force the Lunane to act to put a stop to these disturbances."

There was more though, something he'd not told her. Lottie waited.

"And…" Henrik sipped, grimaced. "*Cold,*" he said. Then he lowered his voice. "Blackwood's got proof that there's another substitute in the Palace."

"Another one?" She was shocked. "But why?"

Henrik shook his head. "They think…"

He didn't seem able to voice the word, but he didn't have to. Lottie mouthed the heretical syllable.

Dead?

He nodded. "They've thought this through. And it makes sense."

"But the Lunane is… the Lunane is *everything*."

"Even he can't live forever. What if he knew his time was coming to an end? Wouldn't he, knowing the disruption his death would create, put a plan into place for his continuation? Isn't that what you'd expect him to do? Like any good father."

Lottie couldn't believe it, but was the idea so farfetched? No one had noticed when Henrik assumed the role. All they had to do was act the part, and let the bureaucratic clockwork run the city as it always had. Sure, and there were enough lonely people in Glassholm who'd be unlikely to be missed much if they disappeared at Dark to make it possible. Or, who knew, perhaps there was even a string of volunteers in the Palace being groomed for the job.

"But what about the journals?"

"Fabrications."

"And what about his appearances? At the Halfdays, on Founding Day?"

"A trick based on costume and setting and indoctrination."

"How long?" She didn't know exactly what it was she was asking. How long has it been going on? Or how long could it continue before it became public knowledge and the city descended into *real* chaos?

Henrik shrugged. "Not long. Though we know it was at least seven months."

"When your ship arrived here. Yes, and the troubles began around the same time."

"Exactly so. Blackwood says the citizens felt the loss, even if they didn't know why at the time. And it's been getting worse ever since. Your city is unravelling." Henrik was shining with it now. Lottie could see how much he needed this logical sort of explanation. It meant he could understand the violence that had been meted out to him, and if these ideas were supported by Blackwood and his cadre, all the better.

She gave what she hoped was an encouraging nod and watched him go off in search of the toilet, but she was far from convinced he was right.

"Top up?"

Lottie didn't know how the chain of discs had got from her pocket to her hand, but she was threading it nervously between her fingers. And she saw the café owner's gaze linger on it before she clasped it away in her fist.

"Please," she said, and watched the woman fill up their mugs.

When she was done, she rested the pot on the table then glanced briefly in the direction Henrik had gone. "I'm surprised to see you back here, Lottie Blake. But you are welcome."

"You know who I am?" Lottie peered at the woman, but other than that first unpleasant encounter here she was certain she didn't know her.

"I didn't at first," the woman said. "It's been a long time since I last visited The Church." She stretched out a hand as if to touch Lottie's face, but stopped half way. "And you're no longer a little girl."

Lottie was surprised and disappointed. If this woman was anything, she was sensible. The speed with which she had reinstated normality to her café after the brief disturbance outside had been a text book exercise in practicality. Her mother had chosen well this time. Why couldn't they just leave her be?

"Look, before you start, I'm not interested in anything she has to say."

The woman looked nonplussed, then understanding appeared in her eyes. "The Mother?"

"*Your* mother. She's no mother of mine –"

"No, no." The woman pulled over an empty chair and sat. "You don't understand. I said I recognised you from The Church, but I've not been there myself for a long time. There was a troubled period in my life when I thought it gave me solace, but…"

"So you're not her agent?" The café owner shook her head. "But you were thinking of going back, weren't you?"

The woman faltered again, but did not deny the accusation. Even if she had it would have been futile. The sorry need that glittered in her eyes was instantly recognisable.

"You don't know what it's like," the woman whispered. "That thing outside. I know what it was. I just…" Now she did touch Lottie's hand. The one that was still cupped over the chain of discs. Her skin was warm. "What do they want?"

Lottie clenched her fist tighter. "I don't know what you mean."

"The silverfish children. What do they want with you?"

"I don't know what you mean," Lottie said again, and was grateful then to see Henrik making his way back to them.

Saying nothing more, the café owner rose and whisked away the teapot.

"What was that all about?" Henrik said.

Lottie shook her head. "Nothing. Can we just go please?"

He shrugged. "Of course."

While he retrieved their coats from the coatstand, she slipped her monkey's gift quietly into her pocket. They didn't look back when they left the café, but Lottie could feel the woman's beseeching eyes on her even once the door had closed, and the word *silverfish* echoed in her mind long after the shop's bell had stopped jingling.

They returned home in silence. Lottie felt so drained that her only wish was to get upstairs and into her own flat without any further excitement, but she was to be bitterly disappointed.

"Don't you run off there, Charlotte Blake. Yer mammy wants a word."

Lottie's blood ran cold. "Hello, Mother."

Euphemia Blake stood just inside the entrance of the close, using her ample frame to block the passage. If anything, she was fatter than when Lottie had last seen her, but she still carried that matronly glamour that had cemented her as the Church's youngest Mother and kept her there for almost as long as Lottie could remember.

"'S a matter? Not going to introduce me to the boyfriend." This was followed by an unseemly cackle. Her curls jiggled in a not altogether natural coquette. "Not going to offer yer mammy a cup of tea at least?"

Lottie caught a twitch of curtain at a nearby window. "All right then," she muttered, ignoring the rapacious smile twisted out of those scarlet-painted lips. "But he's not my boyfriend," she added, although she would have preferred to claim the opposite just to spite the woman who had dared to forbid him to her.

There was no room in Lottie's flat for her mother. There never had been, figuratively speaking, but now that the woman was actually there, wallowing on her sofa, drinking her tea, the point was proved beyond doubt. She consumed the air. Guzzled the light, became luminous while Lottie and Henrik faded into the shadows. She tutted. Constantly.

"Oh, you've let yourself go, so you have, Charlotte, girl," Phamie said, exaggeration in every gesture slopping milky tea into her saucer. "Bit of powder, dab of paint, do you the power, so it would. I mean, how'd you expect to land a decent man in clothes that look like they've come off the back of the clean-up wagon. And as for what you've done to your hair —"

"I like the way Lottie looks." Henrik's interjection was brave, and sadly misguided.

The red lips pursed.

"Thought she said you weren't her boyfriend?" The reply came quick as a kiss. "Mind you, no offence, but you're hardly the catch of the week. No doubt yer puss'll heal up soon enough, but nobody likes a brawler. Not dependable, see? Now, my first man, Charlie —"

"This is all very nice, mother," Lottie cut in. "But what is it you want?"

Her mother shot her a sharp look, a warning Lottie knew well.

"I want you back at the Church," she said simply, at last dropping the affected Dockton argot. "*Daughter.*"

The emphasis pinched Lottie where it hurt.

"Do we need to go through this again?" she said. "You can do what you like, you won't get me back there. Not for anything."

"But you must." She cast Henrik a sly glance. "And *alone.* Will you not take a telling about the company you keep?"

There was something in this that Lottie didn't like. What could be so important to force Phamie Blake off her fat arse and waddle all the way over to Beckon? Something she hadn't bothered to do in all these blissfully quiet years.

Lottie took the bait. "Why, must I?" she said. "What's so fucking important all of a sudden?"

"All of a sudden? Girl, you know better. All of a sudden! It's ordained by the blood. As are all of nature's cycles." Her mother's eyes glittered with unpleasant fervour. "Praise to the blood!"

"What is ordained?" Lottie was losing patience. "What are you talking about?"

"The child's coming, girl," her mother intoned. "The blood has spoken. *The* child." The woman's eyes rolled as her voice rose. She was on the verge of one of her full-on Church performances now. "The patriarchy is coming to an end, and the time of Motherhood is dawning. The Church needs all of its daughters now. And especially you, girl. The Mother's Daughter —"

Lottie had had enough. "Mother, I want you to go." She took a hold of a raised wrist.

Her mother's eyes snapped open. They shocked her with their penetration. Her other hand shot out snake-fast. It touched Lottie lightly on the brow, pressed briefly on her breast, slipped with invasive intimacy between her legs.

The eyes widened. Naked wonder, stripped of pretence and artifice. "*It's you,*" her mother whispered.

"What?" Lottie disengaged from her mother's hand, stumbled away. "What are you on about?"

"It's you," she repeated. "This glorious, wonderful child. Our new queen, will be your child. *My grandchild.*" Tears welled in her eyes. "Oh, Charlotte…"

"Don't be ridiculous." Lottie laughed, although it was far from funny. "I'm not pregnant."

"Of course you are, girl." Her mother stood toe to toe with her. "When did you last bleed?"

"Mind your own business."

"A woman's blood is Church business."

Lottie barely held her fountaining anger in check. "How many times, mother?" she yelled. "How many times? I want *nothing* to do with your Church."

Lottie's mother grabbed at her hand, placed it on her own belly. "Then feel for yourself."

All Lottie felt was fat, unattractive, unhappy. "Get out of my life." She flung her mother towards the door.

Henrik allowed her some time to herself before coming to her room to see if she was all right. "She's gone." He came to the side of the bed, hovering uncertainly.

"I know," she sniffed. "It's like someone rolled the Dark off the moon."

Henrik's attempted smile cost him a wince.

193

Lottie sat up, patted the pillows next to her. He sat down stiffly, but when she laid her head on his chest she felt him unbend enough to slip his arm around her shoulders. *Better.* His free hand went to her hair. Strong fingers massaged her scalp through the rat tails and bric-a-brac. *Better still.*

She felt the tension slip away.

"Is she really that bad?" Henrik had this uncanny knack of changing the mood just when she wasn't expecting it.

"The evidence of your own eyes not enough for you?" she replied.

"Well, she's a handful, I'll grant you that, but she's still your mother. She must love you."

"She's an egomaniacal witch who preys on the superstitions of others for the purposes of self-aggrandizement," she said. "She's got a whole houseful of trained sycophants up there conditioned to love her, but the only person Phamie Blake cares about is herself."

"Sorry," he said. "I admit I didn't understand half of what she was saying but I thought she seemed sincere in wanting you back. She clearly misses you."

"Sincere?" Lottie stopped, breathed, calmed herself. She didn't want to fight with him, but why did he always have to be so *fair* all the time? "She claimed that I'm pregnant with a Queen who will replace the Lunane. How could anyone be sincere about that?"

"Well, it looks as if there's a vacancy. You have to admit her timing's pretty good."

"No," Lottie said. "She's just spinning a story to get me back there, back under her control. I won't have it and that's the end of it."

They fell into an uncomfortable silence.

"Did you mean what you said?" she said after a while.

"About what?"

"About liking the way I look?"

She felt his laugh more than she heard it. "Of course," he said.

"Good," she said. "I'm glad."

The relaxation took over, the rhythm of his fingers. She thought she might have drifted off.

"Henrik?" she said.

She could hear him breathing, but he didn't answer. Perhaps he had fallen asleep too.

"I'm not pregnant, you know."

Lottie didn't know which of them she was trying to convince.

Mortlock waited until the Blake girl and her boy left before entering the café. It was all but empty and sluggish Jane was trolling between the tables, setting out the cutlery for the morning.

Shirley appeared, wiping her hands on her apron. "Oh, it's you."

At first he took that for annoyance, but she managed a smile for him. "Fraid so." He sat at his usual table. Immediately, with his habitual view of the world in front of him, he felt better. "Anything left in the oven?"

Shirley looked at him contemplatively. Then she appeared to decide that whatever was on her mind was not important enough to bring up right now. "There's half a chicken pie left. That all right?"

Mortlock realised that he was consumed by hunger. He couldn't remember the last proper meal he had had. Was it two nights ago? Three? He nodded back with a smile of his own. "Ideal."

And when the pie came, it *was* ideal. The pastry over-fired, but he liked it that way. Hot, savoury and it filled him up. He glanced at the clock. He should probably get back to the Palace, but his shift was almost done. Might be better to use the time to pop down the docks and see if he could uncover a fresh angle on Alfie's murder. He'd learned bugger all from Lytten and wasn't sure why he thought he would come up with anything among the stevedores and sailors. Something he'd seen in the office perhaps, but he couldn't recall what it might have been. Regardless, it was a stone he hadn't turned yet and therefore was better than nothing.

"How was it then?"

The final stragglers had melted away while Mortlock was absorbed in digestion and introspection. Jane had started stacking chairs on tables. Shirley sat next to him.

"Wonderful," he told her. "It's always wonderful."

She put a hand to her brow in mock modesty. "Don't skimp on the flattery now."

"I mean it," he said. "It's a touch of normality, this place."

She humphed. "Now that's real flattery. And I thought you'd lost interest."

"How do you mean?"

She crinkled her eyes, and Mortlock realised that she'd put on make-up. "Well, you've not exactly been predictable in your routine this weather, John."

He shrugged helplessly. "Nothing's predictable these days."

"True enough." Her voice cracked and for a second it was as if her skin was translucent, her brave face the thinnest of glazes. There was a porcelain fragility to her that stopped him from speaking in case the wrong word shattered her.

He wanted to hold her, but he didn't dare. And yet, he suspected, that was the root of the problem. "Shirley, there are things I need to tell you."

"What sort of things?" Her eyes widened. "You've walked out on your job, haven't you? That's why you're in here so early. What has Lytten –?"

"No." That was all that worried her? "No, it's nothing like that. I left the Palace because I was chasing... someone."

"*Someone?*" She looked sceptical.

Mortlock balked. Shirley was a practical woman. Moon bless her. What was she going to think if he started blabbering about cover-ups and spies and children made out of sea water?

"You trust me," he said. "Don't you? I need to know that you trust me."

"Most of the time," she said. Then: "Of course I trust you. What's this about?"

Mortlock still found himself unable to start. It was the window, he realised. Over Shirley's shoulder he was staring directly at the window that the water creature had ended itself on. It was that and the blackouts and the murders and this sudden, inexplicable urgency to be in Dockton.

"Can we go somewhere else?" He was shocked to hear his voice quaver.

Shirley smiled. "If you want to get me upstairs, you only need to ask," she said. And then, when his body started physically to shake, "Oh, John. Love, what is it?"

Somehow, she managed to manhandle him up the narrow staircase at the back of the shop, and soon had him in front of an open fire with a brandy pressed into his hands.

There wasn't much to her accommodation. A bedroom at the front, a tiny bathroom at the back, and in between them this main room that incorporated the stair head and a rudimentary kitchen as well as the few items of comfort that were arranged for a single person's convenience around the hearth. One end of the flaccid couch on which they sat had been edged closer to the heat with cushions, a woollen rug and a brocaded footstool at that same end. To the side, a table had held the brandy bottle and a tumbler.

Mortlock placed his glass beside the bottle, then sank back into the couch. He closed his eyes. "I'm sorry," he said. "I suppose it's been creeping up on me."

Shirley perched on the edge of the other sofa seat. Her hands were clasped on her lap. The picture of attentiveness. "What has, John?"

That was the question. He didn't quite know. For sure, tonight's unbelievable experience was a significant factor, but perhaps it had merely been the final straw. Since he started at the Palace he'd been looking over his shoulder. His memory was getting worse, and that scared him. He'd thought Lytten had his boys spying on him. Now he didn't know what to think. There was all of that. But there was something else too, something he *did* remember from tonight's encounter. Something from the past about him and Alfie and Jenny Garret's father. A memory that felt as if it had been unearthed and then buried again. Only not fully.

So, he started from the beginning and told her everything. When he told her about the Palace's usurping of the investigation into Alfie's death, she took his hand. And she squeezed it when he told her about his former colleagues. She didn't even flinch when he told her about the discs.

"They all had one?" She fingered the chain around her neck. "From a luck monkey?"

Mortlock's instinct was to say *no, not from a monkey*, but he settled for: "There's no evidence where they got them from. It could be coincidence."

He did flinch then from the look she gave him. He decided then and there not to patronise her again.

"Are we in danger?" she asked simply.

"I think we have to consider that I could be," he said. "But I can't believe you are."

"But I'm connected to you."

"Yes, but you're not connected to the Crew." He rubbed his head, as if the agitation would shake loose more of the memory. "We had a sort of club back in the day. Those of us that were off duty at Dark used to get together and go drinking. Once or twice it got a bit out of hand."

"What do you mean, 'out of hand'?"

"There were maybe a couple of occasions that we got an absolute skinful and then we went out to look for known hoods, and when we found them we beat them up."

"What?" Mortlock didn't blame her for her shock.

"I know," he said. "It's not something I'm proud of."

"But you were the police –"

"*I know.*" He broke off for a moment. "Shirley, we were just kids. We were full of bravado and bullshit in equal measure. We thought we were doing the right thing. We prided ourselves on it. We even called ourselves the Clean-up Crew."

"Subtle."

"Like I said, we were young. Most of us hadn't been on the force more than a couple years."

"That's hardly an excuse. What happened?"

"There was a bit of an official fuss, but our station chief, Prunty, stood by us. It was all smoothed over. That's all I recall." He wished he could remember more. Lytten had called them *thugs*. Was it possible that the lads had done something worse than knock a few heads together when Dark came around? Something that might give someone with a better memory a real motive for revenge?

"So, you think these murders are reprisals from some criminal you dished out a leathering to twenty years ago?"

Mortlock shrugged. "It seems unlikely," he said. "There were other victims. Palace employees. I don't know what their connection to the old crew might be. But I can't think of any other explanation."

"You said you were chasing someone," Shirley said. "Was it the person you suspect of doing this?"

Mortlock sat forward, looked into her eyes. "This is where the trust part comes in." He told her about water child. It didn't take long in the telling, and once it was out he was almost embarrassed.

From the way Shirley was staring into the fire, it looked like he wasn't the only one.

Then he saw that she was crying.

He touched her arm. "What's the matter?"

She shook him away. "Nothing."

"I know it sounds crazy, but I swear –"

Shirley was nodding. "It does sound crazy. And I've seen them too."

Then she told him all about her long dead baby boy, and the water children that haunted her with his memory. She called them *silverfish*. Mortlock stiffened, remembering the word on the lips of the would-be assassin, but Shirley protested. These creatures, she assured him, were not agents of agitation but of consolation. And she told him, too, that she and the boy weren't the only ones. These counselling angels were all over the city.

Mortlock woke in an unfamiliar darkness. He was seized with the notion that he ought to be out tracking down Alfie's killer, but the impulse dissolved when he remembered where he was. He felt next to him and found the bed empty. And properly awake now he could hear voices.

He slipped out of bed, located his trousers and put them on. Opening the bedroom door just a crack, he listened.

"Shh, there my lamb, my pet." It was Shirley's voice. Over the back of the sofa, he could see her head rocking. "Shh, and sleep now."

Mortlock knew who she was talking to, but listening to it was horrible.

"Shh, now," she cooed. "Your mammy's here."

"Shirley," he said, and entering the main room, saw her stiffen, heard her gasp.

When he reached her, she was alone. And she was drenched.

And her lap was filled with sand and shells.

Chapter 17

"Hogarth!" Anton's voice was a rasp, his throat dry as paper.

The tentative face peeked through the curtains. "Good morning, sir," said the biographer. In one hand he held his journal, and in the other was a familiar soft grey hood.

Anton groaned. "What day is it?"

Hogarth ducked respectfully. "Why, it's the Halfday, sir," he said. "And I'm afraid we've slept a little late this morning."

Halfday?

He knew better than to question Hogarth, but the last thing he remembered was Muir's bizarre visit on the night of the fifth. Which meant there was another entire day missing from his memory.

Lost. Gone. Used by someone else.

He looked at Hogarth, saw the confirmation.

"Tell me," he said. "What did we do yesterday?"

Hogarth flipped open his book, always happy to be called on to do his job. "Now, yesterday… Ah, yes, it was back to work on our special project," Hogarth said. "We rose very early." This earned Anton a look of reproach. "And we were hard at it until late in the evening."

"What's that?" Anton heart sank like a corpse in the Lunane's lagoon. "Let me see." He grabbed Hogarth's ledger from his hand, ignored the hostile glare. He scanned the pages. The entry that Hogarth had made of their trip to the underground repository, two days ago now, was succinct, bordering on pointless. It was as if the lad, knowing now that it would likely be rewritten or excised altogether, hadn't had the heart to describe it in full.

The following day's entry did indeed start early, and spent more time describing his meals – there was a note about the return of his 'usual appetite' – than their technical activities, but given Hogarth's aptitude that was hardly surprising.

Anton handed back the ledger and then swept back the

bedclothes. "Let's go and see what we've been up to then."

Hogarth stopped him with the grey cowl. "Sir, the Halfday."

Anton sighed with exasperation. "Fine, bring the get-up with you," he said. "But we're going to see the machine on the way."

They settled on a comprise. Anton dressed in the Lunane's Halfday regalia, but not enough of it to entirely restrict his movement, and Hogarth huffed along behind him toting the rest.

When Anton saw the machine, he froze, unable to do anything but stare in horror. Everything that could be removed had been. Cowling and plating lay piled on the floor. Beside them, components were arranged in neat rows. Severed entrails of cable and wiring loom flopped out of the bowels of the beast. Someone had stripped the machine down to its skeleton. The great beam itself stuck up in the air like a denuded bone, picked clean. Only its hard-to-reach spherical ends appeared to have escaped the carnage.

Anton clattered down the stairs to stand amid the wreckage.

"What *happened* here?"

Hogarth appeared to assume that the question was rhetorical, and of course Anton should have known the answer from the neatly arranged evidence around him. This wasn't butchery. This was a surgeon's careful dissection. For Anton this was much worse than being used as a mouthpiece. It was all very well taking a mental back seat at the Halfday and letting the Lunane talk through him. But this? This was using his hands to wreak absolute destruction on the oldest working example of the Founders' art in the city. It was abhorrent.

"This is a disaster." Anton's voice echoed to the chamber roof. "What have you done?"

A damn sight more than you have, Engineer, the voice answered. There was a diffidence to its tone that sounded like self-justification.

"So I see. And you used my hands to commit this atrocity?"

Your hands and your mind.

"But you're not quite the puppeteer you believe yourself to be, are you?"

Anton touched the dismantled beam. He was surprised to feel the buzz of power through the metal.

The machine still functions.

True enough the beam was still pointing at the moon's image in the ceiling above them. As if it was aware of the conversation, it shifted an inch. The movement set up an unhealthy vibration that in turn shivered loosened screws and rivets all along its length.

"I can't do anything to fix this now," Anton said. This admission of defeat surprised him, but it was true. "Perhaps with the little I've learned, I could have made improvements." He gestured aimlessly. "But I can't fix this."

You must.

"Must?" Anton beseeched the chamber. "*Must*, you say. Why can't you understand that some things are impossible, no matter what your wishes are? I reiterate that it might – *might*, mark you – have been possible to extend the working life of the thing by a matter of months. But since you decided to interfere…"

You are too cautious, Engineer. A king must be proactive. A king must lead.

"You vainglorious *bastard* –" Anton began, but was not allowed to complete the sentence. The last thing he saw before the Lunane's impatience overflowed him was, up on the gantry above him, the shocked 'o' of Hogarth's mouth, and the crushing grip he was exerting on the Lunane's cowl.

Lottie hadn't been to the Palace since she was little. All that Halfday petitioning stuff was for old women with too many gripes against the world and too much time on their hands. For most people where she had grown up the Palace might as well have been the moon itself. You were constantly aware that it was there, but it was a long way to walk and interaction when you got there was unlikely to improve your lot in any meaningful way.

The last time she had been here, belted into the hateful red dress and dragged along in her mother's retinue, the grannies around her had chatted incessantly about the price of coal while they waited their turn at bending the ear of the man in the chair. Aged ten she had found the whole thing incongruously funny, and had been summarily skelped for it when she had got home. But if that same ten year old were here today, she would have been scared out of her wits. The grannies were still here, of course – where else would they go on Halfday? – but they had wisely given priority to the grievances of a crowd which had been of a considerable size when Lottie and Henrik had arrived, and had swollen significantly since.

Lottie felt lost. She couldn't understand it. *Pregnant.*

They waited with the familiar faces. The two Boxers, Spitz and Rodrigo, flanked Blackwood, looking more like a pair of rented Dockton goons than sporting men. Frank, the engineer who had brought news of the latest imposter, was pensive. And the others, many of whom she recognised without knowing their names. And they hadn't just come from the Joffries' meeting – there were people here from the markets, the farmers and growers, the Foundry. A group of stevedores came over to Henrik to express their regrets and bestow general threats towards his attackers.

Coming together stoked the general disaffection and anger began to boil off the crowd, hanging like not-quite-visible steam above the heads of the assembly. The guards sensed it. They were edgy from the beginning, brusque in their instructions and over-physical in their attempts to keep everyone in line. Nevertheless, order was maintained, and the people stood in line and waited for the Lunane to descend to them.

The only man she'd been with recently was Henrik on the Fullday, but she'd taken the usual precautions: drunk a whole flask of wrackwater, used plenty of moult paste – her mother's own recipe, even – so there should have been no possibility. How could she be *pregnant?*

Joffries was fretting.

"He's keeping us waiting on purpose," he muttered. "He's scared to come down and face his people." The little man's face was pale, but with feverish pink in his cheeks and a manic glaze to his eyes.

"Calm down, man" said Blackwood. "We'll never have our demands taken seriously if you come across as a gibbering madman."

"Gibbering, is it?" Joffries snapped. "Do you not think it important that our campaign should be presented with passion and belief?"

"Passion is all very well." Blackwood frowned. "And belief is essential, but don't forget that you were the one who persuaded us to adhere to the principles that we are trying to preserve in the first place. *Order and propriety*, you said. *What will we become if we abandon those?"*

Joffries stiffened. "You do not need to lecture me on the subject of principles," he said, but that look did not leave his eyes.

Lottie only half heard the bickering. She was bloody pregnant and she didn't know what to do. Henrik was being gentle and supportive, but he was no *practical* use. The doctors at the Infirmary would be little better. And she refused to even contemplate the other alternative.

Blackwood looked as if he had more to say to Joffries, but Rodrigo nudged him. The crowd hushed. They all looked up.

Stately, slow, the grey eminence of the Lunane descended the staircase. The entrance was perfect. The tower's ethereal light leant him the soft, silver luminosity of a cloud that has momentarily covered the moon, and his measured descent was accompanied by a rain of white down donated by the congregation of crows that looked down on the proceedings from the handrails of the upper levels of the tower.

There could be no one present that was not instantly reminded of the Lunane's place at the heart of their community. His power. And for those that had entertained any fanciful doubts, there was no doubting his veracity. This was no monkey in a suit. This *was* the Lunane.

Silence fell.

People looked away, circled their hearts reverently.

Lottie bit her lip, resisted the urge to kneel.

The silence became strained, but no one broke it. Silence could not be broken until the Lunane allowed, and the Lunane was in no hurry. Reaching the bottom of the staircase he walked towards the great chair in the centre. Then he climbed the dais, and turned to face the crowd.

Lottie had to squint to look at him. The light might only have been the early Spring sunlight lancing in through the tower ceiling, but when it hit the Lunane, he seemed to amplify it. Those soft grey robes became dazzling silver. The throne behind him glowed like a Foundry ingot. The orrery above him twinkled in sedate revolution. You could not escape the impression that it wasn't the sunlight after all, that maybe it was the man himself.

The Lunane spread his arms, at once beseeching and enfolding, and at last addressed the assembly.

"My people."

The voice was a compassionate baritone, and it carried sympathetic vibrations that fluttered Lottie's heart.

"*My people.*"

He was talking to her. He was addressing all of them, but specifically he was talking to her. Lottie leant forward.

"These are troubled times for our city, our haven, *our home,*" the

Lunane said. "Times such as we have not seen since the early years of our founding. The sea has turned against us, our crops have failed, the fishing has been meagre and our friends across the ocean have been quick to take fiscal advantage of our plight. Luck, on the whole, has not been with us. It has not been easy to endure it." The Lunane raised his hands higher, balled them into fists. "But, my people, *we will endure*. This is nothing more than a phase of the great interconnected cycles that have underpinned the fabric of our life since we came to this island. As the moon waxes out of the dark, as the tides calm and ebb, as the monkeys share the luck out, so will Glassholm weather this slough, and emerge soon into a new phase of prosperity."

Lottie felt her heart swell. Looking around she could see there were a number of hopeful smiles on the faces of the onlookers.

The Lunane accepted the patter of applause with a humble nod. "In the meantime," he said. "We will do what we have always done. We will observe our traditions and, in doing so, preserve the balance."

The Lunane climbed into his magnificent chair, and an enormous crow chose that moment to swoop down from the tower heights to perch above his shoulder.

"Bring me your worries," the Lunane said. "And I will try to ease them. Bring me your disputes, and I will try and resolve them. Bring me your fears, and I will try and allay them." He held up a warning finger. "I repeat, *I will try*. Because, like every one of you, I am just a man. At times like these, all men must try to aid each other. Only by striving together will we endure."

With that, he beckoned for the first in the queue – one of the stevedores – to come forward. Lottie didn't know if he had come with the intention of petitioning, but it seemed that when he looked, he found something in his heart that needed to be unburdened. He stepped past the guard cordon, knelt at the foot of the dais and began his petition.

The docker finished and the queue shuffled forward. Automatically, Lottie fell into step. It was an easy compulsion. It would be good, she thought, to tell someone. About the sickness in the mornings, about the swelling of her belly and about the thoughts she had been having ever since her bloody mother had told her about the baby. Black thoughts of the like that would not even occur to her at Dark. It would be good to tell someone who would listen, who would offer the kind of fatherly advice she had never had.

When she saw Joffries shove his way to the front, she remembered why they were there. Grumbles of annoyance rose from among the patient line of former-protesters. Beside her, she heard a confusion in Henrik's, "Hey!" that mirrored her own.

Joffries' purposeful charge was blocked by the guards. They were too far away to hear what passed between them, but the tenor of the conversation was nevertheless obvious. There was no place in this ordered process for those who broke the rules. Joffries began to remonstrate, but his shouted imprecations were snatched upwards by the acoustics of the tower. Then he began to gesticulate too, pointing with rigid arm and fervent finger over the shoulders of the guardsmen, and that was too much. Their leader drew his pistol. He didn't aim it, but its presence was sufficient to make his point. Joffries didn't get it. If anything his face turned redder, his voice became shriller. With a shrug, the guardsman grabbed a fistful of his jacket and dragged the surprised businessman towards a nearby doorway. For a second, the guardsman's fretful gaze met hers. Lottie gasped.

Henrik put his hand on her shoulder. "What is it?"

She pointed. "That's the sergeant who interrogated me and Vickers about that dead policeman."

"He's still an arsehole then?" Henrik said watching their erstwhile spokesman disappear with the slam of a door.

"So it would seem," she replied. "Poor old Joffries. He was the one who was so keen to do this the proper way. The Glassholm way." Until he'd realised that the Glassholm way was doing what you were told, toeing the line and assuming the Lunane's primacy in all things.

The interruption broke the spell. The queue fragmented into knots and clusters. A babble began. In no time it became a racket.

Blackwood and the others appeared at her side. Spitz and Rodrigo looked around, as edgy now as Joffries had been.

"I knew he'd blow it," Blackwood seethed. "The Lunane lapped him up."

"It was almost as if he knew we were coming," said Henrik.

The remark was quietly made, but it created a stir. Suspicious looks flew between them.

It was Blackwood who defused the situation before the accusations started in earnest. "Of course he knew," he said. His voice was heavy with defeat, with the memory of the way they'd all to a man and woman stood obediently in line as soon as they heard the king's voice. "He's the Lunane. This is his city, and who could even dare to imagine they could change that?"

Lottie's heart tightened to see the feisty printer like this. The fight had gone out of him.

Around them the brief frisson was beginning to dissipate too. In moments another petitioner would advance and the queue would shuffle round one more place, and all would be as it always had been.

Then another figure stepped forward. This one was as silent as Joffries had been full of rage, as controlled as he had been demonstrative. Lottie didn't recognise the cowed woman until she lifted her head and gave the king a look of deep sorrow. For an older woman, she had always taken care of her appearance, but now she looked like a life-long resident of Chicken Town. Her clothes sagged off her and were as grey as her skin. Her hair was a crow's nest. Her eyes were dull as old buttons. And she moved slowly, hugging herself as if that might stop the shakes breaking her apart. Lottie had only seen her the evening before. She had been confident, calming, reassuring then, the café owner. It was impossible that this was the same woman.

"It's not working any more." She spoke softly, but clearly. "This... this..." She cast around her, a frustrated finger pointing out the people, the guards, the Palace staff who had appeared on the stairs. Finally it came to rest, via the Lunane himself in his chair, on the too neat, too trite metaphor that revolved patiently above him. Little people in their place moving around. In prescribed circles. Forever.

"...*this machine*," the café owner said. "You pretend... you *lie* to us. You tell us it encompasses everything, but you ignore the rest. The pieces that do not fit. It is convenient to lay them aside. But people are not convenient. Even if they are not perfect cogs, even if they wear out before they can even begin to turn, they are still our children." She sagged to her knees. "Please. My boy... I know he's still alive."

Lottie felt for the woman. As a child she'd witnessed more than once the screaming and the crying when a baby was born sick or dead. She remembered that the sisters sometimes used the word, *incomplete*. Reflexively, her fingers tugged her hair over her bad eye and she thought about the baby in her own belly.

Something odd happened then. As the assembly poured their

sympathy on this woman, it seemed for the briefest instant that there was a change: a flutter of the light, fracturing the mob into isolated individuals, revealing the figure in the chair as no king at all, just an unremarkable man.

She looked. They all looked. But in the next instant it was the Lunane again, only not as superior, not as resplendent. Like an image in a tarnished mirror.

Then there was a shout from further back in the queue. Heads turned. Another shout answered it, joined in. And another, but it wasn't until the fifth or sixth voice was added that Lottie was able to make out what they were shouting.

Three words, repeated over and over.

"*Tear. Him. Down.*"

The cry caught the cooling embers of the crowd's anger, blew oxygen through them and with each utterance attempted to ignite them again. Lottie spotted the shouters, recognised them from the first meeting.

Anarchists, Blackwood had called them, spat it like filth. Which made it all the more surprising to see the printer standing shouting alongside their leader, the slick prick who had offered Lottie death.

"*Tear him down!*"

The guards moved out uncertainly and the returning sergeant brought reinforcements. But it was too late. The crowd's leaking wrath had finally found the spark it was looking for. The Castil tower was ablaze with the shout.

"*Tear him down!*"

Then the crowd erupted in violence. The brash young men laid into whoever was nearest, and their victims responded out of self-defence. The guardsmen who had rifles had retreated around the Lunane's chair, and brandished them at any of the brawlers who looked like spinning in that direction.

Lottie and Henrik escaped to the safety of the wall, but there was little chance of getting close to the corridor they had entered by. A full blown fistfight had erupted there.

Lottie gazed over the heads of the fighters at the object of the people's ire. The Lunane raised his hands in supplication, but even his clever voice could not carry over the riot. She saw him turn his head, taking it all in. Then his head had snapped up and he was looking all

the way over the top. He was looking directly at Lottie.
Despite the distance, their gazes locked.
She saw him smile, then she doubled over in wracking pain.

Anton became only distantly conscious. He could tell that was sitting down, and there was commotion all around him. He felt a bead of sweat trickling down his cheek. The movement of his own jaw, tongue, lips. A voice.

He was at the Halfday ceremony. Slowly his awareness of his surroundings rippled out from the cowl around his head to include the chair under him, the granite dais it sat on, the great tower stretching above him all the way up to the moon.

But something wasn't right.

Gone were the docile petitioners and the temple reverence in which every shuffle and cough had previously echoed like a thunder clap. In its place was a scene unlike any Anton had ever witnessed. The dais was ringed by guardsmen who were barely managing to repel the jostling crush of enraged citizens. Angry shouts echoed back and forth and mixed with the corvine chatter of the white birds that swooped around the chamber, diving from the railings above to rake at faces with their claws.

Something sailed out of the mob, struck the dais step with a crack. Splinters skittered around his shoes and dislodged the huge crow at his shoulder with a rasping *kraaak* and a *whump* of displaced air. The bird launched itself straight towards the thrower of the missile.

Anton didn't know what to do. Something had clearly gone terribly wrong with the petitions, but he couldn't begin to guess what. Nor could he understand why the Lunane should suddenly relinquish control of his body right in the middle of the ceremony.

Another piece of brick hurtled overhead.

On reflection it was fairly clear why the Lunane had withdrawn. If the guards failed to protect him, he might need to look out for another host.

Lottie slumped against the wall. Her belly felt filled with burning eels. Her hips and pelvis felt as if they were being rearranged by a giant's hands.

"Lottie, what is it? What's the matter?"

Henrik was too far away to help. Lottie whimpered with pain. She thought she was going to be sick. She thought she was going to pass out. But before she could do either the sensations eased. In the aftermath she was sore, sweaty, her clothes too tight, but she was able at least to catch her breath, and after a moment or two, to stand.

She managed a weak smile. "I'm okay."

He looked scared. "Is it the –"

"The bloody baby, yes." Lottie ignored his scowl of disapproval.

There was something happening on the other side of the hall. People were pointing towards the stairs. Through the crush, a shape plummeted out of the sky, the light flaring off it as it dropped. The crash when it landed made several of the crowd pause in their hostilities, but by no means everyone had noticed.

"Henrik?"

"What was that?" Henrik craned, trying to see.

Whatever it had been, it was followed by half a dozen others in quick succession.

"Henrik!"

He turned back to her. "What *was* that?"

"I need to get home"

"Okay, yes." He glanced nervously over his shoulder. "Good idea."

He attempted to lift her, but she pushed him away. "I can manage on my own. Just make a path."

Without further comment Henrik did as he was asked, anticipating gaps in the heave and sway of the bodies, pushing in where there were none and dodging the consequent punches swung in his direction. Lottie tucked in low behind him and kept as close as she could.

They made it fifty yards down the corridor that led to the Palace gates before the screaming began.

"Anton!"

It was a full blown riot down there now. There was fighting and there was escaping, but it was impossible to distinguish the one from the other. There were bodies too. Some of the crowd were crushing into the arched corridors, not only the one which connected the tower to the outer gates, but the other passages too. In minutes they would spread the panic to the kitchens and the rest of the servants' areas. The remainder of the mob stayed in the Castil, taking on the guards.

Those were the ones who hadn't yet encountered the crabs.

"Anton!" The voice lifted up out of the mêlée. Anton blinked, then saw a face in the crowd, a hand reaching in his direction.

It was Frank. He was with a group that were trying to persuade him to come away before he got caught up in the fighting, but when he saw that Anton had spotted him at last, he pushed them away and beckoned furiously. The nearest guards were fully occupied trying to unclamp a steel claw from a someone's bloody ankle. Their faces were ashen. The man they were attempting to help did not struggle, did not scream. Anton caught a glimpse of the mechanical crustacean's retractable hypodermic.

"Anton." Frank beckoned again. "Come on. We'll get you out of here."

"Your Majesty!" This came from the opposite direction. There on the stairs were Gerard and Lytten. Hogarth hovered behind them. The secretary's shout barely carried over the racket. Next to him the ashen security chief looked struck dumb. "Your Majesty, this way. Guards, make a passage for the Lunane."

Anton was welded to his chair by a cold seam of indecision. He didn't know what to do. He didn't even know if he could move. He almost wished that the Lunane would take control again, but there was nothing. Not a flicker.

"Anton." Frank again. His companions were physically manhandling him now. "Come on, man!"

Anton stood, tottered on his ridiculous shoes. To his left the guards had almost managed to push the crowd back enough to leave clear passage to the stairs. Gerard stood above them on the steps, exhorting them to redouble their efforts while two of the metal crabs scuttled up and down in a menacing patrol.

Anton gauged the distance to the stairs. Not so far to go. Up there was safety. Up there was his machine and it needed him more than ever. It was the job he was intended for after all. He thought he could manage to go up.

He wasn't at all sure what lay in the other direction. The crabs might not attack him but, if this mob were any indication, out there was a city waiting to stone him on account of the clothes he wore, the face they saw in his features.

Above him, the orrery continued its measured movement. No, he thought, he knew his place in the city-machine, and that was up in his tower.

"Anton!" Frank elbowed one of his friends away, wriggled out of the arm lock of another. "Have you forgotten about Krista?"

He discovered his thoughts of Krista at the back of his mind, further back even than the place that the Lunane resided. They had been put there deliberately, reduced to abstraction. He knew he should feel sadness, shame, but all he felt was that it was right that he should forget her. He was not made for love.

Someone grabbed a fistful of his robe and pulled, and Anton stumbled down the stairs, brushing past the surprised guards and tripping into the throng. At first he thought he was going to get trampled, but he felt strong arms catch him. Then the cowl was tugged off his head, and something heavy was draped around his shoulders.

"Keep low," they whispered, and he felt himself propelled through the jostle of bodies.

Anton did as he was told. Clasping the donated coat at the neck, he kept his eyes on the floor and his feet moving in time with the boots that flanked his impractical shoes. Behind, he heard Gerard's shouts of fury, then the sound of shots. His companions increased their pace, and that was what saved them. Behind them came the ticking thunder of steel feet on stone, the shearing sound of scything claws. Someone among the hundreds of other escapees had the presence of mind to start closing the heavy exterior door. Anton and his companions were the last through before it was slammed shut. The escapees threw their bodies against the wood just in time.

Secretary Gerard sat behind his desk and stared at the room's other chair until Mortlock felt compelled to fill it. "Your report, Sergeant?" The secretary's tone bristled with blades.

Mortlock didn't know what he was doing here. Gerard's office, at the very centre of the secretariat maze, was larger than Chief Lytten's but, aside from the desk and the two chairs, it was virtually empty. If you were summoned for an audience with the secretary, there were no distractions from the reason for your visit. That reason was the magnitude of his failure yet again to protect the Lunane, of course, but surely Lytten could have dealt with that? Indeed he would have taken delight in doing so.

Gerard's gaze suffused him with cold loathing. "Well?"

Mortlock took a deep breath and rattled off the facts as he knew them. The arrests, the deaths from crushing, gunshot and dismemberment by those diabolical crabs. At least he could not be held responsible for the last of those.

"And the injured?"

"Private Lennox has a serious head injury," Mortlock replied, "but we are hopeful he will pull through. And Corporal Ross will be off his feet for a few months. They're both good lads."

"I'm sure they are," Gerard sneered. "What about the injured petitioners?"

"Don't know, sir," Mortlock grunted.

"You didn't check?" The Secretary sounded surprised. "The Lunane wants to know. He cares for the welfare of every one of his subjects, after all."

Mortlock saw a scrap of relief and snatched at it. "Then His Majesty has returned?"

"Not yet," Gerard said. "But rest assured, Sergeant. Even if I thought it necessary to go into the city and search for him, I'd no more entrust that task to you than trust a luck monkey to make his breakfast. The Lunane will return in his own time." The secretary steepled his fingers. "I don't suppose your extracurricular activities have borne fruit?"

"My extra...?" Mortlock felt certain that he should know what the secretary was referring to, but it eluded him. "You don't mean my investigation of Alfie Kremer's murder?"

Gerard's face cracked into a smile then. "The murders, yes. How are you getting along with those murders?"

Mortlock had been nervous before but now, without knowing why, he felt like the ground had fallen away all around him. "I'm not, sir," he managed.

Gerard leaned forward. "There haven't been any more?"

"Not that I've heard. You'll need to ask Chief Lytten –"

"Security Chief Lytten has taken a leave of absence, Sergeant." Gerard's smile slid away.

At least as this was something Mortlock could understand. "Is this because of his… visitors?"

Gerard's face was perfectly blank. "Thank you, Sergeant. You are dismissed."

Mortlock was only too happy to leave.

"Oh, Sergeant?" Gerard's scrutiny was intense. "If you do happen upon another body on your travels, say around the docks area, be sure and report it to me, won't you?"

They chose to hide him in the most ironic place they could have thought of. The complexity and scale of the great clock's workings were so difficult to take in at once that Anton could not shake the impression of having been abandoned in some deep grotto, surrounded by a constellation of glittering metallic geodes. But no, indeed it was a machine. It was Glassholm's most famous machine, and in all his time in the Foundry, looking in vain for inspiration, innovation, even a single new idea, it was the last place he would have thought to visit.

The great clock of the Foundry did one thing. It told the time. The technology involved had changed little since clocks were invented, and it summed up the Foundry in one gloriously fussy, massively over-engineered example.

Every one of the thousands of gleaming gears, spinning capstans and greased chains that turned the eight pairs of hands, struck the bells and whirled out the shaded discs that marked the progression through the month was built with the absolute precision, fail-safed with multiple redundancy and maintained with the utmost care. It all moved around him with a pedestrian measure that was both beautiful and infuriating.

But it did its job. The clock never stopped. Not at Full, not at Dark. Not even for the Lunane.

Anton wriggled to find a comfortable position among the pile of musty sacks but found comfort elusive. He couldn't stretch out without fouling the clock's workings. He was tired, but there was no chance of sleep. The whisper of flywheels displaced the mote-spotted air like the breath of sleepers and the ratcheting of cogs was almost musical, but the sound was unceasing. If that and the constant flurry of wings – roosting pigeons, instead of spying crows, but nevertheless – had not kept him on edge, the knowledge that Frank might return at any moment with Krista would have.

Anton didn't know how he was going to feel when he saw her.

Guilt, more than likely. Anger, disappointment, perhaps. There should be relief, longing, but whatever the Lunane had done to diminish her in his memory had emptied him. For now there were no feelings in him, just the mechanical processes of pulse and respiration.

The creak of wood. Someone was climbing the ladders. A head appeared through the trap door.

It wasn't her.

The newspaper man, Blackwood, heaved himself into the loft, then picked a path around the assorted mechanisms.

"Suppose it takes a lot of gubbins to keep a clock like this right," he said conversationally as he hunkered down next to Anton.

Anton nodded warily. Since his escape, the reaction to him had been mixed. There had been a number of strenuous, whispered discussions during the course of the afternoon that led him to believe that there was disagreement in the ranks. Frank was on one side, while the two bruisers, Spitz and Rodrigo, treated him with open hostility. This Blackwood, it seemed, remained undecided.

"Frank's been telling us all about you."

"Really?" Blackwood was probing, but Anton hadn't a clue what for. He'd already told them everything he knew about what had been happening at the Palace.

"Bit of a maverick around this place, I understand." Blackwood gestured around him. "Not keen on the local rules, eh?"

"Something like that," Anton agreed, but wasn't going to give Blackwood any more than that until he knew if he was safe or in danger. "The Foundry has an awful lot of rules."

Blackwood grunted.

There was a tension in the clock, a scrape of straining ratchet. Anton had been here long enough to remember to clap his hands over his ears before the ratchet *chunked* over, the flywheels flew and the hammers began to strike the rows of bells. Over the course of the last few hours he had become reacquainted with that old children's song. The one that Gerard was so bloody fond of.

Blackwood raised his eyebrows when the last reverberations had died away. "And every man is he?"

Anton shrugged. "So I am told." He was saved further interrogation by another vibration of the access ladder and the sound of voices from below.

Frank arrived first, then he let down his hand to help his companion into the loft. Anton's heart clicked on a notch. Clinging onto the brickwork outside her window had been like dreaming about her, but from the second the crown of her head rose through the hatch Krista suddenly became real to him again.

Her hair shone with chestnut fire in the invading light of the rail egresses.

Her cheeks were flushed.

Her smile was uncertain.

"Hello, Anton," she said.

If there was a feeling, Anton realised that it was closer to anger than anything else.

Blackwood coughed. "We'll need to be reviewing our plans." He left quickly. Frank lingered long enough to appraise the situation and then followed.

Krista stepped neatly through the spars and rails, and sat down cross-legged, not too close to him, but not too far either. She cast him a familiar scorning once-over. "What are you like, eh?" she said.

Knockabout questions like that had once been staple of their daily communication. *I don't know. You tell me*, was the standard reply.

"What am I like, Krista?" The question was freighted with inference, but he couldn't help himself. "Am I still the man you didn't want to marry?"

The pursing of the lips and the look that narrowed to icy needles confirmed, even if nothing else had, that this was his Krista.

"It wasn't as simple as that," she said. "It's difficult to explain."

The anger boiled away. Once he could have sustained it, but now he just wanted to know. "Suppose you try anyway."

So she told him. It both was and was not what he had expected. She had never been to the Palace, never become a Bride. It was simply that she had been having doubts for some time before the wedding, a slow accumulation of distracted conversations, broken social engagements and lonely nights when he pulled all-nighters in the workshop. And on the morning of the wedding she had simply been unable to go through with it.

While she talked, Anton kept expecting his emptiness to be filled, for sadness or anger to sluice through him again, but he remained as hollow as an empty kettle. When she was done, he realised he really didn't care. And what was more distressing was that he recognised this reaction not as the result of the Lunane's manipulation but as a true response. When it came down to it he simply did not care about other people as much as he did for his work.

"Perhaps it's for the best then," he said at last.

Krista's look of shock indicated this was not the reaction she had expected. Her nod was imperceptible but the relief that washed across her face reinforced her agreement.

"Will you be all right?" he asked.

She nodded again, more forcefully this time. "The family haven't quite got over the 'I told you so' stage yet, but my friends have been a great help."

Frank reappeared then. He must have been clinging to the ladder, listening in, to make such a timely return. He didn't have to say anything. The way his hand slipped into Krista's was eloquent enough.

Anton looked at the pair of them. "Take care of each other." He meant it. They would be able to do that better than he ever could.

He felt something break inside him, but around him the clock ticked on.

"What kind of mother am I going to be, Henrik?"

"Don't talk like that. You'll be wonderful."

"Mothering skills don't exactly abound in our family."

He didn't say anything, then he reverted to what had become his catechism since returning from the Palace. "How are you feeling now?"

Lottie heaved herself up off the workroom floor, labouring to make the point. Then, turning profile-on to him, she swept her hands over the bulge of her belly. "I'm hungry."

He gave her a dubious look. Little wonder, as she hadn't strayed far from the bathroom in the past few hours. On the way home the pain had returned and with it, her stomach swelling grotesquely even as she had watched, had come the sickness and diarrhoea, the sweating and the delirium. And now that she looked like a woman into her sixth month of pregnancy and, with the pain subsiding once more, she suddenly found she had an appetite to match.

Realising that she was serious, Henrik said, "I'll make you a sandwich."

In the kitchen, she watched him, deft with the knife, as he

prepared the food. She tore her eyes from the blade, concentrated on the man, on his kindness. He did everything right: left the rind on the cheese, cut the tomatoes thick, spread the butter thin but right to the edge of the bread. One sprinkle each of salt and pepper. Perfect.

He scrutinised her in return as she bit into the sandwich. That first mouthful awakened a new level of hunger so profound it was almost a different kind of pain.

"You sure you don't want to go to the infirmary? Just to check you out?"

Her mouth was filled with crust and cheese, so she shook her head, pointed at the tap. Henrik ran her a mug of water to wash the sandwich down.

"We're not going anywhere near the Palace," she said.

"Lottie, you don't know it's..." He slapped his hands to his sides, exasperated. "What you're saying just isn't possible. There must be something wrong to just balloon up like that. You need to see a doctor."

"Henrik, for the last time, you can't feel what I feel. There's nothing wrong. Apart from the timescale." She took his hand. "Look, I will see someone, I promise. But I won't go back to the Palace."

Henrik frowned. "Where else is there to go?"

She was trapped. He was right, she needed help, and with the Infirmary in the Palace complex too dangerous to go anywhere near there was only one option left to her. She spoke quietly. As if, whispered, it didn't count.

"The Church."

Anton was abandoned for the night in the loft of the great clock. Out of the way, like a piece of family junk or a failed experiment. It was dark, and he supposed it must be cold too, but he didn't feel it. He had become inert. At least they had left him the coat they had thrown around him during the escape. The coat would have kept him warm if he had been capable of feeling such a thing.

When Frank and Krista left, trailing excuses like vapour, Blackwood had returned. "We don't know what to do with you," he admitted.

Anton didn't reply.

The printer tried again. "If what you tell us is true..." He didn't look as if he wanted to believe it, but he was keeping as much distance between them as the loft would allow. "The Lunane can enter the heads of any one of us."

Anton nodded, an oscillation that was damped under gravity until his chin rested on his chest.

"And you claim he's not in you now, but can you really be sure?"

Anton's head was a counterweight on a broken spring, too heavy to lift.

"Mr Dunn?" Blackwood left him alone with his thoughts.

Anton didn't know how much later it was, how many turns of the wheel that went *tchaak-ak* at the start of each new cycle, how many *drrr-sshiks* of the bearings in the ball race that circled his spot, how many times the bells above pealed their tune. All he knew was that his intended function's time had come and gone. He had been used and discarded. By the Lunane, by Gerard, by Krista and Frank, and their friends too. *Revolution*, they said. Didn't they know that revolution meant going round in a circle, and ending up at the place you started? The Lunane was using them all. Of course he cared about his people, because without his people and their adulation, he was nothing. They were all just pieces of his great machine of self-perpetuation.

Everything was mechanical. Close by, Anton found a canvas bundle. It was heavy. It *chinked*. Some engineer's tool roll. He unwrapped it, felt his way along the spanners, chisels, awls. Found what he was looking for. A stubby trimming knife.

It was too dark where he was, so he forced his rusty limbs into motion and crawled to the wedge of starlight from the nearest rail egress.

The skin of his forearm was smooth as canvas. The knife sliced it open in a clean, straight line. When the opening was large enough he probed with his finger. Dark liquid spilled out. But the pain did not begin until he had ascertained that the liquid was not oil, the tendons were not wires, the bright bone was not a steel truss. Then it raged through him like fire. He even imagined he could smell smoke, hear the crackle and roar of flames. Feel the heat.

Anton bound his arm up with the sash of his Halfday robes, and the pain subdued to a pounding beat.

He could still smell the smoke though. And he could hear shouts of alarm too.

His second rescue of the day came with a delicate shake of the ladder. A soft, slender human form, no more than a shadow in the darkness of the loft. A cold, clammy hand on his cheek and a soft, wordless question.

"Hello, Mia," Anton said.

Chapter 18

No one in the city had ever witnessed anything like the fire that tore through the Foundry that night. It was like a maddened beast. People came from all over the city to watch its claws of flame punching holes in the roof, sending slews of slates shattering on the ground. To see window glass shatter before the roar of its voice. To see heavy doors pop open at the flexing of its muscles. They were mesmerised by its wildness, astonished by its ability to leap lithely from one building to the next.

It was only when they realised that it was looking to leap in the direction of the rich dwellings that bordered the Parks that they were motivated to do something about it.

Only once the fire had become a mere glow beyond the rooftops and a whiff of smoke in the air did Anton realise that Mia wasn't taking him back to the Palace. She guided him through the Foundry estate undetected. Where there was light, she found a darker alternative, where there were agitated crowds streaming in the opposite direction she found a quiet lane, a secluded grove, a back court.

She set a pace that, even with the heels hacked off his Halfday shoes, Anton found difficult to match, and she demonstrated her impatience ably.

"Where are we going?"

A grimace.

"Tell me where we're going."

A slash of fingers in the air.

Anton stopped to lean on a lamp post. He was lightheaded now and there was blood dribbling out of the arm of his adopted coat. The delay was met with beseeching eyes and vigorous tugs of the coat's hem.

He shook her off. "I can't."

Mia cast a frantic glance to the road end where the side street emerged onto a square. Anton could see brighter lights, and heard conversation and music. The news of the great plume of smoke above the Foundry had clearly not reached this far.

Mia shook her head, pressed her fingers to his lips, and Anton saw how scared she was. Up until this point he had assumed that this odd journey was by either the Lunane's or Gerard's command, but now he wondered.

Once more she tugged at his coat. Wherever she was taking him, she did not want to linger.

The square was little more than a cobbled pause in the regular pattern of buildings. A handful of shop fronts reflected the golden glow issuing from what should have been a quiet café bar opposite, but the doors were struggling to contain the noise of voices and frantic fiddle music within. It sounded more like Fullday than just after the Half, and very much the kind of place you would want to avoid at that time of the month. Some people's idea of a good time could be dangerous to your health.

Anton craned for a better view, but his line of sight was obscured by a stand of knot trees in the centre of the square, midway now through their patient, monthly unfurling. He tried to find a chink, but it was no use. There was something more solid than branch and leaf in their midst.

Then he realised that it was a Founders' stone.

Nowhere were the discarded remnants of the Founders' machines more abundant than the Foundry estates. Anton had once believed that the defunct machinery was there to inspire the residents to match their ancient predecessors' achievements, but he now thought differently. *The settlers' machines are junk now*, they said. *Innovation is not the answer. Your goal*, your duty, *is to preserve what we have.*

Anton crossed the distance between the street and the trees, pushed through the resisting branches. Take this: *whatever-it-had-been.* This thing that resembled a gunnery shell, but larger, and made of some flimsy white material that was nevertheless as strong as any metal. Whatever function it had performed would have seemed like magic to a Glassholmer. And if the Lunane had his way, none of them would ever see it.

Ssst. Mia, urging him on again.

Anton emerged from the trees, but he'd dawdled too long, appearing at the exact moment that the bar ejected its rowdy crowd. Closing time. Drunken they may have been, but they spotted him right away.

"Evening, Citizen." This was a well-dressed young man with a nasty swagger. The lad smirked, nodded at the copse. "Caught short were we?" Anton had loathed this kind of cocky youth when he had been a student. His responses had never been quick enough to avoid ridicule, and even now with ten years at least on this lad, he found himself stumbling for a reply.

Much of the crowd had already dispersed, but a few loitered in the expectation of a little after hours entertainment. Someone sniggered.

Anton couldn't help looking around the square for Mia. There were dead-eyed windows, deep doorways, but no sign of the girl. He couldn't have looked more guilty if he had tried.

The youth glided over. People like that were always too smooth, too lithe, too fast. "What are you up to?" he said.

"Nothing…"

But the youth was interested now. When he grinned the two halves of his neat moustache rose like tapered tern's wings. His gaze wandered, first down and then back up to linger on Anton's face, and then his eyes widened as some recognition clicked into place. When he spoke his breath reeked of black spirit.

"Hello?" He grabbed a fistful of coat lapel. "Lunane's man are we?"

There was a roaring in Anton's ears. He didn't hear past *Lunane.* The bastard was still controlling him after all. And right now there didn't appear to be one loyal citizen left in the city.

"What do you mean?" Anton's lips fumbled the words.

The youth stroked the lapel between finger and thumb. "Nice coat like this? Keep you good and warm on a cold night, eh? Up there on the watch towers. It's all right for the Lunane's little pack of guard-dogs, isn't it?"

The man's grip tightened, and Anton's spirit managed both to soar and plummet at the same time. It was the military coat that had been recognised, not the Lunane's face. However, any more tugging would reveal the Halfday robes and he'd have no chance of explaining those away.

The youth turned to his companions. "What do we do with the Lunane's men, again, lads?"

"Teach 'em how to fight!" replied the leering onlookers.

Anton searched inside himself just in case, but if the Lunane was still there he could not coax the commanding voice out of hiding. His only chance was to work a little glamour of his own.

"You got me wrong, pal." He hoped it sounded gruff, hoped his trembling couldn't be felt as one by one he prised the fingers away from the lapel. "I bought this old thing down the markets. Only cost me half a selene at that."

The youth grinned. "That so? Then you're a lucky man. It's freezing tonight."

Anton made himself grin back. It felt like a rictus.

"So, what's the big secret in the bushes?" The tone was conversational, almost friendly. It told him that he had got away with the deception so far, but now that he had begun the pretence he was going to have to follow it through.

He attempted a shrug. "Caught me, right enough. After all, His Majesty thoughtfully provided something to piss against – seemed a shame not to avail myself."

The student pushed into the copse. He reappeared a few seconds later. "We chose a good pub tonight, lads." He reached into his jacket, pulled out a sharpened iron bar. "We've got our very own genuine Founders' stone right here. Who wants to help me pay it our respects?" A whoop of delight went up as the clot of students charged off into the trees. In seconds the shouts of joy were accompanied by the more prosaic noises of wanton destruction.

Anton didn't resist when Mia reappeared and dragged him away.

Lottie rode the tram all the way to the Merchantry, changed onto the Hatchard line and rode it back out. The straight line distance would have amounted to a half hour walk, but that was out of the question now. Her belly had grown again overnight. Even in her baggiest sweater there was no disguising it. Fellow passengers stared. The matronly older woman who boarded at The Rottens bestowed her with twinkly smiles all the way up Hatchard Hill. Lottie had no doubt that these were meant to confer membership to the oh-so-precious coven that was motherhood, but if there was secret knowledge in those knowing glances she was damned if she could decipher it. Staring the old witch out gave her meagre pleasure, but at least she left her alone after that.

She felt the baby shift. Imagined it, eyes closed, tiny fingers twitching. But that's all it was: just imagining. She had only known about the pregnancy for a matter of days, and it just wasn't possible for the baby to be anywhere near that well developed. And yet, she wasn't imagining the size of her belly, or the undeniable movements inside it. Even if the Palace infirmary had not been the scene of a riot, this wasn't something the Infirmary doctors would be able to do anything about. No, if you wanted to know anything about the difficulties of childbirth, you went to the experts. Glassholm's self-appointed midwives.

You went to the Church of Women.

It stung bitterly to have to swallow her pride. All her adult life she'd avoided returning to the place she'd been brought up in. Well, if she had to return, she was determined at least to do so on her own terms. She would not be dictated to, she would not be swaddled, she would not be sucked back into their world. She would get the thing seen to and go as soon as she could.

Lottie got off the tram three quarters of the way up Hatchardhill Road. A squally drizzle buffeted her. In the harbour below, the water reared against the solid, stony arms of the sea walls. Twenty foot whips of spume lashed and fell away inches short of the fishing fleet cowering behind the walls like frightened dogs. What was it Blackwood had said? Three months this coming Full since the boats had been out two days in a row?

There wasn't far to go. Mael Street followed the contour of the island's edge. A terrace of tenements with their backs turned to the sea. The stone up here was salt stained. The wind bitter.

Women who came looking for the Church for the first time often arrived in a state of perplexity. Most expected to find a monument of a building: nothing as grand as the Palace, but certainly something befitting the importance of their organisation. Not the Lunane's phallic tower then, but perhaps a building constructed from stone that was as pale as skin, with columns as slender as fingers, and a hearth as welcoming as motherhood. What they got, when they finally found it, after walking right on past the door this way and then that way, was a house. Just an ordinary house, but a house of secrets.

The signs were there if you knew how to read them. In a street of identical abodes, the Church was the one that looked least like a home. Its walls were more soot-blackened and clogged with moss. There were rain-faded slogans and pictures chalked on the pavement outside, as rude, crude and unimaginative as they had been twenty years ago when Lottie had first discovered the words – *darky bitches* – scrawled on the wall. The gate had once been decorated with a mosaic of pink nacre, but had lost many of the pieces to the boots of frustrated husbands, not to mention the wilful fingers of a certain child who had once lived there. Its windows lacked the white flashes of curtain popular with the neighbours, opting instead for swags of red velvet that were supposed to stand out as defiant cardinal flags, but had not been washed in so long that they resembled bloody clots. But none of these indications was as plain as the scandalous front door, painted the glossy scarlet of a whore's lips. This combination of dilapidation and seediness blinded many prospective visitors to the building's true nature, but the women who needed to found it nevertheless.

What did these clues tell you about the secrets inside? That the Church was not universally popular, and not just because it occupied a space that would otherwise have housed ten families. It had started as just one home – the tiny attic apartment belonging to Rebecca, the first Mother – but the years had seen it grow into something that combined all the functions of a refuge, an apothecary, a maternity centre and a coven.

Lottie knew more. You needed to hold the wicket gate up to prevent it squealing and setting the neighbourhood curtains fluttering. And if you didn't want to wake your mother by yanking the stiff chain and filling every floor with the peal of bells, there was a latch key in one of the nooks carved above the lintel.

She stretched, and her fingers found it first time. For all she knew this key hadn't been touched in the eight years since she had last used it herself. It still fit the lock though and the red door swung eagerly inwards.

If the neighbours were watching now, all they would see was yet another unfortunate lass who had got herself pregnant and in her desperation, turned away from the Lunane and towards the Church.

The hall was dimly lit by candles guttering in wax-filled saucers on the staircase. Lottie could hear singing. Ignoring the doors to the left and right – the first the herbalist shop, and the other a consulting room – she tiptoed past and started up the stairs. She wanted to postpone interaction with any of these people for as long as possible.

The singing got louder as Lottie ascended, treading as carefully as if the brown carpet was woven from tinder-dry twigs. Both of the doors here were closed, but on the level above, where the offices and meeting rooms were, it would be almost impossible to sneak past. Fortunately, Lottie knew another way.

She listened, recognising the sweetly sung song. The women of the Church called these devotional songs 'hymns' which, until she had seen the word written down, had seemed to Lottie to be entirely contradictory. This one was called 'The Body' and was often heard on the lips of the nurses.

My body be hale, my body be whole, the woman sang. The words came from the door on the left. That was good because it was the one on the other side she wanted to enter.

The room held a row of neat, empty beds. The former kitchen beyond had been turned into a place to prepare and store drugs. The shelves were packed with labelled boxes and earthenware jars. Lottie ignored all of that and headed straight for the door in the corner. It was thick with sloppy paintwork and looked like it hadn't been opened in centuries but Lottie knew better. With an altogether too loud creak she heaved the door open, and wasted no time in entering and pulling it to behind her.

The forgotten stairs were dark and narrow and filled with dust. They turned, folded back as they connected one storey to the next, zig-zagging clandestinely up the side of the building. Lottie felt her way, climbed ponderously all the way to the top. There she opened the last door and stepped into her old bedroom.

Lottie had half expected to find the room converted into a small office or perhaps her mother's overflow wardrobe. Climbing the abandoned stairs, a resurgent moment of teen-angst brought the notion that she would find it dark and dusty, shut off entirely as if she had never existed in this house.

Nothing had changed. Everything was exactly as she had left it.

The gleeful leer of her Mister Moony peeked out of a nest of other knitted dolls and toys arranged on the narrow bed. The pictures pinned to the walls, faded now and foxed at the corners, mingled modernist prints with her own early sketches. Above her desk was a scholastic calendar for the year 498 with its unmistakeable gradual shading of the days, light to dark to light again. The desktop was cluttered with teenage debris: pencils and make-up pots, a ceramic bowl containing hair grips and a neat stack of clasp-locked diaries. The pages were empty because Lottie had never trusted her mother not to read them.

It was as if not one day had passed, let alone eight years.

Completing that impression, placed on her pillow was a razor-folded slip of snow-white paper.

Lottie unfolded it with shaking fingers. She had always thought her mother's handwriting incongruously beautiful. She admired the tightly controlled loops of the script, the precise crosses, even when executed in this awful red ink. At first Lottie thought the note was another relic, a last blast in the internecine tit-for-tat that communication between mother and daughter in this house had finally become before she ran away. But the paper was too crisp, the ink too vibrant. Only the words were old.

Welcome home, Daughter. When you have settled in, we're having tea in the Chapel.

There wasn't any point in hanging around. May as well get up there and get this over with. Lottie left her bag on her bed, and set her jaw, determined to keep her promise to herself.

In many ways the Chapel was the centre of the Church's operation. If you turned left at the very top of the main staircase, away from the Mother's private apartments and through the various ceremonial rooms, you eventually came to a non-descript door. Behind the door was a heavy red curtain. It looked mysterious, symbolic, but Lottie knew that it was there to block the draught. When you pulled the curtain back and started up the short flight of stairs you quickly found out why.

Hidden from the street, the Chapel was perched on top of the building. Although *chapel* was a grand name for what was essentially just a flat piece of roof overlooking the sea. Lottie had never liked being out here. She didn't like the slipperiness of the lead sheeting underfoot, didn't feel protected by the low railing that was all that saved you from a very long drop down to the distant waves, and didn't feel comfortable being so close to the sky. Up here it felt as if the moon could see into your soul.

No better place in Glassholm for an altar and space enough at a precarious squeeze for a bunch of crazy, praying women.

They weren't praying right now, though. Four ladies sat at the folding table, good crockery pinched between their fingers, chatting away as if this was any Merchantry tearoom. All of the women were middle-aged or older. Lottie didn't recognise two of them, but they fitted the template. Earnest, serious women. Dedicated, able women. Plain, worthy, grey women. Those were the sort that Lottie's mother surrounded herself with. Those and the cackling oddity that was Aunt Ruby. Lottie's aunt didn't join in the respectful pause in their tea-making activities, didn't look up from rolling her crumpet so tightly that jam squished out of the ends to mimic Phamie Blake's twinkly beam of expectancy as the other two so carefully did.

Lottie waited until she'd taken a bite big enough to choke on before speaking. "I'm only here for as long as it takes you to get rid of it."

If Ruby's reaction was disappointingly sanguine, the other two effected a more than satisfying gape of horror. Lottie's mother took the time to drain her cup and dab the corners of her mouth before smiling sweetly.

"Oh, it's much too late for that, Lottie dear. Much too late."

Mortlock decided to pay the Blake girl a visit.

What he *wanted* was to talk to Shirley but he hadn't seen her since her performance in front of the petitioners. There had been signs of life in the café, but no amount of shouting her name had brought her to the door. He wanted to be certain she was well, of course he did, but more than that he needed her to help him make sense. The more he thought about his meeting with Gerard the more he thought that the secretary, in his uniquely subtle manner, had actually instructed him to carry on with the investigation. With Lytten out of the picture – anyone who saw him at the petitioning could see that the man had lost it – and with police resources stretched tissue thin with everything else going on around the city, *someone* had to continue the search. Mortlock's next shift wasn't for two days, or was it three? Which had to be more than mere convenience, surely?

He wanted to ask Shirley about the silverfish children. Wanted to know if they could be trusted. Because they were the ones who had led him specifically to the Blake girl at the café. The girl who found Alfie Kremer's body and – although he couldn't quite see the connection – had been in the thick of the agitators at the Palace.

Mortlock had to do something before he unravelled entirely. He was drinking again. Last night he'd drained the black spirit bottle and he passed out on his living room floor. At least he'd woken up in the same spot, but he'd been visited. The empty bottle, on its side next to him had dazzled in the dawn light, three stripes of multi-hued collage the shape of little fingers marking the dark glass. A cone of damp sand beside it. There were scales stuck to his skin.

So were these Silverfish trying to help him too now? He had a notion that perhaps they were trying to help him remember some vital fact about Prunty's boys, something that he had known but lost with the head injury and the passing of the years. More than a notion, a hope. If those creatures were the benefactors Shirley claimed, chamfering a little at a time off the guilt that she had carried around for twenty five years, surely they might do something similar for him. And that was another reason for chasing down the only lead he had.

And there was one more reason too. He had been a policeman. He still considered himself one. If he *didn't* investigate, what bloody use was he to the city, to Alfie, to himself. What *was* he at all?

Mortlock shrugged on his stiff, old copper's greatcoat. He wasted too long searching for his pistol, which he had managed to misplace somewhere, before settling for slipping his cosh into a pocket and heading out.

The few passengers on the Beckon Hill tram were scared. Scared or guilty. Mortlock stood at the end of the car challenging any of them to meet his gaze. Few would. Not the elderly man with his Lunane's locket held to his heart and circled so fervently that he was in danger of rubbing the silver away to nothing. Not the couple with the shopping bags on their laps that smelled of brine and wriggled in their grips with the sound of clicking claws. Not the teenage girls with their cheeks dusted with a powdered iridescence that, he was shocked to realise, brought to mind those silverfish children, a fashion created for these new times. Even the two young militia conscripts up by the driver's cab looked nervous.

Only the cluster of urchins who boarded at the base of the hill showed no fear.

"Why are you lot not in school?" Mortlock asked them.

Their faces were the picture of sullen innocence, but something about them aroused suspicion. They were hiding someone.

"Well?" He tried to peer over their heads, but they closed together.

An exchange of looks followed that appeared to confer the group voice on a tall, freckly girl. "Shut up, you big pig."

Mortlock drew himself up and noted every one of them flinching. "You know you're talking to a police officer, don't you?"

It was the littlest one who cracked first.

"They sent us home because the bad men threw stones through the windows."

There was no resistance now. Brushing them aside, Mortlock discovered the smallest child of all. Five years old, if that. Soaking wet and shivering in her simmet and socks. They'd tied fish heads and crab claws into her hair.

"She's the Derryman," piped up one of her tormentors.

Mortlock knelt down on the tram deck. "What's your name, pet?" He got no answer. "Where do you live?"

When the child opened her mouth water dribbled down her chin. "The sea," she whispered, and then jumped off the tram as it rounded a corner, pursued by the rest of the gang.

Mortlock was still trying to control his anger when he alighted at Emers Street. *The Derryman*, of all things,

The close that Blake lived in was a half a dozen doors up Farring Street. A dull, unappealing tenement in a long row of equally dour buildings. Of course, the flat was at the very top of the stairs.

Policeman's luck, that.

When he knocked, it was the boy who answered. They stared at each other. The lad guarded, holding the door open just enough to see out. Mortlock with a confusion of almost recognition. He'd not had it the last time he'd seen the boy, but that had been at a distance and he'd been covered in bruises… No, it wasn't coming, but he was certain that he knew him.

"My name's Sergeant Mortlock." It was a long shot that the girl would even have remembered his name, but he saw recognition in the boy's bruised eyes and from the additional frost in the lad's voice it was clear what his girlfriend had told him hadn't been complimentary.

"Right," the lad said. "This is about the policeman at Dark?"

"Can I come in?"

"Lottie's not here right now."

"Can I come in anyway?"

Confusion passed across the lad's face, but then he shrugged and opened the door.

"Henrik, is it?"

He was a tall lad, even slouching against the wall. The complexion underneath the settling bruises on his face was pale, the untidy hair an immigrant blond. A tilt of the head was all the welcome Mortlock was going to get.

"Where's your girlfriend then?"

The sandy brows rose. "She's not exactly my girlfriend."

There was a cocky antagonism there that Mortlock didn't like. "That's not what it looked like when you were stirring up trouble together at the Palace yesterday, but I don't care about your personal arrangements, son," he said. "I asked you where she was."

"That was supposed to be a peaceful protest."

"You're not listening to me," said Mortlock. "Now, unless you want to end up banged up with your pal Joffries, I suggest you tell me where the girl is."

When Henrik answered there wasn't noticeably more respect in his tone, but at least he knew well enough to stop mucking around. "She's visiting her mother."

Mortlock picked his way through the clutter, nosed into the kitchen area, the bathroom, both empty. Then he spotted a beaded curtain at the back of the room. Pulling it aside he found an additional space with a table in it.

Henrik followed. "I told you, Lottie's not here."

"I heard you." There was a tool box on the work table. Mortlock opened it and found an odd assortment of hammers, mallets, snips, grips, pincers and awls. "Do these belong to you?"

Henrik shook his head. "This is Lottie's workroom."

Mortlock remembered. The girl had professed to being some kind of an artist. "These don't look much like an artist's tools."

"Well, that shows you what you know about art, doesn't it."

Henrik lifted a canvas bundle down off the shelf behind him. He unwrapped it with great care, and once he had done so, Mortlock saw why. The bundle contained a dozen glass flowers. But it wasn't their beauty that arrested him, it was a memory of seeing similar before.

Links were forging in Mortlock's mind. The garden he had woken in after blacking out on Darkday night wasn't far from here. How had that happened? Was it possible that some silverfish child had guided him there? Hadn't there been a faint smell of brine in the air that morning? And his subsequent encounter with a silverfish had also led him to this pair. They were linked to everything that was happening. If only he could see how.

At the bottom of the toolbox Mortlock found a knife. The haft was thick, with a rubberised grip. The short blade had a chip out of it that made it pretty much useless for making a neat cut in anything. Mortlock turned it over in his hands. "What does she use this for?"

Henrik shrugged. "I've never seen her use it for anything. It's just an old knife."

Mortlock shook his head. "It's an old gutting knife," he corrected him. "The kind the fisherwives use down at the harbour when the catch comes in."

"Well, whatever it is. It's not been used for anything for some time. Look at the rust..."

Mortlock let the procession of thoughts play out across Henrik's face. It wasn't blood, it was rust right enough. This knife hadn't been plunged into anyone's straining neck, but as sure as Dark follows Full, the murder weapon was close to identical to this. And just for a moment the lad hadn't been sure. He tossed the knife back into the box and strode out of the work room.

Henrik trailed after him. "Sergeant?" he said. "What exactly do you want with us?"

Mortlock wheeled so sharply that Henrik almost ran into him. "What do I want? I'll tell you what I want, son. I want to find out who killed my friends. Tell me, you spending any time near the docks lately?"

Henrik's face set in a mean scowl. "It's where I work. Or did." He indicated his fat lip, his livid eye socket. "My colleagues weren't too happy to have me around."

"You don't say." Mortlock turned away. Something about this

latest nugget of information had his old copper's instinct singing. *Working at the docks, an unfriendly welcome.* He shoved his hands deep into the pockets of his old coat, felt something. "What's in here?" He indicated the closed door at the back of the main room.

"That's Lottie's room," Henrik said. Then, too quickly, "there's nothing in there."

"Really." Mortlock opened the door. There wasn't much, just a bed, a chest of drawers. "Going somewhere?"

Henrik shrugged. There was no point in denying the bag full of clothes. "Can you blame me? Your city's hardly opened its arms to me."

"What about your girlfriend? What about your child?"

Henrik scowled but kept his counsel. A glint caught Mortlock's eye. Something shiny on top of the shirts. A chain of familiar discs.

"And what's this?"

"What?"

"Take a look." Mortlock murmured, stepping back to allow the foreigner to bend over the bag, slipping the rubber cosh from his coat pocket.

"Oh, that? I just wanted something to remember them –"

One swift blow to the base of the skull and the boy crumpled. Mortlock stood over him, seized by the impulse to hit him again, harder, hurt the lad, *punish* him. The urgency of the impulse shocked him, but it passed, leaving him with an aching tension in his body, and that familiar gnawing fear about the state of his mind.

The Beckon Hill station wasn't far, but it was far enough when you had to transport a twelve stone deadweight. In the girl's junk room he found a tin bath with castors fixed to the base. Even getting Henrik downstairs to the street and tucked into his makeshift carriage had Mortlock sweating. Just as well it was mostly downhill from there.

On pushing Henrik through the station's doors, he found Telfer on the desk. "Here's our man, Lieutenant." Mortlock grinned with the satisfaction of doing his bit for the city, seeing the job done.

"This streak of piss?" Telfer looked sceptical. "*This* murdered Alfie Kremer?"

Henrik twitched in his bath, groaned.

"You can believe it or not," Mortlock said. "But I'd get him down to the cells before he wakes up just in case." He retreated for the door.

Telfer grunted. "Not going to give us a hand?"

Mortlock looked over to where the stairs began. Again he experienced a clutch of panic. He shook his head. "I got him this far. I'll leave that to you boys. And besides," he pushed open the door, "I've still got his accomplice to track down."

The question was where to look. All he had was a name and it was a common enough one. How many Mother Blakes would he have to track down before he found the right one?

"Sergeant." The shout intruded on his thoughts. It was a voice he recognised. And it belonged to a face he recognised. Chief Lytten emerged from the doorway of the pub where Mortlock had first met with Telfer. The door had been boarded up, one window broken and fringed with streaks of soot. Another casualty, it appeared, of the unending madness that had engulfed the city.

Mortlock crossed the road. "The secretary said you had been relieved of your duties, Mr Lytten."

Lytten smirked, then ducked through the door. When Mortlock followed he noticed that the wood around the lock had been smashed. And it was hard to reason why anyone had bothered. The interior of the pub was trashed. Glass, paper and shattered furniture lay jumbled on the floor. The carpet was still wet from the hoses used on the fire that had raged long enough around the corner window to turn the walls, floor and ceiling black with blistered ruin. The stench of mingled smoke and damp made Mortlock choke.

Lytten shrugged. He looked haggard. His clothes were unkempt, his eyes glittered. "But you and I, Sergeant," he said. "We know that duty – *true duty* – cannot simply be set aside. Don't we? We *know* that every man has his use in the Lunane's machine and he cannot simply decide to cease his service to the city."

Mortlock felt the same clammy fear that he always experienced in Lytten's office. That feeling of being surrounded by something terrible, something that started with the touch of fingers. He rallied himself. "Is that what your silverfish visitors told you in your late night get-togethers? To be a good servant?"

"Them?" Lytten's face twisted into a scowl. "Sneaky liars. I had to meet them there or they would have come to my home. Do you know what they told me?" He didn't wait for a reply. "They *told* me it didn't matter if that lad got away. That it didn't matter if people discovered the truth about the king's person. They *told* me there was a new cycle beginning, and that none of it would matter. That's what those liars said." Lytten shuffled close with a sly smile. "But we showed them, didn't we, my friend? We showed them that men of duty are not swayed from their service, did we not?"

Mortlock shook his head. "I had no part in whatever this –"

"Ha!" Lytten barked. "But you did. That was why I sought you out from the start. And you performed *so well.*"

The fear again, eroding Mortlock's resolve now. "What are you talking about?"

The chief ignored him. "Except for this one last time. I gave you a very explicit instruction. You were to find him and kill him. But what have you done? You've offloaded him onto an entire police station." Somehow Lytten had moved closer. In an eye blink his splayed fingers were in front of Mortlock's face. Then they were pressing hard on his temple and he felt himself unfold. "Have you still got the knife?"

Mortlock's fingers found their way to a secret pocket in the hem of his old coat. The knife was a short, ugly thing. The blade, none too sharp; the haft wrapped in string that was stained rusty brown.

"Then get over there and finish the job."

Without argument, Mortlock turn and left.

Lottie sat naked, shivering on the bed. She ignored the whispering cabal in the corner of the room. Let them whisper. The longer they talked, the longer before she was subjected to their hands again. Those hands: white, soft, warm. All over her body, as if they owned it.

A conclusion reached, the most senior of the white-starched matrons came over.

"You may dress now."

Lottie just nodded. All of her screaming defiance was long since spent. "So, my mother was right, was she?"

"The Mother is never wrong, dear." A moue of unwelcome sympathy. "You're seven and a half months gone."

"It's not even a month," Lottie said, but saying it didn't change the facts. One month ago she had most certainly *not* been pregnant. Now she was. Impossible, but nonetheless true. Even if she chose to disregard the perverse wisdom of the Church, there was no denying the evidence of her own body.

"This is a most remarkable child."

"Is that supposed to make me feel better?"

When the nurses fluttered out Lottie placed her hands on her belly, now a tight, white distension rippled with straining pink lines. During the two hours of the examination, she had grown over half an inch. *Remarkable*, wasn't the word. She dressed so she wouldn't have to look at it.

The obligatory minion was waiting outside. The pale, bony girl, whose name was Cara, was the same one who had delivered her mother's message the night she found her luck in The Rottens. "The Mother requests…" she began, but Lottie didn't have the heart for any more of that kind of talk.

"Don't speak. Just take me."

The girl obeyed instantly and without complaint. Lottie had occasionally felt sorry for those gullible unfortunates that skivvied for her Mother and the other office holders, but she didn't feel inclined to express her pity right now.

They went straight up to the Bleeding room. Of all of the parts of the Church, this was the one Lottie had always hated the most. Her mother's inner sanctum, where the serious business of the Church was conducted. It was both a heart and a womb, and the symbology employed in the furnishing was as crass as it was extensive. She detested the sight of those velvet hangings, thick as suffocation and dark as menstrual blood, the material rotted through and cleverly mended in a constant battle against the month's destructive force. They were hypocrisy in a nutshell. The celebration of the monthly cycles, of change as a natural force, was all well and good. Just as long as it was done conservatively. Just as long as nothing actually changed.

Lottie hated the walls, ribbed floor to ceiling with the spines of books, lending the impression that this was a place of learning. She knew that the books were set so solidly into place that you could see your reflection in the vitric. She loathed too the acrid, lemon and hot pepper aroma of burning seagrass. The many hours she had spent sitting downstairs with the other daughters weaving the stiff stalks into ceremonial hoops, Lottie considered slave labour.

But all of those were just general observations about the Church and the hypocritical paraphernalia that went with it. Compared to the things that had happened personally to her in this room, they were inconsequential.

Thirteen years old. Up at the crack of Darkday morning and made to bleed into the ceramic bowl forced between her knees. Feeling the heat trickle down the inside of her legs. Being exhorted by the other women, those that were not weeping and wailing with the hysterics of Dark, to join in with the cycle. Her mother's voice: *Come on, girl. You can do better than that. Give us your spent. You're a woman of the Church now.*

Lottie never had *done better*, not the way her mother meant. Her period had never locked with the moon's phasing the way the other women's did. Her body's timing had remained inconstant – wilful and capricious, as if she were doing it out of spite.

Well, it seemed she was now making up for the years of disappointment. Her mother beamed up at her from the cushions scattered in the centre of the burgundy wool rug. The floor around her was strewn with paper – the hand-drawn charts and diagrams whose intelligence the old bitch alone seemed able to interpret with any accuracy.

"There she is." She said it in the same voice she had always used when showing the child Lottie off to the Church's devotees. "The little mother."

Lottie was so weary. "Can I sit down?"

"Of course you can, moonbeam. Pull up a cushion." Her mother wheezed out a laugh. "Better make it a big one, eh?"

The effort of lowering herself to the floor left Lottie short of breath. "I want to know what's happening to me."

Now that it was just the two of them, without the fawning audience to play to, Lottie's mother's face relaxed to embody the kindness that Lottie had forgotten she could be capable of. "Why don't you stop fighting everyone that tries to help you then, hen?"

Lottie opened her mouth to protest, but it was true. Everything that had happened to her since the last Fullday had dragged her deeper into something she didn't understand and, like a vortex, closer and closer to the Church. It might have been lonely up in her little eerie on the periphery of society, but at least it had been peaceful, and she had been able to do pretty much anything she wanted. But then had come Henrik, and Blackwood's little rebellion, and all of a sudden she was caught up in the centre of the biggest upset Glassholm had seen since Lunane knew when – probably Founding Day itself.

And *this*. This was the worst of it.

What had Henrik said? That not one person in Glassholm had free will? She'd thought him wrong, convinced that she lived her life according to no one's whims but her own.

Her mother leaned forward. "Tell me what you know," she said. "And then I'll tell you what I know. And we'll see what we can make of it after that, eh?"

Lottie nodded and then told her everything. About meeting Henrik. About taking him to see Ruby, and about the growing support for rebellion. Then she talked about what had happened to her at the Halfday, feeling the foetus react to the Lunane's scrutiny amid all the furore and the horrible sudden growth that followed, driving her to the decision that abortion was the only option, and she had to come home.

When she finished, her mother was frowning, her fingers fluttering through a sheaf of notes.

"What is it? What have I said?"

"Nothing, dear." A lacquered nail scanned handwritten text before the sheet was cast aside and another snatched up. "It really is the most remarkable thing..."

Lottie plucked the calculations from her mother's fingers. "Tell me."

There was near panic in her mother's face. "He's interfering," she whispered. "That bastard. He knows, and..." Her eyes widened. "*Of course he knows*. And now he's fighting back. He's trying to stop us, cheat us out of our rightful time."

"I don't understand. You're scaring me."

The older woman crooked a finger at Lottie's face. "Good!" she cried. "Good, girl. We should be afraid of him. He'll try every trick he knows to cling on, but his time is waning. It's our time now. The Age of Mothers..."

"Who? Who are you talking about?"

"Why, the patriarchal pontiff hisself, of course. The Lunane." Lottie's mother got up, tottered across the room to a darkwood cabinet in the corner. It wasn't a large piece of furniture, nor was its design especially refined, but Lottie had fervently wished never again to lay eyes on those red-black doors with the rough-and-smooth scrimshawed handles.

She looked away, cast her eye over the drift of paper: all the charts and tables, the diagrams and amateur astronomical calculations. "You're telling me the Lunane's responsible for what's happening to me?"

She heard the snick of the latch, the scrape of a heavy object being lifted off the stone shelf.

"Not at all, girl," came her mother's voice from the other side of the room. The cabinet doors clipped shut again. "Your baby is without doubt the one ordained. It's been in the divinations for centuries. The alignments are quite unmistakeable."

Lottie picked up one of the papers. The sheet was new, the ink fresh and black. It contained some figures, a bunch of indecipherable notes and a sketch that showed the moon – personified with a face, long eyelashes and rose-bud mouth – occluding the larger disc of the sun.

The eclipse that no one had seemed to know about. Was that why her mother's voice held a tremor of doubt? That didn't sound *quite unmistakeable*.

"Except?"

"Except nothing. His time is at an end. His eclipse is nigh, and no amount of moving his moon around in the sky will put off the inevitable." A fat shadow loomed over Lottie's shoulder, a wheezing breath on her cheek. "Clear a space girl."

Lottie sighed inwardly, but did as she was told, clearing the papers to the side to allow her mother to place the object on the floor in front of her.

And there it was. The blood bowl. The Church's most sacred possession. Underneath its thick layer of glassy vitric, the glaze had discoloured and mazed to an uneven moonish off-white. There was a functional beauty to it.

And its contents stank.

There's was nothing as distinctive as the smell of old blood. It brought Lottie right back to this room every time. Old blood. Dark as the wood of the cabinet it was kept in. A viscous puddle, complicated by clots and framed by a spattering of dried-out, rusty splashes.

Her mother retook her seat on the cushions. "Hand," she said.

"What?"

"Give me your hand, girl."

Lottie offered her left hand. Her mother took it with a smile, and then with a swift twist delivered Lottie a jab of pain. Lottie snatched her hand back, but not quickly enough to avoid dripping fresh rubies into the pot. She sucked her thumb as her mother wiped the tiny knife on the rim. The coppery flavour made her gag.

"Don't fuss so, Charlotte," he mother said. "If you were that bothered about a wee prick you wouldn't be in the trouble you are now, would you?"

Lottie scowled at her, but was prevented from replying by a second bout of gagging as her mother spat on her own fingers and then stirred the spent blood with them. Then she did something Lottie had never been permitted to see before, although she had always known in theory how the Church's divinations were produced.

Her mother licked her bloody fingers, rubbed them against her gums. Then she breathed sharp, rolled her eyes dramatically. Her lips parted, revealing the pink stain on her teeth, a gobbet thread of red on her tongue.

"Oh, yes," Lottie's mother mumbled. "He's interfering all right."

"But how is that possible? To meddle with nature like that." *To meddle with me.*

Her mother emitted a sound that was half laugh and half choke. "For the Lunane many unlikely things are possible," she said. "That's how he created Glassholm after all. But what he's doing now, what he's trying to do to you... that's desperate stuff, Charlotte."

"What is he trying to do to me? For once in your life explain yourself in plain terms."

Her mother's eyes opened. The pupils were enormously dilated. She ran her stubby tongue along her teeth. "Plain terms is it?" she said. "If you had paid heed to your lessons –"

"Mother," Lottie breathed. "Please."

That settled something in her mother's mind. A stiff nod. "Very well then, in plain terms. For nearly all of its two hundred and thirty eight years of existence – since the first Mother discovered there was prophecy in the blood – our Church has known that there would come a time when our city would no longer be ruled by the Lunane, but by a woman. A Luness." She reached into the cushions behind her and pulled out a roll of paper. "See here? *When Nature and the Sky agree, according to the testimony of the blood and the moon and stars, the Mother will give birth to a new cycle, a new order, a new way of living.*" Lottie's mother's eyes sparkled. "That's our Queen, that is. *That's your baby.*"

Lottie had always thought the Church's divinations pretty vague, but given all that had happened in recent days the content of this one was compelling. And being here, in this building, this hateful room, made it all seem all the more plausible. "And how is the Lunane trying to stop this?"

"By interfering with your unborn, girl. What you felt at the petitioning. That was him."

Lottie remembered how the Lunane had looked at her just before the burning, squirming began in her belly. "He's trying to kill my daughter?"

Lottie could not tell if the look on her mother's face now was one of fury or fear. "Oh, yes, Charlotte. At the very least."

"Then why didn't he succeed?"

"Because she was stronger," her mother replied, sly triumph slipping into her eyes.

But Lottie knew that with the blood there was always the point where divination passed over into zealous wish-fulfilment, and she suspected that point had just been passed. Not that it mattered. Either way she looked at it, she and her unnatural child were the prize pieces in *someone's* plans.

Chapter 19

After Anton and Mia left the Foundry and its estates behind they came to the mills that lined the upper reaches of the Cord, then they followed the waterside road north to the place where it squeezed in through the city walls. The River Gate. It took them two painful hours to get that far. Dawn was still some way off when they reached the gate, but Mia moaned plaintively when Anton hesitated on the threshold.

Anton had never ventured beyond these walls. He made Mia wait as he took time to appreciate the precisely dressed stone, the wide-flung doors of oak and hammered iron that separated what he knew from what he didn't. The shell of the machine. The hesitation persisted, stretched to the point of incapacity, and the suspicion kindled that his feet were frozen not merely by unfamiliarity, but another's control. He searched himself again, but there wasn't even an echo of a gloating laugh to betray the king's presence. Where was he then? Was he in hiding? Had the machine that tethered the moon finally failed?

This escape was turning out to be suspiciously straightforward.

Anton stretched out with his foot. Nothing happened.

He took one more steadying breath, and left the city.

On the other side, the road under his shoes remained the same grey flag but the sky was bigger, the night darker, the breeze colder, wilder. And the moon, currently on the southern side of the city, was surely smaller. He knew, of course, that the satellite circled not only the city but the entire island and a great area of the surrounding sea as well, but still it felt as if he were leaving its protection behind.

According to his trusty pocket watch, they left the city at two thirty in the morning. When they emerged from the other side of the forest that lay at the end of a traipse through stubbly fields it was gone four. And by the time they sat perched like unhappy gulls on a rocky outcrop topping a cliff that dwarfed any of those that skirted the city, it was close to six.

Anton clutched the watch through the folds of his robe, rubbed its solidity through the material, felt the vibration of each tick.

They waited. The sun rose, turned the sea to furious molten iron. Mia huddled on her rock and stared out at the waves. It appeared that for now their journey had come to an end.

As the morning wore on, Anton's stomach began to growl, but the coat's pockets were empty and the plants around them were wild, barbed things with nothing approaching a fruit among them. With nothing else to do, he watched the waves too. They swelled grey and smooth in the distance, sleek and powerful as the backs of leviathans, and rolled in with a deceptive aggression that only made itself fully apparent with a final roaring lunge and snap of frothing jaws at the splintered, but enduring rocks.

The tide ebbed, falling back to gather its energy and plan its next attack with slow, saurian cunning.

Anton tried to remove his coat to examine his arm. The grey sleeve was stained where the blood had soaked through the improvised sash bandage, and the whole lot was now glued together. While they walked, the pain had subsided, but even tugging gently at the material revived it like waking a sleeping snake. It needed attention, but what were the chances of happening across a doctor out here?

Anton donned the coat again, and crossed over to sit beside Mia. "What are we doing exactly?"

The girl ignored him. Her glossy dark eyes remained fixed on the sea and the glistening exposed rocks down at the shoreline. Her lips moved in her habitual silent mutter.

He tried again, indicated the sea, the cliffs, the sullen trees with a sweep of his good arm. "Is this it?"

It was no use. The girl would not be distracted from her staring and her mumbling.

Anton rose and stretched his stiff muscles, buckled Spitz's army coat tighter to seal out the blustering, salty wind. He looked around. There was a thicket a little way back that looked the likeliest place to search for something edible. The leaves shivered. There, that was encouraging. If there was an animal in the thicket there just had to be food of some description nearby.

Anton's mental image was of a rabbit, maybe a fox, but better not take any chances. 'Animal' was a pretty wide category. Walking towards the thicket Anton clapped his hands to scare whatever was in there away.

"Ay-ay-ay!" he shouted, ignoring Mia's glance of disapproval. There was a definite movement. Foliage rustled. Perhaps something larger than a rabbit after all. He lifted a leafy branch and peered into the thicket. It was dark, but he made out it the shape of a head, the hump of a back or a shoulder. Two huge, round eyes watching him.

Then the thing unfolded to five times the size that it had first appeared. The way it knuckled forward a pace then sat back was familiar. The way it leapt at him was instantly recognisable.

He'd known their flight was too easy. He remembered what Hogarth had said about the Friends being able to find anyone. They had deployed the crabs to defend him at the Palace. They had sent the ugly, metal monkey to retrieve him from outside Krista's window. It was no surprise to see the thing again.

Anton was too slow to sidestep the attack. The impact was like a cannonball hitting him in the chest, and it knocked him clear out of the thicket. He blinked, gasped for breath.

"Augh!" Mia beckoned to him to join her at the cliff edge.

Anton started to scrabble towards her, but a powerful fist grabbed him by the sleeve. His injured arm burned and he found himself staring straight into the monkey's blank eyes. He braced for whatever came next, but the monkey paused. Its tail whipped. Its eyes rolled in their sockets. Its saw-blade jaws worked absently.

Cautiously, Anton tried to prise the fingers from his arm. There was no reaction, but the grip remained unbreakable. He looked to Mia, but she had gone back to her perch and her mumbling.

"I could use some help here, please."

That earned him a scornful glance, nothing more.

When, after some full minutes, the monkey had still not moved, Anton wriggled out of the coat and left it dangling in the steel beast's grip.

"Thank you," he said, sitting down beside Mia, but facing inland where he could keep an eye on the contraption. His injured arm burned where the bloody crust had been ripped away.

She didn't look at him, but he thought her lips twisted into the thinnest of smiles.

"This is the limit of the Lunane's control then?"

A bob of her head.

"Thanks for telling me." Deciding to put up with his hunger after all, Anton found a grassier part of the cliff-top to lie on. "Give me a nudge when the boat gets here."

That earned him a raised eyebrow, a sorry shake of the head. "*Moa?*" Then Mia creased up with silent laughter.

Anton was shaken awake. He was cold and his body ached all over. More than once during the rest of the day and the long night they'd waited here he had resolved to rescue his coat from the monkey machine, but, even though the thing had not moved an inch, it emitted strange squeals and groans. Anton rationalised these sensibly as the metal contracting as the temperature dropped. But they dissuaded him from approaching it again.

He blinked in the daylight. He had slept longer than he would have thought possible.

Mia shook him again.

"What is it?" he said, scrutinising the monkey. Had it moved closer during the night? It didn't seem so, but he couldn't be sure. Mia huffed to get his attention, then pointed down towards the cove. He'd quizzed her repeatedly about why they were here, what they were waiting for, but every time her answer was to point at the waves. Despite everything he hoped that there would, after all, be a boat, but of course there was none. Even so, it appeared that what they had been waiting for had arrived.

She gestured again, impatient. He looked and saw the cove, the rocks the waves, and then he understood. Low tide. They must have missed it by a matter of hours yesterday.

Mia crept to the lip of cliff, her intention all too apparent. The edge bristled with whin grass like unruly hair.

"I'm not going down there," Anton said. "There's no path."

A wicked smile reminded him who knew best out here. Carefully, Mia chose her spot amongst the wind-whipped stalks, and then stepped over the edge and dropped from sight.

Anton lurched to the place where she had vanished, pushing away visions of a broken-doll body spread-eagled on the black rocks.

Despite that, it came as no real surprise to find the girl's upturned face staring back at him, her eyes shining. She waited on a hidden ledge, her eyes shining, her grin gleeful-black through the billowing storm that the wind made of her hair.

A sighing sound blew through his inner ear. It could have been the wind in the grass or the susurrus of the trees, but it sounded like a warning. And he was almost certain the leaden resistance in his legs, the thick recalcitrance of his fingers, were not of his own making.

Mia laughed aloud. The wild ululation would have been unpleasantly out of place back in the Palace, but was absolutely terrifying out here.

Anton peeked over the edge again. The perspective swam dizzyingly. He still didn't know what Mia's motives were, but if she had meant him harm she could easily have exposed him to the mobs back in the city or pushed him over while he slept. He had to trust that she meant well.

Gingerly, Anton eased himself over the edge. His feet dangled in the air for much longer than he would have thought possible before he finally felt the ledge with his toes. He hugged the wall, gripping what he could of its contours. The wind had fists and clutching claws which alternately tried to push and then pull him off the ledge. He opened his eyes. Mia was already a distance along the ledge, beckoning impatiently. Anton's groan was snatched away, but he had no option now but to edge towards her.

The descent took an age. The rock face was precipitous and cruelly faceted. Mia skipped ahead with an ease that indicated a familiarity with this place that made him wonder, but Anton could not go any faster. Not until he stood with shaking legs on a tiny strip of sand. The high tide mark came right up to the cliff wall, a line of weed and shells and other detritus at the foot of the edifice he had just negotiated. A large crab tapped at the rock face in a bemused manner. Anton felt the cliff lowering above him, but he did not, could not, follow the crab's upwards gaze.

He looked outwards instead, and that was almost as bad. The tight smile of damp sand was manageable, the sloping arêtes of wet, black rock even helped by providing a framing enclosure to the view, but beyond that there was too much sky, too much light, too much noise and so much effervescent ozone that his lungs felt like balloons.

From the city, the sky and sea were abstract entities. It wasn't necessary to give them any more thought than that. No one in their right mind – and madness was surely a pre-requisite for the island's fishermen – got closer than this to the sea.

Yet Mia was walking right into it.

"You have to be kidding me," Anton shouted after her, but she laboured on over the skittery rocks. At first he thought she was going to try and climb the great tilted slab that thrust out into the waves like the side of a capsized ship, but the scale of it dwarfed her. Instead she waded along its edge and then, waist-deep so that her skirt floated around her middle, she rounded a mound of scree and vanished.

"Mia!" Panic made him lurch forward into the tongues of the waves, but it was something else that stayed him after the first step. The same inertia as he had felt at the city gates and the cliff's edge. This time, though, the Lunane's voice finally returned too.

You will not go there.

Now the presence was palpable, but it vacillated like the waves.

"Will I not?" Anton breathed. He hadn't fancied wading into the sea after Mia, but being *forbidden* from doing so lent him the defiance he required to splash forward again. Water swilled around his ankles, the sand pliant under his soles.

He felt the mental pull and prepared to surrender control, but the tugging was not strong enough to drag him under. He stumbled another step and felt the Halfday shoe sucked from his foot by the soft sand. The water was cold, but it was also cleansing. Laughing, Anton kicked off the remaining shoe.

"Your hold is not so strong out here," he said, "away from your people."

I should not need to exercise control. The voice echoed, oddly phased. *Your loyalty should be enough. All your loyalties…*

"I have been nothing but loyal to this city," Anton cried. "Much thanks as I have received for it. I have lost my wife's love and abandoned my life's work to help you."

And you failed. Just like all the rest.

"I might have got somewhere if you had not interfered." He threw his hands up in frustration. "It is no wonder your subjects have turned against you."

Turned against me? The mental laugh was lost in the fizzing rush of surf. *Stick to your simple machines, Engineer. The mechanism I have built here is far more complex than you can comprehend. The wheel will turn, the phase will shift, and I will have them back. I will wax again.*

Anton laughed at the sky because there was nowhere else to direct his scorn. "You think this is all part of some cycle? Glassholm has never seen troubles like this. I've seen the journals, remember."

A little maintenance, the voice rumbled, faded. *Is all that's required.*

"It's too late for that now."

Too la... The voice distorted, the volume dropping entirely. Only the sound of the waves and the wind now. The water splashed at his knees. The tide was coming in. If he did not go now his chance to follow Mia would be missed. It might already be too late.

He was stumbling and sloshing through the water in the direction of the gap in the rocks when the voice returned. It was so faint he almost missed it.

There are contingencies, idiot Engineer. There are. Contingencies.

With that the Lunane's presence was finally and completely gone from his mind.

Anton waded on until he reached the place where Mia had vanished, and saw that what had looked from the land to be a continuous finger of rock was in fact a trick concocted out of geology and perspective. And in the gap between the one stratified slab and the next was the inverted vee of a cave.

Anton climbed up on to the shelf, and paused there to listen, but he could hear nothing from within except for the echoes of the echoes of the sounds of waves.

As he turned the corner from Hatchardhill into Mael Street, Mortlock brooded over the wasted time. It had taken more than a day to locate the Blake girl. He'd searched everywhere he could think of. Her neighbours barely knew her. The Promise Centre folks were tight-lipped, and had been reluctant even to speak to him. He suspected that the state his face was in following the latest blackout, the swollen mash of his knuckles, the spray of blood up the sleeve of his coat, had much to do with that, but going home to clean up – let alone worrying about where and how he had got into a fight – would have delayed unforgivably his search for the girl. She'd told no one who her family was. The perfect *Miss Nobody*. It simply never occurred to Mortlock that a girl like that would be connected to the infamous *Phamie* Blake. By the time he made the connection a good deal of time was already lost.

Every copper in Glassholm knew the Church of Women. *Temple of Strife*, the boys at the station called it, in honour of the maritally-related disturbances that regularly took place along this street. Not a popular assignment being called out here. The residents had little love for the Lunane's officials.

Mortlock drew himself up to his full height, took a deep breath and delivered three firm knocks to the blood red door. It swung ajar.

The hall was hushed. A distant gabble of voices indicated activity elsewhere, but here was deserted. The door to his left whose hand painted shingle read, *Remedies*, was shut firmly, but the other door, the one that said *Consultations*, opened and a matron in a starched pinafore emerged.

"I'm sorry, sir." She looked him up and down, offered the thinnest of smiles. "The Church is not open to visitors at present."

"I'm here on Police business," Mortlock said. In his old copper's coat it didn't feel too much like a lie. He looked past her into the consultation room beyond. Chairs lined the wall. "I want to see Lottie Blake. I know she's here."

She had to be – she wasn't anywhere else.

The matron edged the door closed with the toe of her boot. "You must realise that many of our visitors come here for protection. You can't expect us to confirm or deny the presence of any of our guests."

The speech was boiler-plate. They turned away enquiries like this all the time when husbands, families, friends came clamouring. "Fine," Mortlock said. "Then I'll see her mother."

The matron stiffened. "The Mother is very busy, sir. Perhaps, you'd like to make an appointment?"

Mortlock lost patience. He pushed past her, shouldered open the door. "I'll wait."

The matron gave him a look that told him he would be in for a long wait, then headed for the stairs.

Mortlock entered a waiting room. In one corner there was a desk, and a door that presumably led to the consulting room. The chairs around the walls were an odd assortment. One of them was occupied by an old lady swathed in a voluminous quantity of purple fabric. Her arms were folded under her ample bosom and she was snoring like a flatulent monkey.

Mortlock took a seat at the end of the row.

The music of the Church of Women filtered through the bones of the building. The drone of voices, the measured pulse of footfalls, the occasional line of song. The room was airless. Mortlock rubbed his eyes. His cheek, jaw and knuckles throbbed heartbeat slow. He wasn't sure if he'd slept in the last forty eight hours. He popped open his shirt collar button, took a deep breath.

Someone entered the room above. They crossed the ceiling – once, and then back again. Again and then back. *Trip, trip, trip – pause. Trip, trip – pause.* He wondered what was going on up there. What did they do, these women? *Church* was a foreigner word from the Jealous Lands where people were ruled by invisible kings instead of a real, living one. Vaguely he thought it might have had something to do with having a communal faith in something that would never happen.

Young boys around here scared each other with stories of ritual sacrifice, dared each other to creep up to the red door. When they were men they knew better, but the place remained tainted by suspicion. These were the people who would turn up when your wife went into labour, perform their mysteries and leave you with a child in your arms. And that was all the contact you were wise to have with them if you didn't want to be one of those men who came chapping at the door, pleading for an audience with your own wife.

Shirley had related only the bare bones of her own tragic experience, but was it really possible that they had stolen her child, telling her it had died at birth? These women might have strange ways, but they weren't monsters. They were just people like everyone else, as subject to the rule of the Lunane's law as the rest of them. Listening to the easy rhythm of the house, it didn't feel like a place of dark secrets. It was a place with heart, a nurturing centre for those in trouble, a safe place to be.

He woke up. There were fingers gently cradling his scalp. The wrong fingers. These fingers were soft, fat, warm. And instead of that drained, groggy feeling he was used to, his skin tingled now with energy.

"Shh, now son," someone said.

"What?"

"Shoosh, now Jonathan. You've got a real mess in this noggin of yours. Sit at peace and let your Auntie Ruby sort it out for you."

Mortlock's eyes snapped open and he was confronted with a

weird landscape of ancient skin, pale and veined as aged cheese, and so wrinkled that it was only the winking of a rheumy eye that identified it as a face.

He pushed away, chair clattering the wall. "What are you doing?"

The little-girl pout was obscene. "Nothing you're not needing, Jonathan, son. Don't look so shocked, you must be used to the salving by now."

"What do you mean?" And then: "How do you know my name?"

The old woman sat down beside him and folded her hands demurely in her lap. "As to the first," she said. "I mean that your wee memory's been messed around with so much it looks like a monkeys' nest, so it does. And don't look at me like that." Her wagging finger forestalled interruption. "I take pride in my work, and I wouldn't have left my old husband with a brain in the state yours is in. Which brings me to your second. I might be old, son, but I never forget a face – or a name to go with it. You've been to see me once before, Sergeant John Mortlock, but it was a long time ago. You were a very frightened, very angry young man. And you had something you wanted very badly to forget."

Mortlock stared at the woman who called herself Ruby. "I don't know you."

Ruby laughed. "Naturally. When your memories are buried by Ruby Blake, they stay buried, son." Her brow furrowed. "Only…"

"What?"

"Well, whoever has been messing in your head is none too skilled. And someone else has been in there too, unpicking the corners of the stitchery… things are coming loose."

"Loose?"

"Mmm." She stretched her fingers towards his forehead. "If you've got a couple of hours to spare, I'll see what I can do to tidy you up some."

Mortlock shuttled onto the next chair, repulsed by the idea of the woman touching him again. "I'm not going to be here that long."

Ruby shrugged. "Suit yourself," she said. "Seems a shame though. A nice lad like you."

With that she stood and then shuffled out. Mortlock listened to her laboured breathing, her feet on the stairs, and then he was alone with only the sounds of the Church going on above.

A couple of hours?

He waited, but in the end he found that he could stand this place nowhere near as long as that.

It began to rain as Mortlock returned to the Beckon station house. A cold slap in the face that stung almost as much as the frustration. He took a belt of black from his flask, and then another, but the drink did nothing to erase the memory of Ruby Blake's fingers, or the images that flashed in his mind as he walked.

The ache in his fists; he recalled raining punches on Henrik in his cell. The loup in his cheek; Telfer landing him one to get him to stop. Mortlock yelling about service and duty. About checks and balances.

Checks and balances. That was what Prunty had always said. Checks and balances kept things from getting out of hand. Sixteen, Mortlock had been, in his new uniform with the hems adjusted by his proud mum. His first shift at Dark had showed him how wife-beaters were kept in *check*, the unpleasant methods that had sometimes to be employed to make sure that *balance* was maintained. And he'd joined in, sure enough, because he was a good lad and he did what he was told.

Mortlock stopped, forced himself to breathe. Ruby Blake had told him the truth. That his amnesia wasn't caused by the accident after all. That he'd *chosen* to forget.

The rain came on harder at the bottom of the hill, but it didn't obliterate the stain of smoke from the pub across from the station. And now he remembered Lytten with his hard fingers and harder instructions. And he remembered times before, the blackouts that were not blackouts but ripped-out pages, erasures to keep him useful for service, to prevent him for remembering what he did...

He could not. *Would not.* Remember.

In the station house there was no obvious sign of rumpus, nothing broken, nothing spilled. No blood, no mess, no noise.

No people.

A half-eaten apple browned on the booking desk, a stack of reports set out for vitricking. "Telfer?" There was no answer, but he didn't expect one. Little point in searching up here, he had to go down to the cells.

The descent was like walking into the waters of the Lunane's lagoon. The sudden weight that made his feet drag on the steps, distended his stomach like he'd swallowed one the clouts they used to weight the corpses of the dead.

A long-hidden parcel of memory fell open, like the wrapping of a Founding Day gift, probed and loosened by impatient childish fingers.

And now he remembered, following Lytten's elisions, the company of children. Wet fingers, tugging ineffectually at his brutalised memory. He thought now that the crucified monkey was left for him, to try and shock him into remembering. To make him stop.

But stop what? Even now he *would not* remember.

Charles Lytten's hackwork and Ruby Blake's older, neater stitchery unravelled together as he passed the table and chair at the stair foot, the stack of dark-wasted novels, the board nailed to the wall with its numbered iron cleats, each dangling their own black key. The passage led around the corner to the cells themselves. There were five solid steel doors. Dread flooded him like sea water. There was even a fishy taint in the frigid air.

Mortlock shook it off. He wasn't sixteen any more. He grabbed a fistful of keys from the cleats. "Telfer?" In the silent passage, the doors stood like closed faces. He tried the first. The cell was empty. The lamp in the wall sconce exposed a regimented bunk, a neatly swept floor. The next two cells were the same. He approached the remaining two doors with caution, wrinkling his nose at the growing stench of rotting fish. The old brown brick at the passage end had been chipped. The splatter marks confirmed that there had been a struggle here. Mortlock scraped with a fingernail. It came away rimmed red-brown.

The cell door on the left was ajar and, as soon he entered, Mortlock knew that this was where they'd kept Henrik. His knuckles throbbed as he remembered the scuffle that overturned the bed, tumbled its thin mattress, spilled the piss bucket across the floor. He remembered knocking the boy down, but having to leave him to deal with Telfer.

Aside from the mess, though, the cell was empty. There was only one place left to look.

When he tried to open it, the door to the last cell stuck against something on the other side. Mortlock pushed harder, then gagged. The overpowering stink of rot was ten times worse than it had been from the passage. The cell was piled high with crab carcases. Telfer had said something about that hadn't he? That they'd been forced by the sheer numbers of these bastards to scoop them up off the streets and store them in the cells.

Mortlock held his nose and saw that a path had been cleared through the carcases. The contents of another parcel came to light.

Blue brick, yellow brick, green brick, black.

Decades of boot scuffs and Dark attrition had worn the paint down to almost nothing, but there were traces. A corner of blue, a rim of yellow. The green might have been algae, the black only dirt, but if you knew what to look for, knew where to step, you were rewarded with a wobble underfoot, a depression and a click. With a groan of masonry a door-shaped section of the rear wall swung inwards and revealed a stair head. The dread weight dragged Mortlock down once more.

If the air in the cells had been as cold and suffocating as the sea, that at the foot of the crumbling steps was like trying to breath at the bottom of the ocean.

Mortlock groped in the darkness and found a rope handrail cleated to the wall. He inched along, feet scuffing, free hand questing ahead. If the passage was built to the dimensions of the station house above, it could not be as long as it seemed, but a subjective age passed before his fingers met something more than air. The something was a cold, inconstant, stranded thing that swung away from his touch. He felt the movement of air and then the edges and planes of the thing brushed against his face with a silvery jingle. Another memory unwrapped.

His heart went cold.

Knowing this for what it was, Mortlock's fingers snared a strand of the curtain, and he yanked it violently from its fastening point in the ceiling.

He knew too that the door at the end of the passage lay only a few steps further on. And he knew what he would find when he opened it.

The Dark Room.

The room was large and roughly square, the walls uneven, hewn directly from the rock. Candles had been left burning. They did not quite show Mortlock everything, but exposed enough. The organic, layered patina on the floor might have looked at first glance like some coppery species of lichen, but Mortlock knew it was blood. Old blood, and not so old too. The hinged iron grate from which could be heard the distant rush of water was where most of the blood had collected. Along the wall there were chairs with manacles.

Mortlock remembered, and his body began to shake the way it had when he'd been a good-hearted lad of sixteen.

The Crew had done things here. Extracted information, punished the deserving or, sometimes, just let off a bit of steam. But it hadn't just been crooks. Amazing how inventive the mind could be when dreaming up justification. *Bad family, wrong crowd, teaching them a lesson before they got started.* Prunty had helped them, not only in fiddling the duty logs and cleaning up afterwards, but he'd had his own chair down here. He had sat there and watched many of the terrible deeds done in this room.

Mortlock had been a good lad sure enough, a conscientious boy. He'd followed orders. But that wasn't what he'd employed Ruby Blake to help him forget. And it wasn't why Charles Lytten had sought him out, given him a job when no one else would. A special task. A dedicated service to the city. The shame burned through him.

Not so very many Darks had come and gone before he was offering suggestions, coming up with innovations that earned him kudos from the rest of the lads. Oh, how he had hated himself when the wax dawned. When he'd been clobbered on the head it had been a piece of luck for everyone. It'd been such a relief to distance himself from all of this, a public duty to drown those Dark instincts in black spirit in private every month.

The chairs were occupied. Five police uniforms, glistening sticky and red-black from collar to waist. The last five of Kremer's crew.

Mortlock approached the closest of them. Telfer's features were distorted in pallid agony. Mortlock hadn't particularly liked the lad and wondered now if Kremer had introduced his new Crew to the Dark Room. If perhaps there might be some justice found here. Even if they hadn't taken up the old practices, they knew about Henrik. Who he was. And had therefore been a danger to the city.

There was something clenched between Telfer's teeth. Mortlock could only see the rim of it, but he didn't need to prise the boy's jaws open to make sure. They would all have one on them.

Mortlock unclenched his fist. The jingling curtain had been a set up to warn those at work in the Dark room that someone was coming. The strand he had torn free had become knotted into a ball. Carefully he unwrapped the chain of linked discs.

Chapter 20

The cave became a tunnel, a rough bore through the rock. Anton quickly found himself in darkness but he stumbled on, tripping on stones, slipping on weed, sloshing through invisible pools, all the time cognizant of the tide rushing in behind him. There was no sign of Mia, and he became fixed on the notion he had been tricked into entering a dead end passage from which there was no escape.

Nevertheless he fumbled on. His bare feet burned, as painful now as the wound in his arm. His outstretched fingers slipped as he tried to feel his way along the walls, slick with slime or perhaps his own blood. His sodden robes threatened to trip him. His heart sped up because the echoing of the waves at his back was getting louder. He stopped. *Definitely louder.*

Anton broke into a blind run, only to emerge into a dazzle of sunlight. He stopped in surprise, and then took a shocked step backwards because his feet were inches from a precipice, a ragged lip that had trapped a knot of wrack, a scree of shells and the desiccated carcase of a crab. Beyond was a shaft of golden air that lanced through a cavern that rivalled the Castil tower in dimensions. The light's source was a blinding fissure in the distant ceiling. Everything else was in shadow.

He located Mia by her mumbling. There, perched on a rock at the halfway turn of a precipitous staircase that led to another beach. Anton stared. The Mia he had come to know in the Palace had always seemed a pale abomination, a transplanted thing at odds with her surroundings. Here, though, she was in her element. Out of the direct light, the shadows clothed her perfectly. Her rock was at the edge of a fatal drop, but she showed no concern. The smile on her black lips was for once without malice and her eyes darkled with contentment.

Joining her, he saw more of the dusky beach below. It was fringed by caves, around which were fishing nets spread out for mending, the hummocks of the hulls of black boats and moving smudges that had to be people. Mia's people. These could only be the Indigenes that the biographies told had been eradicated from the island back in the founding days.

Mia slid off her perch and offered him her small hand. He hesitated but then took it and found that, far from the clammy fish-flesh he had always imagined, the girl's skin was smooth and warm. Together they descended the switch-backed stairs, and before long Anton's aching toes were burrowing in soft, cool sand. Weariness turning his legs to tar and he sank to the ground.

"Thank you," he said.

Mia sat down beside him, legs crossed underneath her skirts. They were close to the water here. The waves rolled listlessly up the sand, so diminished from the continual thrashing assault that ringed the island that these spent rollers resembled the returning survivors of some gargantuan mythic war. The strange acoustics of the cavern even made the rhythmic roll and hiss sound like whispered war chants.

Anton sat up. He had been on the verge of falling asleep.

He *had* been asleep. The light that shafted in through the chink in the ceiling had dwindled to a glimmer, so clearly he'd been out for some hours. Sitting up, he realised that during that period of unconsciousness someone had taken care of him. His outer robe had been removed and placed over him, and his arm had been cleaned and properly dressed. He rubbed sand from his cheek, stretched out his legs, then yanked his feet back from the freezing water that had crept up on him unawares.

A soft laugh came from nearby. Anton peered into the gloom. He was not alone, but the bulky silhouette blotting the moonish lanterns that hung outside the caves was not Mia. The laugh tailed off to a rhythmic murmur that merged into an ongoing whispered conversation between the waves and the sand. It was a man's voice, and as Anton's ear became attuned he realised that it was counting. "... *two... three...*" he heard, the words rolling off, half submerged in the surf of the man's breath.

"You're awake, kingling" the silhouette said. "... *four... five...*"

Kingling? They knew who he had been, then. Of course they did. Mia had brought him here. To the scene of one of the Lunane's great victories, where he had slaughtered the Indigenes and claimed Glassholm for his own people once and for all. Only, some of those Indigenes had survived, and lived on, somehow, in secret. And five hundred years was a long time to nurture a grudge.

"I'm not *him*," Anton said.

"No? ... *six*..." The voice was musical, amused. The counting was bizarre, more like a subconscious tic than intentional utterances. And the speed of it seemed to dictate the frustrating pace of the man's speech. "I understood that in Glassholm, the Lunane was every man ... *seven... fifteen thousand four hundred and ninety eight...*"

"That's just a saying," Anton replied. "A patriotic children's song."

"... *one*... Yet it is true nevertheless. Or are you not living proof? *two*..." The man rose. "... *three*... My name is Coombs," he said. "Come in to the village. You must be starving."

Anton gripped the extended hand and was hoisted to his feet.

"Thank you," he said and followed the slow ... *four*... *five*... *six*... up the beach towards the lanterns at the cavern's rear.

In the ethereal illumination, Anton saw Coombs clearly at last. In the dark, with only the voice to go by, his mind had conjured a misshapen brute whom nature had gifted a pleasant sounding voice as some sort of compensation for whatever physical deficiencies generations of cave living had meted out. It was logical that people who lived in such a place as this, who had driven the Lunane to attempt to obliterate them, who put forward Mia as an acceptable representative to send to the city, could not be well-favoured by nature.

But that was Lunane's logic. It was the reasoning of balance, the arithmetic of conservation.

The figure that stood before him was that of an ordinary man. More or less. A little shorter than Anton himself perhaps, but he stood straight enough for a cave dweller, and if he was as pale as death about the face, that was understandable. His eyes were a watery blue, but he shared with Mia his thick, slick hair. That and, when he smiled, those black lips and razor teeth.

Coombs indicated the way along the lantern string. Past the boat caves was a deep crevice. Around it had been arranged a loop of those lamps, which Anton now saw were made from egg-cases, inflated and vitricked and fitted with candles.

"Who are you?" Anton's whisper followed Coombs into the narrow fissure, washed off the walls and fizzled away beneath the slow, steady beat of his companion's subvocal enumerations. Anton's initial instinct had been to dismiss this tic as symptomatic of the oddness he expected of the Indigenes, but it wasn't a tic. It didn't irrupt through Coombs' demeanour but rather underpinned it, as natural to him as breathing.

The counting man stopped. "It must be obvious by now ... *four...*" he said. "Every child knows who I am, Mr Dunn." His teeth glittered. "I'm the Derryman."

Anton's appreciation of the machine the Lunane had created out of Glassholm grew. Everything on this island had a place in it. Even children's fables had a function. There really was a monster lurking outside the city, waiting to pounce if any child dared to stray. Without recourse to the journals most people would only know of the island's Indigenes as one of the early obstacles that the Lunane had overcome in the Founding days. One of many hasps of gratitude that had bound them to their king in those early times. But he hadn't killed the aborigines. Here they were to this day, living in secret on the periphery of the island. Turned into figments and cautionary tales. But why? There had to be more reason than frightening children.

A moment later the question was forgotten.

It was a minor thing, some subtle change in the air, that made Anton look up to see that where he had assumed the crowding wedge of rock would continue, there was instead open space. The fissure walls had gradually spread apart so that he found that he was now standing at one end of another cavern easily as big as the one they had just left. And the cavern was a city.

No. It was no longer a city. There were enough dwellings, Anton guessed, craning his neck to count the levels, the strings of globe lanterns making it like peering into a velvet-lined box of pearls, enough staircases and gangways and colonnades to house thousands. But thousands would have been visible. Thousands would have deafened him with their chatter. Thousands would have crowded the place with life.

Once there had been thousands of Indigenes here, scraping themselves a new city from the rock, but they were long gone. This was an upturned bowl with a handful of souls rattling around inside.

"How many of you live down here?"

Coombs' face was ghostly. "... *one...*" he said. "One hundred and fifty."

Anton shook his head. "As few as that?"

"It isn't … *two*… as easy living underground as you might think."
Coombs held Anton's gaze and then, when he intoned a hushed, "…
three…" there was a soft rag to the echo. Coombs smiled. "… *four*…"
he said, and it was there again. Other voices had spoken the word in
unison. Coombs' arithmetic affectation was a community activity.

They climbed some stairs, and came upon a fire blazing in a
central hearth. Smoke and embers spiralled upwards from it, and
standing and sitting, and working, and lounging too on thick blankets
around it were more of the outcasts.

"… *six*…" the occupants of the cave said, their lips moving in
unison, the sibilant echo of the word like a shiver in the air.

"Do you have visitors from the city often?" Anton whispered.

Coombs shook his head. "No," he replied. "No visitors."

A clutch of children, engrossed in a complicated-looking shell
game, stopped their yabbering and turned their ghost faces to follow
Anton's progress.

Some weren't as ghostly as others though. One girl, there, with
her frizzy, auburn hair, and a touch of stubborn pink about her cheeks,
was surely as far from being related to these people as he was himself.

Anton's blood ran cold, reminded again of the *Derryman* story.
The bogeyman from the sea who stole the errant children of
Glassholmers. Surely that part of the story wasn't true as well? He
started towards the children, and the girl looked up. That was when he
saw the ruin of her face, a weird discontinuity that split her upper lip
and distorted what would otherwise have been a pretty nose.

He saw he lips moving. "… *fifteen thousand five hundred and twelve*…"
she murmured along with the rest of the congregation.

Anton froze. He had never seen the like. He had thought Mia
ugly, and had expected worse from her kinsfolk, but this… this was
absolutely shocking. Real children were not born this way.

He felt Coombs' hand on his arm, and allowed himself to be
drawn away. Near the fire they joined a quiet, shuffling queue.
Something was pressed into Anton's hand. A plate. It bore a children's
design that had been in vogue a generation ago. Its surface was rough
with scuffed up vitric and it was missing a chunk of its edge so that it
resembled the moon three or four days after Full. Anton stared at the
plate as he joined the line. He clung on to the familiarity of the cartoon

design even when it was obscured by a dollop of slop, and tried to conjure in his mind the domestic scene when this plate had last seen the moon's light.

A family evening meal, he thought. *Maw and Paw and a couple of kids in a modest two bedroom tenement flat in the low district of Hatchard Hill. Nothing fancy, but still perfectly respectable. There's beef stew in the pot – it's been beef stew for the last three nights, but since Dark is only a few days away, they're using the last of it up. No one complains. It's that time of the month, and by the time they're on their fourth dinner of mealy pudding, they'll be savouring the memory of tonight. Little Thomas – he's been given the job of setting the table. He gets the plates out of the dresser one by one. Paw's plate, Maw's plate and Betty's plate are big creamy circles. They were new just last Founding Day, and he has to be very careful – especially this close to Dark. There's one for him too, but he does not like it. The last plate he lifts out of the cupboard has been his one as long as he can remember, and he loves it because it has Mister Moony on it. The plate old and rough now, but he won't eat off anything else. Thomas is excited by his new responsibility – proud that his mother trusts him and that he has never, ever had an accident, but scared at the same time. He treads slowly, placing each foot with care, just like he does every night, but this time Dark catches him out. He's almost at the table when he snags his toe on a rumple in the carpet and pitches forward. The plate cracks against the table, a limb of it shearing off. Paw consoles him as Maw clears away the pieces and Betty gets the other big, plain plate out of the cupboard. "There, son," Maw says. "Nothing lasts for ever."*

True enough, Anton thought. *But all Glassholmers are like Thomas. They do think that their world is eternal.*

"You'll have questions." Coombs took him to a spot on the periphery of the gathering where they could sit with their backs against the rock and shovel at the fishy concoction with their slabs of flatbread.

Anton shot him a glance, but didn't know where to start. He was talking to a man who had hinted at abducting children, after all. Instead of answering, he copied Coombs. The dinner didn't taste of much at all, but it was the first hot food he had eaten in who knew how long. For the next few minutes he had no thought other than to devote himself to the simple act of eating. He was mopping up the last of the sauce when he realised that Coombs was watching him with some amusement.

"As you can see we eat like kings here. You must feel right at home."

"But you live like outcasts," Anton replied. "You can have no great love for our Lunane, then?"

Coombs, finishing the last mouthful of his own meal, smirked as he sucked his long fingers. "What do you think?"

A wave of temper washed hotly across Anton's skin. He didn't like being toyed with like this. "I'm not sure whether I should be scared for my life or only my loyalty," he snapped back.

"Your life, Mr Dunn, is safe enough while you're here," Coombs said. "As for your relationship with your maker…" Here he made a face that Anton could not interpret. "… well, I'm sure that's your own affair."

"My *maker*?" Anton was surprised by the anger that edged his voice, but the accusation stung as if the man had taken a knife and sliced open the wound on his arm again. Anton knew he had not been thinking clearly back in the Foundry clock tower, but wasn't that exactly what he had felt? That he was some sort of mechanical part, broken and no longer fit for purpose. A busted, manufactured thing.

"What are you getting at, Coombs?" He asked this with less fire because this was the perfect opportunity to gain new information, an outsider's perspective on how Glassholm had turned into the thing it was. It couldn't have been by design right from the start, but somewhere in those early years something had happened that had turned the settlement from a camp of desperate refugees concerned merely with survival into an engine of conservation. It had taken a little social engineering to turn survival into prosperity, but the Lunane had become addicted hadn't he? Their need. Their dependency. And the longer he'd continued to be needed, the more he'd shaped his city into the form of a machine at which the notion of his *absolute necessity* was the centre. The capstan, the vital, master cog that ran everything, and held it all together.

A notion, mind. Because Anton now knew that that was all he was. A consensual, living idea that existed inside people's heads, tethered there as constant and bright as the moon itself.

And what would happen if the people started to question that idea? What would happen if the Lunane's moon left the sky?

No wonder the king was panicking.

Coombs nodded as if he were following Anton's train of thought.

"We're keeping him alive," Anton said.

"Bravo, Engineer." His companion pressed his palms together in mimed applause. "All of that, up there. All of your Glassholm, is no more than an elaborate device to preserve *the idea* of a man who died nearly half a millennium ago. A generator whose sole purpose is your Lunane's own personal myth."

"Positive feedback," Anton murmured.

"Quite so." Coombs squeezed out a difficult smile. "And the only role in the engine of his myth for this land's rightful owners is that of the vanquished savage."

This matched what Anton had learned from the biographies, but he narrowed his eyes. "And yet here you are, living in secret and stealing our children."

Coombs ignored the bite. "We're as much part of his machine as you are. Whether we like it or not." He sighed. "When the Lunane was founding his city we were routed, but we were not slaughtered. Not all of us. He's a smart one. He knows that people are usually of more use alive than they are dead. He killed just enough of our ancestors to make it clear that we had no future, then he came to us with a deal."

"A deal?"

Coombs nodded. "This was some years after he had driven our people to the fringes of the island, and they were finding survival hard. Before the Lunane came we were a race of fishermen. We knew the sea like a lover, we were masters of her tides. But when he brought the moon here, the sea turned against our island and it took a long time until we learned to fish anywhere near as successfully as we once had." Coombs noticed the furrow on Anton's brow. "But that is all by the by," he said. "The Lunane waited until things were desperate, and not just for us. His new city continued to struggle, on the verge of disaster. He was in his second or third body by then, but he was far from strong. Thus far his leadership had engendered loyalty, but the people were becoming restless. He needed more than leadership. He required fear too, but more importantly he also needed *conformity*." Coombs spread his hands. "And so the Derryman was born."

Anton was confused. "You're saying he *asked* you to steal into the city and snatch children?"

Coombs looked disgusted. "And you call yourself a rational man," he said. "Examine yourself to see how deeply the myth is laid? No one snatches children from their cradles, Anton."

"So, how do they get here, then? These children. They are not of your line."

Coombs stood up, brushed a few crumbs of bread from his trousers. "Walk with me," he said. "I'll introduce you to some of our family."

As they walked back towards the fire, Anton noticed that the gathering had largely dispersed. Those that remained had all found themselves some task – raking the coals, gathering up the blankets or sweeping up the debris of the meal. A child approached them carrying a stack of dirty plates. She was as careful not to trip as Anton's imaginary Thomas. Coombs added their own crockery to the top of the pile.

"Thank you, Sadie," he said.

When the child smiled back at them, Anton saw her split face. It was the same girl he had seen when they arrived. "Hello, Sadie," he said.

She raised her pretty eyes to him. He held them, trying valiantly not to let his gaze drop.

"How long have you lived down here?" he asked her.

She touched the gap in her lip absently, traced the red line where the skin fused. It was at once a touching gesture and a horrific one.

"You mustn't be shy of Mr Dunn," Coombs said gently. "He's our friend. Do you remember when you came to live in the caves?"

At first Sadie shook her head, but then she opened her mouth to speak. However, all she said was, "... *two*..." It was perfectly synchronised with Coombs' own intonation, and softly echoed by the cavern's other inhabitants. Anton realised he had become so used to the counting that it had almost ceased to register.

"You came to us just after you were born, Sadie," Coombs said. "A long ... *three*... time ago. Off you go now and take those dishes down to the pool."

They watched her careful progress across the rubble-strewn floor, as protective of that pile of chipped crockery as if it were the Lunane's own china.

"Sweet child," Coombs murmured. "You don't see many like that on your city streets, do you?"

Anton was unsure whether he was talking about her sweetness or her ugliness. "I've never seen the like," he admitted.

"No, I don't suppose you have," Coombs replied. "Sadie's face is just a minor accident of birth. And such idiosyncrasies happen more often than you might think. Why do you suppose you don't see people like Sadie in the homes and streets of Glassholm, Anton?"

Anton shook his head.

"Because they are brought here as soon as they are born. Keeps the population consistent. No one stands out. Uniformity is a very important part of the machine."

This put a new slant on Coombs's earlier comment about the Lunane being Anton's *maker*. Anton was horrified. "You're telling me the Lunane is breeding our people to be subservient?"

"Breeding?" Coombs mused. "No, that's too strong. But there's a longstanding undertaking to winnow out any that stand out from the crowd. The midwives have great talent at spotting those types, not just the physical abnormalities – those are obvious – but there's something in the blood, they tell me, that can indicate those who are different mentally as well." His gaze was penetrating. "I've been thinking, Anton, that it is a wonder that we did not see you down here a long time ago."

Anton was going to protest that he was no different to anyone else in Glassholm, but a nagging thought stalled him. His strong-willed mother, ignoring the demands of family and neighbours, birthing her son at home without the aid of either the Infirmary or those cultish midwives. Perhaps that had set the pattern for his life after all. Made him the individual, the rock that always seemed to be struggling against the common inertia. The Adamant.

"I must have slipped through the net," he muttered.

Coombs raised an eyebrow. "Perhaps," he said. "Or perhaps the king was prepared to run the risk of a little disaffection if it meant some clever little boys and girls were able to grow up into clever engineers. He must have been aware that the old devices would fail eventually."

Anton nodded. "There's been a department of the Foundry dedicated to their so-called understanding for as long as anyone can remember." He rubbed his eyes. Coombs' allegations would have been far-fetched in Glassholm, but here in this underground exile they made a weird sort of sense. There was a mechanistic elegance to it that Anton admired. It wasn't natural, but he now knew that life in Glassholm was far from natural. In taking the moon for himself and making his city under it, the Lunane had bent nature. Glassholm had been artificial from the start.

"I think I understand now," Anton said. "After all of his work and determination it must have been desperately frustrating for him to know that he was dying, and then when he discovered that he had survived – maybe *persisted* is a better word – because his people needed him so badly, he must have felt ordained to complete the work."

Coombs's shrug indicated that he didn't much care how difficult the Lunane had found it. "Come this way," he said. "I have one more thing to show you. The reason we brought you here."

Anton had become used to delving down into the earth. Glassholmers were raised to believe that everything of value was above them but recent experience had taught him quite the opposite. So, it came as no surprise to him to find that steps had been hacked out of the floor at the rear of the cavern. Leading down into darkness, away from the light and the influence of both moon and king.

A scuff echoed from the stairwell, a light grew within it, and then Mia was there with a candle. She cradled a stack of books in the crook of her arm.

Their covers were black.

"I believe your biographer is ready to show you the other story of the Lunane's life," Coombs said.

The trip down these stairs was easier than the one that had led to the other journal repository. Barely two turns of a loose spiral brought them to another cave. This one had been shelved with slabs of slate, and it was these that held the black-bound journals. In the candlelight they formed organic towers and looming aggregates that Anton first misidentified as stalagmitic formations of the cave itself. Where book and rock met were the slumped distortions of the oldest journals under the twin pressures of gravity and decay.

Mia led him to a clear space and tugged his arm to make him sit. Then she handed him a journal, opened it at the place she had been marking with her finger. By contrast to much of the cave's contents, this journal was relatively new. The batters were stiff, the pages crisp, the ink black. He rubbed the paper between his fingers and cast Mia a questioning look. "No vitric?" His voice echoed flatly.

Her black smile was pretty, her eyes twinkled.

Of course not, she was saying.

"Is your disregard for the Lunane so low?" He sounded like Gerard, and Anton decided against talking for the time being. Instead he looked to where Mia tapped on the page.

The contrast to the official journals was immediately apparent. Where those records had been made in the tight, controlled script, that by Hogarth's time had become more of a professional requirement than a mere matter of style, the writing on these pages was made in a looped, organic hand that filled the paper from margin to spine. And instead of the concise sentence structure that suited the daily journals' simple reportage, here the writing was complicated by clauses and parentheses, inclusions and score-outs. Even the occasional squeezed-in drawing, suggesting that not only was the biographer's sense of structure suspect, but their vocabulary was often insufficient for the task as well.

Anton offered Mia an uncertain smile.

She nodded impatiently at the page.

There was no date to the entry, and only a hasty line separated it from the previous piece.

It is night. He read. *It is not Darkday, but my moon is missing from the sky. My moon has deserted me, and without her controlling power the city's streets resound with laughter and jeers. I have climbed to the top of my tallest tower to persuade my moon to return, but there is no sign of her. All I can see is the sea. It has breached the harbour. It has overflowed the Cord. The streets are flooded, like shining fingers seeking out the Palace. Now my city is drowned. The people are silenced, the buildings, the streets, sunk. The waters are rising now around my tower.*

Anton stopped reading. It was nonsense, but he also had the strange feeling that he'd heard the story before. "I don't understand," he said.

Mia sighed, pointed again to the page. To a drawing of a domed tower surrounded by waves, their peaks drawn so that they looked as if they were reaching towards it.

I stare into the water, knowing what I will see, but am unable to stop looking. There is a glint of light in the dark, deep water. Like the moon's reflection but not, because my moon is gone from the heavens. I'm falling. Falling towards the waves. The suffocating, vengeful water. And what lies beneath.

Anton's heart thumped alarmingly. He looked at Mia. "Is this all?"

She nodded.

"But this is a fantasy," he said. "It's more like a..."

Mia nodded again. She put her palms together, raised them to the side of her face and closed her eyes to mimic sleep.

"*A dream?* These are the Lunane's dreams?"

Mia pointed at Anton.

"This is *my* dream?"

The girl mimed applause. It explained the familiarity, the dread that both he and the Lunane would have felt when experiencing a dream like this. "But I don't remember this dream," he said. "You're right. I know I had it, but I don't *remember* it."

Quick as a bird Mia stretched towards him. Her slender, white fingers touched his temple and then withdrew, slowly, as if drawing a thread from his head.

At last, Anton understood what the night biographer did. The purpose of Mia, and her mother, and all those that went before them. What the pact was that the Lunane had made with the Indigenes who, after all, possessed special talents. The other reason that he had not wiped them out all those years ago.

They recorded his dreams.

"But why do you do it?"

Mia grinned. Then she flipped backwards through the journal. From the number of pages that fluttered under her fingers, Anton guessed that they were passing beyond his own link with the Lunane. The passage now under Mia's finger carried no residue of recognition, although in other respects it was very similar to the one he had just read.

I'm on the deck of a ship. Glassholm, my island, my city, my people – my moon, all of it, recedes behind me, slow and inexorable as the unrolling of time. The ship is empty of both passengers and crew. No one is steering this ship, but its course is…away. As my island, my moon, dwindle on the horizon, the waters around the ship chop up. I know what that means. I don't want to look over the side, but I have to see. And sure enough, It is down there. Unfettered. I spy it, deep, deep under the snatching waves.

I recognise the ship. It's one of the Fleet. The original Founders' vessels, cannibalised and scuttled so long ago. And even as I realise this the ship starts to break up, to founder. To sink.

To draw me down.

Anton went on and read the next one too. This was similar again, involving the Lunane isolated, in some way losing his island. Clearly a recurring nightmare, possible flavoured by whoever's head he was using to experience the dream.

"You're like those women, aren't you?" Anton said. "But instead of covering up unpleasant memories, you salve the Lunane of his nightmares."

Mia nodded, but she wagged her finger. He wasn't quite right. Again she mimed drawing the thread from his head, but this time she finished the action with a jerk. A break.

"Ah, you do more than make him forget," Anton said. "You actually remove the dream?"

Mia mimed sleeping. Fluttering her closed eyelids and snoring this time for effect.

"As he is dreaming it?"

Abruptly Mia snatched the book from his fingers, tossed it carelessly behind her. It fluttered erratically, landed heavily across a rock like a broken-winged crow.

"And you bring the books of dreams here, where they can be dumped and forgotten, because...?"

Mia grinned manically. Sticking out her tongue, she crossed her eyes and waggled her head from side to side.

"The Lunane would go mad as a month of Fullishness."

And if that happened, the dreams of Glassholm's destruction might well come true. Perhaps not as drastically as the king appeared to fear, but the great machine could surely not function with such discord at its centre. At the very least, it would keep the king's mind clear and untroubled for the duration of the day.

"Unnh!"

Mia thrust another volume into his hands, one that had evidently been discarded here many years ago. The batters were dirty, the pages pulpy, the writing faded to tired brown, distorted in places by water spots and obliterated by mould.

He opened it at a random page.

The machines are finished, he read, and his mouth dried at the unexpected mention of the Founders' devices. *Seizing up and rusting where they stand. The city is drenched under an iron red snow.* From there, though, the dream returned to more familiar territory, the overwhelming of the city, the Lunane's fear of the water, and something within it.

Piqued now, though, he worked his way through the journal looking for more anxiety about the machines. The soft paper tore between his impatient fingers. The fate of the machines was a recurring factor in this volume. Anton imagined that it had been around this point that the Lunane had discovered that the machines they had used to found their city were beginning to reach the end of their useful lives. There was no mention, however, of the machine, *his machine.*

He thrust the journal back to Mia. "Where is it?" he said. "There's something in here about the machine that controls the moon, isn't there? Something that you want me to know."

Mia merely smiled her sweet, black-lipped smile and shrugged her skinny shoulders.

Anton stood up, went to the nearest pile of journals. "Where is it, Mia?" He picked a spine at random. "Is it in this one?" In heaving the journal free, he toppled the stack across the cavern floor. "Or what about here?" Another stack spilled.

Mia rolled her eyes. Then, tired of the game, she got to her feet and produced one more journal from behind her back.

She laughed like a seal when Anton snatched it from her fingers.

"I'm in the room at the heart of my Castil," he read aloud. "The room where they installed the machine that tethers nature and holds the symbol of my power in the sky, but the view in the dome above me is blank. The machine itself is dead. It should point down!

"Now I'm passing through the repository where my ongoing history fills the shelves. The door opens. The stairs. I am compelled to descend, although I am terrified by not knowing whether it will be waiting for me or whether it will be gone."

Anton closed his eyes, tried to think this through. He was so close... There was something about the machine's relationship with the moon. *"It should point down"?* It was no use. There was still a missing piece to the puzzle, and whatever waited through the door in the repository. Something below.

Anton snapped his eyes open. "What's down there?"

Mia was gone.

Up the stairs, the cavern-city was deserted. He shouted for Mia, for Coombs, but the rock swallowed his calls. Only after negotiating the crevice entrance and blundering his way back to the beach did he discover where everyone had gone.

They were camped around the perimeter of the beach. The organic lantern glow cast their huddles in a familial light that rung an unexpected pang in Anton's chest. They were still counting, but now they were doing so with a full voice. As a community.

Coombs was hunkered down near the front. His arm was around the shoulders of little Sadie and their attention – along with everyone else's – was directed towards the tide rolling high up the beach.

"*Two!*" the assembly cried in unison as the wave rushed up the sand and then slunk back.

"What's going on?" Anton demanded.

The little girl smiled her beautiful and unfortunate smile. She opened her mouth but Coombs put a finger to her wasted lips. "Ssh," he said. "Watch the waves, love."

He spoke to Anton out of the side of his mouth. "You've come on a special day."

Another wave had begun frothing up the beach. "Whoahhh... three!" came the cry as the wave reached a foot higher up the sand than its predecessor. Anton thought for a moment he could see movement, like many somethings wriggling in the damp sand, but it was only the glitter of evaporating moisture.

"Let me tell you something, Anton." Coombs tickled Sadie's ear then pretended to look the other way when she turned round in surprise, but Anton knew that the group's spokesman was watching him. "Before your Lunane and his people came here, we had a long established relationship with nature. We lived by its rhythms, most of all the rhythms of the sea. And because we respected nature, we lived well."

Coombs pointed, indicating to Sadie to watch the next surge of the tide.

"Whoahhh..." the girl shouted along with the crowd as the surge raced up the beach. It was as if they were encouraging its efforts. "Four!"

"And who wouldn't want to live well, Anton?"

"What?" Anton had become distracted – not by the spontaneous round of applause that had broken out, but because this time he was certain that behind the edge of the receding wave the effervescent sand shivered for an instant or two with activity.

Coombs carried on with his story as if nothing had happened. "But when the Lunane arrived, he found a way of imposing his will on nature, didn't he? Like a giant clockwork that trapped the land, the population, even the moon into serving one purpose – the perpetuation of his people, and himself. There are those who will tell you that the

Lunane's actions were necessary, that they saved thousands of lives from flood, from starvation, from plague. But whatever the reasons, nature is not to be contained. She adapts. Would you believe that before Glassholm was established, Full and Dark were barely of more significance than any other time of the month? Or that luck was distributed naturally without the need for monkeys to carry it? Nature was greatly disturbed by the stealing of the moon, but she is patient. And she is ever inventive in finding ways to fight back. Perhaps you've seen her children about the city?"

Anton shook his head.

"No, well, I don't doubt that you will before this is over. They're the real Derry-men."

Anton's own eyes were now fixed on the tide too. He watched it roll back, turn, and begin the next assault.

Coombs' murmur blended with the hush of the waves. "Do you know, Anton, that it used to be reckoned that the moon influenced the tides? Maybe that was true, once, but your king's usurpation of the moon's natural path severed that link. The world's waters are too vast and the factors that govern them too wonderfully complex to be ruled by one petty egoist."

"Whoahhhh... five!" The receding wave was chased by applause and an excited cheer. The wet sand sizzled with life again, but once more it settled before Anton was able to see the cause.

Coombs stopped clapping and resumed his lecture. "Now down here, Anton, we're about as far from the Lunane's influence as you can get on this island, but you have seen nevertheless how he has drawn us into his machine. And you can see also," here he swept his arm around the assembly, "how in spite of that bastard we maintain our link with nature."

Anton shook his head. While it was obvious that something was being demonstrated to him, he couldn't see what.

Coombs laughed. "Here we live by the rhythm of the sea. You can feel it Anton, can't you? The count of seven in your heart. This way we keep a tenuous grip on the pulse of nature that we once knew so well. We no longer live well, Mister Engineer, but at least we do not live as slaves."

"Whoaaaahhhhh... six!" There was palpable excitement as the sixth wave fizzed across the sand. This time the sand flurried up in a dusty cloud as the water drew back.

The crowd quieted each other, held a collective breath.

"And every now and then, Anton," Coombs murmured, as the tide gathered all of its strength and rushed up the beach. "Every now and then, nature rewards us for our faith."

"Seven!"

The tide drove farther up the beach than any wave yet. It swept up to within yards of the onlookers, but then tired and fell away. Like two lovers, separated and trying to find each other again. Close, but always too far away. And as the sea withdrew, the surface of the sand rippled behind it like the ghosts of the waves. Then the beach exploded, throwing up another cloud of sand, this time mixed with something else. In the next instant the cavern resounded to a sound like a thousand Fullday firecrackers. Something landed near Anton's feet. He picked it up, turning in his fingers a ridged casing about an inch long. A thing of hardly any weight, translucent brown and cracked open along its length.

There followed a moment of relative silence, save for the pattering rain of similar casings on the sand, before the humming began. At first Anton thought the sound was coming from the crowd. Some part of the ritual, a low threnody to follow all the hoopla. But then he saw that the cavern roof was now obscured by a different kind of cloud, a sort that no longer had anything to do with sand. The cloud was vibrating. The cloud began to scintillate. Flashes of colour winked and sparked, and the hum grew louder, developing undertones and harmonics that, as soon as Anton distinguished them, complexified still further.

He had identified what the cloud was. "It's insects," he said, mainly for his own benefit because he could not quite believe that mere insects could create such an awesome din.

Next to him Sadie too stared upwards, her jaw hanging and her hands clamped to her ears.

Coombs must have been reading Anton's lips because he surely could not have heard him over the noise. "We call them storm flies," he shouted.

"I can see why," Anton bellowed back.

Impossibly, the cacophony was still rising.

Coombs grinned, nodded. "I've always thought that was a little harsh on them, but the noise isn't the only reason. Watch."

275

Anton saw what he meant. As the volume rose, so did the frequency of the lights, and instead of individual flickers there were now pulses of staccato brightness within the mass. These lightning flashes stuttered, faster, brighter until the cloud of insects became a throbbing brilliance that lit the cavern like a summer's day.

The din was deafening now, and Anton joined the rest of the crowd – not just the children – in protecting his ears. "What are they doing?"

Coombs squinted at him through the glare. "They're mating, of course," he shouted. "The storm flies breed once every seven years. That's how long it'll be before the tide comes so far up the beach again. This is what we mean about the rhythm of nature, Anton. This is the way things are supposed to be."

As the noise of the storm flies finally relinquished, the light began to stutter once more and the first of the spent insects dropped to the beach, a shout of warning went around the assembly. Adults covered the children's eyes and hair, and pulled their own coat collars tight. Anton – watching one that had plopped to the sand beside his foot; wings limp, its abdomen beating erratically , apparently all but dead, but still trying to burrow into the sand – was unprepared for the ensuing torrent.

In the shocked silence that followed, Anton joined the rest of the community in plucking the twitching, ticking bodies from his hair and clothes. After such a sensory crescendo, he was glad to have something to concentrate on so that he didn't have to speak. And he was glad too to see that he was not the only one whose heart was rattling like a caged lunet bird.

"We should return you to the city," Coombs said at length. The show over, the cavern's citizens had begun to filter back through the crevice, some of them gathering handfuls of insects on the way. No doubt they tasted better than the fish stew.

Anton saw Coombs' lips move, but he heard a hundred odd other voices murmur it. "*Four.*" He didn't need to look over at the bay to know that the tide was now once again retreating from the beach.

"That's it?" Anton said. "That's all you're going to tell me?"

Coombs shrugged. "We've told you all we know. We've broken our pact with the Lunane by showing you the night journals. You were expecting something more?"

"I was hoping…" Anton shook his head. What had he been hoping? He had hardly begun investigating the journals, and in his few short hours in this dim place he had begun to feel comfortable. Had he really thought though that perhaps the Lunane had conveniently managed to dream the complete blueprints of the machine? Had he really forgotten the urgency in the city, the lengths the Lunane had gone to try and stop him leaving? He laughed at his own naiveté.

Coombs caught his arm, held his gaze. "You have work to do in the city, Anton," he said. "We hope you have learned enough to finish your task."

There were layers of meaning in this, but Anton couldn't peel them apart. "What do you mean?"

"You'll figure that out for yourself." Coombs was walking away. "We all have to be true to our own nature in the end."

When Coombs had gone, there was only Mia left. The girl handed him a bundle wrapped in cloth tied with string. Journals. Then she wagged her head in the direction of the switchback path and led him back towards the city.

Chapter 21

The house was filling up. It resounded with chat, the fervour of song and, worst of all, the interminable wailing of the inconsolable ones. They arrived in packs now and were sleeping in every spare inch of floor space.

Only Lottie of all the women in the house had special status. Her old room was hers alone and it became both her sanctuary and her prison. She was constantly exhausted. Her belly had swollen to an alarming girth, and the baby shifted constantly, as if anxious to escape. She knew how it felt.

Cara brought her meals three times a day. Great hearty platefuls that the thin girl eyed with poorly disguised hunger.

"I'm guessing the rest of you don't get as much as this," Lottie said to her when she brought lunch.

Cara shook her head.

"How many are there now?"

"Nearly three hundred, Daughter."

Lottie pushed the tray back. The aromatic steam rising from the lamb stew had her mouth watering. "Take this away. Share it amongst the women that need it."

It was an empty gesture. Lottie knew that there was not one woman in this place that would begrudge her this meal. She hated the relief she felt to see the girl shake her head, and refrained from attacking the plate until Cara had backed out the room. The truth was she was ravenous. She was always ravenous.

Three hundred women, though. Three hundred women had quit their jobs and abandoned their families to come here. She wasn't conceited enough to imagine that the sole reason for this was her impending freak-of-a-child. There were greater issues. She thought about the mayhem at the Halfday. She wondered just how bad it had got since then.

"What's happening out there?" she asked Cara when she returned for the empties.

"I'm sure I don't know, Daughter."

"You must know something," Lottie said. "What are the women saying?"

Cara wrung the napkin between her fingers. "The Mother said you weren't to be bothered with such trivia."

Lottie hated herself for putting on her best smile, her mother's voice when she replied. "But my mother is not carrying our future Queen, is she now?"

Cara was happy to be obedient as long as she knew whose orders to obey. She dipped her head. "Daughter."

Lottie patted the coverlet next to her on the bed. "Well?"

Cara hesitated for just a fraction longer before acquiescing. "Oh, miss." She breathed it like pent-up steam. It was only partly girlish scandalising; Lottie also recognised genuine fear. "It's terrible. The city's on fire."

"What do you mean *on fire?*"

Tears now. "The Foundry was first, then some of the big houses in the Parks, but now it's the Rottens too. It's fallen into the river."

Lottie slugged back cold tea to slake the sudden dryness in her mouth. "What about the hills? Garton? Hatchard? What about Beckon?"

A tiny shake of the head. "I don't know, miss, but it's bad all over."

Lottie sank back on the bed and covered her face with her hands. She sensed Cara hovering, probably uncertain of whether she ought to offer comfort, and was relieved that in the end the girl chose simply to flee.

She pressed her fingers tight together, trying to blot out everything. Instead of darkness she saw Henrik's face. *Poor Henrik.* She had managed so far to avoid thinking about him by focusing on her frustration with her mother and the baby, but every time the child shifted or kicked – as it did now – the plucky, hapless foreigner's face floated into vision.

He was going to get killed out there.

Lottie got up and went over to tug up the window sash. Her belly made the stretch difficult, but she managed to raise it an inch. Enough to feel the breeze on her cheek, and be reminded of the city outside which, just as it had in her childhood, might as well have been across the sea as at the end of her street. The breeze was cool, and – Cara hadn't lied – there was a taste of autumn to it, when the knot trees were razed back in preparation for winter. A stench of smoke.

Lottie stretched again, up on her toes now. Tried to budge the sash higher, but the wood had suffered too many warps during Dark to remember true. Then something bulled its way onto the ledge, spreading itself and blocking out the sky.

Lottie shied away from the window, overbalanced and sat down painfully on the floor.

A golden eye regarded her through the glass.

The crow opened its beak and *kraaked* a sound like a warning.

Anton hurried through the woods, chasing in Mia's wake, connecting those stretches of cleared vegetation recognisable as path with the signs of her passing: ripples on puddles, shivering branches. His breath rasped, his feet slipped in shoes borrowed from Coombs and the path threw up roots and rocks too fast to do anything but stumble over, but he careered on and in the rare moments that he had breath to spare, he laughed.

The chase was a game. Ahead he could hear the shrill ululation that was Mia's own, unique laugh. She may have been born in those caves, but her position of privilege had allowed her a taste for the wider world. She travelled this route at dusk and at dawn, and she relished this freedom.

After the recent events in Anton's own life, he knew something of how she felt.

It wasn't only the fun of the chase or the thought of losing his guide that spurred him on. It was having an inkling, at last, of how to fix the machine.

Anton clutched the bundle of journals to his chest. They were the key. After leaving the caves, Mia had insisted on waiting until dawn before even attempting to negotiate the forest, and while she had rested Anton had used the time to locate the monkey statue, prise open its fingers and retrieve that blasted coat. Then he had toppled the beast, opened it up with a sharp rock, ripped out the battery leads, sparked up a camp fire and settled down to read.

He hadn't learned much more than he had back in the cavern, but by sheer repetition it eventually sank in that the machine operated inversely to how everyone thought. *It pointed down.* Which meant that it was directed not at the moon itself, but whatever waited beneath the Palace. It probably even used the moon's own power to do so. If you wanted to keep someone permanently moribund, he imagined you'd probably have to find a way somehow of modifying the lunatropic rays into the nadir phase. It'd be like Dark every day.

The question was, who or what was being subdued?

Anton didn't know. But he knew where to go to find out.

He blundered on until the trees thinned and he found himself at the edge of a potato field. Out of breath, he rubbed his side to ease a stitch and looked around for Mia.

"Where are you?" There was no sign. This early in the year, the furrowed runs contained only stubby shoots. There wasn't much in the way of cover.

Anton spun slowly around. The day was still young, the weather uncertain and the light insipid, but to the south he could just make out the smudged finger of the Castil tower against a boulder of cloud. No, not cloud. *Smoke.* He felt the bite once more of that old urgency. It was a good few hours' walk yet, but he would not lose his way from here. He didn't want to return alone, though.

Anton turned to face the tree-line. He leaned against the trunk of a hefty chestnut, slipping off his borrowed shoes and massaging his feet. The girl had simply vanished. Was this part of the game? Or had this been the plan all along, to bring him far enough that he couldn't go wrong, and them leave him.

"Mia, are you there?"

It occurred to Anton that people would be up and about soon. Perhaps Mia didn't want to rely on her shawl in broad daylight. Not when there was so much anger among the citizens. On meeting her for the first time, Anton's own reaction had been one of shock. He could only imagine what some of those hotheads would make of her.

And what if they were no longer limiting their attention to the city?

"Mia, come on. The fun's over."

He turned around one more time, hoping to spot her ghostly face peeking around the bole of a tree or sticking up among the shaws.

The sound came from above. A gentle *snick*, followed by a tumbling rustle. A broad-leaved greenstick branch hit the ground nearby. Anton stared at it, unable to process the strange smear that clashed so with the vivid green of the leaves. Stupid of him, though, not to anticipate that Mia had climbed the tree. She would be sitting up there right now, laughing at him and plucking another branch to throw.

"That's very funny." Anton looked up just in time to register the falling shape and dive aside. This was far bigger than a bit of twig and leaf. It hit the earth with a sickening thump, and lay there, dark and inert.

It was Mia.

And she had been twisted into an awful shape.

And she was dead.

Anton knelt beside the poor, pretty, black-mouthed girl. He tried to rub the garish blood from her pale skin, but there was too much. He barely sensed the shadow, felt the draft, before he was gripped and lifted bodily into the sky.

Wind and tears blurred his vision, streaking everything to smears of vivid red and green and poor, soft white. He hung helpless and furious as the scythe-beaked crow bore him with unhurried beats of its massive span away from Mia's corpse and the bundle of precious journals at her side, and towards the city, the Palace, the tower and its immortal occupant.

Anton's brain was as numb as his frozen face and fingers, but he still recognised the unpleasant itch, and knew what was coming.

Welcome home, Engineer, the Lunane said. *You have unfinished business.*

Mortlock traipsed the streets, looking. Sometimes he forgot who he was searching for. Sometimes he knew it was Henrik, but he couldn't remember why. Only one thing was constantly in his thoughts: the Dark Room and the things he had done there.

He walked the crumbling docks, he walked the dry hills, he walked the smoking Foundry and the deserted Parks. He slugged the black until his flask was empty. His coat fitted him, snug and right: with the blood stains on the sleeve, the cosh in his pocket and the knife tucked close to his heart.

Lytten caught up with him in the Merchantry. There was some sort of massed protest on Sali Boulevard. It had been repelled by the

Palace guard and the side streets were thronged with angry, frustrated citizens. As Mortlock bullied a path through them, the chief grabbed his sleeve and pulled him into an alley mouth.

"What *use* are you?" Spittle flecked his lips. "You had him and you let him go."

The alley was cool, dim. The sounds of the crowd were distant. "You've seen Henrik?" Mortlock said.

Lytten flashed out a slap that caught him around the ear. "Of course, Henrik. Who else? He was skulking around the house where those women congregate on Mael Street."

Morlock's ear was numb. Everything was numb. "I didn't see him. I went looking for his girlfriend there. But I didn't see her either."

Lytten made to lash out again. "What use? Eh? What *use?*" The slap turned into splayed fingers that sought Mortlock's temple. "How many times do you have to be told?"

Mortlock batted the arm away. "I know what to do. Remove the lad, and his girlfriend…" His fingers slipped inside his coat.

"At last the penny drops." Lytten glanced towards the crowd, lowered his voice. "See that you finish the job this time."

"… and everyone else who knows," Mortlock completed. The knife felt good in his hand. Then he threw the chief against the wall, pulled his head back and opened his throat to the air. Silenced him.

He made a mental list of people who knew about the sailor. Shirley was on it.

The cobbles outside the Gull were strewn with debris; sticks and rocks and ripped-up public information handbills advertising that the coming eclipse was now due before Fullday, not after.

The café's street was quieter than most but still rang with shouts and the sound of scuffles. Mortlock didn't even bother knocking. Shirley wouldn't answer anyway. He prised open the shutters of the nearest window, smashed the glass with half a brick and let himself in.

The stillness inside was inhibiting. Cracks in the shutters admitted random spears of daylight, isolated spots of trapped brilliance amid the forest of upturned chair legs. The atmosphere constricted his voice. "Hello?" It came out hoarse. He opened the door at the rear, cleared his throat, tried again. "Shirley?"

The stairs were silent.

"It's me love. John."

It took a matter of seconds to scale the stairs, and he knew from the moment that he poked his head up into her living room that she was gone. Her home was empty.

There was a note though, and it was addressed to him.

You'll find this if you come looking for me, and I know you will eventually. Probably sooner than later, I think, but that can't be helped. I know you've got important things to do, but I need help too.
The truth is I can't stand it anymore. The children come all the time now. I need to know why. I need answers.
I hope your luck turns out better than mine.

S.

Mortlock slumped on the sofa, rubbed his forehead. Another one slipped through his fingers. It was so hard to think. Where would she have gone to? She was a widower and her parents too were long dead. Had she mentioned a sister? He didn't think so.

Shirley's brandy bottle was down to sips and vapours. He downed most of what remained in a swallow, sank back in the cushions again. Dust motes dropped from the rafters. The cutesy stoneware vase on the mantle was stiff with a clump of moonsmilk, the lintel littered with curling black petals and orange stamen fuzz. Shouts, perhaps chants, dopplered along the street outside. He knew he had to go back to the Church, but not without – in his mind the word he used was *seeing*, but he knew what it stood for – Shirley first. The weight of duty paralysed him in this still room. It would be easy enough to stay here a while longer.

Mortlock looked into his tumbler. Barely a dribble left. A noise made him pause as he made to drain the glass. Reluctantly, he stopped. Listened. The silence stretched long enough almost to convince him that he had imagined it, but then it came again.

A *slosh* and a *swirl*, followed by laughter.

A child's laughter.

It was coming from the bathroom.

Mortlock heaved himself off the couch. The springs protested, but there was no call for stealth. They knew Mortlock was here. The bathroom was squeezed into the end of a passage that ran between the eaves and the stairwell. Hanging from the door was a small collage picture made from glued-on bits of shell. It depicted a tower, the flattened cone of a limpet in the sky above it. The artless thing could have been bought in the Dovene market, or it could have been made by a child. Mortlock guessed the former, but suspected the latter as being the reason Shirley had purchased it.

Splash – heh-heh-ho.

Mortlock pushed the door. It swung slow. The window at the end of the room was made of that cheap glass, imperfections compounded by vitric so that the panes strained the light like the surface of a pond. Like being under water. Beside the window the toilet pan, then the wash stand, both of them glistening with liquid drops. Finally, closest to the door, the bath tub itself. There was water in the bath, and there was something in the water.

In the aquatic light, the figure in the bath tub resembled that of a child waiting for someone to wash its hair. There was a curve of spine, a slimness of shoulder, the nape of neck, the dripping curtain that hung down in front of the face. There was even something about the play of light on the shape that suggested pale, wet skin. Little wonder a woman ridden by the guilt of a lost child could not stand to be around them.

But then the creature moved, and Mortlock recognised the silverfish for what it was. Not in the water, but of it.

The creature turned its head towards him. A shoal of minnows crossed its face like a fleeting smile. Higher up, a shell tumbled like a wink. Water swirled and an arm raised out of it. A finger took on definition and beckoned for Mortlock to come closer. He did so, and saw that there was something else in the water. A glittering thing, submerged below the surface.

Mortlock knelt and retrieved the object. The water was shocking cold, and the child laughed like it was being tickled.

The object was a disc. Two lengths of sundered chain dangled from it.

Shirley's luck.

"I don't want to kill her" he told the child.

The child looked crestfallen, and then its arm stretched towards him. Mortlock closed his eyes and waited for the cold fingers to touch his skin.

The afternoon brought a succession of visits. Two nervous girls arrived bearing linen. Lottie glowered. Shortly afterwards came the matrons. In a pack, like a yardful of geese, and today it seemed to take seven of them to perform the same tasks that it had taken one the day before.

"Do you know something I don't know?" Lottie challenged.

The matrons bowed heads to murmur together. The leader – the one with the coldest hands and the firmest grip – answered for the collective. "All in good time, dear."

Later still, her mother came with her lancet and bloody bowl. "Well? What?" Lottie snapped as she straightened up, wiped her chin.

Phamie glared at her as if it was Lottie's recalcitrance that was making things difficult. "I don't know, child."

Lastly, Aunt Ruby ambled in, flopped into the chair by the window. "Nearly there, Lottie, hen," she said. "Don't look at me like that. You don't have to talk if you don't feel like, but you'll be glad of the company when it comes." She grinned her yellow teeth. "This one's going to be a bastard for sure." With a smug purse of the lips at her own joke, she settled herself and then pulled out a pair of knitting needles and a ball of hairy, purple wool.

It might have been the boredom, or it might have been hypnotic *clacking* of Ruby's pins, but Lottie slept. When she woke, the room was so dark that she thought at first she had been out for hours, but then that evil-looking crow hopped off its perch on the sill and it was day again. Lottie cursed the Lunane's bird with a whisper.

She took a sip of water. "What time is it?"

"Gone four, hen." Ruby raised an eyebrow but didn't break the rhythm of her needles. "Don't worry, you won't sleep through it when it comes."

Lottie was thinking of a retort when there was a noise from downstairs. They all heard it. Something between a banging and a shouting. It made Ruby still her needles and ruffled the feathers of the bird outside the window. The sound became a growing commotion, a rumpus that resolved as it grew louder. And closer. The voices were mostly shrill, but one stood out. It was male, accented. Blessedly familiar.

Henrik.

Outside Lottie's door, her mother's thin peeve cut through the hubbub. "Now, son, I've got to ask you to stop. You're disturbing our residents, many of whom have had a traumatic time of late, so I can't allow —"

Henrik's voice was pitched too low to make out his reply.

"It *was* Lottie's room, that's right." Her mother was spinning for all she was worth. "When she was a wee girl. But now we use it for our most needy convalescents, so if you'll —"

Henrik cut her off with something serious and final. When the door opened, Lottie realised she had never been as glad to see anyone in her life.

"What's all this?" Ruby moved with surprisingly litheness to stand between the door and Lottie's bed. "You getting a bit confused again son? Forgetting yourself are you?" There was no sympathy in her tone.

"Looks like a rescue party to me." Lottie found herself laughing. It wasn't funny. The whole situation was ridiculous, sure, but it wasn't funny in the slightest. "I see you came prepared."

He had indeed. Henrik looked at the gun in his hand. A solid piece of ironwork with a hefty wooden grip. And it was dripping wet, with a tail of emerald weed poking from the muzzle. "A gift from the... *someone...* I met on the way here." Something in that last sentence confused him. He shrugged it away. "Got me in here, didn't it?"

Lottie's mother cleared her throat. She wore an expression of serene fury.

"I don't care where you got the gun from, it doesn't frighten me." To look at her you'd believe it. "And I'll be expecting you to pay for the bloody, great hole in the wall downstairs, thank you very much."

Henrik had the decency to look ashamed.

"And as for a rescue, *what rescue?* Charlotte's here to be cared for by her own kind. People that know what's good for her."

Henrik shook his head. "There's nothing good for her here. I'm taking her away."

"Away!" The mother pumped the word with scorn. "Away where?"

Henrik addressed Lottie. "There's a ship leaving this evening. Remember those places I told you about. Sissaloniki, Bergamel, the Magdriatics, New Russland? We can go there. To all of them if you like. It's all arranged."

Lottie propped herself up. She felt her lips curve into the

unfamiliar shape of a smile. The images she had painted on the Promise Centre wall unfurled in her mind. Beautiful, exotic. Unreal. "What about the baby?"

"Well, when the baby's born –"

"'When the baby's born?'" Lottie's mother's tone was scathing. "Have you no eyes? This baby's more overdue than the Lunane's promise."

As if aware that it was being talked about, Lottie felt the baby give an impatient wriggle. And again, but this time more than a wriggle. Her face must have left no doubt to anyone in the room that something was happening because they all reacted at once.

Henrik reached her first. "Come with me. Now."

She shook her head at Henrik's naiveté. "It's too late."

Lottie's mother took hold of Henrik's outstretched hand and drew it down. Her voice was gentle for once. "She's right enough, son. This pregnancy is like nothing we've ever seen. The baby's grown miraculous quick. It's ready to come out, but Charlotte's body hasn't been able to adapt fast enough. She's not ready. So we're going to have to cut her open and take it out. Otherwise…"

Henrik went pale. "Lottie could die?"

"They both could. And we can't be having that, now can we?" She passed Henrik's unresisting hand on to Cara, who drew him away as the matrons busied themselves around Lottie. One of them opened an expanding wooden box, its many compartments filled with glittering instruments. Another laid a white sheet on a stool, and a third who had brought the blood bowl placed it reverentially on the cloth. The last one opened the window and made *shooing* noises at the crow on the sill. The bird cawed menacingly and snapped at the woman's fingers.

"Take the lad downstairs and make him a decent cup of tea," Lottie's mother told Cara.

The girl nodded and tugged at Henrik's sleeve, but he shook her off and with a final worried glance made for the door under his own steam.

"Wait." Everyone turned to look at Lottie. She forced a smile through the pain. "Come here."

Henrik did as he was told, knelt beside the bed. She put a hand behind his head, pulled him closer, relishing the solidity of his shoulder, the fierce tension in his neck. Lottie drew as much strength from the kiss as she thought Henrik could afford to lend her. She heard the Lunane's crow chattering with agitation and redoubled the passion of the embrace.

"Thank you," she said when they broke apart. "And please, I need you to stay." He nodded, and that was enough.

Out of the corner of her eye she was aware of the bird flustering and stamping and trying to prise open the window. It didn't like Henrik's presence at all. It began to *kraaak* again, a hoarse and bitter noise.

Lottie let go of Henrik's shoulder, biceps, wrist, fingers. Gun. It was weighing him down like a ship's anchor. Gently, she prised it from his fingers. He let her take it and backed away. The women gasped collectively as they realised what had happened. And again when, with both hands, Lottie clicked back the hammer.

Lottie smiled to herself, and everyone but Henrik began talking at once so that it quickly became impossible to distinguish their imprecations from the damned crow.

She aimed the gun, fired it.

The percussion was shockingly loud. The reverberations froze the assembly into a tableau of fright.

And for a few seconds at least, as everyone watched the settling snow of bloody white down, the silence was beautiful.

Lottie pointed at the nearest matron. "Get that cleaned up will you?" She waved the gun around the rest of them. "And now we're free of observers, let's get on with the business of getting this baby out of me."

She had no doubt that the baby was aware of what she was saying. Even Lottie had to believe that this was a supernatural child, and although she hated to give credit to the Church's stupid prophecies, what else could it be but the Queen in waiting? The pregnancy alone was proof that the child was determining the timing of its own birth, irrespective of the Lunane's attempts to interfere.

This time it caused such a ruckus inside her that she screamed with the pain.

Chapter 22

Nature was taking its revenge on Glassholm.

The crow flew Anton in along the line of the cliffs. Below them, the sea renewed its assault on the city. Waves spumed up the encircling cliff walls like grasping claws. Each barrage loosened a fistful of rock, a slab of slate, the foundation stones of someone's home. The harbour was awash. Untethered boats drifted in the Dockton streets. The Cord burst its banks in numerous locations as the tidal bore thrust at the city's heart. The floodwater submerged Sump Street, knocked out one of the slender supports of the Mason's Bridge and washed away the remains of The Rottens before surging on towards the Palace to make mud of the ornamental gardens.

The people retreated to the hills, the higher buildings of the Merchantry, what remained of the still smoking Foundry. Anton could see them down there, roaming the sodden streets in search of reasons.

In the avenues that led to the Lunane's Palace they were rebuffed by the combined efforts of what looked to be the police and the Palace guard and a nervous ad-hoc militia that had been conscripted from the Palace staff. They were rebuffed, but they did not disperse.

The Lunane's machine was in sorry shape. The citizens may never have seen themselves as cogs in the city's engine, but at some level they clearly knew. And, with no sign of their Lunane in their time of need, each one of them would have an emptiness inside their heart where their loyalty and sense of duty had been. Cogs no more, they disengaged from the machine and sought new purposes.

Some, he expected, would gather in flood-damaged coffee shops and Merchantry pubs where that gap might be filled with the fire of revolution. Some would lurk in alley shadows and have the gap filled drop by cold drop with whispers of corrosion and revenge. And some, whose gap flooded with blind rage like the sea into Dockton, stomped from cobble to puddle, lashing out at the multitudinous crabs with snatched-up weapons. The crustaceans suffered the brunt of this frustration because ten of them were easier to hit than even one of the monkeys that now swarmed the city, scampering from street to window to gutter to roof, seeking out recipients for the worst kinds of luck.

A few souls, light-headed and loose, wandered like flotsam, the gaps in their hearts perhaps containing nothing more substantial than the ephemeral spume of hope. Like cogs that continued to turn when they were meshed to nothing but air.

The crow deposited Anton in a Palace courtyard. It did not do so gently. Though it swooped low enough that the fall would not break bones, the impact jarred him from head to toe. He caught his breath, then raised himself into a sitting position. His hands burned, raw from gravel abrasions, and his shoulders ached where the mechanical talons had gripped him.

The crow perched on the pitched roof of one of the surrounding buildings and watched him with its ball bearing eye. With a crack, a piece of slate beneath its talons splintered off and skittered to the ground.

An image of Mia's broken body flashed into Anton's mind.

Forget about that traitor. The instant the Lunane's voice echoed in his head, Anton's mind blanked. Like forgetting a dream on waking, he was aware that he had been thinking about something, but could not for the life of him remember what.

Never mind. It wasn't important. There was a touch too much glee in the Lunane's tone. *You do remember what's important, don't you?*

Anton stood, shook the grit off his coat. "You sound like you're pleased to have me back," he said. "Does that mean I'm more than just a body to you now?"

You know that your expertise is valuable. Under the *bon homie*, the Lunane was snappish.

"You mean you've still not fixed your machine yourself?"

I was wrong to attempt that.

"Really?" Anton was surprised. It was the first time he had heard the Lunane admit fault in anything. And now he sensed that there was something else different about the king too. A diminishment of presence, perhaps? A lack of command?

A glimmer of something, then it was gone.

The Lunane snarled. *I've already admitted as much. Do not try my patience, Engineer. Now tell me what you learned from* them.

"Them?" Anton's palms throbbed. His hands were bloody and

gritty. The gash in his arm pulsed as if in sympathy with these new injuries.

The freaks and the cast-offs.

"Oh, *them*." Anton picked shards of stone from his skin. The pain brought another flash. It was something to do with Mia.

Where was Mia? Had she stayed behind?

"You mean Mia's people?" he said. "The people that take away your unwanted dreams and your unwanted children?"

Those people know their place in my city, the Lunane said.

"*Outside* your city, you mean?"

It is for their own protection. The populace would not accept them.

"Don't give me that," Anton snapped. "You just don't want anything to rock your preciously balanced boat."

A dry chuckle, and Anton felt a soothing peace settle through him like snow.

He balled his fists, squeezed. Pain flared like fire. The image flashed again, a shape curled on the ground.

I allowed you to leave the city, didn't I? Was there uncertainty in the tone? There was certainly less force now, like it had been at the shoreline.

"You had no choice. Your control only extends so far."

Do you really think so? Engineer, I was with you all the time.

"Then why do you need to ask what I learned?"

There was silence.

Anton squeezed his fists tighter. They became blooming roses of pain. Now he remembered Mia's corpse clearly. He remembered the peaceful setting, the awful violence of what had happened. He remembered the handful of moments before the crow snatched him away in which the only sound had been the susurrus of the leaves, as rhythmic as the waves.

"I'll tell you what I... learned." He paused to listen, but heard only the in-out of his own breathing. "I learned enough, perhaps, to bring your machine... back in line. But I will see to that in my own time. There are more important things to be getting on with first."

He felt the surge beginning, beat it back with pain and the refusal to forget Mia's death. The swell rose, a black wave rolling in. Anton ground his palms together, focussed on a lolling little head, a snapped spine, a pale throat stained scarlet.

The wave receded.

When Anton looked around him again, he recognised this courtyard, and he knew how to get to where he needed to be.

"... *one...*" he muttered under his breath as he strode towards the nearest doorway.

Mortlock followed the tramline. The silverfish walked at his side, kept him on course between the steel rails. The silverfish, with their gentle touch that hadn't been strong enough to unpick the work of Ruby Blake or Charles Lytten but now stirred his thoughts with whispers like shells on the seabed. They told him where Shirley was.

The route saw them cross the Cord and skirt its little sister, and every time the tracks brought them close to water the entourage grew. The creatures slipped out from under the warehouse jetties and climbed up from the sewers. The ones that emerged from the waves lapping the rubble of the Rottens were dark and had bellies fat with crabs. They paused momentarily to drop their cargo on the cobbles with a *splash*, a clatter of carapaces and a clicking of questing claws.

Mortlock climbed Hatchard Hill and listened to his companions. The sun dipped behind his back, and by the time he had reached Mael Street all that remained was a molten blob that cast the city below him in bronze. It looked like a sunken, man-fashioned thing, lost and rusted solid.

He recognised that such imaginative a thought was likely not his own, but that failed to concern him unduly. He had orders to follow, and that was all that mattered.

By the time he reached the gate of the tenement church, the last of the sun had slipped away and the red door was illuminated by the moon. That stopped him. The moon was in the wrong place, too early past the eastern finial and high, *high*, above the horizon.

Ocean-cold fingers touched his hand, directed his attention back to the door. Under the moon, the paintwork was glossy and dark. How flagrant was that, a door that colour? *The colour of a cunt. The colour of a promise that could be delivered or snatched away on a whim. What gave those bloody women the right, eh?*

Mortlock heard Prunty's justifications in those words. A cheer from the crew.

Bloody right.

They were all in there: the Blake girl, protecting her murdering boyfriend – only, no, he hadn't turned out to be Alfie's killer after all because that had been *him*. Well, orders were orders, Kremer understood that. No matter, the lad had to go, and the women whose petticoats he chose to hide behind had to go too.

And that Shirley. She'd be first.

They told Lottie they were going to cut her open, but that was hours ago. The passage of time was measured in the rotation of matrons around her bed, the frequent blood readings, and the not-nearly-frequent-enough steaming mugs of whiteleaf infusion. Lottie had changed her mind about her mother's favourite tea. She still didn't like the taste but those minutes after she greedily gulped each cup down were a blessed relief. The child inside her grew more impatient with every hour that passed and, every time Lottie slid back into lucidity, the pain redoubled.

In between heaving gasps for breath, Lottie whispered to the baby. "It's not my fault, Your Highness. I can't do any more. Please be patient, love." *Listen to yourself*, she thought. *You'll say anything to make this more bearable.*

Amid it all, there was Henrik. He sat with her, he read to her, he held her hand. None of it helped particularly, but she clung to his solidity when she felt herself getting tugged along by the rising tide of the Church's fervour.

And it was seductive. The building was filled with serene song, an unbreaking liturgy of calm that Lottie found comfort in, even at her most anguished moments. As an air of aid, it buoyed her, but it was a paean of praise too. Praise for the child, and praise for its mother. The matrons became reverential in their ministrations. Where their fingers had been rough and efficient before, now they were tender as they rubbed ointment into her belly and her spine, their strokings bordering on yearning. Even her mother's attitude had changed. The scorn was replaced with murmurs of encouragement and assurance, and there was a gleam of something in her eyes. It might have been pride, but that Lottie chose to interpret as the anticipation of power.

Lottie drank her tea and drifted, roused only when someone came to fetch her empty cup. She heard them enter, heard the delicate *chink* of the crockery, heard them humming under their breath. For a change it wasn't a Church song. That pricked her curiosity, but her eyes were too heavy. A pause followed, stretched into nervous silence. The visitor did not retreat. Then there was a rustle of skirts, and breath at her ear. Lottie really tried to look now, but she was just too tired.

"You've got to get out of here," the visitor whispered.

"Can't…" Lottie's lips were barely able to form the word.

"They'll take your child away. Send it to exile in the caves."

Lottie managed a sloppy shake of the head. "Queen…"

The voice cracked. "Don't tell me you actually believe that? Look at yourself, girl. This child is unnatural. It will not be accepted." Lottie felt fingers brush the hair away from her bad eye. "You know all about acceptance, don't you? How welcome would you have been, with your tiny blemish, if not for who your mother was? For your baby's sake, *flee.*"

When Lottie woke next, night had fallen. Outside the window, stars winked in the black like sunken coins. *Was it them that cast this strange, aqueous radiance in the room?*

"What's happened to the light?" she murmured.

"Shush, love," Henrik said, but he wasn't listening. "There's not long to go now."

Lottie raised her head from the pillow. The lamps were burning with their usual brightness, but there was an extra shimmer. "No, listen, there's something wrong with the light."

"Shh." Henrik pressed her gently back down again, and the question went further unanswered because the matrons chose that moment to return. Six of them, like Palace guardsmen. The military impression was compounded by the precision of the creases in their aprons, the uniform angle of their starched hats. Lottie did not like this.

"Time to get you properly attired, Your Highness," the eldest said, and one of her subordinates unfurled the cloth bundle she was carrying, revealing it to be a night dress. It was white muslin but glittered in the odd light, and Lottie saw that there were designs embroidered into it in silver thread. And such designs. The flowing patterns covered every inch of the fabric, the needlework so fine that the garment, as it spun in the light, looked from one minute to the next as if it were made from water or spiderweb or steel.

"That's so beautiful," she said.

"It is the work of many hands," said the matron. "And many,

many years."

Lottie had always despised the women who came here and spent their time sewing, patching and mending the Church linen and the women's ageing clothes. Who would have guessed that the best of them were permitted to work on this: The Queen Mother's birthing robe? The reward for their skill and labour, to be sworn to secrecy, unable to tell anyone that such a thing even existed. She stroked the material. So soft. She had expected a degree of stiffness from so many layers of thread upon thread, but it was pliant and silken.

Lottie pulled back the bed clothes, shifted herself into a sitting position and raised her arms above her head. Two of the matrons took an arm each of her plain flannel nightdress and tugged it over her head. Even that simple exertion made her sweat, but the baby for once remained quiet.

One of the matrons had begun rolling up the hem of the beautiful gown to make it easier to put on. The stitching glittered even more brightly than before, close to dazzling now. Lottie cast a frown around the room. The lamps looked even dimmer now. The cause of the dazzle was elsewhere, but she could not identify it.

"What is wrong with the light in here?" she demanded. "Where is it coming from?"

The matrons shared looks. Their serious faces betrayed uncertainty. It was Henrik who told her.

"It's coming from you love," he said.

Lottie did something then she had tried to avoid in recent days, she looked at her body. It was true. Her skin was radiant.

It hadn't been so obvious in the natural pallor of her arms, but with her naked torso exposed, there was no denying the light emanating from within her skin. Her breasts were bright as moonflowers in full blossom, but it was the fat, veined stretch of her belly that shone brightest.

"You didn't tell me about this," she said.

"We didn't know, Charlotte." The matrons parted to let her mother approach, reach out and place five scarlet tipped fingers on Lottie's blazing stomach. In the strange illumination, her rouged lips looked slathered with blood. The smile was unnatural. "But if this is just a hint at Her power," she whispered. "Imagine what changes your daughter will soon make of the world."

Anton expected more resistance on his way into the Castil. From the look of the relief squads he encountered – chiefly comprising kitchen porters, vintners and clerks – it seemed that the security effort was concentrated on the perimeter of the Palace compound. Those already within the walls, Anton surmised as he strode through the halls unchecked, were deemed to have a right to be there. And generally everyone looked far too busy to bother about the purposeful-looking man in the military coat. It was a welcome alternative to unending obeisance.

In one vaulted passage he encountered three old men sweeping up a litter of crab carcases and dirty white feathers, and sluicing gore and guano from a magnificent mosaic. When he entered, the pensioners froze, stared at him in the same dissociative daze he'd seen in every one of the loyal workers who had stayed to protect their king. It had to be the shock. A month ago no one in Glassholm would have been able to believe that an attack on the Palace was possible.

It *had* to be the shock, but that faraway look reminded Anton of his own experience of the Lunane, and that raised another possibility.

Surely not all *of them?* No, that had to be beyond even him.

He hurried on. In the Castil tower, the depopulation was especially eerie. Anton had so quickly grown used to the presence of guards, porters, clerical staff that he had stopped noticing their presence, but now their absence was shocking.

In the emptiness he heard a sound. A music of whirrs and ticks like the secret workings of the world. The orrery mechanism. The suspended brasswork swept regally around the empty throne as if it had never missed a tick, but now it was no longer accurate. The jewelled moon that circled the dais lagged the position of the real moon Anton could see projected in the tower's dome. Alice Muir had been right about the speeding up of the orbit.

The orrery still ran, though, and the machine it represented was not yet broken beyond repair. And that meant the Lunane still lived. The question was: where?

The quiet *tick-tick-ticking* filled the hall, and the longer Anton listened to it the more agitated it made him. Its rhythm was too regular, too exact. Not natural.

"… four…" He hardly heard himself say it, and surprised himself further a few moments later by knowing exactly when to follow it with "... five..." There was a soft well of pressure behind it, like waiting for a tap to drip. There was a rightness to it that did not exist in the orrery, or anywhere else in the city.

Approaching the great staircase, Anton received the soft applause of wings as three enormous birds landed on the steps above him. These crows had been in the wars: their beaks were chipped, their feathers ravaged. One of them was missing an eye, but that only seemed to intensify the penetration of its gaze.

The birds hopped and shuffled. They weren't sure where the Lunane was either. When Anton took a step onto the staircase they flustered up to watch from a higher banister, but they let him pass for now.

The library was shut up. This perhaps was the greatest sign that everything had come off the rails. In all his time here, the library had been a place of quiet industry. The librarians were always shuttling through these portals on some purposeful errand, and you could hear the muted telegraphy of the typewriters at any time of the day. A reminder that the history of the city was an unstoppable process.

Or at least it had been until now.

Anton stole a glance up the tower. The levels above were just as quiet. They couldn't have all gone to defend the Lunane, could they? Even the astronomers? Even Gerard's bureaucrats? He couldn't imagine those grey robes bearing arms up on the Palace walls, but this was the heart of the machine. Here people were at the furthest remove from the influence of the sea. They would be the last to desert. No, they would protect the heart at all costs.

"... seven..." Anton murmured.

There was no lock on the library doors, but his shove met resistance and his hand came away gritty from the white patina that coated the handle. Anton sniffed his palm. An acrid tang.

He put his shoulder to the door, felt it give a little, but not enough to give him hope that he'd be able to budge it. Something bulky had been employed as a barricade. Which meant that someone was still inside.

"Hello?" The echo of it fled up towards the Castil roof. "Muir?"

Anton placed his ear against the wood. Was that the sound of something shifting inside? Anton hammered. "Alice? Are you there?"

Another sound from within. This time, a soft exhalation that tailed into a compressed, but unmistakable, sob. "Go away."

Anton recognised Muir's voice. He remembered the state the woman had been in the night after she'd taken them down to the journal repository. She'd cracked, albeit briefly, under the pressure of something. *Dreams*, she'd said.

Well, Anton knew about dreams.

He tried again. "Muir," he said. "There's no one here. Only me. I need your help." He paused to listen. He might have been talking to an empty room. Then something heavy scraped against the wood. The handle turned and the door opened. Anton caught a glimpse of a face retreating into the gloom. The librarian looked terrible.

Inside, Anton had a moment to appreciate the effort Muir of removing all of those books so that the stout shelves could be used to barricade the door, before the door slammed and the light was gone. Behind him Anton heard something being dragged, shoved and wedged once more under the handle.

"Muir…"

"Shut up." The voice was quiet, but close.

A match scritched, flared, a fizzing hole in the dark. Then it was applied to a candle and light returned. The haggard cast of Alice's face made Anton think of the corpses that sometimes escaped their shrouds and weights and floated up in the lagoon.

"Who are you?" The librarian squinted suspiciously.

"You know who I am, Muir. And who I was. My name is Anton Dunn. I'm an engineer."

The candle dwindled as Muir disappeared behind the cases. "Yes, yes, yes…but who are you *right now?*"

"Just myself. He's gone. For good this time. And I'm not letting him back in." It felt like the truth, even if it wasn't.

The candle stopped. Anton could see the tip of the flame winking like a golden star.

"Muir?" he whispered. "Do you understand me?"

"*They told me to trust you.*"

The candle hadn't moved, but the voice was closer. Anton whirled, looked directly into Muir's deathly face. The librarian's lenses were pitted like moons. Alice removed them, wiped them on her robe. It made no difference. It was a wonder that the woman could see anything. A step closer, Anton finally recognised the crusty substance was. Salt.

"Who are *they*?" Anton asked.

Muir's lips squirmed as she tried to tame them into something approximating a smile. The taciturn woman had never been much of a one for smiles anyway, but this took effort.

"There is so much knowledge, Anton Dunn," she said. "But so many secrets too."

Anton's spirits slumped. Alice appeared to have unravelled completely.

"That's what *he* does, isn't it? Keeps us in the dark. Keeps us in line."

"The Lunane would tell you that such measures are not for his benefit but for the good of everyone," Anton said, probing.

Muir's laugh was desiccated. "No doubt he would," she said. "He might even flatter you with trust. He'd puff you up with the idea that you were the custodian of the city's truth." That laugh again. "But loyal as you are all your life, he'd still demand secrets of you. And guard his own jealously."

Muir grabbed at Anton's coat sleeve, tugged at the insignia at the cuff. Two silver crescents indicated that the boxer who had owned it had been a Lieutenant.

"Doesn't matter how loyal you are, Mr Dunn." Muir said. "Or what you have to do to maintain that loyalty. In the end it's not enough. It's not worth it. He'll never let you in on his secrets."

The librarian was rambling now but Anton thought he knew what she was getting at. "You're talking about the door, aren't you? The door in the underground repository."

Muir nodded. "Yes, they told me…"

"The children in your dreams?"

She removed her spectacles. Without them she blinked like a child. "I don't believe they are dreams anymore."

Anton's guess had been right. What had Coombs said about nature fighting back? About children in the city? The real Derry-men? He didn't know what exactly it was that had been visiting Muir, but when you thought about Mia's people, about the patient, spectacular storm flies, what other secrets might the limitless ocean keep from these ignorant self-absorbed city dwellers? Clearly something strange enough to make a woman lose her faith in her king.

It wasn't important who had been talking to Muir. The important thing was opening the door in the repository.

"You know what's down there, don't you?" Anton said.

Muir widened her eyes. Then she nodded.

"I need you to show me."

It took substantial persuasion to prise Muir from her hidey-hole. Anton's various threats, blandishments and promises were rebutted out of hand.

Muir maintained her protests as Anton half-pushed, half-dragged her down the tower staircase. "It's no use. The door only opens for the Lunane. I've tried. So many times."

"This time will be different," Anton assured her.

In front of the throne, Muir dug her heels in. "Different how?"

"I've got a theory." Anton turned towards the exit, but Muir folded her arms. "Very well. Listen, we know from the original journals and from what Gerard told me that when the king vacates one body, he moves directly into another. His consciousness has to be somewhere, doesn't it?"

Another nod.

"So where is he? Why hasn't he returned in all his glory to lead the defence of his Palace? The way he manipulates public opinion, you'd think he'd jump at the chance for a bit of grandstanding from the Palace walls."

Muir remained sceptical. "I imagine it would take more than that to regain the public opinion," she said. "The children are very persuasive."

"Maybe." Anton pointed at the vacant throne. "But the question remains: where *is* he?"

Muir shrugged. "And you think you know?"

"Yes, I do. And I think I can persuade him to open that door for us too. Come on."

On the way to the winery courtyard, Anton paid attention to everyone they encountered. He'd been incredulous when the notion first occurred to him, but he'd been unable to dismiss it. Now he was looking for evidence to support his theory. A trio of guardsmen, carrying a colleague with a poorly dressed head wound to the infirmary, eyed Anton and Muir with vague interest. A pair of kitchen girls scurrying by with brimming pots of water also paused to watch them pass. A boy wheeling a barrow piled high with hoes and rakes from the gardens awarded them similar unfocused attention.

All of them shared the same air of distraction he'd noticed earlier. Anton felt sure he knew where the Lunane had gone. After all, there really was safety in numbers.

They had to hurry though. Who knew when the king might decide to abandon his control of the Palace's defence, thinly spread among the loyal staff, bolstering confidence and shoring up failing loyalties, and return to one person's body. Anton thought he might be able to defend himself, but if the Lunane chose Muir for his vessel there was nothing he'd be able to do.

Muir's key let them into the wine store. In the bottling area they saw that the elevator had already been used, and whoever had used it hadn't returned.

Muir arched an eyebrow. "Maybe this answers your question about where the Lunane went. He's there ahead of us."

Anton shook his head. "Not necessarily." He hoped he sounded more confident than he felt.

Muir leaned on the heavy handle. There was a distant *chunk*, and then a grinding noise that grew in volume, became a rattling rumble. As the lift platform rose to the surface another sound could be heard. The sound of whimpering.

"Hogarth?"

The terrified biographer's attention snapped between Muir and Anton. His eyes were wide. "Mr Gerard said you were dead." He sounded disappointed that it wasn't so.

"The secretary is prone to exaggeration when it suits him. What on Earth were you doing down there?"

"I was..." A flick of the eyes to Muir and back again. "I was hiding."

"Hiding from whom?" Muir asked.

Hogarth flinched at her tone.

"You have nothing to fear from us, Hogarth." Anton hoped that was true. Although he believed that he had rebuffed the Lunane, he had been counting on either himself or Muir having a tiny piece of the king in them. Not as much as the Palace staff, but enough. Now, however, the question was academic. If anyone was an open conduit for residency, it was Hogarth.

The lad breathed out, a shuddery exhalation. "I'm such a coward," he said. "I just wish things were back to normal."

Anton seized on this. "We can make it like that. If you help us."

As Anton's words sank in, the lad's expression shifted from one of relief to one of hope.

"How?" He got shakily to his feet and revealed that he had been sitting on his trusty ledger.

Anton and Muir joined him on the elevator platform. "By fixing the machine in the tower," Anton said. "But first we need to see what lies at the bottom of all this. What do you say?"

The life was returning to the biographer by the second. He opened his journal, flipped hurriedly past a sheaf of blank pages to the one marked with that day's date. "I'm ready," he said.

Muir wasted no time in taking them down. At the bottom of the shaft she opened the door and led them to the door in the back corner.

Hogarth poised his pen, then realised his companions were looking at him expectantly.

"Me?"

Anton nodded. "The Lunane is every man. And, at the moment, it seems that among the loyal Palace residents every man really is he."

"Except for us," Muir added.

"You're our best chance," Anton said.

The lad nodded and reached out until his hand was an inch from the handle. Then he dropped it again. "I don't think he wants me to." His voice had a faraway quality.

Anton and Muir exchanged glances. Then he took hold of the lad's elbow, Muir the other one. "It's not important," Anton said.

"Don't stress yourself," Muir murmured.

Together they propelled the lad towards the handle. Touching the metal, the biographer's hands gripped by instinct. His arms went rigid and the others were physically repelled from contact with his body.

The handle dropped and the door swung open.

"Are you all right?" Anton asked the dazed biographer. His skin was slick. He looked like he might vomit. "Perhaps you should wait here." Anton looked for Muir. She must have gone ahead. "While I —"

"Don't leave me." Hogarth's grip was as tighter as those of the

Lunane's mechanical friends.

Anton prised his fingers off his arm. "Very well," he said, anxious now to be away. "Let's go together."

Beyond the door was a plunging stairwell in which electric bulbs dangled from the ceiling at distant intervals, marking the descent like the lambent lures of gloomfish. The cold air carried an acrid taint. The steps had been hacked hastily out of the rock. Even the passages of the Indigenes' cavern had been crafted with more care. The edges were crumbling, and they glistened treacherously, but using them was the only option.

Anton listened for Muir ahead of them, but he heard only the soft choiring of the air and the musical dripping water. Even those sounds were close to inaudible next to the ragged panic of Hogarth's breathing. Anton shot the lad an exasperated look, and then began his descent.

The going was slow without the stability of even a handrail on those treacherous steps, and proved trickier still when the lights turned out to be far enough apart that the illumination dwindled close to nothing between them. It made Anton think of the average person's descent through the months, the passing into Dark with the memory of the previous Full distant behind you and the prospect of the next an equally far away hope yet to come. They had to take the Dark slowly, a shaky step at a time, with the knowledge that soon enough the light would improve and things would get gradually easier.

He laughed at himself. He'd got too used to the Palace's obsession with symbolism. The engineer in him knew the bulbs were sparse because to run more would have overtaxed the generator. And you could never see more than one light ahead because the passage was curving. It started off as an imperceptibly gentle bend to the right, but the longer their descent went on, the tighter it became. A clockwise curl that reminded him of the stairs of the Castil tower. He wondered if, when they reached the bottom, they would find a replica of the throne and orrery above. That would be like the Lunane, a place to sit and giggle at the Dark time of his month. A refuge of counterbalance. Imagine the surprise of the citizens. They had always been educated to believe that their king was the impervious, undying fulcrum around which every aspect of their lives revolved. To discover that the Lunane underwent the same trials of the spirit as they did at the opposite ends of the month would be a shock. It might even go some way to increase his standing among his subjects again. But there was more to it than that. There was the machine as well.

There were no more bulbs.

Anton and Hogarth stopped together on the last step. They could see only the barest outline of its edge. After that they could be stepping into a void for all they knew.

"We're not meant to be here." Hogarth's timid whisper came out flat, compressed by the oppressive acoustics.

"We have every right to be here. We need to know what it is the machine controls. Do you feel him in you?"

"No, not now."

"Then he can't stop us, and…" Knowing the way the Lunane thought, Anton was sceptical but he said it anyway. "Perhaps he's allowing us to do this. Perhaps it's time for the people to learn a few secrets."

Anton heard Hogarth's breathing ease. He reached for the lad's arm. "We'll take the steps one at a time. We'll count them. Are you ready?" He guided Hogarth forward, and tried to keep the vertiginous flip in his own belly from being transmitted through their contact.

"One," he said. Hogarth's joining in was a faint echo that was yipped off as they stepped out. For a heart-stopping moment even Anton panicked that there would after all be no next step. Then his toe found the stair exactly where it should have been. Both of them choked out a sigh that became a laugh of relief.

"See? No problem. Next one?"

"Okay."

"Two…"

The remainder of the descent took an age. They weren't even able to tot up the number of steps because Anton found the numeracy subconsciously problematic. Every time he got to seven, he had to start again.

The last step brought them back into the light and on to the shingle shore of a vast lake. Anton scooped a handful of pebbles and shells, let them rattle through his fingers. This reminded him of the place where the astonishing storm flies had burst forth from the sand, but then again it was nothing like that at all. The water lapping at his feet was sterile. It lacked the life of the waves. Anton could not imagine Coombs' people connecting in any way with this flat, black expanse.

Neither would they have permitted the irruption of the Lunane's technology through the centre of the cavern roof. It was too far away to identify more than a gleaming conglomeration of brass and steel, something spinning fast like a flywheel, and of course the one thing that Anton had expected to see.

The great lens that focussed the phased lunatropic rays down here.

Which left the question of what it was focussing them on. Something in the water. Something terrifying, according to the Lunane's dreams. Anton peered at the lake but it was a mirror.

He looked up again confused. Where was the light coming from? There was no obvious source in the contraption on the ceiling. Was it possible he had made a theoretical misassumption? He had always thought that the visible light component of moonlight and the lunatropic component were separate, but could it be after all that properly filtered lunatropic rays also possessed visible properties? The light in this cave had in fact that exact spectral quality that made moonlight unique.

Fifty yards to his left there was a rocky protuberance that struck out from the wall like a boxer's nose. Anton scrunched eagerly across the shingle to climb it. He scrutinized the lens again, and could see now that there was a spot of silvery brightness on the glass. Then he saw his error. The soft glow on the lens glass was a reflection. The source of the light was the lake itself. Or at least, the terrible something that he now saw lurked beneath its surface. The something was round and flat and impossibly large. The something was pallidly luminescent. The something twisted and flipped in the murky depths in a manner that was altogether too familiar to Anton. He had watched this so many times in the dome window of the machine room. The night journals had said as much, but Anton realised only now, despite all the impossible things that he had witnessed of late, how little his rational brain had wanted to give credence to mere accounts of dreams. But it was all true. The machine's purpose was to imprison this thing in the water, not the moon.

As if sensing Anton's scrutiny, the something slid towards him. Bow waves broke against his rock. Instinct made him scrabble higher, but that just allowed him to see better the scale of the beast, because in coming closer it was also rising to the surface and as it did so the light became dazzling.

Anton had seen the like of it in the fishmarkets, spread out over ice on the fishmonger's tray. The wiry fins and tail that pushed it through the water were similar, the bulging sideways eyes too. But you could not buy a fish in any market whose back you could walk across; a journey that would take the same time as crossing the Castil tower floor. You could not kill a fish whose rough skin was patterned with circles and shadows identical to the familiar contours of the moon's face. You could not cook a fish whose body glowed with such beautiful radiance. All of it, except the slowly shrinking crescent of darkness near the tail.

A moonfish.

It was all so simple. The Lunane had not captured the moon, not directly anyway. He had caught a fish. An inconceivably enormous fish, sure, but a fish all the same. Had anyone even known that in all of the world's deep waters there was a fish that guided the moon in its orbit in a natural and unbreakable bond? Had the Lunane, desperate to find something, *anything*, to give his people the will to struggle on, just got lucky when he found that keeping the fish prisoner brought the moon to the city too?

The tranquil eyes regarded him. The sickle-shaped mouth blew sad bubbles under the surface. It didn't take any great empathy to see that the fish was terribly unhappy. Who wouldn't be after five hundred years of manufactured Darkdays?

"You couldn't stay away, could you, Engineer?"

The voice echoed oddly in the cavern, but it was still instantly recognisable. Anton turned away from the water to look into the face of the king, and was instantly enthralled. The Lunane sat with his back against the rock wall. His refined features shone with charismatic life. His bright, dark eyes, twinkled with danger, and his smile carried a stiletto mischief that gave the impression that he had materialised out of thin air.

Then Anton realised that Hogarth was gone.

Anton looked again, and this time he saw past glamour. The hair was straggly. Long hanks pooled in the collar of the grey robes. At the end of the gaping sleeves, the fingers were nail-bitten and inky.

Anton wondered whether poor Hogarth was even aware that this conversation was taking place.

"I had to see it all. The whole system," he told the king.

"Of course you did. It's in your nature." There was a bemused smile about the regal lips. "People like you always want to know everything. Even when that knowledge is not in their best interests."

"Well, that's the risk you run in allowing people like me free reign in your city. People who might think differently, or look differently, or speak differently from everyone else. From what I understand, *people like me* usually end up in a dark hole in the ground before they are old enough to make any trouble."

"An unfortunate necessity for the greater good." The Lunane's eyes were cold coals. "Really, Engineer, I thought you might have understood something of kingship by now."

"Well of course," Anton said. "You can't expect a mechanism to run smoothly unless all of the components are fit for the job."

The Lunane's smile was colder than moonlight. "There, you do understand. Although, it's a much rarer occurrence than you seem to think. Someone has been filling your head with stories." He got gracefully to his feet. Even in Hogarth's body he was tall and solid. No evidence here of the sloped shoulder or the cowed head. This was a man long used to confidence and pride, and in whatever physical body he inhabited these qualities engorged him.

"But we're not talking about machines here." Even to his own ears Anton's words sounded irrelevant. He knew it was just the Lunane's effect, and concentrated on seeing round the corners of the personality, looking for the poor subjugated lad underneath. "We're talking about human beings, we're talking about nature itself."

The royal brow crinkled, and Anton felt a rush of sympathy that threatened to crush him. Instantly, he understood why so many people queued up every Halfday for this man's comfort.

"Oh, Anton," the Lunane murmured. "You should have been born in Abergaard back before the floods. A mind like yours would have helped to create the most wonderful contrivances. In Abergaard we had machines for everything. Social engineering was fine art. The conquest of nature? Is that not what mankind has been striving for since he discovered fire?"

The soothing honey in the words conjured images in Anton's mind of a city of enormous gleaming devices. Clean, efficient, precise. Application built on knowledge built on experience. He thrilled with the prospect of understanding, *really understanding*, and inventing genuinely beneficial applications for that knowledge.

And that was the secret of the man who always seemed to give the people what they wanted. The skill of spinning the dream. The comfortable lie.

The Lunane was speaking about a past that was lost to him. Even if his nostalgia was sincere, such a city could never arise from a place like Glassholm.

Anton turned away. "You're a liar."

The Lunane didn't reply. Anton watched the water. The fish had retreated to the deeper centre. A flick of the tail-fin took it under, its light diffusing once more to that easier, silvery sheen. The waves rippling out from the place where it went under broke one after the other against the rocks with a grasping frustration.

Anton counted them.

One... two... three...

"I come down here sometimes." The Lunane's voice was so close to Anton's ear that it might have been inside his head.

"To gloat over your prize?" The bitterness in that surprised even Anton. It was worthy of Coombs himself.

"Hardly, Mr Dunn. In my own way, I respect nature."

Hogarth's robes billowed past where Anton stood. The king crouched by the water's edge, wriggled idle eddies with his fingers.

"I come to thank her. And to apologise." The ripples from the motions of his hand appeared inconsequential, but Anton knew that nothing that this man did was ever inconsequential. "For many years that seemed to be enough."

In the centre of the lake, the light swooped, down and up. Then it began once more to edge their way.

"And your apology is no longer adequate?"

The great outline of the fish became visible behind a bulging bow wave that raced towards them. The water broke off the Lunane's knees, soaked his robes, but he didn't move. His hand continued to stir the water until the fish's crater-patterned face was inches from his fingers. The jaws opened, revealing a snaggle of needle teeth, then closed again.

"It is no longer a matter of apology," the Lunane said, reaching out to stroke the beast's skin. It regarded him with a woeful look, but did not pull away. "Circumstances have merely changed."

"What circumstances?" Anton said. The intimacy on display between man and fish was uncomfortable. At first it had resembled the relationship between a man and his pet, but the longer he watched the exchange at the water's edge the more it made him think of the behaviour of unhappy lovers.

"A cycle of nature has come round again. One that we didn't factor into the original calculations."

"Hence this additional strain." Anton saw it. There had never been any malfunction with machine in the tower. It would have operated forever, but a new force – an immensely powerful force – had been introduced that the equipment could not cope with.

"Until recently there was no great problem with housing her here. This cosy cave or the open sea, she saw no difference, but now she needs to leave." The Lunane tapped the fish between the huge eyes and it slipped away once more from the shore. "And I cannot let her leave."

They watched the fish furrow back towards the lake's middle. Then it returned to the surface and emitted an awful sound that was half moan and half steamy gasp. In the next instant the colossal creature executed an unbelievable roll that threw up gouts of spray before diving once again below the surface.

This time it did not resurface, but Anton had seen what he had been intended to witness. The bulbous sac that accreted like a cyst to the pale underflesh of the beast's belly.

"It's going to die?"

The Lunane shook his head. "More than that. I talk of the Moonfish as a she, but technically she is an 'it'. The Moonfish might be the oldest animal on this planet, but it is nevertheless as bound by nature's law as are we all."

If the king was aware of Anton's incredulity at this irony he did not acknowledge it.

"The Moonfish, you see, reproduces asexually," he continued. "It has to, being the only one of its kind. How *could* there be more than one creature to guide the moon, after all? Its spawning cycle, it turns out, is a little over five hundred years long, and now it has come round. In the wild there is a place in the sea where it goes to spawn. The young one you saw there is already consuming the parent from the inside."

"How do you know this?" Anton hadn't intended to bolster this self-important monologue, but once again his curiosity got the better of him.

"Because it was the young Moonfish that I was so very lucky to come upon out in the sea. Floundering around and subsisting off the remains of its mother, dazed and hungry and full of energy. It was hard to catch, but I did so and brought it here to save our people."

Towards the end the speech took on a rousing tone, and the well-timed crack in the voice hinted at honest emotion. It was just possible that the Lunane had been spinning his legend for so long that he really believed it. No, that was unfair. It was true after all that the colony had persisted by having faith in their new leader, and the acquisition of the moon had been the focus of their belief.

Nevertheless, it was at an end now. As much as the Lunane's people had known about harnessing nature, they had not been omnipotent. The Abergaardians had been caught out by the floods, and now they were caught out again by this big old fish.

"So now it needs to return to where you found it," Anton said. "The spawning ground."

The Lunane didn't answer. Not at first. Anton watched his shoulders begin to shake, and thought he had been given a glimpse of what happened when the Lunane came down to this private place. He admitted defeat.

Then he recognised the sound the king emitted as laughter. When the Lunane stood and turned, his features were stretched in a manic rictus, his eyes blazed cold with delight.

"Come on, Anton," he bellowed. "Where's your engineer's spirit? Once we're over this hump, the machine will resume normal operation. All we have to do is persuade these Moonfish that their spawning ground is here now. Of course it will be difficult this time round, but at the next spawning the resistance will be less. And at the one after that…"

"The next one? The one after that? How long do you intend to go on?"

The eyes gleamed. "Go on?" the Lunane said. "I have no intention of stopping."

The water was so flat now that it looked to be frozen. "So, you're going to restore things exactly as they were before. Use the last of those glorious machines to constrain us with conservatism, restrain us with routine, when we could be rediscovering those lost technologies, making Glassholm greater?"

"That knowledge is lost."

"We could regain it. The people of this city have so much potential. Are you afraid to let them try?"

It was nothing more than a curl at the edge of the lips, but the expression told Anton everything about the petty tyranny of the man who had become king in times of necessity, but who found himself unable to give up the reins long after that need had passed into history.

"I said that knowledge is lost, Engineer. Experimentation is divergent, and divergence is a risk to the integrity of the machine. The machine *works* and it must continue to work."

Anton thought about the Lunane's great, complex system, worked his way through the linkages. "Not with my help."

The Lunane moued. "Why so churlish? This is the zenith of your career."

Anton shook his head. "No. The central component is defective, and beyond my skill to repair."

Mock dismay. "I'm hurt."

"I'm not doing it."

This time the Lunane's laugh ripped through the cavern. "Oh, Engineer," he said. "Do you still believe that you have any choice?"

Anton was ready for the attack. He closed his eyes, lips already moving as he sought out the rhythm of the world outside the machine. His breaths and heartbeats were his own, ungovernable by anyone else. Counting them linked his body to the air and the sea and all of the rest of the natural world in the midst of which this island was nothing but a tiny anomaly. The technique beat back the mental surge easily. Familiar with the touch now, it wasn't so hard to minimise the king's hold over him.

Two fists grabbed his lapels and Anton's eyes popped open. But instead of rage the Lunane's face was radiant with projected disappointment. It cored into Anton, shredded his resolve. Shame washed through him.

He imagined the shame as waves, and kept counting.

The Lunane's borrowed fingers found his face, stroked his cheeks in a conciliatory manner. The shame lost rhythm, became a torrent, but through the contact Anton felt a thin pulse. He counted the biographer's heart beat instead.

The fingers found his throat and squeezed. Red dazzled before Anton's eyes. The fish's radiance began to pulse light to dark to light again, and it was accompanied by the distant sound of water, the insubstantial lapping of waves.

He lost count.

He lost consciousness.

Then he was falling, the jarring pain of impacts blossoming in has palms, elbows, shins. He lay in the shingle, braced for the next assault but it didn't come. The Lunane was fighting with someone else. *Muir.* The librarian stood knee deep in the water, and soaked as if she had emerged from the lake. She must have been hiding, watching all that took place and waiting for the opportunity to take revenge on the king that had betrayed her. Muir had taken the opportunity, but she was in trouble now. The king used Hogarth's height to push the librarian into the water.

Anton rose, intent on helping but Muir, gripping grimly to her opponent diverted her attention long enough to mouth the word: "Run."

Anton lingered, torn between saving himself and helping the librarian. Then Muir changed her tactics. Instead of resisting the Lunane's force, she gave in to it, catching him off balance and pulling him down into the water. What happened next was hard for Anton to recount later. The water around the entangled couple foamed and rose, and formed itself into the shapes of child-sized figures. Hands and arms rose out of the lake to grasp and wrap around the thrashing, panicking king and his combatant. Liquid heads oversaw the proceedings with grimaces made of the skeletons of fish. Pieces of jet tumbled like dispassionate eyes.

"Run!"

It was the last thing that Muir was able to say before both she and the Lunane were dragged under the waves.

Chapter 23

The moon was shrinking. Across Glassholm the people watched with alarm. The Palace issued notices of reassurance from the astronomers. *An unusual atmospheric effect that only made it seem to be shrinking.* The crowds encamped outside the Palace entrances tore the notices off the gates. Behind the walls the guards to a man and woman felt their righteous bravado drain from them. Scared and confused, they braced themselves for the next onslaught of bricks and cobbles.

There was a running battle at the Foundry gates. The charred skeleton of the clock tower watched over the fight as the Foundry's engineers barricaded the city's gas supply against rioters. They lost, and all across Glassholm the lights went out.

All except for the Palace. With its own electricity, the city's white heart outshone the moon. The satellite, in its turn, continued to rise, continued to roll around the northern sky where for a few minutes it angled directly into windows of the tenements on Hatchard Hill.

The light that filled Lottie's room triggered desperate activity in her belly.

The child knew the touch of moonlight.

It was time.

Lottie couldn't have kept the fact from the matrons even if she had wanted to. All she could think of now was getting it over with.

The years of meticulous preparation paid off as the Church's plans swept smoothly into motion. Lottie observed it in a distracted fashion that she attributed to increased dosage of the whiteleaf concoction.

Somewhere, someone was wailing.

Lottie marvelled at the matrons' efficiency. The production of steaming basins and cloth-covered trolleys. The careful scrubbing and exchange of urgent murmurs. It was all very impressive.

She wished that whoever was wailing like that would just shut up.

Then she realised that the wailer was herself.

Lottie took a deep breath, and managed to form words. "Where's Henrik?" she said.

"There's no room in here for that big lug." A matron tucked in Lottie's sheets. "He'd just get in the way now."

"But I want him here."

"He's waiting for you downstairs, love." Another laid a blanket across the bed.

"What are you doing?"

"Hush your mouth, girl and act like a mother of this Church."

Her mother's face leered down, resplendent in its mask of rouge and paint. Lottie's light threw dark shadows under her fat chin.

"Is everything ready?"

"Yes, Mother."

"Then let's go."

Two of the matrons were at the foot of her bed, two of them went to the head. Another matron held open the bedroom door, and those that were left carried all the paraphernalia and followed the Mother from the room. Then, in concert, the four women at the corners of Lottie's bed heaved, and to her astonishment it too rolled towards the door.

She was flabbergasted. When exactly had they put castors on the legs of her bed? It must have been since she returned to the Church, or at least since her mother knew that she was with child. She refused to even consider that her mother and her bloody prophecy had fingered her for the Queen Mother all along.

The matrons rolled her along the landing. At the stairs they were met by a pack of women. Cara was among them, her face shining with pride, along with a handful of other faces Lottie would not readily have associated with the Church. There was Innes, the widowed ironmonger from the Dovene Square market, and her stupid daughter too, and behind them the sallow-faced girl who ran the public baths, a silver-haired police woman, in uniform, who Lottie recognised as a regular in the Rottens, and that nice woman who ran the café in the Merchantry. What had been her name again? She had been so sensible, so supportive and free with good advice, until she'd fallen apart at the Halfday petitions. It saddened Lottie to see someone like that fall back on the crutch of the Church. Then she realized that, while her gaze was as intent as the rest, instead of bathing her in milky adoration, it scoured her with pity.

Lottie remembered the whispers at her bedside. *They'll take your child away*, the woman had said. But that was what she wanted wasn't it? To be rid of it. For this all to be over.

The women mobbed Lottie's bed and then, like drilled soldiers, at a single barked command lifted it clear of the ground. Powerless, Lottie lay back, closed her eyes and tried to keep the effects of all the jostling and bouncing behind her clamped lips.

After the staircase, they trundled her through the ceremonial rooms. Then the scrape of curtain rings. As the bed was transported up the rise, there was a commotion. "*... not of the blood...*" A scream of frustration that was cut off and instantly forgotten. Rumbling on the roof, the bed was rolled into its final position.

The night air was shocking. It cut through the residual whiteleaf torpor and the pain that had now begun to ebb back into her awareness. Lottie opened her eyes and looked up into the uncaring eye of the moon. Like all Glassholmers, she had lived all her life under its gaze; so familiar to her that she couldn't remember the last time she had really looked at it. She did so now, and decided that, yes, it was a magnificent, beautiful thing. Cold and remote though the moon may be, it was still the closest thing she had to something she could rely on.

The matrons bustled into activity. Behind them a nervous crowd waited. But Lottie used the moon to distract herself from all of that. Close to Full, when people were susceptible to all sorts of persuasion, you often heard it said that the patterns of shadow resembled the Lunane's face. The pale smudges that could be eyes, and underneath, the dark 'o' of a mouth, were there sure enough, but Lottie had never been convinced. Perhaps she had been more influenced by her upbringing in the Church than she thought. No, to Lottie, the moon was not a person. It was a place. A beautiful, remote place, and at that moment she would have given anything to travel there. She imagined herself travelling without moving. The moon did not get closer, but the pain inside and activity around her receded.

Someone touched her and she snapped back to the Chapel. Gentle fingers lifted her head. Fragrant steam warmed her face.

"Drink this," they said. "It's time now."

The infusion had an instant effect. She felt both like a stone weight on the bed and like a paper husk, light enough to float away. If she could find a way to separate the two parts, she felt that she could reach the moon. She could leave Glassholm forever.

"Ladies of the Church." Her mother's voice was distorted by pride and self-importance. Hateful and jagged. "Ladies of the Church. This is our hour."

Lottie ignored the cheers, focused on the voice. Made it a tool. Every word sawed at the strands that tethered Heavy Lottie on the bed to Light Lottie straining to rise into the air.

"This is the hour foretold by our blood. By our mothers' blood. And their mothers' blood too. The hour when our greatest prophecy is fulfilled."

Lottie flew. As the detestable voice dwindled, the moon grew closer. Soon she would cross the sky and would be too far gone to ever come back. The tiny voice was a mosquito whine.

"This is the hour that our Queen will finally be born to the world."

"Our Queen," chorused the onlookers. Lottie could not have cared less, but she found she could not quite ignore it.

"We will raise our Queen in the ways of the Church," Lottie's mother continued. "It is the duty of every one of us."

"Our Queen," came the hungry clamour. The neediness of it twanged the last strand that tethered Lottie to this place.

"And in turn, our Queen will overthrow the patriarch and lead our city in a thousand years of our own making. No more will we suffer His *grace* to follow the destiny of our blood. No more will we pay the tax of conscience in return for his permission to follow our creed. No more will we pass judgement on the city's children. That is ended."

That was a curious choice of words. Lottie remembered what the café lady had said, and the thought snagged her attention like a twig trapping the tail of a straining kite.

Lottie's mother carried on. "We will build a Palace on the rubble of his tower of man," she cried. "A Palace for our Queen."

"Our Queen." Their fervour reached all the way out to where Lottie floated for the moon. Her attention, however, remained tethered, and it seemed that the last strand was too strong after all to be broken.

Their Queen? Lottie thought. *It's my damn baby. No one is passing judgement on my baby. It's for me to say whether she grows up a royal or a ragamuffin. And it's for* her *to decide what to make of her own life. No one else.*

She realised she meant that. With all her heart. The solid truth of it scared her. She looked to the moon again, but it was as remote as ever. And now, slowly, it appeared to be vanishing.

Lottie had spent much of her life distancing herself from the things she found difficult, but there was no escaping this. It had to be faced. "Are you going to deliver this baby or not?"

Her mother's glossy lips twist momentarily into a snarl. "All in good time," she murmured from the corner of her mouth.

"Well you'd better…" Lottie grimaced as the child somersaulted, "…hurry up." She indicated with a roll of her eyes. "Or – myself aside – you're going to run out of light to see what you're doing. And believe me, I don't want that any more than you do."

Her mother couldn't help herself. She glanced up, and every face in the congregation did the same. Uncertainty stained the rapture in their upturned faces, and the uncertainty pooled and spread until it became a cloud of fear.

The sliver of darkness at the edge of the lunar disc grew as they watched. It looked for all the world as if the month had been speeded up and thrown into reverse.

"There is nothing to worry about." The mother tried to exude calm pragmatism. "We've all seen an eclipse before, surely."

"But it was not forecast until after the Fullday," one of the matrons said.

Lottie's mother seized the opportunity. "And is that not precisely a sign of the Queen's power? She is not yet born and already she controls the moon."

"Our Queen!" The chant was less certain than it had been, but it came again. "Our Queen, our Queen!"

Lottie's blankets were snatched away. The cold enveloped her like a bright, effervescent energy. Like the light that was now pulsing from within her own body, illuminating the nightgown like a skin of jewels.

Not your Queen, my baby, Lottie thought again. *Me. Mine.* For the first time in her life she was the centre of something. Everyone was watching her. All the faces staring, wanting, needing.

It was terrifying.

No wonder the child inside her was anxious.

As soon as you are born, she told it. *We're getting out of here.* She didn't know how she intended to achieve that feat, but she made the promise all the same. No child of hers was going to be subject to this madness.

"Hurry it up, now."

A hand squeezed her jaw and a strong, strong dose of whiteleaf was slopped into her mouth, spilled carelessly down her neck, into her hair. It kicked in immediately, but she was still aware of the nightdress being yanked up to her chest. She still saw the glitter of the sharp, sharp blade.

Sensed the child still in anticipation.

Saw the sparkling arc of the scalpel.

Felt it pierce her skin, and her blood flow.

Mortlock rubbed his shoulder. Getting in to the tenement was straightforward, if painful. The red door gave after the third attempt. The atmosphere of the place was eerie. Still, like a breath caught in anticipation. Whatever was going on was important enough that they hadn't even left as much as a guard.

Stupid women.

A silverfish touched his hand. A cautionary gesture. Calming, cool.

Mortlock stopped to listen and heard the distant sound of chanting or cheering. He peered up the stairwell. He saw nothing, but that was where he had to go.

Mortlock climbed the stairs. His companions left a trickling cascade of water, a litter of shells and sand. The fervent cheers grew louder and, by the time Mortlock reached the landing second from the top, they had almost resolved into words. Then he heard something else. Other voices in urgent conversation.

Mortlock approached the closest door. Wet hands grabbed his coat but he shook them off. He knew those voices. The door opened onto a darkened hallway, but light shone underneath another door at the end. Under the blow of his shoulder it flew in and stopped the conspirators in mid-conversation.

Shirley and Henrik were huddled on a bed, her arm around him like a mother around her child. There was nothing sexual in their intimacy but the expressions on both their faces was as if they had been caught in the act all the same, and Mortlock felt a dim twist of jealousy.

"John?" Shirley withdrew her arm. "What are you doing here?"

Mortlock looked from her to the lad who flinched visibly under his scrutiny. "My job," he said. He felt the outline of the knife inside his coat, but these two could wait. During his trip here the silverfish had convinced him where the real danger lay. "Where's his girlfriend?" He inclined his head. "Taking part in the festivities is she?"

Henrik grimaced. "She *is* the festivities."

As if on cue, the chanting began again.

A voice whispered to Mortlock from the hall. "Then it's time to put a stop to the fun," he said.

Henrik shook his head. "You can't get up there. We've tried."

Another whisper. "We'll find a way."

Shirley peered past him. "Is there someone with you?"

There was a sluicing sound in the darkened hallway and then one of the silverfish slipped past Mortlock into the bedroom. A diminutive specimen, which as it fixated on Shirley, took the form of an even younger child. The silverfish held out its arms to her.

Henrik recoiled. "What the hell is that thing?"

Shirley's expression hardened. "*That* is a bloody lie. They told me my baby was given away. They didn't tell me he was a *monster*. Oh, the Mother was *quite* forthcoming on the subject. She thought the truth would convert me to her cause. But the midwives are every bit as guilty as the Lunane himself." Her reactions were faster than those of the silverfish. She snatched up a daisy-patterned bowl and ploughed it through the torso of the child, scooping most of its substance away with an almighty splash. As the bowl clattered to the floor, the remains of the silverfish disintegrated. The water drained through the boards and left a spray of sand and a handful of winkles spinning to rest.

The whispering from the corridor was urgent now, compelling. Shirley and Henrik ceased to be important at all. What was important was the Blake girl. The remaining silverfish led the way. Behind him Mortlock could hear someone calling his name, but he had no interest in turning to find out who it was.

On the stairs, someone shouted from behind: "Stop. I'm warning you. I won't let you hurt her." But the silverfish trooped on, and Mortlock followed in their dew-dark footprints.

In the enclosed space of the stairwell, the shot was cacophonous. Mortlock felt the bullet tug the flap of his coat, saw it tear turbulence through the heads of two of his companions before splintering the wall tiles on the landing.

Mortlock climbed on without pause and then followed the

silverfish through a succession of rooms. The water things stopped at a
curtain the colour of old wine. Mortlock tried to draw the curtain back,
but the closer his fingers got to the velvet, the less inclined they were to
complete the task. Only the urgings of the silverfish made him grasp
the material and yank it along the rail.

"Not so easy is it?" Shirley and Henrik had followed him. The
lad's arm swung like a pendulum, weighted by a lump of steel. The gun;
but that was irrelevant. Mortlock lunged for the knob but he could not
get closer than six inches. He strained until sweat sheened his cheeks.
He dropped his aching arm, gasped for breath. The silverfish inclined
their heads and choired a question. Mortlock shook his head. "I can't
do it."

"It's the blood." Shirley's voice. "See on the handle, and on the
lock, and all around the jamb?"

Sure enough the brass and wood were smeared with something
dark.

"You can't get through that door unless the blood in your heart is
the same as theirs."

The nearest silverfish whispered something. A solution. "Yes," he
grinned. "But it only applies if you *have* blood." He stepped back and
the silverfish that had spoken launched itself like a wave. All three
humans ducked in an unsuccessful attempt to avoid a soaking. When
they looked again the doorway was dripping, the brass handle gleamed
clean.

It turned easily.

The climb back up was exhausting, but the pulsing fire of adrenalin
made it pass in a blur of exertion. On his return to the repository,
Anton leaned against the door frame, listened for signs of pursuit. He
wasn't sure which he dreaded most: the solid step of a human being or
the dripping footfalls of Alice Muir's impossible allies.

He was forced to admit the probability that Muir and Hogarth
both were dead. And if Hogarth was dead, the Lunane would have
found a new host. Anton couldn't help have sympathy for the unlucky
recipient, but it did not matter where the Lunane was now. There was
work to be done.

"Sir?" A bedraggled Hogarth appeared at the staircase door.
Anton instantly recognised him as an empty vessel. Nothing of the

Lunane remained within him.

The biographer knelt and retrieved something from the floor. His journal. The lad looked at the book as if uncertain of its purpose.

"Are you all right, Hogarth?"

The biographer trembled. "I'm sorry, sir," he said. "I appear to have killed Miss Muir."

Anton bit his lip, although the news wasn't entirely unexpected. "It wasn't your fault. It was the Lunane's doing. Do you understand?"

Hogarth nodded then, automatically, peeled open the book.

"You don't have to write it down, Hogarth. Not any more."

The biographer fished his pen from within his sodden robes. The confusion in his face was painful. "Sir?"

Anton understood in that one syllable just how fully the biographer was defined by his role. Without it, he was unable to function.

"Very well," he said. "Write if you wish."

A smile ghosted into the biographer's face as he began his scribbling.

"I shall have to see Mr Gerard about a new pen, I fear, sir." Hogarth gave the implement a shake.

"Fine." Anton sighed. "Let's go and see him right now."

Mortlock couldn't see her through the forest of anxious women, but he knew she was there. The ones at the back craned over the shoulders of their colleagues. Someone began to sing, a clear voice raised to the heavens. The ethereal melody was taken up by others, turning to frosty vapour as it left their mouths. They hugged each other too or held hands. It was a strong bond, as strong as the seal on the door, and the exhortations of the silverfish to push through, to get to the girl, *get to the girl*, faltered in the face of that bond. Mortlock looked for a way around the circle, but it stretched from one side of the roof to the other. They were only women, but their backs were a forest so dense that the shadow of it consumed the moon, sucking the light from it. The moon shrank further as Mortlock watched.

The voices of the silverfish washed over him. *This was the heart of the evil that was unmaking his city. Never mind the riots, never mind the murders, this one event would destroy everything.*

This was Mortlock's chance to make amends for every crime he had committed at Dark.

The shadow covered the moon. A frisson of excitement passed through the women.

A child cried. An orgiastic chorus: "Our Queen!" that faltered even as soon as it began.

The knife was in his hand. Mortlock moved.

Chapter 24

Twelfth of Haffey Wax, 507UM

When the moon was eclipsed, people brought their own light to Glassholm's darkened streets. Some brought flames, some brought lanterns, and those who remembered the old ways brought glowing jars that held the writhing blue grubs of the Gibbous moth, but all of them brought their own fervour. Fuelled by their fear, it fizzed like lit magnesium.

The city's straining unity fractured, and everywhere those splintering factions met sparks flew. Those loyal to the Lunane sought out the silverfish, beating down the water creatures and their dazed human companions indiscriminately. The protesters at the Palace gates fell to infighting. The anarchists, who had long since ceased to require the encouragement of the silverfish, fought with anybody they could find.

In the centre of it all, the Castil tower blazed like a pillar of solid moonlight. Luminance filled every window and the great dome shone with such unearthly silver light that rumours circulated that the moon had finally come to earth. For some this was incontrovertible evidence of the Lunane's continuation. A sign for the faithful and faithless alike. For others it was yet another example of the flagrant abuse of privilege. With the entire city plunged into darkness, the king took the light for himself.

Lottie stared at the place where the moon had been. She tasted iron, smelled blood, and tried to ignore what was happening lower down.

Pierce, draw, tighten.

"Where…" Her whisper was tugged away by the stab, the pull, the cinch. She tried again. "Where is…" This time it was the scurry of the busy matrons that swamped her effort. Lottie wondered if she had actually spoken or whether the whiteleaf brew had left her voice too weak to escape her lips.

"Where is my baby?" A face came into view. Her mother.

"The Queen..." She faltered. "Charlotte. Your child is born dead."

Dead? How could such a vigorous, vicious wee thing, so impatient to be born, be dead?

"Show me." Lottie's mouth was dry as sand.

A nervous ripple passed through the congregation. A young matron came forward with a bundle.

Phamie stepped in again. "I don't think it's appropriate..."

"Not appropriate?" Lottie raised herself up. The effort brought pain lower down that made her gasp. When she breathed, it throbbed. She ignored the pain and filled her lungs. She wanted them all to hear this. "What kind of *mother* are you?"

The congregation gasped gratifyingly. Lottie's mother leaned in and placed her pudgy fingers on her brow. They were feverish. The lacquered nails began a skittish descent down the side of her face like a nervous luck monkey finding a way down from the rooftops, but they stopped at the corner of her bad eye, her imperfection. Lottie felt the talons hook there.

"The kind of mother who has had to make difficult decisions for her children," Phamie said.

"How *terrible* that must be for you."

The new voice was thin as wire. It cleaved the circle of watchers. Lottie recognised its owner. She remembered the café owner as the very hearth of human warmth, but the woman that advanced on them now could not have exuded more bitterness if she had taken lessons from Lottie's mother herself.

The matrons closed ranks in front of Lottie's bed. "That's right, hide it away," she screamed at the Mother, but appeared distracted. "That's what you do with your *difficult decisions*, isn't it?"

"I seem to recall that you were asked not to participate in this event, Shirley." There was steel in the matriarch's tone, but there was a creak of fatigue too. "You are no longer of our blood. I wonder now if you ever were."

Shirley's gaze skittered around the congregation. She frowned, and visibly mastered her rage. Quietly, she said: "Don't be a monster all your life, Euphemia. Allow the lass to hold her child."

At last, Lottie's mother nodded, and the waiting matron placed the bundle in Lottie's arms. It was so still that it could have been no more than a twist of linen. Except for the birthing shawl, in every way as beautifully crafted as Lottie's gown. Except for the exposed features, pressed in a frown of consternation as if the baby had been confounded in the very act of working out what life was all about. Except for the skin glow.

Lottie untucked the shawl, plucked it away from the child's – *her child's* – chin. The face grew. And grew. It was too big, too round. Those shadows around its eyes, the dark bruising of its lips. The mottled patterning of the white skin that was stretched thin over the impossibly large, hairless skull.

"Tell me truthfully, Euphemia." Shirley had come forward. "If the child had lived, would you really have had her as your Queen? Or would you have sent her down to spend her days in darkness with all the other freaks?"

Lottie tore her gaze from her amazing, moon-headed baby. There were tears in her mother's eyes. "It would have been kinder," Lottie said.

Phamie squeezed her eyes shut, but the tears would not be dammed.

"And besides," Lottie wrapped the shawl once more around the little body, "it's a boy." She stroked his cheek. Saw the pulsing shimmer. Felt the *huff* of breath. "And he lives."

She spoke it quietly, but the Church broke into an uproar of dismay that quickly changed tenor into one of fear.

Lottie saw the terror leap to the faces of those around her too. Then she saw the children. They capered in front of the terrified onlookers, feinted lunges and laughed silently at the panic they caused. She saw the little pieces of sea-stuff that floated in their watery bodies and remembered the figure in the shadows the night she had got her luck in the Rottens. She smelled salt and remembered the night that something had collided with the window of the café. How long had these things been following her around the city? But it wasn't just her, was it? This panic wasn't merely the fear of these strange creatures in themselves. For many, it was the shock of discovery. These were the sparkling children that came to the people in dreams and made promises.

Moonlight fell on the gathering, a bright revealing terminator. The eclipse was ending.

Then someone appeared at her side, snatched the baby from her arms and bore him away into what remained of the darkness.

An explosive report rang through the machine level. Anton raced through the darkened anterooms, heart in his mouth. He skidded on some sort of spillage on the floor outside his laboratories, but he didn't stop to see what it was.

There was a second bang. This time it was followed by a mosquito whine.

A ricochet.

Hogarth caught up with him, eyes wide. "Is that...?"

"Someone's shooting."

The chamber door was open. There was a puddle in front of it, a strand of lurid weed in the water.

Hogarth's face had turned to chalk. Anton hadn't asked how much he remembered of the tussle between himself and Muir, but it seemed he remembered enough. The biographer hung back.

From the top of the steps Anton looked down on a bizarre tableau. The machine was dormant, but appeared undamaged. There were no scorches on the casing, no blackened wires. It just sat there, waiting. A glance showed Anton the murkiest outline in the projection dome. The moonfish had gone deep. It was waiting too.

Gerard stood next to the machine. His robes were drenched, his face was ashen, and the outstretched arm that held a guardsman's revolver shook. Anton had never seen him lose his composure so completely. He could hear the heave of his ragged breathing over the slow trickling of water that spilled from the gantries like a circle of rain.

There were figures on the gantries. Far from the lithe, vindictive water creatures that had come to Muir's aid, these were the size of Dockton bouncers. They were bloated and sluggish, their bodies heavy with something that squirmed inside them. One of them approached the handrail. Gerard spun and fired. The secretary may have been on the verge of panic but his aim was remarkable. The bullet made a fountain as it passed through the head, struck the wall and zinged off at a tangent. Anton dodged the ricochet by instinct, and only caught a glimpse of the way the figure tottered, shuddered, collapsed like a shoreline breaker and cascaded down to the floor below. The water took the crabs that had snuggled in the thing's belly with it. Glossy black creatures they were, big as cats and with pincers the size of a man's hands. The crabs righted themselves from the fall with a skitter of feet and cracked their claws in the direction of the machine's cabling.

Gerard fired again. One of the crabs flipped over in a spray of shell shards. The other two continued to advance towards the machine.

Anton descended the stairs and instantly made himself Gerard's target.

The secretary sneered. "I'm surprised to see you here, Dunn. Have you come to persuade me to abandon my duty as you abandoned yours?" The gun's black muzzle twitched like the dilated pupil of a Fullday burn-out.

Anton spread his hands. "My goals were the same as yours. I just wanted to achieve them on my own terms."

Gerard dropped his arm.

Anton allowed himself the luxury of breathing.

The gun went off. Two thunderclaps that shook Anton's skull like a brass bell. The sound of claws behind him was stilled.

Gerard's grin was like a deathshead. "It's academic, Engineer. You failed. There's no hope now. But we have to protect what remains for as long as possible."

"I didn't fail," Anton replied calmly. "I know how to fix the machine."

Gerard's face was a perfect mask of disbelief.

"I'm not saying that I can make it good as new again, but in theory I think I can refocus the mechanism, make it work more efficiently so that things don't deteriorate any further."

Anton felt his heart hammering, counted the beats like skittish waves, steeled himself for the expected attack.

Gerard's shoulders and spine straightened. His tough defiance and ragged hope vanished in a swimming of features. His face became a mask of hauteur as the king's glamour slipped into his skin.

The Lunane raised a mocking eyebrow.

"Is that so?" The voice deep and sweet.

"It... it's simple." Anton faltered again in the face of the king. He swallowed before going on. "The machine's output slipped due to the extra strain of subduing the fish's spawning instinct, right? Like a dog tied to a railing, it's been trying to worry itself loose, and while it's not done enough to get free, it has managed to loosen things up. And the looser the tether feels, the harder it tries. The leviathan has been shaking itself loose of the lunatropic damping. The machine wasn't built to overcome such an unanticipated and strong imperative, but the Founders always did build well."

"So what is it you think you can do, Engineer?"

"Cement the railings, tighten the leash," Anton replied. "Nudge the lunatropic lensing back to full antiphase and your big, old friend down there will go back to swimming round and round in sad, obedient circles, until it's time to give birth and die. After that you'll have five hundred odd years to figure out how to stop it happening again."

The Lunane swept an arm towards the machine in a grand and compelling gesture. "Then I suggest you get on with it."

Sensing the change in circumstances, with a slosh and clatter, the remaining water creatures around the gantries emptied themselves.

"And make it quick."

Anton patted the housing. Felt for life. The thrum of power was there sure enough, but it was a sickly pulse. "I know what ails you," he murmured. Slinging a tool bag over his shoulder, he clambered up on to the housing and began to slide down the great steel beam towards the end that pointed down through floor, down through the tower, the foundations of the Palace and the rock beneath them. Hand over hand, he pull himself along. The metal was cool, slippery and progress was slow.

The Lunane started firing again.

"Hope you've got enough bullets." Anton was answered by another round of shooting. The beam flinched and Anton gripped tight, glad that he was at least astride the thing not standing beside it. Which didn't mean that he wouldn't be flung off at any moment.

"Hush now. It'll soon be over."

When the tremor did not repeat, he risked a look forward. He was over halfway and from this angle the sphere at the beam's end hid the Lunane like a mocking eclipse.

The remainder of the journey passed in concentration. Knowing that the beam could take his weight was not the same as knowing that it would, and the closer Anton got to the end the more nervous he became of any change in vibration. When he reached the sphere, a quick twist of his screwdriver opened the shell like the carapace of a moonbug.

"I hope for your sake you know what you're doing." Anton glanced over. The crabs now circled the king. They snapped at the hem of Gerard's robes and took turns to lunge at looms and component arrays. The king dealt one of them a savage kick that snapped off a leg and sent it spinning into the shadows.

"I said *in theory*," Anton shouted back. He peered into the open sphere. "The application is another matter entirely." The rectification he wanted to make should be a simple matter of adjusting the lenses to rebalance the interferometric array. Now that he knew that's what these spheres contained. If only he knew which ones.

"So?" The Lunane held a wriggling crab by the hind leg. Its claws worked frantically but could not reach him. "Can you or can't you?" The gun blew a hole clean through the beast's shell.

Anton unclipped one of the lens mountings from the edge of the array. It was incredibly fine. The glass was really no more than a sliver, the mounting crafted with utmost precision. Hundreds of years old, and irreplaceable. A single component doing a simple job, but in concert with its neighbours achieving an incredible result. "It's not so much a matter of whether I can fix it," he said, sliding the mounting back into position, clipping it home with satisfying solidity. He selected another tool from his bag, hefted it to make sure it was the right one for the job. "It's a question of whether I should."

Because Anton was not a component. He was not part of a machine. He had a mind of his own and he could make choices.

He drove the screwdriver blade through the centre of the lens.

The Lunane screamed. One long bellow of outrage that Anton felt more than heard as a mental surge. He weathered the assault and worked systematically round the array until just one irreplaceable piece of glass remained. He paused, his hand stayed by wanting. He could take just one of the lenses away for use in his own work, couldn't he? Just one? But that one lens might be enough to keep the moonfish prisoner, to keep the old machine just about running.

Anton smashed it to splinters.

"Engineer!"

The Lunane looked up at him with utter hatred. He raised the gun. Squeezed the trigger.

The gun made an impotent click and the enormous, black crabs launched themselves, slicing at the man's legs, hooking at his clothes, and dragging him to the floor.

The king didn't bother trying to defend himself. Blood seeped through gashes in his robe, poured from an open cheek wound, but his gaze never left Anton for a second.

"The machine is not so easily scrapped, Engineer." The Lunane's lips frothed with bloody spittle. "Don't forget. *Contingencies.*"

Then he was gone, and Gerard was screaming as the vengeful crabs dismantled him piece by methodical piece.

The sea's talons raked at the shore as if grasping for something. That was how it looked to Mortlock. Up the cliff face, up the city wall, up the storm-scarred stonework of a back-of-nowhere tenement building. Up on this roof, the edge of which his toes overlapped, the wind snatching at his coat. Beneath him, the sea continued to grasp at the land. Was it searching for him or for the bundle in his arms?

"John?"

The voice was drowned out by a surf-rush of whispers.

He picked at the layers of wool and cotton, uncovered a face. The skin was smooth and sheened as a vitricked vase, but it was shadowed by sickness.

"John?" It was Shirley's voice. She was scared. The tide of whispers rolled in again, but this time could not wash her words away. "Step back from the edge, love. Please."

Mortlock turned around and saw that he was cornered. The women of the church, Henrik, the girlfriend would be there somewhere too. Shirley beckoned to him. "Give Lottie back her baby, John. There's no need for this."

He looked at the sleeping bundle. Slipped the material away from the face to see it properly, then wished he hadn't. Its head was a monstrous shape.

Then he felt something. An almost imperceptible shift of consciousness, a mental tickling, as of something searching, flittering by and passing on. Slight as it had been, the feeling flooded him with emotions: love and guilt and pride all at once. Most especially pride.

It felt exactly like being close to the Lunane.

Then the baby opened its eyes and smiled. It was a smile brighter than moonlight. It inspired utmost devotion, and in that instant he would have done anything for that child.

It was his duty. Because here indeed *was* the Lunane.

Protect me, the baby said. *I am in danger.*

Kill it, kill it, kill it, said the sound of the waves.

All Mortlock had ever wanted to be was a good copper. To do his bit for the city. Since his first day on the force when he had taken the king's selene in his hot hand, the symbolism of the circle meant more to him than the value of the coin, his first week's pay, when he had presented it to his mother. *You're a good boy, John. You've always had a good heart. You've always done right.*

Except, sometimes at Dark...

Mortlock fumbled in his pocket. Metal discs spilled and tumbled. He slipped one into the baby's mouth.

Save me, the child pleaded.

"John? John, what are you doing?"

"I'm giving him the Lunane's coin," he mumbled. "Reminding him of his promise."

"John, please, you're confused."

They had all been good boys. They had done their best for people. A lot of bastards out there in the Dark, but they had always done their best.

He felt inside his coat once more, the secret pocket in the lining. The knife. Only one way to save someone for sure, because no matter how good your heart, you never knew what you would find yourself capable of down in the Dark Room.

He remembered everything now. He'd seen good coppers torture petty criminals for the fun of it, turn the act into a gambling game. He'd seen good boys punch pretty girls until they mumbled bloody, snotty, hysterical promises of sexual favours, and then take full advantage of what was offered. And sometimes, on the darkest of Darks, there had been the children. The hideous, unfortunate children. Lunane knew where Prunty had found them, but those good boys had known what to do with them right enough. *Derryman*, they had cried them, and allowed the superstition to make them into demons worthy of annihilation. But every one of those good, good hearts had known that, really, they were only children.

Children like these, gathered round now among the shocked women. Children like this deformed little mite in his arms.

Only one sure way to save you from the dark of your heart.

He put the tip of the blade to the baby's neck. The skin so pale, it glowed.

Kill it, the children chorused.

The baby's eyes glittered. There was danger in them, not innocence. *I command you, Sergeant Mortlock*, the baby said. *I command you to protect me with your life. You took the coin, you made a promise. Now fulfil it.*

Mortlock looked around the assembled faces, every one of them a mask of shock. Didn't they know he was a good man? Couldn't they see that he was only doing his job?

In the end it wasn't the disgust of the people that stopped him from drawing that simple line on the white skin. The line that said *No More.* Nor was it the Lunane's command that all his life he had done his utmost to obey. It was the touch of Shirley's hand. Warm, whole, real.

"Do what's right," she said.

He let the knife drop to the ground.

He heard the first wave coming in the form of running, wet feet. The silverfish impacted Shirley from the side, knocking her down. The second wave came directly at him. The child was fast, hit him like a battering ram. Mortlock barely managed to shield the Lunane-child with his coat when the water struck. Off-balance, he was forced back a half-step, then another. Felt the air under his heel, and threw himself forward.

Mortlock planted his feet and braced himself. The third wave struck him, then the fourth. Water streamed down his face, weed plastered his skin, salt stung his eyes, but he held firm.

Ha-ha! the baby cried. *You're a good man, Sergeant. My rock. Dependable to the last.* Then the child began to laugh, and everyone heard it. The deep, sonorous laugh of the Lunane coming from that tiny child was obscene.

The fifth and sixth waves struck Mortlock together. The force almost lifted him off his feet, but somehow he dropped to his knees and, hunched there just like a rock, weathered the onslaught.

In the lull that followed, the water dripped and trickled, but no one moved, least of all Mortlock, because everyone knew that the seventh wave was always the biggest.

They heard it coming from deep down and far away. They felt it building, sensed it rushing, felt the tug on the chains that bound their hearts.

The Lunane sensed it too. The baby was no longer laughing. *Traitors*, the baby cried. *You're all traitors.*

"Look!" Henrik was the first to see it. Everyone followed his pointing finger, saw the waters boiling down in the harbour. Boiling with light. There were gasps of amazement as the turbulent brightness moved away from the island. And they turned to screams of alarm when it became apparent that the moon, *their moon*, was following it towards the horizon.

The seventh wave came quietly, but the force was irresistible. The last silverfish put its arms around Mortlock, gentle as a mother's love, and enveloped both him and the baby. The water soaked through his coat, through the child's swaddling, into its mouth, its eyes, its ears, and down, a steady trickling over the rim of the roof, down to the waiting sea below.

Do what's right, Shirley had said. During their embrace, the last silverfish had repeated those words, and added, *End it.*

Beneath it all, in his good heart, Mortlock knew what was right. He clutched the baby to him, stepped backwards into the air and waited for the waves to swallow them both.

On the horizon, the moon set.

Epilogue

They held the Lunane's funeral at dusk on what would have been Fullday. They watched from their boats in the harbour. They watched from the cliff tops above silted Dockton. They watched from the tenements on the hills.

Blackwood's people arranged everything, as they seemed to be arranging so much in the aftermath of the king's demise. They laid Gerard's body in a fishing boat. Since he had been the last man in Glassholm to have held the king's glamour, it seemed a fitting reward for his loyalty. Even if, at the end, the Lunane had deserted him. The craft rode low in the water because of the journals stacked around the functionary's body, but the waves were calm enough to offer little danger of an ignominious capsizing. The sea had been still for three days now. Since the moon had left the city and returned to wandering the world.

They waited until the satellite appeared over the Castil tower, then they poured fuel onto the journals, put them to the torch and heaved the vessel out into the current.

Initially Anton decided not to watch, choosing instead to return to the remaining wing of the Foundry where he had taken interest in some intriguing water-powered contraptions from the formerly restricted archive. But when the hour came he relented, opened the window and watched the flaming boat drifting out beyond the harbour, sparks and billows rising into the sky. Some complicated aspect of the currents, no doubt, kept the vessel directly underneath the moon. Anton didn't know much about currents but he knew someone who did, and made a mental note to talk to Coombs soon. There was no such thing, after all, as bad knowledge.

"I suppose that's that." Anton turned to his companion. Her auburn hair was tied in a creamy white bow. "Now, back to work. Can you get me a number three magnifier please?"

Sadie smiled her unique smile and skipped off on her errand. It wasn't a pretty smile, and she and her kind had challenges ahead if they wished to be accepted into the new society. But Anton would defend their right to do so with every ounce of strength not devoted to helping Glassholm to move on at long last.

The engineer returned his attention to the device on his desk, dismantled and sectioned, and ready for his study.

In the harbour, another vessel waited its turn to leave Glassholm. The *Lycea*, out of Haverland, had berthed in the harbour the day after the seas relented. Now its engines rumbled to life, ready to depart.

From the deck, Henrik and Lottie watched the funeral boat until it vanished over the horizon in a final flare of flames that reached into the sky, stretching for the setting moon that would now, forever, be out of reach.

As the ship edged out of the harbour, Lottie stared at the horizon. Henrik squeezed her hand. The world waited for them to come and make their place in it. Alone and together. And at no one's whim but their own.

They did not once look back.

Author's Acknowledgements

Thanks are due to my agent, John Jarrold, and to Ian Whates and his team at Newcon Press for their faith in this book and its author. Also to the people who provided the various nuggets of golden advice that helped transform the story into an actual working novel: Hal Duncan, Phil Raines and everyone else at the Glasgow SF Writers Circle (especially Duncan Lunan, for the loan of his name), Jeff Vandermeer, Tessa Kum and Gio Clairval. And also to Emma Taylor, for everything.

This book is dedicated to Eleni. She always wanted to read this story when it was finished, and I'm so sorry she can't.

Neil

About the Author

Neil Williamson's fiction has been published in a variety of magazines and anthologies, both in the UK and internationally, including *Interzone, Lady Churchill's Rosebud Wristlet, Logorrhea: Good Words Make Good Stories, The Third Alternative* (the forerunner to *Black Static*), *Solaris Rising 2* and several Newcon Press anthologies. Many of these stories can be found in his British Fantasy Award nominated collection *The Ephemera* (Elastic Press / Infinity Plus Books). Neil's short story "Arrhythmia" was shortlisted for a British Science Fiction Award, and *Nova Scotia: New Scottish Speculative Fiction* (Mercat Press), which he edited with Andrew J Wilson, was shortlisted for the World Fantasy Award. *The Moon King* is his first novel.

Neil lives in Glasgow, Scotland, where he works as a technical writer, performs cabaret and occasionally plays in a band. He is a longstanding member of the notorious school of literary pugilism known as the Glasgow SF Writers Circle, and has the internal bruising to prove it.

Neil's website is: www.neilwilliamson.org.uk.

NEWCON PRESS

Publishing quality Science Fiction, Fantasy, Dark Fantasy and Horror for seven years and counting.

Winner of the 2010 'Best Publisher' Award from the European Science Fiction Society.

Anthologies, novels, short story collections, novellas, paperbacks, hardbacks, signed limited editions, e-books…

Why not take a look at some of our other titles? To date, NewCon Press has published work by:

Neil Gaiman, Brian Aldiss, Kelley Armstrong, Alastair Reynolds, Christopher Priest, Tanith Lee, Joe Abercrombie, Dan Abnett, Nina Allan, Sarah Ash, Neal Asher, James Barclay, Stephen Baxter, Tony Ballantyne, Chris Beckett, Lauren Beukes, Aliette de Bodard, Chaz Brenchley, Keith Brooke, Eric Brown, Pat Cadigan, Simon Clark, Michael Cobley, Storm Constantine, Peter Crowther, Hal Duncan, Jaine Fenn, Gwyneth Jones, Jon Courtenay Grimwood, M. John Harrison, Amanda Hemingway, Paul Kane, Leigh Kennedy, Kim Lakin-Smith, David Langford, Alison Littlewood, James Lovegrove, Una McCormack, Sophia McDougall, Gary McMahon, Ken MacLeod, Ian R MacLeod, Gail Z Martin, Juliet E McKenna, John Meaney, Mark Morris, Marie O'Regan, Philip Palmer, Stephen Palmer, Sarah Pinborough, Rod Rees, Andy Remic, Mercurio D Rivera, Adam Roberts, Justina Robson, Mark Robson, Robert Shearman, Sarah Singleton, Martin Sketchley, Kari Sperring, Brian Stapleford, Charles Stross, Tricia Sullivan, Adrian Tchaikovsky, Lavie Tidhar, Lisa Tuttle, Ian Watson, Freda Warrington, Liz Williams, Neil Williamson and many, many more.

Join our mailing list to get advance notice of new titles, book launches and events, and receive special offers on books.

www.newconpress.co.uk

Lightning Source UK Ltd.
Milton Keynes UK
UKOW01f0902130916

282876UK00005B/183/P